RISE of the VIRAGO

BY ZA'CHARY WESTBROOK

The Silkhaven Trilogy
- Neon Jezebel
- Rise of the Virago
- The St Lawrence Fire

Silkhaven Serials
- Silkhaven Pulp
- 13 is not a Number

Rise of the Virago

Za'Chary Westbrook

Book 2
of the Silkhaven Trilogy

For Pimley, my most reliable source of enthusiasm

CONTENTS

Prologue:
The Confession of Vivienne Walker

September 25th, 1920. Silkhaven.

Bless me, Father, for I have sinned. It has been three days since my last confession, but do not worry, I did not have a particularly interesting weekend. There is an old sin that I have carried since I was a girl. It was a lie; a lie of omission, but all the same. I cannot say that I have ever forgotten about it, but it never weighed on me until recently. My brother has been gallivanting around playing detective and something in one of his stories has brought it all back.

It started the summer I turned sixteen. I had, at long last, begun to flower into womanhood and I was vain about it. No more than one would expect from intemperate youth, of course. I was finally getting attention from boys at the beach; something my friends had been enjoying for a season or two already and it was my turn to join the club. There was one boy, in particular, whom I hoped to impress that year; not in any licentious way, merely in the way all young people hope to be recognized as adults.

You see, I had a cousin who was a few years older than me. Everyone called him Rooster, due to a chronic cough he had developed as a child. Each morning, his family was awakened by one of his coughing fits and the nickname was a sort of joke that brought levity to the fear that one of those fits would someday be the end of him.

Growing up, Rooster and I had been bosom friends. When his father, my Uncle Cecil, had moved the family business down to New York, Rooster and I continued our relationship through occasional letters. However, each summer, our families would gather at a vacation house Uncle Cecil bought in Montauk. From the moment we saw each other to the moment a carriage took one or another of us off, we were inseparable. That is, until Rooster started university.

That was when I was fifteen. Rooster had been too busy carousing with the uncles to pay me much attention that summer. So, you can see why I had such expectations for the following year. I fancied that I looked just like the sort of girls a college boy would meet. Again, I had no romantic feelings for Rooster; though, if he and I had taken up together, I imagine the family would have tolerated it.

No, I merely wanted my old friend back. I wanted him to see me as an equal again.

As the carriage was approaching the house, I was downright giddy. When the house came in sight, I nearly leapt out before the horses came to a stop. I found Rooster, no surprise, in the library. His condition had always made him prefer academia to the rougher forms of masculinity. He was friendly enough, not effusively so, like when we were children, but I accepted this as a sign of adulthood. We passed a few companionable hours with him reading poetry to me before the announcement that Aunt Lydia and Uncle Herbert were approaching.

That news lit up his face as my appearance had failed to, which was a blow. Outside, my father and Uncle Cecil greeted their sister, Lydia, with a great and energetic affection that shattered my newly forged conviction that adults were calm and rational about meetings after long partings. Watching Uncle Cecil sweep Aunt Lydia up in his arms and twirl her around with my father trailing behind like a hopeful suitor was another wound. Then, Rooster trotted to the carriage and did the same thing to our cousin, Maybelle, who was only eight-years-old. That was the final insult.

I ran inside and up to the girls' room to cry. Naturally, I did not dare explain to anyone the cause of my tears. Instead, I honed them into a sharp bitterness which I would turn on Rooster at the first opportunity. Maybelle and her older sister, Vera, brought their things up to the room that we three would be sharing for the duration of the reunion and I did my best to help them get settled.

Vera and I had never been close before, despite her being only a year younger than I. However, with my heart turned firmly away from Rooster, I was in search of a companion. In that way young people so easily can, Vera and I became the most intimate of friends in the few hours between their arrival and dinner. We had a great deal to discuss, of course, having passed very few words in the past.

We talked about school and songs we were learning on the piano. We had just broached the topic of boys when the dinner bell was rung. The adults had not yet caught on to the turmoil in my relationship with Rooster and had left my long-accustomed chair beside him open. Before I had the chance to refuse it and show Rooster what I thought of him, he was calling for Maybelle to join him.

The whole dinner, Rooster was entertaining Maybelle with the funny voices and silly stories that he had created for me; with me, in fact. I looked about at the adults and, when they took notice of Rooster's comedy, they beamed at him. Aunt Ethel, Rooster's mother, even commented on what a fine father he would make one day.

I spent that dinner in agony as I watched my most ancient friendship sink below wave after wave of disregard. By the end of the reunion, there was nothing left in my heart for Rooster. I returned to Silkhaven and spent the rest of the summer enjoying the usual pastimes of girls without thinking of him; at least, not with any hope or happiness. When I caught boys looking at me, I no longer wondered if Rooster would be as impressed by me as they were. Instead, I began to appraise all the ways they were his superiors. None of them seemed as skinny as him. To a man, they were more robust and vigorous, never once breaking into a fit of hacking coughs.

I held a boy's hand while caroling that winter and had my first kiss at the King Louis house with an entirely different boy that spring. All through it, I was writing almost weekly letters to Vera. As the year went on, our similarities began to slip. She was not so versed in fashion as I was, nor so airy in regards to young men.

Unbeknownst to me, Aunt Lydia and Uncle Herbert were having financial troubles. Uncle Herbert's business had begun a downward spiral from which it would never entirely recover. As is so often the case, he was turning his hopes for financial salvation towards marrying Vera off. If nothing else, it would mean one less mouth to feed.

Vera was as apprehensive as one would expect a then-sixteen-year-old girl to be about the prospect of marrying a man some fifteen years her senior. She said nothing unkind about the prime suitor in her letters. Rather, she damned him by faint praise. Being tall and knowing how to dance was as good as he got in her estimation.

All of this set the stage for the following summer.

Uncle Cecil's family always arrived a few days early to oversee the preparation of the house, which did not have a staff except when they were present, only a pair of groundskeepers who also looked after two other houses in the area. If a storm broke a window, they would inform Uncle Cecil and wait for him to reply with the money to replace it and so on.

When my family arrived, Rooster was on the veranda, smoking with his father. Seeing us, they both stood and Rooster immediately doubled over coughing. At university, Rooster had picked up the idea that smoking might strengthen his lungs in some indescribable way, though I am inclined to believe that he had merely felt left out.

Niceties passed between myself and Rooster. He even went so far as to carry my things up to the girls' room. For a little while, I entertained the idea that he had reflected on his behavior towards me and was ready to make amends, if not actually apologize. That was dashed about an hour later when Aunt Lydia arrived and Rooster discarded polite gallantry for that high-voiced enthusiasm one expects from a bachelor uncle greeting his niece.

Maybelle was delighted to see Rooster, of course, he knew far more jokes than Vera and was less familiar with the intricate society of her dolls, who lived lives of intrigue that put Jane Austen's characters to shame. As Rooster crouched beside Maybelle's bed, being regaled by the gossip of the dolly season, Vera and I made ourselves scarce.

Over the many years of summers at Uncle Cecil's vacation house, Vera had partaken in very few of the recreations, volunteering herself as Maybelle's nanny. That summer, though, she seemed happy to let Rooster watch her charge and go off with me to wander the grounds, exercise the horses, and learn to shoot a rifle. The most exciting thing, though, came towards the end of the reunion.

On our last Friday evening, the grownups decided that we cousins should be allowed a bottle of champagne to drink among ourselves. You can imagine the commotion this caused. Most of us had had a glass or two at dinner, but this bottle was to be shared without our parents present, making it the first "adult" drink most of us had ever taken.

It is curious to think about, really. When one imagines the rites of passage among tribesmen, at least one parent is present, possibly even leading the ceremony. For us, it was the absence of parents that made it momentous.

The younger boys were all in a tizzy about it, but Rooster begged off. He was much more accustomed to drink, having beer with some regularity at university. Instead, he offered to take Maybelle out stargazing, saying he knew a lovely spot for it. I knew exactly which spot he meant. He and I had spent many evenings in a certain small clearing a few minutes' walk from the house.

Rooster was well-versed in both astronomy and mythology from a young age. We would lie on the grass and he would point out constellations, then retell their stories with delightful irreverence. There were melodramatic voices and a few jokes of the sort that Ovid would have approved of. At nine, it was agreed that Maybelle was still too young for champagne and, in my teenaged thinking, that left a bit more for the rest of us. It all seemed perfectly natural to me.

Vera protested.

She made a dozen arguments to her mother against the stargazing and became so worked up that Uncle Cecil threatened to withdraw the offered champagne if she did not calm herself. Of course, by then, Rooster and Maybelle had already snuck off and were halfway across the lawn. I do not know what Vera had seen in Rooster that night. She had seemed content to leave Maybelle in his care, so far. All I know is that, in that moment, I was blind and Vera was not.

We only got one glass each out of the bottle. Though, I made sure that my brother and the younger boys got smaller portions than myself and Vera. She was gloomy the whole time and I began to resent her, I will admit. The boys allowed themselves to act more drunkenly than they could possibly have been and my one hope for escape from their noise was ignoring me, only staring forlornly off into the shadows of the surrounding forest.

Once the champagne was gone, the boys—declaring Vera a wet blanket—took themselves off to find other entertainment. Despite my own feelings, I stayed with Vera as she held her vigil. We silently leaned on the veranda's rail and, once I had settled into it, I began to enjoy the quiet.

The adults came out to tell the boys that it was time for them to go to bed. They claimed that it was unfair, as Maybelle was not back yet and she was younger, but—our parents contended—she was with Rooster who was as good as an adult. Vera broke her silence to make a bitter comment about sending the boys to stargaze, as well. Aunt Lydia did not like her tone and that was that.

Even when the adults announced that they were retiring, Vera and

I remained on watch.

It was nearly 10pm when Maybelle emerged from the forest. She was running full pelt towards the house and, when she saw us, she burst out into sobs. Vera did not wait and ran out to meet her. She swept Maybelle up, even as Rooster appeared. Vera demanded to know what Rooster had done to Maybelle, but he only gave a tired, non-answer. He followed as Vera brought the crying Maybelle into the house.

Seeing the child in such distress, I was moved to take up Vera's questioning. I put myself bodily between him and my girl cousins, but he only said that there had been a misunderstanding. Maybelle's sobs roused the adults and turmoil overtook the living room. Faced with the parents, Rooster became apologetic and played up his cough a bit. He claimed that he had given Maybelle a scare, meant to be playful, but it had touched her more deeply than he had intended.

Uncle Cecil and Uncle Herbert both chided him, though in terms that belittled Maybelle even as they corrected Rooster. When it became clear that no punishment would come to Rooster, Vera began crying herself and—still clutching Maybelle—ran up to the girls' room. I followed her and we did our best to comfort Maybelle until she fell asleep.

"He hurt her, Viv." Vera told me. "I knew he would." She could not bring herself to elaborate further, but I began to see.

With only a week remaining to the reunion, concerted efforts were made to keep Rooster and Maybelle separate. It was generally agreed that, whatever had happened, Maybelle would get past it in her own time. My father declared the next morning that the men would be taking their meals outside. It was played as a rugged and masculine thing, to eat out on the grass, but there was no masking its true purpose. The younger boys took no issue with it, often dressing for meals in their swimming costumes so that they could seamlessly move from eating to swimming.

The appertaining depression that clung to Maybelle was covered by Aunt Lydia as ordinary sickness. She had caught a chill while stargazing was the story and even I began to remember that night as unusually cool. It was even made a lesson to the boys. This was why they had to go to bed so early. Children that stayed up too late, especially when it was cold, took ill.

However, the only true illness I saw was in Rooster. With each passing day, he grew more sickly; not with remorse, but with something more like a jilted suitor. All of his humor was gone and every time I took note of him, he was gazing up at the house. I remember wondering how it was possible for a man of twenty to pine for a girl of nine.

The holiday ended uneventfully, with Aunt Lydia and Uncle Herbert deciding to leave a few days early, hoping that returning home would improve Maybelle's condition. Once my own family returned to Silkhaven, I immediately wrote to Vera to inquire about Maybelle. She had indeed improved, but Vera had no forgiving words for Rooster. In fact, she refused to write his name, referring to him only as 'R—'.

Over the next few months, her furor grew; or perhaps it was her boldness in expressing it. As time made the event more remote, I began to feel that Vera was making too much of things until she finally wrote the two words which would plunge me into the true darkness of that evening: 'unnatural desires'. I had read enough detective stories to understand her meaning and I fairly reeled at the implication. Yet, I could not forget the longing I had seen in Rooster; that he had been, in the most diabolical sense, a jilted suitor.

The event galvanized Vera and she became intent on marrying. It was not lost on her that her fiancé, Roger, was more her senior than Rooster was Maybelle's, but—as she put it—a man of fifty desiring her would be more natural than a boy of fifteen desiring a girl of ten.

It was a Christmas wedding and we all made the journey to Toronto. Rooster was conspicuously absent, supposedly too absorbed in his studies, which may have been true. The groom far exceeded my expectations based on Vera's letters. He was far more handsome than I had expected and dignified in a way that improved his appearance further. I could not fathom how he was unmarried until I learned that he was a widower.

My mother explained it all to me. He had married at the usual age, only to lose his wife in childbirth. By then, he was of an age where the women in his set were all married or of unsuitable reputations. So, he had no choice but to seek a young bride. My letters from Vera post-nuptials portrayed him as a gentle and respectful husband, though not so attentive as a young woman would prefer. He did have his own company to attend to, after all, which was a large part of why Uncle Herbert had pursued the match. Wed, Vera was thrust into the very grownup world of family finances, but was still young enough to discuss them openly in a letter.

By spring, Vera was pregnant and, with the year's reunion

approaching, she gloried in how her station as a married woman—and one with child, no less—would give her the authority to cut Rooster off from Maybelle entirely. By then, I was convinced that Rooster was a fiend. I cannot say exactly what opened my eyes to his fiendishness, but open they were.

July rolled around and we descended again upon Uncle Cecil's summer home. When Aunt Lydia and Uncle Herbert arrived, we heard them from a mile away. Roger's addition to the family had, for the time, reversed Uncle Herbert's fortunes and they had decided to get a car, rather than horses. Seeing the car, Rooster rushed out to meet them, giving himself a coughing fit from the exertion. He recovered himself and was immediately thrown into a doldrum when he saw that Maybelle was not with them. She was coming with Vera in Roger's car.

Uncle Herbert warned Rooster that Maybelle had not entirely forgiven him, yet, and that he should not expect any warmth from her. Then, I heard Rooster say: "Did she not get my letters?" That word—'letters' in the plural—chilled me. The very idea that a grown man would write to a child repeatedly with no response was the final confirmation.

Uncle Herbert told him that she had not, for fear that they might upset her. This threw Rooster into a rage that was tempered by another fit of cough. Uncle Cecil intervened then and, while I did not hear what was said, Uncle Herbert came away from it cowed and ashen-faced.

I rushed inside and found my mother. In private, I told her what I had heard. She added to this that Rooster had brought a dollhouse to Montauk that was intended as a gift for Maybelle. "What are we going to do?" I asked her. "He is a monster!"

Mother grabbed me firmly by the shoulders and said: "He is the first son of the first son. He is the prince. You cannot call him a monster unless you can show the world his fangs."

When Roger and Vera did arrive, we all gathered to greet them. Rooster was last, bringing out the dollhouse and nearly shouting for Maybelle to look, look: a dollhouse that they could paint together. Vera would not hear of this and another row broke out. When Uncle Cecil tried to intervene, again, Roger waved him away. Whatever power Cecil had over Herbert, it was nothing to Roger.

Roger said that he did not know much about the old argument and that he did not care to. All he knew was that Rooster's behavior was disturbing his pregnant wife and that he would not permit it. This idea awoke in the aunts a new power and they immediately swooped in to agree. Yes, of course, it was most unhealthy for a pregnant woman to become upset like this.

Aunt Ethel, Rooster's mother, even told him to "think of the baby", a sentence which turned my stomach, but nonetheless forced Rooster to relent. The favor of the queen was on Vera's side.

For Vera's part, she insisted that she needed Maybelle's constant assistance in her delicate condition. She was not so far along as that, but Aunt Lydia brushed aside any possible argument, saying: "You know how anxious one gets with their first child. Besides, Maybelle adores helping her about the house."

And thus, it seemed, order was restored and Rooster was blocked from causing any further damage. That is, until I saw Rooster talking with Roger.

Cut off from Maybelle, Rooster took every opportunity to charm the newest addition to the family. His rapier wit came out in full force and he played up his condition to make himself appear harmless. His coughing fits were all the more dramatic that summer and he needed longer than I had ever seen to recover from them.

Vera and I were alike disturbed by how well he got on with Roger. By the end of the first week, Vera came to me on the verge of tears to tell me that Roger had entreated her to forgive Rooster and let him make his apologies to Maybelle. He had even criticized Uncle Herbert for not giving Maybelle his letters. How could the girl get over what had happened if she could not hear the apologies? Vera was livid.

So far, she had been able to shield her sister, but she felt that ability being chipped away at. The way she told it, Uncle Cecil had an almost hypnotic power over the family and it was only a matter of time before he tired of them all denying his son something he wanted. She feared that Cecil would make a proclamation and Maybelle would be delivered directly into Rooster's arms.

I then began to see how little effort was being made to keep the two apart. It was really only accomplished by myself and Vera, while the rest of the family only avoided things that may cause a confrontation. Even Roger's once valiant defense was reduced to him fraternally telling Rooster: "Pregnancy does enflame the emotions, old boy. Best not to stoke the fire."

There he was, a man grown leering wolfishly at a child for all the world to see and the most anyone could muster against him was a concession to a pregnant woman's irrationality. Something shifted in me that morning. Something cold began to show me how Rooster's energy had not declined an iota and that Vera was stretched to her utmost already. It would come down to the two of them with the family acting only to keep the peace. I alone was left to tip the balance.

Perhaps I could protect my cousin, but then I wondered if a wolf could ever be satisfied with one lamb. If he could so easily charm Roger, who could protect the other little girls in the world? That cold thing began showing me all the people looking fondly at Rooster, so skinny and pale with his terrible cough, as he ingratiated himself to another little girl. "What a sweet man." They would say. "It is tragic, really. All he wants is to be a father and yet he cannot attract a wife."

That cold thing tightened in my chest and I was resolved to bring all of this to an end.

Vera was sitting on the bank of the inlet before the house, watching Maybelle and the other children play in the water. She shouted, "Not too far," and sounded exactly like her mother. An inlet is not so much fun as a lake, with the constant threat of a current pulling a weak swimmer out to sea.

Of course, with Vera at the waterside, Rooster was confined to the house by the unspoken rules that still stood. He was perched up in the library, staring out the window. Hardly knowing what I was doing, I approached him.

"It is a lovely day." I said. "Let's take the boat out...for old times' sake."

There was a little rowboat tied up to a short dock. The uncles kept it in good repair for fishing, but Rooster and I used to take it out when we were still fast friends. He would always just sit there while I swam around, occasionally splashing him or making menacing faces at him like I was a water nymph and he was Hylas.

When he was unmoved, I added: "We can watch the children swimming without the veranda in the way." It would have given me a chill to say that, but I was already cold from the thing clutching my heart. He agreed, then, to my disgust and relief.

Twenty minutes later, we were both in our swimming costumes and walking down to the dock. With me as an escort, Vera made no objections and so neither did anyone else. He rowed us out into the water and we began to reminisce. We reminded each other of summers past, and for a few moments, I forgot that he was anything but my cousin, a fond figure in childhood memories. Then, his eyes drifted to the shore where Maybelle was splashing around and he sighed like every romantic hero in poetry.

"Remember when that was us?" I said, still feeling unsure of my purpose.

"Yes," he said. "So innocent. So pure." He said it in the tone he might use to describe a wine.

"Let's get in." I said.

"Oh, Viv," he shook his head. "You know I cannot swim to save my life."

In that moment, my purpose crystallized. With a naiad's smile, I stood and put one foot on the side of the boat. I had dived from that little craft a hundred times as a child. My foot was planted exactly where I needed it to be. Thrusting my weight down in preparation to jump, I tipped the thing completely over, throwing both myself and Rooster into the water.

I heard him scream for a second before submerging. I surfaced and cast about looking for him. When I did not see him, I sank myself and looked through the clear water. The salt stung my eyes, but my resolve kept them open. When I caught sight of his dark form thrashing towards the surface, I swam over and grabbed him by the shoulder. Looking up, I saw the shadow of the boat and I pulled him up with me until I broke the surface in the pocket of air trapped underneath.

My hand was still on Rooster's shoulder, an arm's length under the water.

I held him there.

He battered my arm weakly as he tried to escape, but he quickly fell into convulsions as the exercise brought on his cough. It is a terrible thing to cough underwater.

Once the fit had passed, he tried again to free himself from my grip, but his attempts were even weaker than before. Finally, he stopped moving at all and I felt his body rising against my hand with only its natural buoyancy. In that moment, I remembered a day years before on the beach with my father. There had been a commotion and out of it came a man carrying a boy who was limp in his arms. I had cried out, thinking the boy was dead, but my father had comforted me, saying: "There may still be life in a body that has stopped moving."

We had watched the adult man pound on the boy's back until he coughed up a gout of water and began to gasp.

"You see," my father had said. "They got him out in time."

So, I waited. Holding onto the inside of the boat, I waited for Rooster's body to fall away from my hand. I waited until Maybelle was safe, until every young daughter of Uncle Cecil's friends was safe, until Rooster was beyond the excuses that shield a prince from reproach.

When he finally sank, I followed him down. I let him go and swam under the surface for the shore. When I was out of breath, I came up and that cold thing released me. Suddenly, I was wracked with sobs. Rooster was dead. A member of my family, my blood was dead. No one I had ever known had died before. Even my father's mother, too weak to make the journey down to Montauk, was still somewhere in Silkhaven playing cards with her twilight friends. And my grandfather had passed when I was too young to remember.

I crawled up on the shore and sat with my face in my hands. It was my brother that found me. He asked if I was okay and I bawled: "I killed him!"

"No," Cranston told me. "It was an accident, understand? We are going to find Rooster. He is going to be okay. You will see."

I did not say anything after that; not for a long time.

Everyone on the beach had seen us go under. The uncles had been called and they all swam out with some of the staff, while the younger boys ran along the shore to bear witness. Cranston wrapped me in his arms and shouted that he had found me. Not long after that, I heard Uncle Cecil wailing and splashing, desperately calling his eldest son's name.

One of the grooms rode into town to get a boat that could handle the open sea and inadvertently put the Coast Guard on the search for Rooster. The next morning, a boat was trawling the inlet hoping to recover his body, but it had evidently been swept out to sea.

The local authorities got the story from my parents, from Cranston, from Vera; everyone but me. They said they saw us go out and that I tried to dive in. They said that Rooster and I had always been thick as thieves during these vacations and took the boat out all the time. They said that I had grown, that I weighed more than I used to, that I had not realized that a woman could not dive from a boat like a girl could. Rooster must have had one of his fits. That it was all a terrible accident.

And I never corrected them.

PART 1
The Crime

Chapter 1:
A Favor for Vivienne

Rebecca Costa-Cortez, left to her own devices, would be naked all the time. It was a complex she had picked up at a very young age.

One Sunday, furious at her mother over the lack of bows on her new church dress, she had petulantly taken the bland thing off. When that did not faze her mother, she had taken off her stockings, pants, and vest, then went running into the bedroom she shared with her three sisters. Her sisters fled the room, partly because they had been raised to be very modest girls and partly for fear of parental wrath falling indiscriminately upon the room. For whatever reason, though, Rebecca's parents had simply decided to leave her behind and took the rest of the family to mass.

Rebecca's family, being Italian on her father's side and Puerto Rican on her mother's, was at church until it was nearly dark and young Rebecca experienced—for the first time in her life—real solitude. She immediately fell in love with the quiet, the freedom, and the access to her mother's immodest story magazines. Through the magical thinking of children, she remained naked for most of the day, thinking that putting any clothing on might bring the whole family back home.

When she finally decided she was getting lonely, she returned her mother's story magazines to their place and then put on her own pajamas. From then on, any time she wanted to be alone, she would strip naked in an attempt to relive that one glorious Sunday. It was hit or miss, but it developed into a key part of her personality.

This great love of personal nudity had led her to apply for work at a burlesque club in New York. While working there, every so often, a gentleman would tell her, "You are so good, you should be in Silkhaven." And one day, she believed them.

Silkhaven had been good to her. The Mermaid Club, while offering more salacious entertainment than the places she had worked in New York, attracted a well-to-do clientele and well-to-do men gave women whom they enjoyed seeing naked some of the very finest fashion available: French dresses, Apache jewelry, and Virginian underwear.

She kept a mental catalogue of who had given her what. When a particular gentleman moved on from her, his contributions would find their ways into other girls' wardrobes. At the moment, the lion's share of her wardrobe had come from a sweet, but troubled man named Cranston Walker. He was as shameless in his courting of her as he was in refusing to make an honest woman of her. No customer of the Mermaid Club attended on his own so often, nor asked for a girl so consistently. It was always 'Pearl' and maybe a friend if he was feeling expansive. And in two years, he had not once, not even drunkenly, asked her to marry him.

He was perfect.

For his first few visits, Cranston had been what the girls called a fisherman; paying for a dance, then dismissing the dancer and asking her to send another mermaid up. Then, Rebecca had walked in, introduced herself as 'Pearl', and before he could order her a drink, she tried to suffocate him with her breasts. That had sealed it.

Whenever Cranston came in, he requested Pearl and being who he was—a *Walker*—he got her, even if she was with another sailor at the time. She gave him whatever dance was encoded by the drink he ordered for her, then would usually lounge in the private box, the 'shell', nude for a while as they talked. Some days his eyes were solidly on hers and sometimes they wandered up and down. Rebecca had never minded; she got ogled on the street any time she wore less than a winter coat. And Cranston was so different than the other men she met at the club or any club before.

Most men were composed of wants; things they wanted to get, things they wanted to do, things they wanted to destroy. Cranston was all stories and opinions. She was unreasonably familiar with the workings of the Walker Corporation and had learned quite a lot of history. Thanks to Cranston, Rebecca knew all the best restaurants and shows for the rare occasions when she had a night off to go to one. Most of the time, Cranston's reviews of the show were more entertaining than the show itself, even the ones he liked; but it bought her lots of kudos from the other mermaids.

Stories and opinions were all Cranston was supposed to give her, besides cash. Rebecca's sex worker license only permitted her to perform 'exhibitions'. Between that and the club's rules about gentlemen keeping their hands off the dancers, Rebecca had enjoyed greater safety as a mermaid than any of the places she had worked in New York. However, it had not taken long for Rebecca to decide she wanted more from Cranston. She wanted him getting fresh as a daisy and to keep his hands anywhere but to himself.

When a sex worker took you back to her place for some off-the-clock fun, providing some manner of recompense was the done thing. That was where the clothes came in; from beautiful gowns to lingerie which required an instruction manual. Cranston had even gotten Rebecca's hints about costumes. If she wanted to be herself, she could just be naked, and if she wanted to be someone else, she wanted to be someone exciting.

Rebecca's current collection included a belly dancer outfit composed of seven diaphanous veils, a nun's habit that left her legs and breasts completely exposed, and a Viking girl costume that was mostly just a bear-skin cloak. Being an educated man, Cranston had also acquired a few interesting historical costumes. There was a beaded dress made from a real fishing net that was supposedly Egyptian and an Ancient Greek dress that was just two squares of fabric stitched together on one side and then tied and pinned into shape.

They did little plays together with those. He never had a costume, though. Cranston was always a penitent or a time traveler or a man visiting a far-off land on business; someone who wore a suit. The fantasy was all for her. Not that he didn't get anything out of it, but being someone else was Rebecca's fancy. Cranston was just the sort of man who liked giving a girl what she wanted. In return, Rebecca made sure the characters she played were the sort of women Cranston wanted: equal parts sexual aggression and kindness.

He wasn't around on this particular Friday morning, though. So, Rebecca had pulled her rocking chair into a sunbeam and sat down to read *au naturel*. She had managed to get a copy of Delmira Agustini's *Cantos de la Mañana* and had been slowly working her way through it, savoring each poem. Sometimes she spent the whole morning just reading and rereading one of them, letting her mind drift through the words and imagining the broader story; to say nothing of the more illicit acts alluded to.

Rebecca had only ever played with other women in a professional context, but Delmira's too-feminine knot did sound...

Knock, knock, knock

And private time was over. Rebecca grudgingly got out of her chair and reached for the housecoat her male visitors did not like; all opaque cotton and buttons. No one showing up unannounced deserved see-through lace or bows of silk ribbon to be rakishly tugged open.

"Who is it?" Rebecca called as she buttoned up the housecoat.

"Vivienne Walker," was the reply.

Mierda, Rebecca thought. *¿Por qué vendría ella aquí?* Then, with alarm setting in: *¿Cómo sabe ella dónde vivo?* "Just making myself presentable." She answered.

Rebecca had met Vivienne a year ago when the older woman had brought some clients to the Mermaid Club, supposedly on Cranston's recommendation. She had returned to the club twice since then, always with clients, and once with Cranston, which had become excruciating for him and delightful for Rebecca. (Of course, Cranston had 'punished' her for it later, which had also been both excruciating and delightful.)

Opening the door, Vivienne somehow looked taller and thinner in the light of day. Though some of that was likely the pinstripe suit.

¡Caray! Casi se ve mejor con un traje que su hermano.

"Vivienne! Doll!" Rebecca grinned. "I ain't seen you in a blue moon. Come on in."

"Thank you," Vivienne strode in and scanned the room.

Rebecca's apartment only had two rooms: the bathroom and everything else; being a large bed, three wardrobes, the rocking chair, a book case with only three shelves, a dining table with only two chairs, and as much kitchen as ten horizontal feet would allow.

"Have a seat." Rebecca gestured at one of the dining room chairs. "Can I get you something, doll? The water's clear and I got milk and beer in the icebox. Have you heard of Yippity? It's this new beer they make for ladies."

"That is fine." Vivienne said, setting her bag on the table and sitting with her legs crossed at the knees. "I do not think I will be staying long."

"Oh, dear. Now, you got me thinking something's wrong."

"There is, but it is a society emergency; crucial and urgent, but also nothing to wring one's hands over."

"You got a society emergency and you came to *me*? Doll, I think things are worse than you know."

Vivienne grinned as she removed her gloves. "This afternoon, there is a picnic to celebrate the opening of Saint Moon's new factory in Régence. Saint Moon is our latest big client, so it is important that Cranston and I both attend. However, I learned just last night that the president of Saint Moon is taking the opportunity to debut his children to Silkhaven society. One of his children happens to be an exotic young woman of about twenty-two, which means I need Cranston to arrive with a woman on his arm."

"'Exotic'?" Rebecca asked, still catching up with Vivienne's rapid-fire lips. "How d'ya mean?"

"Her mother is oriental. Probably Chinese, but somehow no one seems to know for sure."

"Just her mother?"

"Have you heard of Edward Blake?"

"Nah, who's he?"

"He is the president of Saint Moon and as Anglo-Saxon as they come without being blonde."

Rebecca made a mock gasp. "And he miscegenated? How progressive."

"I will admit to a good deal of curiosity there, myself. Now, I know that Cranston can restrain himself from flirting with any intention, but I sincerely do not believe he knows how to talk to women without flirting at all. And I have seen the *crème de la crème* of Silkhaven women drape themselves—sometimes literally—over him when they feel they are not getting enough of his attention."

Rebecca nodded. "It's the smile."

"*Is* it?" Vivienne asked genuinely.

"Oh, yeah. He smiles at you the way you've always wished someone would smile at you, even if you never gave it much thought before."

"Interesting. I thought it was how he carries himself like a bootblack while wearing expensive suits."

"That helps, for sure, but it just makes him look fun. Lots of men look fun and you don't have to be on their arm to get it. That smile though, a girl just wants to put it in a box and hide it under her pillow."

"Fascinating,"

"Okay, so you don't want your client's daughter going gaga for Cranston, at least not where Daddy can see, so Cranston's gotta turn up with a dame?"

"'Gaga'?"

"Silly,"

"Ah, yes: no. We cannot have Miss Gabrielle Blake trying to put Cranston's smile in her box."

"Okay, but ain't this a high-falutin kind of thing?" Rebecca asked. "Not that I don't appreciate the invitation or nothin', but...um...what do English dames say? 'I haven't a thing to wear.'"

"Well, as I said, I only learned this last night." Vivienne's voice took on a careful cadence. "So, it is a last-minute invitation and society women rather bristle at that sort of thing. You, as a licensed sex worker, might—I thought—be more amenable to the practical considerations underpinning said invitation."

Rebecca considered without knowing how to feel about that. The idea of being Cranston's emergency date tickled her, but it would have tickled her more if Cranston was extending the invitation himself. Nothing Vivienne had said was untrue and she had said it as politely as she could. There certainly were women for whom this kind of thing was their bread and butter, but Rebecca had chosen to work in a club because of the regular hours and all that entailed. Something about this did not feel good, but she could not put her finger on what or why or even how much.

"I will admit," Vivienne continued when Rebecca did not reply. "That I am unclear on the exact nature of your relationship with my brother and I do not need fine details. However, I know he likes your company and I am more than willing to remunerate you for your time, the same as I would any other professional."

"So," Rebecca said slowly. "This is a business call."

"Again, not knowing your arrangement with Cranston, I was not sure if this should be business or social. Whichever is your preference, I will accommodate."

Rebecca then realized Vivienne was out of her element. She wasn't sitting there all straight-backed and business-like because she thought she was more important than Rebecca, but because she felt she may say the wrong thing at any moment. Like the hygiene people might say, she was a few degrees out of her comfort zone. They both were. The club certainly was not Vivienne's usual sort of place, but it had rules and procedures. This situation did not. Or rather, what the rules were was unknown to both of them.

"I can't take money for this." Rebecca said. "My license doesn't cover it and there's always someone who checks."

"The mayor will be there, possibly the governor, so yes, we should avoid breaking any laws until they break them first. Fortunately, my set has a way around that sort of thing. We call them 'favors'." She winked.

"Wait, really? You wanna call this a favor?"

"Is that a problem?"

"No, it's just I never did a favor for...someone...." She didn't want to say 'rich'. "Well, someone of your station."

"You know Cranston." Vivienne said seriously. "If a pretty young woman from the East invites him to motorboat, do you really think he will say 'no'?"

"Motorboat?"

"The picnic area is along the East River."

"Charming," Rebecca fawned for a moment. "But you're right, he's a man."

"Only more so. And keeping him from endangering this contract is worth a substantial favor, yes."

That felt better, though she still could not pin down why. "Yeah, I'll take a favor, but I still don't have anything to wear."

"I knew that was a possibility. We have an appointment at Quirk's Department Store in thirty minutes."

"I'll throw myself together." Rebecca said, standing. "You know, if Cranston had come with you, you coulda saved that favor."

"That is good to know, but that is also the catch."

"Oh, dear."

"Cranston is somewhat indisposed with a project and I suspect that pulling him away from it will be difficult. Less so for you, I imagine."

"You mean there's seduction involved in this?"

"Of a sort, yes."

"You should have opened with that, doll. What's his project?"

Chapter 2:
Pearl–Rebecca

August 5th, 1921. Silkhaven.

One Globe. Two Worlds. Three Telegraphs. Four Posts. Five Journals. And a Phoenix. All in a stack.

Still in his pajama bottoms, Cranston sat on the floor combing through this week's pile of newspapers fetched for him by the dutiful captains of Walker Trading ships. He had a large logbook at his side, a pen and ink, a jar of paste, and a pair of scissors. He had been at this for eight months and had only filled about half of the log.

He was looking for a hole in the words; one shaped like a woman who got halfway to becoming a bird. If she had been spied on by some reporter, it wouldn't be printed in any reliable newspaper, but maybe the story would be written around her and he could catch her shape in what went unsaid.

Della Caine was, it seemed, still working for Benjamin Syme's Atlantic Network. Both company and owner appeared in newspapers from time to time, as did Benjamin's newly elected senator brother, Henry. That was where Cranston started. His logbook was full of the names of clients, associates, friends, rivals, and people filing lawsuits.

At that moment, Cranston was reading about the death of a union treasurer in Wheeling, West Virginia, right on the America-Iroquois border. Back in February, the Ferryman's Union of the Ohio River had been in a dispute with three companies—two American and one Iroquois—regarding the effects of import taxes on shipping costs. Iroquois had dynamic tax rates, which made it impossible to calculate them into an annual contract. After a particularly turbulent winter, the Ferryman's Union demanded the companies pay these taxes directly, instead of taking them out of the ferrymen's payments.

One of the American companies, Two Creek Coal, had hired the Atlantic Network as strikebreakers, even before a strike was officially declared. Nothing apparently came of it and an agreement was signed in early March. Through the spring, the agreement had become the topic of much discussion in the papers. The Iroquois began issuing European-style tariffs, removing the shippers from the equation; something which had ramifications, both real and imagined, for American and Canadian companies.

The death of the Ferryman Union's treasurer seemed unlikely to be related to the dispute, the Atlantic Network, or Della Caine; but clues were so thin on the ground that Cranston couldn't chance it. He was so engrossed in the story—the treasurer died of a fever that no one else in town had—that he missed it the first time his name was called. When it came again—"Cranston!"—it nearly made him jump.

He turned to see Vivienne standing there with Pearl. The latter was wearing a pale violet day dress that appeared to have at least a yard of fabric dedicated to masking the large ratio between her waist and hips. The world of fashion, in its infinite youth, was spurning the sumptuous silhouette of the Victorian and consigning women of Pearl's proportions to great, flowing sheaths of fabric which made them look like silk-festooned pillars with heads and arms.

Cranston scrambled to his feet and smoothed out his pajama bottoms. His shirtless chest was not something either woman had not seen, but he was far less dressed than they were, and made him feel disadvantaged in some way.

"See?" Vivienne said to Pearl. "He has been doing this for months."

"Why don't you have a desk?" Pearl asked, looking around the room.

Of all the horrors Cranston had witnessed, his sister and his favorite paramour commenting together on how he had appointed a room was at least a contender for the top ten.

"I..." Cranston stammered. "I haven't gotten around to it."

"He says it," Vivienne drawled. "As if he would have to carry the thing up the stairs himself."

They were in the penthouse of the Walker Grand Hotel. This particular room had been a bedroom back when their paternal grandfather had been alive, and Uncle Cecil's family lived here with them. Cranston had barely begun toddling when his grandfather died. Once Cecil had full control of the company, he had moved his family to New York, hoping to eventually relocate the company headquarters there.

When they left, Cranston's family had moved in, partly to look after Grandmother. In all the intervening years, this room had remained officially empty. There were times Cranston had used it as a playroom, but his mother had forbidden any permanent installation of toy boxes or blanket forts. Now, being the man of the house, he had decided to assert ownership of the room. In his excitement to begin his search for Della Caine, he had not thought about furnishing the room, and by the time his excitement had died down, he was used to the present situation.

"What are you two doing together?" Cranston asked, still too unbalanced for tact or charm.

"We have just come from Quirk's." Vivienne answered.

"Yeah," Pearl stepped forward. "What do you think?" She asked, giving a little twirl.

"It's lovely." He said politely. "What's the occasion?"

"The Saint Moon picnic is today." Vivienne said. "You need to get dressed."

"Oh," Cranston said. "Damn, I forgot." He could see what was happening, and his resistance to it was bolstered by his distaste for Pearl's dress. "The thing is..."

"The thing *is*," Pearl interrupted. "I just spent three hours getting pinned up in this rig, so you can be damn sure I'm going to take my turns around that fancy picnic or whatever it is y'all do. And I insist you escort me because, if you don't, I have ways of making you miserable."

Cranston had to chuckle. "I had no idea you were on the guest list."

"There are all kinds of things you don't know," she said, stepping close enough to draw a finger down his chest. "Like what I got on underneath this thing."

"Oh, dear." Vivienne groaned.

"Brand new, too. Imported." Pearl bit her lower lip suggestively. "You couldn't even begin to guess."

Despite the presence of his sister, Cranston found himself responding to this suggestion with a tentative redistribution of blood flow.

"Mmm," Cranston growled, falling into his usual mode with Pearl. "That does appeal to the lesser angels of my nature."

"Are those angels quick dressers?" Vivienne blurted with obvious discomfort.

Cranston pulled himself out of his flirtatious tone to say: "They can be persuaded."

"Good, I am going to dress." And Vivienne excused herself rapidly from the room.

"You know," Cranston said, flirting again. "She's going to be a while."

"Hold your horses, cowboy." Pearl flattened her palm on his chest. "Once I'm out of this dress, it's going to take an engineer to get me back into it, and I have hardly begun to enjoy playing that I'm one of your society dames. So, you are going to get yourself into a suit and show me a good time before I show you..." she leaned as close to his ear as their height difference allowed. "Some red, Virginian leather."

Pearl pushed him back, then spun and swished out of the room. "Vivienne," she called as she made for the door. "I'm coming to help, doll."

Cranston, alone again, turned to look at the great stack of untouched newspapers. Part of him was certain the clues he was seeking were there, right there. If he could just spare the time to find them. If only the world would conspire with him. Another part of him knew how unlikely that was. That part of him knew he may never find her and, with her, the cure to his nightmares. That part of him remembered that, until a cure was found, Pearl was the woman best at helping him keep said nightmares at bay.

He sighed and crouched down to close the logbook and tidy the newspaper he had been reading. Then, back up and out to find his seersucker with the light blue stripes. Of his day suits, it would look the best with Pearl's faint purple 'rig'.

Two and a half hours later. Régence, King Charles Island.

Régence had been established east of Silkhaven some seventy years prior as a place for new money men to keep their wives and children in idylls while they painted Silkhaven red. Thanks to some unusually strict real estate laws, Régence had managed to spawn a sort of new world gentry that had successfully resisted being absorbed into Silkhaven since the turn of the century.

Of course, they had also driven their property values to remarkable lows. Somehow Edward Blake had managed to secure a large parcel where he could build Saint Moon's newest factory. It reeked of dirty dealings, but then that had been why Walker had pursued this contract in the first place. They had to get close if they were going to find out what he was planning.

The factory, when they arrived, was not merely new; it was the sort of new that made you realize how old the neighboring buildings were. Here, neighboring involved almost a half mile of travel, but nonetheless.

It was all bright red brick and glossy, steel doors. The parking lot was half full of branded trucks and three double-decker buses, presumably for ferrying in workers. A flat-topped iron fence wrapped around the property that was tall enough to discourage jumpers without the decoratively menacing spikes. The front gate had the company's name wrought in iron letters, and while it was open, there were two young men in crisp, pink uniforms and white peaked caps informing guests there would be a tour later, but that they should park at a place called Charpentier's Dock.

Williamson, their driver, parked on the far side of a characteristically charming park hardly improved by the banners and streamers marking it as the picnic area. There was a tent set up for drivers and other help that had tagged along while the employers recreated in the open.

Vivienne trailed behind while Cranston walked with Pearl into the scattered guests doing their best impression of *A Sunday Afternoon on the Island of La Grande Jatte*. The women's hats were too small and there was not a bustle in sight, but other than that, they were doing a fine job. Cranston's mind made the leap to *Le Déjeuner sur l'herbe* and part of his brain started working out the logistics of recreating that one for a decadent occasion, maybe his birthday.

But that thought would have to wait. They approached the nearest cluster of guests.

"Bertie!" Cranston raised his free hand to the first member of the pack to make eye contact with him.

Bertrand Bly stiffened noticeably but smiled. "Cranston," he replied with polite coolness and extended a four-fingered hand. Bertie had been a pilot in the Army Air Service and lost his right ring finger and half his pinkie in a crash landing. Now, he was deputy vice president of his uncle's bank.

With him were Leonard Schiff—who had been a judge advocate during the war and was now working in the district attorney's office— and Jerome Daraiche, who had been an infantry captain in Africa and since then Cranston had heard nothing else. They were with their wives, and introductions were made all around. Cranston had been preparing for this.

"This is Miss Rebecca Costa-Cortez," Cranston had had to ask for her full name in the car as it had never really come up before. It sounded like an alias to his ear. "A woman of independent means from New York."

"Lord," Mrs. Schiff exclaimed. She and Cranston had had a flirtation the summer he was sixteen, which had climaxed with nothing more than some light petting on a rowboat. "He is importing them now."

"Shows you what he thinks of us," said Mrs. Daraiche, with whom Cranston had danced a few times over the years.

"I imported myself, thank you very much," Pearl—*Rebecca*—replied with a haughty grin and an unfamiliar accent.

The ladies laughed companionably, though Cranston could see the gossip-lust in their eyes. "Don't tell me," Mrs. Schiff said. "They don't have men like Cranston in New York?"

"Oh, we do," Pearl—*Rebecca*—nodded. "Only less so."

Mrs. Schiff feigned a defeated sigh. "That's how she did it," she said to Mrs. Daraiche.

"No surprise," Mrs. Daraiche replied before turning to Pearl— *Rebecca, Rebecca, Rebecca.* "That is precisely the sort of thing Vivienne would say." Her eyes turned to Cranston. "You Walkers; it is bon mots or bon voyage with you." Then she hugged her husband's arm close and looked up at him adoringly. "Give me a plain-spoken man any day."

Cranston leapt in. "Jerry, what is it you're doing these days?"

"Still in the service," he replied as if daring Cranston to make a wisecrack about it.

"Well done, Captain," Cranston replied amiably.

"It's Major, now."

"Well, that's egg on my face," Cranston smiled to the group, getting none back from these men he had gone to school with. "Thank god we're not in uniform, or he'd have me doing push-ups for that."

"I'm sure you'd talk your way out of it," Leonard muttered.

Cranston assumed a more sober tone and said: "That *is* what Uncle Sam trained me to do. Just following orders and all that."

"For all the good your gang did us at Verdun," Bertie replied.

Apologetically, Cranston said: "I had been moved north by then, but I heard it was a most dynamic battlefield. I imagine by the time their reports were ready, the information was out of date."

"All the reports in the world," Bertie continued, his chest swelling a little. "Are not half as good as a photograph."

"I don't suppose so, no,"

Mrs. Bly was rubbing her husband's arm soothingly.

"That's all history, now," Cranston said. There was a long silence as no one verbalized agreement. "It was good to see you all safe and sound."

"Sure thing." Leonard answered sternly.

"Have a good day, then." He and *Rebecca* took their leave of the stony-eyed men and somewhat bewildered ladies.

Pearl pulled herself close to Cranston's ear as they walked away. "They looked ready to fight you."

"I told you: the Praetorians were unpopular."

"I know, but...damn it, they looked at you like you were a sympathizer."

Cranston just let out a weary breath, disinterested in explaining things further; the paranoia and wild gossip that had been directed at him and the other men with eagle heads stitched on their shoulders.

Pearl went on. "Did you meet them over there?"

"No, in school. Bertie and Leonard were part of my set in secondary school and university. Bertie, I've known since grammar school."

"Golly..." Pearl just clutched his arm tighter.

"Cranston!" He was summoned to a cluster of conversation, this time. It was Jonathan Cabot, a small, wizened, and humbly dressed man who was chairman of the Walker Corporation's board of directors. He stood with a crowd of much better dressed people of his own generation, with the exception of the young-ish woman on his arm.

The woman towered over Cabot not only in sheer length of form, but in the imperious way she carried herself. She was about Cranston's age, but with the peculiar tightness in the skin one saw in career sailors. Her bright blonde hair contrasted starkly with her suntanned skin and she stood with one hand propped on her hip in a subtly unladylike way.

"Cranston Walker," Cabot said as they approached. "You know

Herbert Cowles and his wife, Mamie."

"Yes, of course," Cranston extended a hand to Admiral Cowles, retired, and tipped his hat to his wife. Cowles had been a friend of Cranston's grandfather and made frequent recommendations regarding captains hired from the ranks of the FS Navy.

"George and Grace Weld," Cabot continued. George Weld III owned the shipbuilding company Walker exclusively bought from; a firm that had operated since the ships were made of wood.

Lastly, Cabot introduced: "Ellis and Helene Longworth." Ellis Longworth was a prominent lawyer, though he had had no direct dealings with the Walkers.

"And who is this charming lamb?" Grace Weld asked, reaching out to stroke Rebecca's free arm.

"Miss Rebecca Costa-Cortez," Cranston said, still feeling like it was a stranger's name. "A lady of independent means from New York."

"It's very nice to meet you, Miss Costa-Cortez." Cabot said, kissing Rebecca's hand. "Cranston, I had no idea you would be accompanied."

"It was news to me as well." Cranston replied.

"I insisted." Rebecca added.

"As one often must." Cabot nodded approvingly. "Allow me now to introduce Miss Odile de la Porte, recently arrived from the Caribbean Confederacy."

The tall, bronzed woman reached out a hand to shake Cranston's. It was a firm, manly shake and Cranston knew immediately what this woman's trade was back home. "Bonjour," Miss de la Porte said.

"Bonjour," Cranston replied.

"Hi," Rebecca said, shaking Miss de la Porte's hand before letting out a little squeal, followed by a giggle. "Quite some handshake you got there."

"Mr Walker," Mr Longworth asked, eyeing Rebecca approvingly. "How does one find a lady of independent means these days? I only ask because we were just discussing the trouble our own grandsons were having finding suitable wives."

"Oh, dear," Cranston chuckled. "Well, if I were to offer the young men any advice, I would tell them to familiarize themselves with a local tea room or some comparable haunt of the fairer sex. Display their finest manners and wear their ignorance of the feminine arts on their sleeves. Any good woman over the age of twenty-five is an eager teacher of such things."

"What do you think of tennis, Mr Walker?" Mrs Cowles asked. "I see it is very popular with young ladies these days."

"In my experience, if one is to get a lady's attention on the tennis court, a gentleman must either be very good at it—to arouse her competitive nature—or very bad at it—to evoke her nurturing instincts. Women who are only middling at the sport, it seems to me, enjoy the game for the female companionship it affords. Beginners may seek out very skilled men to teach them, but you are not likely to see them more than once or twice. Very serious novices, of course, will hire a teacher."

Mrs Cowles shook her head in frustration. "Alas," she said.

"Now, do excuse me, please," Cranston said. "I have yet to see our host and I would not want my escort to get a better offer."

They said their goodbyes and continued on. When they were away, Rebecca whispered to him. "A better offer? The kind of women they're looking for are the ones who refuse to vote."

"Or worse," Cranston whispered back. "Vote how their husband tells them."

"Horror of horrors." She giggled, then said: "Can you imagine a female president? If we ladies really set our minds to it, I bet we could get it done in ten years."

Cranston did some quick math in his head. "Alice Longworth for President 1932."

Ahead of them was a pronounced crowd of guests branching out on two sides from a husband and wife. Edward Blake wore jaunty, light blue trousers with a navy jacket and a dark orange bow tie. The small woman at Edward's elbow was the mysterious Mrs Martha Blake. She wore a close-fitting dress ending just below her knee, which would have been a scandal before the war. From the gleam of the sun coming off it, Cranston could tell at a distance it was silk. He may have avoided learning the ins and outs of the family business as a boy, but he knew very well the parts of import and export that made girls swoon.

Mrs Blake's dress had a high collar and short sleeves. The silk was red, but had an ornate design of large flowers on a vine done in gold thread. Her jet-black hair bloomed in bunches of little curves around her ears and a thick lock was glued to her forehead in short waves with so much wax it shone more than her dress.

Vivienne appeared at Cranston's elbow. "We should make our introductions."

"I wouldn't dream of doing otherwise." He replied.

They approached their hosts with Vivienne in the lead. Her couturier, Madame Jojo, had made her a suit in pale green with trouser legs so wide they could be mistaken for a skirt on casual observation.

"Pardon me," Edward told his little court. "Vivienne!" He proclaimed.

The whole crowd turned to her.

"Good afternoon, Edward." They shook hands.

"I have the distinct pleasure," Edward continued. "Of introducing you to my wife, Martha."

"It's a pleasure to meet you, Mrs Blake."

"Likewise, I am sure." Mrs Blake bowed with her hands folded across her stomach, her accent permitting no R's and making her sound more severe than her face suggested. "Though, we did meet once before."

"Did we?" Vivienne asked.

"It was a long time ago. It is no surprise that you do not remember."

"That is very gracious of you, but I should like to hear about it."

"Oh, you will." Mrs Blake smiled knowingly.

"Until then," Vivienne said, moving on. "This is my brother, Cranston."

Cranston stepped forward. He proffered a hand and kissed hers when it was offered. "Charmed," he said.

"Charming," she replied with a coquettish tilt of her hips, eliciting delighted laughter from the crowd.

"Careful, darling," Edward smiled. "This one might really put you to the test."

"I think he is spoken for." Mrs Blake gestured subtly at Rebecca.

Cranston touched the small of her back and brought her forward. "May I introduce Miss Rebecca Costa-Cortez?" It sounded real, this time, and that gave Cranston a twinge of melancholy. He missed 'Pearl' already.

"Edward Blake," he kissed Rebecca's hand.

"Good afternoon, Miss Costa-Cortez," Martha bowed.

"It's nice to meet you, Mr Blake." Rebecca said. "Mrs Blake...Knee ho."

Mrs Blake's thickly outlined eyes opened a fraction wider. "好開心見到你." She said.

Rebecca nodded. "Hi ah."

"午安." Martha said slowly with a patient smile.

"Isn't this cosmopolitan?" Edward said to the onlookers unnerved by his wife's departure from English.

Cranston, standing behind the ladies, noticed a younger woman in the same sort of tight, calf-length dress as Mrs Blake, only in deep blue with turquoise birds stitched on. The younger woman certainly bore an ethnic resemblance to the woman he assumed was her mother, but her makeup was completely different, giving the impression of sharper cheekbones and an altogether more angular face. She was also vibrating, something Mrs Blake's demeanor suggested she was incapable of.

"Darling," Martha said, as if on cue. "I think we have taken too much of Miss Walker's time." She nodded at their apparent offspring.

Vivienne turned to the younger woman who rushed forward to clasp Vivienne's hand with both of hers. "Vivienne Walker?" The younger Blake said, her almond-shaped eyes starry. "You don't remember me, do you?"

Cranston watched as his sister was hauled off by the younger, elated woman who had begun telling her a story in terms akin to a Scandinavian epic. He and Rebecca made a polite exit from the elder Blake's court and began strolling.

"I didn't know you spoke Chinese." Cranston said to Rebecca.

"I only know a few phrases." She replied. "You share rooms with all kinds of girls in my line of work."

They walked for a few more minutes, Cranston quietly identifying other members of Silkhaven's elite as they were scattered about the park's gentle slope. Then, he spotted a young woman in a dress that was out of place for reasons he couldn't put his finger on. It had the loose, sheath-like quality of modern dresses and the large bow on the hip was not exactly unfashionable, but not quite what everyone else was wearing. He also couldn't place the material.

"Her," he said. "I don't know."

Rebecca looked for a moment. "That's Thursday Johnson." She said, surprised.

"A colleague?" Cranston asked, noticing the brunette woman in the odd dress appeared unaccompanied.

"Nah," Rebecca said. "But her mother is."

"Oh, really?"

"Thursday's a reporter. She does club reviews and such." Rebecca waved as she tugged Cranston towards the improbably named reporter. "Thursday!" She called.

"Rebecca?" Thursday Johnson's face lit up with recognition. The two women embraced. "What are..." she cut herself off. "Cranston Walker," Thursday said in a voice like a master of ceremonies introducing the next act. "Silkhaven's third most eligible bachelor and the terror of the city's restauranteurs. Nominal CEO of the Walker Trading Company, though word has it that his big sister is the real power behind the throne. Care to comment?"

"Vivienne Walker was at her father's elbow for fifteen years before inheriting his chair." Cranston said in the tone he used when giving his secretary dictation. "The company could not have asked for a more informed or competent successor." He switched tones. "Something like that?"

"Well," Thursday cocked her head and hips in opposite directions. "I was hoping for something in the first person, but a girl makes do." She turned back to Rebecca. "Don't tell me you've convinced this one to settle down."

"No!" Rebecca laughed. "He'd be the one doing the convincin', doll. But he's good company for as long as any company can be and this sounded like a hoot. What are *you* doin' here?"

"Same as you," Thursday replied. "Working."

"You get a promotion or somethin'?"

"The opposite." Thursday sighed. "But I do have my eyes on an exclusive." She nodded surreptitiously to her right.

A dozen yards away, a young man in a crisp suit stood under a tree. He had his hands clasped in front of him and looked beleaguered by two much older men talking, not so much *to* him, but *around* him. Cranston recognized one of the men as a manager at Saint Moon. The sad-looking boy had a clean, Anglo-Saxon jawline and narrow, oriental eyes.

"Michael Blake," Thursday said without actually looking. "Saint Moon president, Edward Blake's only son and heir apparent to the family business. While his twin sister is collecting Silkhaven's bachelors like a mother duck, the young ladies of the isle seem unsure about the brother's Eastern charms. I, on the other hand, am *fascinated* and Mama taught me plenty of ways to make a man chatty."

"Oh, dear." Cranston said, matching Thursday's frankness. "Part of me feels I should protect the boy, but also, he must learn somehow."

"Don't worry, Mr Walker," Thursday raised a succubus' eyebrow at him. "No one's ever regretted an interview with me."

"No, I imagine...wait," he said. "What do you mean I'm the terror of restauranteurs? I've never raised my voice to a waiter in my life and I always tip generously."

"They're afraid you'll come only once." She said. "One visit from Cranston Walker means you're on the map. A season without a second visit means you best close up shop."

"Really?" He said, feeling a sudden burden of valor. "Is that why I have so few bad meals in this city?"

"They'd rather toil in obscurity than see you just once."

"I will make a note of it."

"Now, if you'll excuse me." She said and sauntered off, her hips swinging and the dress shifting in ways that made it look like it might fall off.

"That young man is in a great deal of trouble." Cranston mused.

"Jealous?" Rebecca asked.

"A little."

Chapter 3:
Atalanta

June 15th, 1905. Lake Placid, New York.

Gabrielle had been excited to visit the club. Papa had spent weeks regaling her and Michael with descriptions of all the summer sporting things they would do. Her mother had been hesitant and Gabrielle had gleaned that there had once been a bad man at the club, but he was gone now. They were going to have two weeks of great fun.

Except that there were lots of bad men. Certainly, there were lots of mean boys and there were men and women standing by doing nothing as they called her 'squinty' and 'pug face'. Her parents were off doing something that was just for grown-ups and left her and Michael with the other children and some minders.

At first, Gabrielle had told the mean boys to stop. Stop stretching their eyes with their fingers. Stop making buck-toothed faces at her. Stop calling her "celestial". She was only seven and didn't know what "celestial" meant, but she knew that she didn't like their tone. When none of that had worked, she had contented herself with the idea of telling her father when he got back and then thoughts of all the trouble those boys would be in.

That comforting fantasy only carried her along for about twenty minutes. Finally, the mean boys had gotten her to cry. Michael, who had seemed immune to their teasing, now wheeled on them and socked one in the face. That boy had gone down crying. This crying, a boy's crying—a *white* boy's crying—had brought the minders running in.

Michael was scolded and told that the boys had only been playing.

When he protested, a woman grabbed him by the arm and began hauling him away. Another minder had come for Gabrielle, then, and she ran. She didn't know why she was running and certainly had no idea where she was running to, only that she didn't want the minders to get her. She tore pell-mell into the forest at the edge of the club's lawn.

"Whoa there!" A male voice called as Gabrielle nearly plowed into him. "Where's the fire?" He chuckled.

Gabrielle looked up to more boys, older boys. They were smiling, mostly to each other. Glancing around, she was deep in the forest and had somehow run far enough that she had lost sight of the club buildings. It was just her in the woods with three boys almost twice as tall as she was. They wore knickerbocker suits without ties and one of them was holding a cigarette.

"If you aren't careful," one of them said. "You'll tear your stockings."

"Where's your nanny?" The third one asked. He was less smiley than the other two. He had that impatient look of grown-ups who don't like children, even though he wasn't a grown-up.

Gabrielle felt a hard, cold lump in her throat and said nothing. If she opened her mouth, she knew, she would cry and one did not go crying to older boys.

"Well?" The third boy—this one in a dark brown suit—pressed.

The first boy, in a light blue suit, leaned down so that his face was almost even with hers. "Do...you...speak...English?" He said loudly, pausing unnecessarily between words. "Englishy? Speaky Englishy? No speaky Englishy?"

"She really mightn't." The second boy, in light brown, said with some private delight. He turned to her and shifted his voice up into his nose. "Wong cow shoe baba pow cow shoe wong kaka kapow." Then, he paused like he really thought she would respond to that. "Huh, I'm not sure she can speak at all."

The boy in blue suddenly grabbed one of her pigtails and yanked. Gabrielle yelped and then tears flowed. All her reserve was exhausted. Gabrielle fell to her knees, certainly dirtying her stockings and dress, and sobbed for all she was worth.

"Shush her up!" The boy in dark brown said, snatching the cigarette. "We'll get it if anyone finds us."

A pair of hands were then lifting Gabrielle off the ground as she screwed her eyes tight against the flood of tears. She kicked wild and blind and one of her feet connected with something. "Golly!" One of the boys grunted and then Gabrielle felt herself sailing through the air, then hitting the twig-covered ground.

"Vicious little beast!" She heard him say then, his voice dripping with wrath. "You'll pay for that!"

Gabrielle willed her eyes to open, but the tears made a blur of the woods. She began crawling in the dirt and rocks and sticks before hands were again grabbing her. One hand came over her mouth and she immediately bit it. The boy screamed, but kept one arm around her waist, hauling her off the ground.

"Shut up!" Another boy hissed as Gabrielle fought against the arm holding her tight.

Then, something entirely new happened. Something smashed into Gabrielle's head. It echoed for a moment inside her skull the way a knock on a wooden door does. Pain like she had never known flared and dizziness swept over her. There was this strange, slow second where the pain didn't hurt. She felt it, knew it for what it was, but with a detachment like it was a mere memory of pain. In that brief instant, the pain seemed like a ball of hot color that she might pluck from her hair and hold in her hand for inspection.

All too soon, that detached moment collapsed and there were no more tears, only screaming. Gabrielle thrashed out in all directions, feeling her heels connect with firm, but yielding human flesh. Her eyes cleared just before she was dropped. Her feet failed instantly and she was on her hands and knees.

"What were you thinking?" A boy chided.

"I thought I'd knock her out!"

Again, Gabrielle was crawling. She was trying to get up on her feet to run, but a hand caught hold of her dress. As she rose up, the hand tugged her off balance and she careened to one side. Her shoulder struck a tree and she fell onto her backside. A hand covered her mouth again, the thumb holding her jaw shut, and pushed her head against a tree.

"Quiet you!" The boy in light brown whispered harshly. "If you get us in trouble, we'll gut you like a fish. Do you understand?"

He was on his knees, staring dangerously into her eyes. Part of her wanted to claw at his eyes and try to run again, but another part of her suggested that, maybe, if she did as she was told, they would stop being so brutish. She had, after all, kicked and bitten at least one of them. Perhaps all this rough handling had been her fault. When they asked her questions, she had rudely said nothing. In the end, might this all be her fault?

This line of thought was interrupted by the snapping of a twig under a boot several feet away.

"Get off her!" A woman's voice bellowed. "Get away from her, now!"

The boy in brown scampered back in surprise and Gabrielle turned to see the towering figure of a woman in trousers and a broad-brimmed hat that looked, in the moment, like the nimbus around the head of a stained-glass saint.

"She's a wild animal!" One of the boys protested as the woman tramped closer.

Gabrielle had never seen a woman in trousers before. From the stuttering surprise in the three boys, neither had they.

"Yes..." another joined in. "She was kicking...she kicked me."

They had gotten into a line and Gabrielle wondered if this woman was their governess or school teacher. Whoever she was, she walked directly up to them.

"She kicked me." The boy in blue repeated, quieter.

Like a bolt of lightning, the woman slapped the boy across the cheek with sufficient force to double him over.

"Did I ask?" The woman growled.

"See here!" The boy in dark brown added only to get the back of that same hand across his own face.

"Scoundrels!" She shouted. "Rapscallions, villains, bottom feeders; sniveling, arrogant, simple, spoiled, two-horse, scrawny, stinking, tilted-capped ruffians!" They were cowering before her as she drew in a breath and continued. "Yellow-bellied, litigious, sons of whores!"

"Hey!" Dark brown suit exclaimed. "How dare you..." He was interrupted by another slap.

"Thus!" The woman declared. "I dare thusly, you glass-gazing, super-serviceable, finical rogue!"

"Hold on," the boy in light brown chimed in. "That's King Lear."

The woman's head swiveled towards him, the one boy she hadn't slapped yet, and he jerked his face as far away from her reach as possible. "Oh, joy!" Her voice rumbled. "There is a scholar among us."

His jaw trembled as he said: "I'm going to tell my father what you did."

"Do." Now, she wheeled on him, moving close enough that he had to incline his head to keep looking her in the eye, even as his teeth chattered. "Tell your father that you went into the woods to smoke, you little, googely-eyed goop! Tell him you found a child there and beat her into the dirt. Tell him you were caught by the incarnate vengeance of the New Woman! Tell him what she did while you stood with your legs crossed."

They were almost nose to nose and the boy's eyes were beginning to water.

"Go!" The woman shouted. "Run!" And they did. Discarding the communal cigarette, they turned back for the club and ran for all they were worth. "Run home, puppies! Tell your daddies that you met Atalanta and her bow is already strung!"

She watched them go, her breath quick. With two long strides, she went to the smoldering cigarette and picked it up, gave a sniff, and then took a breath of it. "I will give them one thing." She said, seemingly to no one. "They steal the good stuff."

Now, the woman turned to look at Gabrielle. One more breath of the cigarette and she snuffed it out on a rock.

"How bad was it, baby?" The woman asked, kneeling down in front of Gabrielle.

"It was horrid." Gabrielle managed before falling to sobs again.

The woman reached out and the girl gladly slouched into her embrace. "There, there." She patted the girl's back. "They are gone now, and I will see to it that they catch hell. You do not happen to know their names, do you?"

"No," Gabrielle mewled.

"That is alright. I suppose they will give themselves away in no time." She pulled the girl away from her, then. "Let me take a look." Gabrielle tried to stifle her cries while the woman inspected her face. "Well, that is going to be a bruise, but it will be gone in a few days."

That was of no comfort, but she tried to be polite and not resume crying.

"Go on, baby." The woman said. "Cry it out. You are entitled to that much."

Gabrielle accepted the invitation and buried her face in the woman's shoulder, careful to keep the part of her face that throbbed with pain in the open air. The woman lifted her off the ground and carried her back towards the lodge. She heard the sounds of the other children playing and clung tighter to the strange woman.

"Oh dear," a distant voice called. "I can take her!"

"I found this girl being molested in the woods." 'Atalanta' sneered at this new voice, doubtlessly one of the minders. "Where were you?"

"She ran off, ma'am."

"A *child*? Ran off?" Atalanta bit back. "Oh, yes, I can see how you would be completely unprepared for such an eventuality. I think I will find her parents, myself, if you have no objections."

"No, ma'am."

"I thought not."

"Madam!" A grown man's voice said urgently as heavy footfalls approached.

Atalanta was walking again.

"Madam!" The man said again, his voice harsh, but quiet. "You cannot wear trousers here! There are children present!"

Atalanta stopped and turned. Gabrielle saw nothing, keeping her eyes pressed against her rescuer's cotton shirt.

"Say my name." Atalanta commanded.

"I beg your pardon." The man's voice cracked.

"You called me 'madam'. Say my name."

"I...I don't..."

"Walker! Vivienne Walker!"

The man sputtered a few nonsense sounds before grasping onto: "I'm sorry, but that is immaterial. We cannot have women wearing trousers in front of children...boys!"

"Would you like me to take them off?"

"No!" The man's voice went falsetto for a beat. "I must insist that you go inside."

"You mean you would like me to continue walking in the direction that I was walking before you started calling me 'madam'?"

"I..." he made a humming sound. "Yes, posthaste. Please!"

"You see, because I would be inside now if you had not stopped me."

"Of course, please continue."

"So, why did you stop me?"

"You are indecent!" The man squealed.

"Garçon!" A second man's voice called, calm and warm. "You best change your tone."

"Sir," the first man recovered himself. "We cannot have ladies parading around in trousers in full view of children."

"And I cannot have men taking that tone with my sister. Do you see the position I'm in? It's terribly awkward and it's all your fault."

"There are rules..." the man insisted.

"There are rules for lots of things, old man." The brother continued. "Like dueling."

This, at last, the first man had no reply to.

"Cranston," the woman holding Gabrielle said. "Three boys came running out of that forest a few minutes ago. Would you be a lamb and round them up for me? Two of them are likely to have swollen cheeks."

"I'm on the case." The brother replied. "You two, make yourselves useful and help me find these junior woodsmen, would you? Quickly, now."

It didn't take long to find Gabrielle's parents. Mother swept Gabrielle away from Vivienne and back to their rooms to apply liniment to her injuries. A little later, Father came in and doted on her while Mother insisted that they leave. She was in an intractable mood and Father agreed. They spent the night and were gone first thing the next day.

Gabrielle didn't see her rescuer again, but she never forgot the name. The young girl inscribed it on her heart and carried it with her into womanhood, around Cape Horn and back, until one afternoon she could finally speak it again.

August 5th, 1921. Régence, King Charles Island.

Vivienne sat, half reclined, on the great picnic blanket Gabrielle Blake had staked out for herself. It was an excellent spot for watching the river, but Vivienne's eyes were tightly shut, bracing against the memory of herself as a young woman. Even as Gabrielle narrated their first meeting, Vivienne hazily remembered the event. She wished she could deny calling herself 'Atalanta', but she had developed a tendency for the theatrical in those days.

"And I simply cannot believe how fate has brought us together again." Gabrielle said, her legs folded underneath her on the blanket. "It is simply too wonderful that I should return to America to find you here to greet me."

"It is not as if I met you on the dock." Vivienne smiled, trying to inject some levity into the girl's smothering adoration. "But you are right that it is a curious twist of fate."

"I was so worried." Gabrielle continued, beaming at her not unlike a certain kind of suitor. "You know, I have heard so many times about people encountering a heroic figure of their childhood and, in adulthood, finding that they are not half so admirable as they had seemed. But you..." and Vivienne swore the girl's face was shining with inner light, now. "You're not even married! Not that you could not be, of course, and it is nothing against my parents, but they are of a different time, you know? But I was afraid that I might one day learn that you had married—and if you had, I would have wished you every happiness—but I feared that he may not be worthy of you. So many women marry beneath them, in regards to character, at least. I had hoped that you knew your worth, not that I sincerely doubted such, but the world is cruel to women and perforce you may have accepted marriage to a bore or a tyrant or a fool in order to escape some greater cruelty."

Gabrielle took a loud breath.

"But to find you unwed and unbowed and..." she searched for a word that never came. "Well, you are still your own woman, as it were. You understand. Finding you in your present strength, it means just everything to a girl. After all, here you are surrounded by women in corsets," she lowered her voice briefly. "And even some in bustles—but you wore trousers!" She gestured at the voluminous legs splayed out like skirts on the blanket. "I wanted to wear trousers today, I did, but Mother has her heart set on bringing the cheongsam into vogue and I can't bear to disappoint her. I'm sure you understand."

"Yes," Vivienne said quickly, jamming the word in at the first opportunity. "It is a very charming dress. Did you get it in Hong Kong?"

"In a manner of speaking, I suppose." Gabrielle took a moment to smooth the silk over her stomach. "Mother and I have a seamstress, Bo Myeong, that we took on in Hong Kong. She has become indispensable to our mode and Mother hopes to make the cheongsam the next great fashion. Father had to call in favors to do it, but he got Bo Myeong permission to come with us. He even found her a little shop with an apartment near our house in the city."

"Oh," Vivienne said brightly, relieved to be on any topic but this veritable stranger's high opinion of her. "You are living in Silkhaven? I had not heard. The arrival of a rich young woman is usually cause for some talk."

"Indeed," Gabrielle turned to look behind them, where a cluster of young and presumably unattached men were waiting for an opportunity to speak with the island's latest bachelorette. "Excuse me," she called to the mob. "Could I trouble one or two of you to fetch us some refreshments?"

There was a clamor of acceptances, and the crowd tightened as the boys cast looks about for these spoken-of refreshments. A fight nearly broke out before three of them made a break for a well-appointed table. A couple more went after them, a few stayed to wait for the next opportunity, and two of them accepted total defeat and wandered off to try their luck elsewhere. One started to approach, but Vivienne warned him off with a look.

"Are the men here always so eager?" Gabrielle asked quietly.

"Under the right circumstances, yes," Vivienne told her. "But there is no telling how long they can maintain that eagerness. And you, Miss Blake, are singular in Silkhaven society, so all bets are off."

"You mean because I'm oriental?"

"I do, and I hope you take no offense."

"How could I be offended by myself? I *am* oriental."

"Cling tightly to that attitude!"

"It was not so different in Hong Kong. There are plenty of Eurasians there, but they are usually brought up in working-class homes. You know, growing up in a wealthy family offers certain protections to children that can be seen in their faces as they reach adulthood. So, despite being of no unusual parentage, I was considered 'a rare beauty' there, as well."

"Excuse me, Miss Walker," came the sharp monotone of Martha Blake's voice.

Vivienne turned to see the woman—who must have been at least forty, but hardly looked ten years her daughter's senior—looming over them.

"I need a word with my daughter," Mrs. Blake added.

"Of course," Vivienne rose. "I should find my brother before the tour."

"I will see you in the plant!" Gabrielle said, rising smoothly from her kneeling position to a height of no more than 5'2".

Vivienne said her farewells and walked slowly away. As she scanned the crowd for Cranston and Rebecca, she heard Martha and Gabrielle talking in what she assumed was Chinese. That would be a fine skill to have, she thought; having a private conversation in the middle of a crowd. She mused for a moment about she and Cranston having a secret language, but it was far too late for that.

And that thought opened a door to regrets about their childhoods, their youths, really the whole of their lives before he had been shipped off to the war. She caught a glimpse of all the ways she could have been a better sister. A dozen imagined, better versions of herself were idle— she discovered—in some waiting room deep in her mind. A lump began to form in her throat and she slammed the door shut.

Chapter 4:
Thursday, Thursday & Friday

"Johnson!" J. Percy Bridge, her editor, shouted from his office door. "Get in here!"

Thursday had a mouth full of potato salad. In the time it took her to find a napkin, Alphonse Johnson was on his feet and smirking for reasons known only to him. "Coming, Chief!"

"Not you, Fruitland!" Percy barked. "Why in tarnation would I say 'Johnson' if I wanted you?"

"My name is Johnson."

"The heck it is! Sit down! I don't want to see you on your feet unless you're putting your coat down for Johnson to walk on."

"Why would I put my coat down for *Thursday*?"

"In case there's a puddle!"

"We're inside."

"Golblastit, Fruitland!"

Thursday stood and brushed rye crumbs from her skirt. "On my way, boss."

"One of these days," Alphonse growled.

"Your balls will drop." Thursday replied. "We know. We're all rooting for you, buddy."

The newsroom at the Silkhaven Journal was a tightly packed collection of desks and neurotic egos. All the typewriters made it a bit like working in a rainforest if the pitter-patter of rain on palm leaves was amplified by a factor of ten and the birds sounded like bell chimes.

Thursday shut Percy's door behind her. He didn't have it much better than anyone else. The walls didn't reach the ceiling and there was only enough space between his desk and the door for said door to open, but he could take off his pants after lunch and that was all the luxury a certain kind of man needed.

"You and Fruitland could take Vaudeville by storm." She said.

"Fruitland couldn't take North Carolina by storm if he was the Wicked Witch of Winter." Percy tossed a peppermint candy into his mouth and crunched it. "Are you trying to kill me, Johnson?"

"Of course not. The cops planted that arsenic in my desk, I swear."

"Did Billy DeBeck write that one for you?"

"He couldn't afford me."

"That I believe." He threw a folded sheet of paper at her. It was her latest article. "You're trying to accuse Saint Moon of murdering babies with nothing more than a few bottles of beer and women's intuition? If I tried to run this, Kinneman would strap a pair of antlers to my head and tell me I got a five-minute head start."

"I never used the word 'murder.'"

"You never gave an address, either. You said these families all lived in the same neighborhood, but then forgot which neighborhood it was!"

"How would their addresses make any difference?"

"Because it makes them all sound like they live in bordellos, damn it! We can't accuse Saint Moon of murdering children of prostitution unless you've got photos of Edward Blake brandishing a bloody knife. You understand me?"

"Who's accusing anyone? I just pointed out that the uniting factor in these deaths is Saint Moon Milk Fortifier and Yippity."

Percy popped another peppermint. "Babies die every day, Johnson. Survival of the fittest. Darwin. A third thing. If we implicate a company that powerful in the deaths of some infants of ill repute, their lawyers will sue us for libel and then our competitors will hit us with exposés until our only readers are licensed *filles du roi*."

"Do you want me to find some rich women who've lost infants?"

"No, I want you to tell me how the duck is at *Genoa* and whether *Blue Lagoon* or *Eskimo Flo's* has a bigger dance floor. I pay you to write about the kind of fun girls your age can't actually afford to have, not the sob stories of professional mistresses. Now, get out of here. The next time I see you, you better be in a party dress and hungover!"

Several hours later, Thursday stood in front of a gaudy mirror bedecked with short candelabras, so that one may look at themselves in the always flattering light of flame. It also had a pair of small handles on either side so that a gentleman positioned behind you could be treated to a certain, singularly erotic experience. Thursday was alone in the reflection, bound into an impractical corset, garter belt, and stockings.

All around her was a room intended to only be seen by candlelight. Everything in it looked very expensive and just old enough to be sentimental when the lights were dim. When the electric lights were flipped on, as they were now, the spell was broken. The Grand Bedroom of *Madame Juteau's* was designed to make the storied madame's clients feel that $100 for the evening was a bargain, while being itself decorated at a bargain.

For now, the place looked like it had been through a hurricane. Hannah Juteau, the most feted sex worker in the city, had thrown open drawers and cast lingerie about, searching for just the right thing for her daughter. Hannah was somewhere around fifty—even Thursday didn't know exactly—but on the rare occasions that the two went out together—never in Silkhaven—they were generally mistaken for sisters. It was only Hannah's confidence and spirit of command that tipped off the shrewd observer that she might be the mother.

Of course, almost none of that was on display as she gleefully fussed over Thursday. The corset was clearly Virginian; the cut being designed to make men swoon or run for their lives. It cinched only part of her waist before narrowing and plunging to a short, sharp point just above the split in her legs, as if the gentleman might need directions. There was another point that rose up in the center of her cleavage, highlighting rather than supporting her exposed breasts.

"Found it!" Hannah called from one of the room's many wardrobes. She returned to the mirror with a short-sleeved robe that trailed a long ribbon. "This is the showstopper!"

She helped Thursday into it. It was weighted at the hem and cuffs in such a way that Thursday had to shrug to keep it on while her mother showed her how to close it. The edge of the right panel had a long ribbon that went through a slit in the left panel. Pulling that through left a long tail remaining. Another ribbon on the left panel went through a loop on the outside of the right panel. Here, the two wide ribbons could be tied into a pretty bow that disguised the slit.

With the bow tied, the dress stayed on of its own accord.

"One tug," Hannah demonstrated, standing behind Thursday and reaching under her arm. The knot came undone and a moment later the dress was a puddle on the floor. "I put two men in the hospital with this dress."

"I still need knickers." Thursday said.

Hannah kissed her behind the ear. "No, you don't."

There wasn't much that could scandalize a girl that grew up in a bordello, but this got close. "I'm going to a picnic."

"You're going to a seduction." Her mother corrected her. "The frenzy that bastard is going to be in when you pull that ribbon, anything between him and your cunt is going to get torn up. And anyway, you don't want to dampen his enthusiasm with unnecessary obstacles. Good sex is in how you use your body. Great sex, darling, is in how you feel doing it. Rapturous lust is a delicate bird and something as simple as shuffling off the laciest of bloomers can clip its wings."

"Golly," Thursday said, looking in the mirror and trying to imagine seeing herself through a man's eyes. "This is going to be rough, isn't it?"

"Oh, yes!" Hannah laughed. "Unless Eddy-boy is far worldlier than he lets on, he'll come at you like a beast."

"It's not Edward I'm after," Thursday said. "It's his son, Michael."

"Oh...yes, you said that." Hannah suddenly mewled happily. "Oh, I'm just so proud of you." She gave Thursday a tight hug from the side.

Thursday had to laugh.

"No, really." She said. "You're a good person and I'm not saying that just on account of you being my daughter. You didn't have to come when I called or listen to my girls tell their stories. Good people deserve to have the power in this world and the only way you're gonna get that power is by prying it out of men's hands." The hug tightened. "When I think of what those people did to my girls, to their babes." She started crying. "Destroy them." She whispered through the tears. "Burn them to the gawd-damned ground."

August 5th, 1921. Régence, King Charles Island.

Michael Blake had even less worldliness than Thursday had expected. The kid might have been a virgin for all his cunning with women. Her initial approach had made him flinch, which suggested that he was a lonely sort. Lonely men had no stomach for love games. When a woman started playing with them, they felt the potential loss more acutely than the chance for gain. So, she had shifted to something softer, almost innocent.

Once Thursday had gotten him away from the party, she had suggested a private tour of the plant. Guilelessly, he had said the tour would be starting soon. "Yes, but when I look at big, powerful machines, I like privacy." He still hadn't gotten it. Or, if he had, was still too unsure to take it. So, she had cupped a hand around his ear like she was telling him a secret and blew softly on his skin before giving it a slow lick. "Don't you like privacy?" And that had done the trick.

Now, they were in the main office of the plant; three stories up and surrounded by windows looking out on the silent, pristine machinery that would soon be making Yippity—the near beer "for ladies"—and milk fortifier, a powder undernourished mothers could mix with their breast milk. She wondered just how much dynamite it would take to destroy all the steel and ruin this place. There was a desk with several, neat stacks of papers on it. A few of those were her best chance for what she really wanted up here; what she about to trade her body for.

Thursday put that thought into a passive, but conscious part of her mind and focused her active thoughts on how she was going to seduce Michael. This boy seemed to know nothing of women and Thursday had learned to fuck from *the* Madame Juteau. He was going to be as putty in her hands, a slave to her whims; a little love zombie and she the licentious witch doctor.

She savored these thoughts, letting them arouse her.

"Wow," Thursday said, pulling free of Michael's arm to go to the windows. She set her purse on the floor, then placed her hands on the wide frame of the floor-to-ceiling window and leaned her upper body forward, while tightening her lower back muscles to lift her ass towards him. "That's quite a view." She said.

"Yes," Michael managed. "Quite."

The boy was already tongue-tied. Thursday had never been with a man who was younger than her and she wondered if they were all like this. She had teed him up so easily and he had still failed to swing. Thursday spun around, shifting so that her back was to the frame, not the glass. She ran her hands down her stomach to her legs, unnecessarily smoothing the dress. Michael's loose trousers had grown a lump in the center. No wonder he couldn't speak, there was not enough blood getting to his brain.

So much from so little.

He wanted her. It was so obvious on his face, but he was almost quaking with virginal fear. She was sure of it, now. She was about to take this boy's virginity. She was about to own him. That thought did it. Thursday felt herself moisten, which made her a little impatient, normally a bad thing in a seduction, but there was a tour starting soon.

She braced her head against the window frame so that her back was not touching it, then tugged on the dress's bow. The weighted fabric pulled itself free of her body and Michael went visibly weak in the knees.

"Uh," he said.

Thursday crooked a finger at him, but he did not move. "Come here." She said, her voice throaty and self-assured. He staggered towards her and she grabbed him by the tie to pull him close. "All you have to do is be a good boy." She said. "Will you be my good boy?"

"I...yes."

"Say you'll be my good boy."

"I'll be your good boy." He half-whispered.

"Now, kneel." She tugged his tie downward to get the motion started and he offered no resistance. He went down on his knees until her cunt and foppishly trimmed bush were at eye level. "Kiss it."

Michael leaned forward and gave her vulva a chaste little peck.

"No, good boy," she said. "Kiss it like a man, with your tongue." Thursday put a hand on the back of his head a pulled him in. He did his best. Naturally, he had no technique and she saw him wince at the taste of summer sweat and cunt water, but he did as he was told.

Thursday began rolling her hips against his confused, random gestures of lips and tongue. Eventually, he just extended his tongue and let her do the work, which was fine. This boy was richer than Croesus and she was using him like an overstuffed pillow. That put fresh verve in Thursday's hips as she pressed her clitoris up against his nose. She could hear him gasping for air when he could, but he didn't move.

Her own libido pushed her away from the frame. Thursday got both hands into his rich, black hair and bent over him. She threw one leg up onto his shoulder and rapidly rubbed herself against his face. "Good boy," she growled as he bravely held his position. "Mistress likes a good boy."

And she was 'Mistress'. She had the control. She could slap him and he'd be grateful. She owned him. Thursday just kept cycling those thoughts as her throbbing labia smeared their fluids all over his face. The tingling in her toes told her she was close and her muscles began flexing and releasing in waves, like electric pulses making her body ripple. With each wave the muscles got tighter and tighter, almost painfully so until, like a cork popping, everything went loose.

A jet of fluid sprayed itself into Michael's open mouth as Thursday grunted out the excess energy stored in her lungs. She went lightheaded and steadied herself on Michael's kneeling form.

That passive part of her mind also slackened and she remembered the papers. Thursday released Michael and said: "Follow me." Walking away from him unsteadily, making for the desk, only turning to sit on the edge. Michael was scrambling to his feet, but not getting closer.

"Um..." he said. "I'm sorry."

Shit. She thought. *He's going to bolt.* But he just stood there gesturing at his groin. The lump was still there, but less than it had been.

"I need to clean up." He said.

"No," she replied. "You need to come here."

As he approached, she realized that there was a dark spot in his black trousers. "I'm sorry." He said again.

"It's okay." She replied. "You are my good boy and you deserve a treat."

His eyes were locked on her breasts, which was a good sign. A more experienced man might have had the clarity to extricate himself from the situation or felt shame too great to continue facing her. This virgin boy, though, was so overcome with lust that the mental rinsing of release could not wipe it all away.

When he was close, she stood. In her heels, she was a little taller than him, which she had not noticed before. Perhaps he was slouching, now. She kissed him, then; their first. Again, he tried to kiss her like she was his sister. Thursday had to pry his lips open with her tongue, while her lips glided along the paler skin around his mouth, getting a taste of herself in the process. Michael started mimicking her and once they found a reasonable rhythm to the petting, she reached down and began undoing his damp trousers, then untying his trunks.

When his half-deflated manhood was in the open air, Thursday pulled away and grinned devilishly at him. He gave her a confused look before she dropped to her own knees. He, of course, was unshorn and his cock tasted of sweat and garlicky semen, but Thursday powered through, licking him clean. Again, his knees began knocking, but there was still a flaccidity that she did not want. So, she ducked her head and licked his fuzzy sack, which caused him to yelp and nearly topple. Her tongue returned to his pole while he righted himself, testing for rigidity, then returned to his balls while her hand gently massaged his cock. This time, she took one ball in her mouth and she felt his shaft jump against her fingers. Another moment's suction and he was as hard as diamond.

Thursday rose and spun, bending herself over the desk. One hand landed on a stack of papers while the other reached back for his newfound hardness. With little more encouragement, Michael stepped forward and sank his cock into her weeping cunt. He was a comfortable size, big enough to feel, but not so big that it hurt. It only took him a few strokes for his hips to reach the cushion of her bottom.

Some ancient instinct kicked in, then. He clasped her hips and began driving himself in and out of her in fast, but uneven strokes. It felt good enough. Thursday had had enough time for her post-orgasmic sensitivity to fade and his cock was not going to tear anything. That left enough of her brain free to understand some of the words on the papers in front of her.

Thursday exaggerated her pleasure as an excuse to spread the piles out. As Michael continued his rutting, Thursday surveyed the documents. She saw a truck schedule with the words "Yippity" and "milk fortifier" on it, as well as a report on a "vaccine project" that included the words "beer" and "milk". That was as good as she could really hope for, but she needed Michael's eyes diverted.

She raised herself up a little and reached back with both hands, grabbing Michael's wrists and pulling his hands to her breasts. This got a whining moan out of him, before she bent down again, bringing him with her. He continued thrusting, though with shorter and more sporadic strokes while his hands mauled her breasts uncomfortably. Importantly, though, she could feel his forehead on her back. He would not see her grabbing the truck schedule and vaccine report and stuffing them between her corset and her belly.

"Good boy," Thursday said, not daring to grab any more papers. "You're such a good boy. Finish for mistress. I want to feel you finish inside me. I want to feel your hot manhood slather my cunt. Come on, good boy. Do it for mistress!"

He released her breasts and braced himself on the desk for a few more rapid strokes and then he froze. His semen sprayed up inside her, sending a tide of warmth all through her. Then, he collapsed on top of her. They lay there on the desk for a few moments. He held her awkwardly, but sweetly and his breaths on her back were pleasantly intimate, while she let herself forget who he was and enjoy the moment.

When he finally pulled himself free, he looked dazed. It was funny, seeing him still in his suit with his lower half bare to his socks. Thursday cheekily grabbed his kerchief to soak up the trickle of semen coming out of her. He looked like he might object, but she moved faster than he could speak.

Suddenly, the door flew open and an oriental woman in a tight, red silk dress with gold flowers on it marched in and screamed. "Michael!" Then, she flew into a babble of some other language.

Michael hid his cock with his hands and tried to say something, but was drowned out, cut off by the angry woman. There was anger without sadness in her face and Michael looked embarrassed enough to vomit. This must have been Martha Blake, the dark horse New York socialite who had risen from "the only Oriental at Wells College" to a mainstay of the New York salons by virtue of her inexhaustible charm and erudite explanations of Confucian philosophy.

The charm was not now on hand, so Thursday had to assume that this was the Confucianism at work.

She put on her best Dizzy Sheba voice to say: "We was just having some fun."

The matriarch turned a blazing stare on Thursday, who smiled like nothing at all was wrong. "Do not speak!"

"Hey, you ain't *my* mother." Thursday got up off the desk and sauntered, hips at full swing, over to her discarded dress.

"You are a whore!" Martha Blake shouted. "How can you be shameless?"

She shrugged. "Luck?" Then bent at the waist to retrieve her dress and purse.

Another, likely obscene, string of foreign words poured out of Martha, who looked on the verge of pouncing. Of course, she would not. Any seasoned society lady knew that physically assaulting someone would get her in the papers. Murder, you could keep quiet, but a brawl would make the front page.

Then again, maybe the old lady just needed to keep herself presentable for the tour.

"I'm going." Thursday said, tying her dress shut. "I'm going." She blew a kiss to Michael before walking in an arc around mother-dearest to the door.

Outside, there was a younger version of the screaming woman in a similar blue dress. She observed Thursday carefully, but without emotion. Memorizing her face, it seemed. This had to be Gabrielle, the twin sister. There were two men running for the stairs as well. The sister turned as their feet began clanging on the stairs, coming to investigate the shouting.

"Sirs," the sister said. "Please escort this woman off the premises."

"Mind your manners, boys," Thursday said, smirking. "I got an invite to this party, after all."

The men had frozen.

"As long as she does not make a scene," the sister said to the men. "Gently escort her out." To Thursday, she asked: "Do you have a car?"

"No," Thursday answered the ridiculous question.

To the men, she added: "Take her to the visitor's desk and call her a taxi." Back to Thursday: "I'm afraid you will have to pay your own fare."

"Always, honey." She smiled and went with the two men that she planned to put out of a job as quickly as humanly possible.

Chapter 5:
Woman-in-red

August 5th, 1921. Régence, KCI

The tour group was drunker than they should have been, resembling a class of reasonably well-behaved children more than a train of investors, partners, and upper-class hangers-on. Almost an hour before, Edward Blake had announced that there would be a delay and had refreshed the drinks and hors d'oeuvres. Cranston suspected that the post-tour phase of the afternoon—the one with real food, not just a variety of creams dolloped onto crackers—would be short.

The way these things went, people were supposed to gather, take the tour or watch the unveiling, then stand around talking about how wonderful it had been. With how tipsy everyone already was, Cranston imagined that quite a few people would leave at the first polite moment to do so. It was the ladies that were the deciding factor. If they started sobering up before the tour ended and the alcohol flowed once more, they would start feeling tired or sick and demand to be taken home.

As Edward led the crowd through the wrought-iron gates, Cranston saw his wife and daughter waiting by the loading dock; no sign of Michael and the mischievous reporter. Cranston himself had two women on his arms. Rebecca was on his right, per tradition, and Vivienne had taken his left. There was half a foot's difference between them and they were still searching for their collective stride.

Edward dashed from his position and vaulted up onto the loading dock like Douglas Fairbanks. "Welcome!" He bellowed, throwing his arms wide. "To King Charles Island's own Saint Moon factory!"

The great door lurched and slid open with dramatic volume. A big wooden ramp, tipped up on its short side, was wheeled out to the edge and then dropped down on the pavement with an almighty crack. This made several people jump and the ladies giggled with relief. The fall revealed Michael Blake in Saint Moon coveralls.

"If you thought our food was good," the younger man called out. "Just wait until you try it factory-fresh!"

There was a moment's silence before the crowd realized that the theatrical portion of the tour was over and gave it a round of applause. The Blake men drank in the claps for a second, then began gesturing everyone up the ramp and into the factory.

"Are your openings like this?" Rebecca asked.

"No," Vivienne whispered behind Cranston's back. "Ours have taste."

"Our openings," Cranston said quickly, as they were in a crowd. "Are christenings. There's a band and a considerably larger crowd."

They proceeded into the factory and listened to Edward and Michael take turns announcing various statistics about the machinery that surrounded them. The factory's roof was three stories high to accommodate large vats for brewing and storing drinks before bottling. There were two offices suspended from the ceiling where on-site managers could oversee the work. A series of catwalks sprawled across what would have been the third floor, with flights of stairs leading up to it at regular intervals. The catwalks bloomed into platforms around the taller pieces of equipment and various types of elevators.

It all looked exactly as one wanted a factory to look: ordered so efficiently that a casual observer felt they understood the assembly line even if they did not know what each station was actually for. It also had enough machines and conveyor belts around that one could almost imagine the place running automatically, the humans merely maintaining the line. It was very modern to portray factory workers as a type of engineer rather than, for instance, melancholic Lithuanian immigrants.

Still, it was a factory. One could only find so much entertainment in a room full of sleeping contraptions, and Cranston less than most. If marvels of modern engineering could have held his attention better, he wouldn't have seen the blur of red out of the corner of his eye. Up in the catwalks, something had gone by with admirable quiet.

Cranston cast his eyes up, hoping for another sighting. Peering through layers of metal floor, stair, and rail, he saw a large patch of red hovering beside one of the vats. He craned his neck to align a gap in all the steel to see that there was a curvature in the red. Then, it moved—fast and silent—but Cranston saw that there was a face under the curve. There was a person up on the catwalks wearing a wide, red hat and seemingly red everything else. That struck him as too much for even the Blakes.

"Vivienne," Cranston said quietly. "Take my hat and move to the back of the crowd. Rebecca, go with her."

"What is it?" Vivienne asked.

"Hopefully, the Blake's next bit of theater, but perhaps not."

Vivienne took his hat, which raised a few eyebrows, but not as much as when he removed his coat and handed it to Rebecca before the two women walked slowly to the rear of the tour group.

"Mr Walker?" Martha interrupted her husband, as Cranston left the group removing his cufflinks as he did. "Is something the matter?"

He gestured up, but said nothing. In a moment, every eye was turned up and Cranston was rolling up his sleeves as he mounted the nearest stairs as quietly as he could.

"Mr Walker!" Martha shouted. "I must insist that you stay on this level! Do not go up the stairs!"

Then, on the opposite side of the factory, the figure in red dashed across the catwalk. Making his way up on a landing, Cranston had a better view. Whoever it was under the wide hat wore a mask that covered their nose and mouth. It was a feminine form in some sort of ankle-to-shoulder leotard under a long coat of very lightweight silk that fluttered as she ran.

An outfit that outrageous could only belong to a vigilante.

Gasps rose from the crowd as she was spotted. Hearing these, the figure stopped and turned to address the gathered people. Cranston continued up the stairs.

"Murderer!" The woman shouted in a French accent; not continental or Quebecois, but distinctly francophone. "This man makes poison! Poison in the beer! There is poison in the beer!" She shouted before raising one gloved fist that had a long string in it.

As Cranston reached the catwalk, the woman-in-red opened a lighter with her other hand and Cranston realized that it wasn't a string, it was a fuse.

"Run!" He bellowed before sprinting across the clattering steel.

The fuse flared to life and the gathered onlookers screamed. Vivienne was already halfway to the loading dock with Rebecca trailing behind her and the pair of them shouted for others to follow. The woman-in-red, seeing Cranston racing for her, dropped the fuse and ran, counterintuitively, in the direction of the supposed explosives.

Wartime discipline had given Cranston clarity under adrenaline. The woman-in-red had given a speech, so she wasn't trying to kill anyone. She was running in the same direction as the burning fuse, meaning that there was safety to be found there. Whatever explosives she had set, they had to be small; enough to sabotage equipment without bringing the whole place down.

Then again, she didn't look like an engineer and—Cranston realized as he watched the fuse burn—she barely knew her tools.

She had used a cheap safety fuse, the kind one could get at a farmers' supply store. Rated for civilian use, they burnt at less than a mile per hour. Cranston overtook the flame and extinguished it with a few stamps of his foot. The clanging of his shoes on the catwalk made the woman-in-red spin around and glare at him. Her eyes were all that was visible of her face between hat and mask, all made from the same red leather, and they were outlined in black so thick that she resembled a comic strip Sheba.

"What outfit are you with?" Cranston called to her, but she replied by doffing her hat—revealing a kind of tight, leather hood—and charging him.

He dropped into a boxer's stance. She ran right up to him, her head about the height of his shoulder. On the last stride, she spun and kicked. Cranston took the kick with his forearm. The collision sent heat crackling down to his right shoulder. Her foot slid across his guard and she planted it behind her in a fighting stance. A second later, that same foot was coming up to kick again; low and on his left.

Cranston saw the strike and tried to grab her leg. The moment she felt contact, she pulled her foot back, but instead of retreating, she just raised the leg and kicked at his ribs. Cranston blocked with his arm and she immediately raised her leg again to kick at his head. Cranston threw a right cross at her knee, but she withdrew the kick before he made contact, then lunged to grab his right arm with both hands.

This move tipped her forward, but her retreating right leg had the momentum to pull her body back into balance. In the same move, she might have unbalanced him, but Cranston whipped his arm upwards, which pulled her grasp in the opposite direction of her balance while stabilizing his own. Then he jabbed with his left.

The woman-in-red released his right arm, then swatted with open palms at his left fist. As she did, she stepped a few paces back. Each step landed at the exact same moment that one of her hands smacked his fist. Cranston abandoned that strike and the two of them retreated from each other. The woman assumed a very wide stance, feet stretched beyond her shoulders.

Planning his strike, Cranston hoped to get her to do the swatting again. If she did, he was sure that he could get a hold of one of her arms and from there overpower her. He took a feinting step towards her and she shifted her weight onto her back leg, then kicked with her front. It was nowhere near Cranston, but when that foot landed, she leapt from her back leg and spun sideways in the air.

As her foot came down towards his head, Cranston raised both arms to grab it. It hit his palms with more force than he had expected and the shock loosened his grip. Her leg slid out of his hands and she landed, hip-first, on the catwalk. A moment later, she windmilled her legs around and somehow got both of them inside his stance. Her feet came up behind him and she dug her heels into the front of his thighs even as her own thighs pressed against the back of his calves.

This threw Cranston off balance. He started to fall backwards but grabbed the catwalk's railings with both hands. The woman-in-red bent at the waist, pulling herself towards his crotch with a fist winding up to cause some real pain. Cranston heaved with his right hand and twisted his body to the left. This put the woman's head on a trajectory with the railing. She abandoned the punch and grabbed for the railing's vertical bars. With Cranston's momentum turning his body counter-clockwise, the woman—her legs still entwined with his—pulled against the railing, adding more force to Cranston's own motion.

Cranston dropped his left hand to the catwalk and grabbed the railing with his right a moment before colliding with it and pushed away. As he did, the woman disentangled her legs and scampered away on all fours like a dog. Cranston hit the catwalk shoulder-first.

He let himself slump onto his back. Looking the worse for wear encouraged another attack, but he knew he could get back on his feet in a flash. The woman was sitting with her legs bent and hands up like claws.

"Listen," Cranston rasped through exaggeratedly heavy breaths.

"If you have proof...that there's...poison...in the beer. I'd like to...to see it. Please."

"Je ne suis pas..." she panted back. "...dupe facilement." She pronounced the 'J' too softly. A winded Quebecer would still have a little voice in it, but hers was almost a 'sh'.

He spent too long thinking about that before he heard the hiss of the fuse, which she was sitting on, burning anew.

"Tabarnac..." Cranston rolled up to his feet.

In the same moment, the woman jumped up into a squat, punching forward with both hands. He wasn't in his stance yet and the woman took the moment to start punching.

Outside, the frantic crowd was met by a small army of men in Saint Moon jumpsuits. They were coming out of an adjoining building, evidently awaiting a cue to enter the facility and fire up the machines. Most of the fleeing guests turned right, heading out the gates and back towards the park. Vivienne stayed her course, coming to a stop at the line of delivery trucks. Going back to the park felt like abandoning Cranston. It lifted her spirit, for some reason, to see that Rebecca was staying close as well.

"You men get in there!" Edward Blake shouted.

The men in jumpsuits looked instantly poised to run.

"There's a mad woman with dynamite!" Edward continued. "Stop her!"

The men wilted. They silently looked at each other.

"Come, now! One of my guests is in there fighting her. None of you has his spine?" Then he just stared at the silent mob for a moment. Vivienne caught two of them having a conversation with eyes and eyebrows. "If she destroys the factory, you'll all be out of a job."

"*We'll* go." One of the men said; one from that facial conversation. "We were sappers." With a nod from Edward, the two men broke from the group and began jogging for the entry. That broke the dam. Most of the rest of the men followed. A few shook their heads and stepped back towards the trucks, trying not to be seen.

Edward watched the workers run half-heartedly into the building. Then, he turned to Vivienne and winked. "That's why you never hire union men."

The woman-in-red was not running. Cranston took that to mean she had used small charges; or what she thought were small charges. There was no telling how much she knew about the dynamite. He did not actually mind if some of the equipment was destroyed. Doing business with Saint Moon had never been the goal.

She came at him swinging, stance wide and low, but advancing with remarkable speed. None of her punches looked like they had much force behind them, but they were fast and numerous. As he retreated down the catwalk, deflecting the punches outward, he had the impression that she was only trying to create chaos. She wanted him confused so that he wouldn't see the real hit coming.

Her right fist was coming in at a sharp angle and Cranston decided to step into it; confuse her first. It hit his pelvis and before she could pull the arm back, Cranston got his fist around it and pulled. The woman's balance shifted forward and she did a no-hand cartwheel, flipping her feet up and over her head to bring them both down on his; but Cranston was already moving forward. He got inside the arc of her feet and grabbed her waist with his right hand, pulling her out of the air.

The backs of her thighs hit his left shoulder and he propelled her towards the catwalk before letting go. Her legs were already flipping in the opposite direction and she landed in a push-up position. Cranston bent to grab her again, but spun on one palm to windmill her legs up into his face again. This time, Cranston got his arm over one leg and trapped it in his armpit. Already bent forward, he belly-flopped. The woman scrambled and got most of her body out of the way of his falling torso.

He caught himself with his free hand even as her free foot shot out to punch him in the face. He recoiled and rolled, pulling her leg with him, which shifted her body so that the kick angled too high, but she just brought it straight down, aiming her heel at his face. Cranston grabbed her ankle with his free hand and pulled it past his face. The woman followed this trajectory with her whole body until she was straddling his chest and punched down into his face.

Cranston released both of her legs to deflect her punch. The woman got her feet under her and leapt into a roll that took her over his face. She landed chest down and tried to kick at the top of his head, but Cranston had seen that coming and was already rolling to his feet. The woman pulled her feet in and rose up, spinning on one knee to face him.

He tried to kick at her, but she whirled again and wrapped her whole body around one of his legs, then kept turning. Cranston heard something pop and felt the disconcerting move of a bone in a direction that it was not meant to go before thick, red pain shot through his foot and up his leg, radiating from his already smarting ankle. The pain got the better of him and he went down. The woman released him, rolled backwards up onto her feet and ran. She picked up her hat, made for an intersection in the catwalk, and disappeared behind a polished piece of industrial equipment.

The fear of dying hit Cranston and he cast about, looking for the fuse. The spark was creeping along a few yards away. He limped as fast as he could for it. As he went, he shut his mouth and worked up as much spit as he could manage. Once he was on top of the fuse, he licked his left palm, wetting it as much as he could before closing a fist around the flame.

It snuffed and Cranston allowed himself to collapse and groan through the pain still coursing through his leg. The men in the jumpsuits would find him, no need to call out. With how upper crust the guest list was, there was bound to be at least one doctor at this party. The fight was done, the danger past, and he could let himself just be injured.

PART 2
The Detective

Chapter 6:
Rebecca's Bosom

Vivienne had thought she had another day, but such were the vicissitudes of biology. Her period had come on just before lunch, which was a minor kindness. She had a stately blue box of Kotex pads in her desk, and her office afforded her the privacy to put one in without the shameful march to the ladies' room. However, the stiff, bulky 'cellucotton' pad was too evident through her trousers.

She could insist on remaining in her office the rest of the day, but her father's old chair disagreed with the backache she knew was coming on. So, she phoned her driver, Williamson, down in the valet's lounge. The drivers all took their lunches at 10, so they would be on hand when the executives went to lunch at noon. The last of the general staff were arriving as Vivienne walked briskly for her car. Staggering the general and executive lunches had been one of Uncle Cecil's innovations.

The intention had been to prevent 65-minute lunch hours, but it had proven beneficial to morale and, by extension, productivity. With the boss out of the office, people eased back into the day's work. They had time to be chummy, which made the atmosphere more amiable in general, kinder. Not to mention that those who were sleepy as they digested felt less pressure to get things done and made fewer mistakes. Even if the boss did not return, as the CEO at least would not today, they all tended to be back in the swing of the day's work by one o'clock.

Vivienne would be spending the rest of the day convalescing with Cranston. After his showdown with the woman-in-red, whom the newspapers had dubbed 'The Masked Virago', Cranston had been tended to by a trio of doctors who were attending the Blake's picnic. Once his ankle was set and bandaged, she and Rebecca took him home, where Rebecca tended to him further while Vivienne took the opportunity to do a brief audit of the hotel's operations.

She had suggested that Cranston bring his women home, hoping it would make him more punctual to the office. However, she had not considered the psychic ramifications of being in the penthouse while Cranston 'entertained'.

So, when she stepped off the elevator into the penthouse, removed her shoes, and saw a very startled and very naked Rebecca fling herself from one of the living room sofas—grasping at a discarded robe on the floor—Vivienne let out an involuntary yelp and bolted for the nearest door, slamming it shut behind her. Instantly, one very sharp emotion was replaced by another.

Vivienne was in her father's study.

For four years, now, the room had gone largely untouched. Blankets had been thrown over the upholstered furniture, and a fine coat of dust lay on the various surfaces. At least one day a month, even in the dead of winter, every window in the building was opened to discourage mold and disease, but the maids had not done much else.

Vivienne herself had avoided this room. On the days when she missed her parents most, she indulged the fantasy that they were here, behind the door, reading. She could take that false comfort and leave them undisturbed. But now, the door had been opened, and they really were gone. To Vivienne's own surprise, she felt relief. The room was empty, and that was a weight off of her shoulders.

She had known this day would come, and she had been putting it off, thinking it would be a difficult day for her heart. Perhaps the relief was the dread leaving her because, looking at this room that had once been a sanctum to her parents, she did not need to cry. Indeed, she did not feel the stabbing loss of her parents' deaths renewed; she felt that a thousand mementos had been returned.

There were the books she had read at her father's suggestion. There was Mother's ivory pen and the little table she had used to write thank-you cards. There was Father's real chair; not of the CEO, but of the man. Vivienne crossed around the desk, tidier than it had ever been, and she pulled the blanket off the chair. She waved away the dust and let the blanket clump on the floor. As she settled down into it, she entertained a quick fantasy that it would perfectly support her back and the menstrual pain there would vanish.

Vivienne eased back and was overcome by a burst of laughter. It was worse than the one in her office! Good gracious, how had the man ever been comfortable in this thing?

She did not get up, though. Instead, she took a quiet moment to see the room as he had, to note the angle of things, to feel a fresh thread of connection to him, likely for the last time. And then Cranston knocked at the door.

"Are you alright, Vivienne?" He called. "Terribly sorry to startle you, old girl, it's just I didn't think you would be home so early."

"Yes, I am fine." Now, she rose and went to the door, making a mental note to try Mother's writing chair, à la Goldilocks. "Rebecca did not hurt herself, did she?"

"No, I don't think so." Cranston replied. "May I come in?"

"Are you decent?"

"Quite,"

"Alright,"

He opened the door cautiously. It seemed that he too had been harboring a certain dread. "Hmm," he grunted, looking about, then added a long exhale through barely parted lips.

"Agreed," Vivienne said.

He made an intentional survey of the lowest shelves of the bookshelf on the wall opposite the desk. He crouched down and pulled a thick magazine from the shelf. It was a 1903 issue of *The Dutiful Wife*, a pornographic literary magazine that had only run for two years. "I learned a lot from this." Cranston said wistfully.

"No!" Vivienne declared. "I have been too close to your amours already, today."

He continued to gaze sentimentally at the respectable-looking cover. "There's a letter for you by the phone."

Seizing the opportunity, Vivienne went to the living room, glaring at that one sofa for a moment as if it had personally wronged her. The letter, which had no postal markings and must have been hand-delivered, was from Gabrielle Blake. In terms befitting a love letter, Gabrielle was inviting Vivienne to take her out on the town. Vivienne found it endearing: this young woman educated in British manners trying to invent a new genre of epistle: the please-host-me letter.

This had always been a possibility in the plan. The Walker

Company needed to deepen its ties with Saint Moon if they were going to learn the truth about this 'vaccine project' that was in the works. Eugenicists had long recommended mass sterilization of "the unfit", never meeting with more neutrality than horror, much less support. The leading theory among the Rose & Chain was that Saint Moon was developing a vaccine for something like tuberculosis, which mostly affected the poor. In this vaccine would be something that carried a high risk of sterilization.

Such a scheme could take years or even decades to discover, especially if the vaccine was primarily given to children. Then, the company could claim ignorance of the side-effect long after the "unfit" population had been decimated.

It was imperative that the Rose & Chain, via the Walker Company, discover what this project really was before it could be implemented. To that end, Vivienne had pursued a deal with Saint Moon like a lovesick schoolgirl and, now, needed to earn the trust of Edward himself. She was about equidistant in age between Edward and Gabrielle, so the notion of a friendship with Gabrielle as an alternative to Edward had been suggested from the beginning.

"Hey, doll, um..." A mortified Rebecca had come down the stairs in a simple day dress. "Sorry for...I guess I'm not sure."

"Soiling the sofa?" Vivienne suggested.

"Did we?" Rebecca looked alarmed.

"I have not had the stomach to inspect it yet."

"Look, I just wanna say that you don't owe me nothin' for this. I sorta missed Cranston at the club last night, so I wanted to see how he was doin.'"

"He seems well." Her tone made Rebecca shrink a little. "Actually, since you are here, I bet you know lots of places that a young bacheloress would like to visit." She held the letter up.

"Oh, maybe. I know diners and that sort of thing, you know? I ain't a tour guide for the great and the good."

"I suspect you are selling yourself short." Vivienne said. Even if this failed, it twisted a pleasant knife. "Gabrielle Blake has invited me to invite her on a day on the town. She is about your age. Why not come with us? We can go all the places the young women of Silkhaven dream of going, entirely on my bill."

The blush had drained from Rebecca's face and taken the regular supply of blood with it. "That's...I mean it's generous, but.... A party where I gotta talk proper is one thing, but the places I know? Sometimes they don't mop the floor."

"It need not be places you 'know'. What are the places you girls read about and dream of one day going? That is what I need. And I could make it worth your while."

"I'm sorry, doll. I ain't your girl. It's a real nice offer and all, but I can't."

Vivienne assumed that tone Cranston used when he wanted to apologize without having to say he was sorry. "Would it help if I said I envied your bosom?"

Rebecca, well-versed in Cranston's modes of speech, visibly relaxed. "Doll, that just makes you human."

"Well, the offer stands."

"Thanks. And I don't want you thinkin' I'm gettin' comfortable here. You don't gotta worry about me tryin' to change the curtains or nothin'."

"I would not mind you getting comfortable. It might be quite nice to have someone to gang up on Cranston with."

A look of pity washed over Rebecca and Vivienne was not sure whom it was meant for. "If you need Cranston on your side, you should try bein' nice to him. He...um...he ain't seen a lotta kindness in the last few years, if you know what I mean."

Vivienne did not and she knew with dread certainty that she did not. It was granted that Rebecca knew things about Cranston that Vivienne was ignorant of, but she had never considered that some of those things might be things she wanted to know.

"Thank you," Vivienne said, her heart sinking a little.

"I'm gonna get out of ya hair."

"That is not necessary. Shall we have a drink? I have some of that Yippity you mentioned; Edward sent us a whole crate."

"That's sweet of you, doll, but maybe you and Cranston could do with some brother-sister time, yeah?" She added a little wink.

Once Rebecca was gone, Vivienne returned to the study. Cranston was sitting on the floor with his back against the bookshelf, reading some dirty story out of their mother's old magazine.

"I think I will use the writing desk." Vivienne said.

"Is there ink?" Cranston asked, looking up from his reading.

"Yes, corked even."

"Don't let me stop you." He said.

Vivienne went to the window and pulled back the curtains, casting afternoon light over Mother's writing table. She sat down and arranged the various implements to compose a reply to Gabrielle. It took her a few tries and she and Cranston passed an hour or so in quiet. He occasionally chuckled at his reading and she asked for editorial input on her letter once or twice.

When she finished the letter, he suggested that they go out for lunch, as if he had been waiting for her. She needed to change first, but accepted. She would have the study dusted immediately.

Chapter 7:
St Peter's and Belmont

August 8th, 1921. Silkhaven.

They called him Big Red, partly on account of him standing half a head higher than any man on the dock and partly because he was Irish; proper Irish, born in County Clare, though his family came to the Americas before he was old enough to have any memories of it.

His father had been one of the three McGettigan Brothers of McGettigan Brothers Stevedore & Transport Company. Big Red had grown up on the docks, starting his apprenticeship when he was just eight. Back then, he had spent hours learning the various knots one found on the dock so he could get them untied quickly. They sent him scrambling up the crates to tie or untie the securing ropes until he was strong enough to handle the crates himself.

He'd learned to fight on the docks, too, and being the biggest lad in sight, as well as the bossman's son, he became the company's enforcer when an argument broke out or the whites started picking on the negroes. Before the war, no company employed more negroes in Silkhaven than McGettigan Bros. They built them strong and tall in Africa and that's what a stevedore company needed.

The war had been good for the company. One of the government's wartime policies had been banning protests, which gutted the dockworkers' union's power. So, when the shipping companies started cutting their people's salaries, the best of them had come to McGettigan Bros. They were a private company, after all: the government couldn't stop them from negotiating contracts. Then, the military contracts had started rolling in.

When the war ended, Big Red's cousins—who handled the books—decided to retire on the nice piles of money they'd made. It took a while, but they found someone to buy the company. Big Red hadn't been happy about losing the name, but he wasn't going to curse himself with the bookkeeping, so he took his cut of Saint Moon's money and signed over his stake in the business.

Big Red had asked to stay on with the company after the sale. The man wouldn't know what to do with himself in retirement. Saint Moon had been more than happy to have him. He couldn't lift like he used to, but he could still drive the trucks and, more importantly, he could keep the boys in line. It didn't matter how much grey was in his beard, no man on the docks wanted to get on Big Red's bad side. Even the marines showed him deference.

The new trucks Saint Moon bought had inspired some grumbling among the drivers, just because they were new. Fellows got sentimental about their machines. That ended when Big Red gave one a test drive and declared them the finest trucks he'd had the pleasure of operating. And it was the truth. They had the smoothest gear shifts that Big Red had ever used, hardly any grinding at all. Add to that the comfortable seats and the mirrors mounted on the doors.

The real marvel, though, was in the back. Saint Moon made their own crates and all their products were sized to fit snugly inside them. Uniform crates made it possible to build racks for the trucks that the crates could slide into. They even put little wheels on the racks, so you could load them faster than anything. The racks were on an incline, so when you took one out, the one behind came down of its own accord, and the rack had this lip on it to keep them all from falling out. No more ropes or loose crates to worry about.

"I may be dumb as a stump," he had told the others. "But I know clever when I see it."

Big Red was proud to drive a Saint Moon truck. That first day of making deliveries from the factory instead of the harbor, he felt like he was trotting around on a prize stallion. He bet this is what boys felt like when they struck it rich and bought themselves a Rolls-Royce. (Not that Big Red couldn't afford a Rolls-Royce, now, but he and the missus were saving to send their second boy to college next year; he was the smart one.)

He waved to the folks he knew, happy to talk up the truck to anyone that commented on it. The kid in the passenger seat, Billy, he didn't get it, but that was okay. Billy was there to do the lifting and if Big Red's chit-chat gave him more time to relax, he couldn't complain. Of course, Billy was also in charge of navigating. Coming from Régence meant new routes, but both of them would get the hang of it soon.

They pulled to a stop at St Peter's and Belmont, on their way to the general stores in Dockside, when Big Red heard a woman scream and then something landed on the hood of the truck. He saw a blur of red before a cataract of oil sprayed up on the windshield. The engine gave an almighty, metallic gnashing and then died. Billy screamed and Big Red shouted: "Out of the truck!"

He threw his door open and jumped out onto the street. Looking back, he saw a woman dressed head-to-toe in red stepping up from the hood onto the roof of the cab. There was a long piece of metal sticking out of the hood, like a spear through the skull of a bear. It was straight up, like the woman in red had dropped out of clear blue sky directly above them.

But how she'd done it was small potatoes, right now.

"Get down from there!" Big Red shouted as he marched back to the truck. She ignored him.

Then he saw her pull a flask out and start pouring the contents onto the wooden crates. Big Red could see where that was headed. He took one long step and grabbed at her ankle. Quick as a whip, she kicked his hand away. It smarted, but he could take it. Next, Red jumped halfway up with both arms reaching out to encircle her legs. She was watching him, though, and jumped out of his reach. She tried to spin and kick him in the face. Red saw that boot coming and he got both hands on the leg attached to it.

Red let himself drop, bringing her down with him and thinking she'd get banged up on the trip. Instead, she kicked off the truck with her free foot and arced away from it, landing on her hands. That free foot swung up over her captured one and caught Red in the face.

In a bar brawl, you can't see half the time anyway, so Red just groped around with one hand. Her ankle slid out of his grip like it was a wet fish. She put some distance between them, which was fine. Red didn't much care what happened to her as long as nothing happened to the truck.

Billy came tearing around with a fist wound back for a haymaker. The woman grabbed his punch right out of the air then kicked him three times—leg, stomach, and face—so fast that Red barely saw her do it. When her boot hit his jaw, she let go of his hand and Red watched Billy's body rise off the cobbles before dropping back down like a wet sack.

Big Red had never seen anyone fight like that. It seemed that she liked kicking though and the big man knew how to handle little kickers. He charged at her with one elbow high up, like he was going to bring it down on that broad-brimmed hat pinned real tight to her head. Half a stride away from striking distance, he halted his feet. Sure enough, her leg was coming around to get him in the side and that's when he brought his other fist down, right on her calf, just below the knee.

She dropped into a squat that kept all her weight on that back leg. This gal knew how to take a punch. Big Red saw her next attack before it came. She launched herself up at him, hellcat style, and he got his hands up to grab her sides, then he spun her around, meaning to throw her, but she tucked her legs in and got them around his ribs. Red's arms were long enough that she couldn't swipe his face, but she was squeezing on his lungs as best she could.

If he let her go, she'd whip up and go for his eyes. Red lifted his chin while launching himself at the ground with her to break his fall. He let go at the last moment to save his knuckles and the woman scrambled halfway up him before they landed. He got an indecent face full of leather trousers and she screamed for a second before her legs were squeezing his head and flipping him up onto his side.

A punch was no good, but Big Red had mitts as big as this girl's head, so he just swung one up and clapped her on the spine. That got him one of those grunts where you lose the wind halfway through. He decided to keep rolling and shake her loose. She released him and rolled up to her feet before he was done with his alligator move. She was halfway to the truck before he could haul himself up to his feet, but he had twice the leg that she did.

Big Red barreled towards the woman, thinking he might pin her against the truck. She heard him coming—ox that he was—and dove headfirst into the cab and out the other side before he could get to her. Then, jumping like a puma, she was back on the cab's roof. Red didn't try to get her the same way twice. He pulled himself up on the truck's hood and yanked the metal bar up out of the engine. It was smooth but had a rubber handle around the middle of it. The thing was an honest-to-God spear.

He swung it around, just about to smack her with it when he saw the match fall. That tiny flame dropped onto the crates and there was a whoosh that threw the woman into silhouette. Instinct made Red throw up his hands, and a second later, he felt both her feet collide with his forearms. But he knew how to fall too.

Red turned over as his feet left the truck hood. He sent the spear flying. Hands outstretched, he caught himself—just like she had—in the push-up position. Before he could rise up, though, he felt her weight come down on his neck.

The next thing Red knew was the burning pain of a broken nose. He was looking at the street sideways, and for a little while, it didn't matter to him. Getting knocked out did that to you. It was a real calming experience. He always thought that was funny in the time it took him to recover.

When he rolled over, he found he was sprawled out in front of the truck. The grill looked sort of like a face and the fire from the burning cargo was kind of like some crazy hair. He could think in those terms when he was dazed, punch-drunk.

Then, there were people coming to him, asking if he was okay.

"Where is she?" He managed to ask, not really caring about how much pain he was in.

Whatever the people said, he didn't hear it, not really. Slowly, the world got real again. All the neighbors were out in their housecoats and pajamas. They were getting a bucket brigade going. It wouldn't do the truck any good, but you couldn't have the fire jumping to the houses. Sure, they were all brick jobs, but even those places had a way of burning.

Big Red found Billy. His face was swelling up something awful, but he could walk. The two of them sat on the curb, waiting for the coppers to arrive. They'd have to give a statement and all that. It was alright. Big Red didn't have anywhere to go; not tonight and not tomorrow. He pulled out his smokes and offered one to the kid.

One for the road. He was retired now.

Chapter 8:
Cranston's Bargain

Cranston stood naked in the small room, feet on either side of a drain. Two men approached in gaudy vestments, carrying a large wooden bowl suspended from two staffs between them. The robes were unique, but of a kind. They were primarily made of vibrant, purple velvet with gold accents running along the cuffs, collars, and hems. The first man was decorated in embroidered vines and flowers of the sort one saw in illuminated manuscripts. The other had Greek sentences writ large across his robe. The first wore a tall, fur hat bedecked with gold chains that wouldn't have looked out of place on a Czar; while the second had a cushioned, silken hat of some Renaissance design. Both men wore masks—gold, of course—like the death masks of ancient kings.

These two, dressed in the richest finery, set down the bowl at Cranston's feet. Soapy water sloshed gently inside, along with two sponges. With ring-bedecked fingers, they took up their sponges and began to wash Cranston. It was a thorough bathing. They took turns holding him up so the other could wash one of his feet, getting between his toes with their bare fingers. Their sponges scrubbed every nook and cranny of his groin, even between his buttocks and beneath his scrotum.

Whoever they were, they were practiced hands at this. When it came time to wash his ears, they used fingers—pruny from the water—to daintily clean every fold. It reminded him immediately of his father, bathing him as a child. They massaged the last of the soapy water into his hair. Once they were finished, they silently gestured him forward, through the door they had entered from. Cranston walked through to find himself in a room with a long, narrow pool.

The pool was tiled with depictions of the burial of Christ: the sealing of the tomb, the visiting mourners and, finally, at the far end, the rolled-away stone. Cranston, never much of a swimmer, sat on the edge, letting his feet adjust to the cold water before sliding in. It was only about four feet deep and he submerged himself to rinse. Ideally, he would stay under for the entire length of the pool, but he wasn't confident enough in the water to stay under that long. He pushed off the wall behind him and surfaced wherever pleased God, as the fellow once said. When Cranston pulled himself out of the pool, he stood, dripping, on a mosaic of Christ's funerary wrappings.

There was another door through which he found two more purple-clad royals that handed him his initiate's robe: a colorless burlap sack with holes cut in it for his head and arms; immediately itchy. As soon as he was dressed, one of the monarchs rang a bell to summon the washer kings and the five of them went together into the rotunda.

The large, circular room had a balcony where more kings and queens stood, while on the floor, unmasked beggars sat in plush chairs behind a dais. The kings left Cranston standing before the dais and mounted the stairs up to the balcony; their finery unfit for a comfortable chair, they had to stand.

I should have consented to this before the war. Cranston thought. Mother and Father should be here.

A moment later, Vivienne entered through another door also in a burlap sack, flanked by queens who left her for the balcony, too. Cranston had the childish impulse to grab his big sister's hand, but dismissed the thought.

From among the comfortable beggars, a very old man—with deep wrinkles and sunken cheeks—stood and took to the dais. He propped himself up with a walking stick of grey, unfinished wood. Bent and shrunken on the small stage, his head was barely higher than the Walkers'. Then, in a cracked, but resonant voice, he addressed the rotunda in what was either Italian or Ecclesiastical Latin.

"Bondservants of Christ," a king shouted from the balcony.

"Serviteurs des Jésus Christ," a queen shouted.

The old man continued. His speech was translated by two or three people for each language. Some listened while the others spoke, so that the old man never needed to pause. It was cacophonous, at first, but

Cranston tuned his mind to the English and the French disappeared into the background.

"We are gathered to bring two more into our fold. They are permitted by right of ancestry and not forbidden as their history is of good conduct. If things were as they should be, their parents would stand here and bear testimony to their children's worth. Alas, our siblings, James and Lolita Walker, were taken from us by evil happenstance. So, we remember to make the best use of the time we have, for the days are evil. Whether their passing was by the will or the permission of God, we do not know, only that time is unforgiving. Whether it is the rising and falling of the sun or the turning of the spheres of the sky, this world, this universe cares nothing for us. It is a blind, dumb, dead clock ticking its unrelenting minutes. Only God, who stands apart from time, cares for us. So, that is where we lay our hope and our treasures.

"This society is dedicated to this wisdom. In ancient times, the Pharaohs of Egypt sealed the riches of their nation in their graves. They murdered those they loved to have their bodies laid beside them. What did it gain them? Their tombs were burgled by thieves and are excavated by scholars. Their mummified bodies were taken far from their native soil and made spectacles or firewood. Their treasures decorate a hundred museums and their names live on not in remembrance of their kindness or humanity, but for their decadence; for all the glorious and glittering things they deprived their nation of. Decadent fools.

"But we shall live in wisdom. We remember the ancient wisdom: the last shall be first and the first shall be last."

Here the old man paused and the whole gallery chanted together: "Novissimi primi, et primi novissimi."

Cranston and Vivienne had been silent, so the old man looked at them both. "Seite consentitis?" He said.

"Êtes-vous d'accord?" A woman called.

"Do you agree?" Called another.

"Yes," Cranston said at the same time Vivienne began: "Novis..."

They looked at each other for a second, then together told the old man: "Novissimi primi, et primi novissimi."

"Infer le vites!" The old man called.

Two kings and two queens descended from the balcony behind Cranston and Vivienne. Each pair carried a metal chain of sharp, square links entwined with silk rose blossoms.

Again the old man began to speak and the interpreters went to work.

"Do you, Cranston Walker and Vivienne Walker, make yourselves bondservants in Christ? Accepting the love of the Savior and the suffering of being his disciple?"

"Yes, I do." Cranston answered.

"I shall." Vivienne said at the same time.

"Do you vow to live by the wisdom of this society, submitting yourself to beggars that your pride may not keep you from the Kingdom of Heaven?"

"I do." He said. "Yes," she said.

"Will you regard the treasures of this world as dross compared to the riches of Heaven? Wielding your earthly privilege, power, and wealth as a weapon to defend the despised, weak, and poor?"

"Yes," he said. "I will." She said.

"Alligant loro manus." The old man said.

The four royals crowded in then. One king took Cranston's hands and held them together at the wrist, while the other wrapped the chain around them, tight enough to bite into his skin, burning like it might draw blood if he struggled. The queens did the same for Vivienne.

As they did, two beggars brought wooden goblets out. The man who came to Cranston was Ferdie Bouchard, whose family owned—to one degree or another—every gold mine in Quebec. They knew of each other, though had never been friends. From Ferdie's inability to look Cranston in the eyes, he assumed that he knew about Cranston's war record.

Still, he held the goblet to Cranston's lips and helped him drink from it. As the Walkers drank, a cheer went up in the rotunda that evolved into a hymn.

August 9th, 1921. Silkhaven.

The rotunda was all but empty. The elders were sat around the dais, as if it were a conference table. Cabot was there, chairman of the Walker Corporation's board; Mrs Hopkins, eternally knitting; and three others that Cranston had never been properly introduced to.

As Cranston approached, Cabot gestured towards an empty chair. "Thank you for joining us, Mr Walker." He said. "I know these confines are not especially comfortable for you."

"Thank you for having me." He addressed the table as he sat. "I know I'm not your favorite operative."

"Mrs Hopkins, you know." Cabot continued, ignoring Cranston's sly comment as always. "We are also joined by Mr Plumber, Mr le Clare, and Mr Gates."

"We understand," began Mr Plumber. "That you engaged the Masked Virago at the Saint Moon factory."

"Oh," said Cranston, taken aback by the harsh language. "Yes, I suppose you could call her that."

"Not me, not originally. It's what the papers are calling her."

"Ah, sorry, I haven't seen the papers lately."

"Not the Silkhaven ones." Cabot added.

"We'll come to that, Jonathan." Mr Plumber said. "You did engage her?"

"Yes," Cranston said. He gave them a brief description of his fight with the woman-in-red.

"You found her formidable?" Mr Plumber asked, Cranston having glossed over the details of the fight.

"Indeed, though I was not trying to hurt her. So, I was somewhat restrained."

"Do you believe she could overpower a pair of deliverymen unassisted?"

"Depending on the men, certainly."

Mr Plumber took a long breath. "Initially, we invited you here simply so that we could hear your story and discuss what to do next. However, circumstances have changed." He lifted a briefcase onto the dais/table and removed from it a newspaper.

MASKED VIRAGO STRIKES TRUCK went the headline. A quick scan showed that the woman-in-red had attacked a Saint Moon truck and set it on fire, then disappeared in broad daylight.

"We have decided," Mr Plumber continued. "That we would like an interview with this Masked Virago. Whatever her vendetta against Saint Moon, it may aid our investigation into their 'vaccine project.'"

"I had the same thought." Cranston told him.

"Why," now it was Mr Gates who spoke. "Did you not use the Voice on her?"

Cranston shifted uncomfortably. "The Voice is not as potent as the army believed. The subject must be paying attention to what you are saying. The more intent on the conversation they are, the more susceptible they become. All those posters showing a Praetorian shouting back a charging line of huns were pure fantasy."

"What if she were captured?" Mr Gates asked. "Would it work then?"

"Perhaps. It may take some time, though. We had prisoners that took days to crack. The officers were easiest. I think they expected us to try to trick them into revealing information. It made them careful listeners. The rank and file would sometimes just shout at us for hours."

"So, you would be willing to use the Voice on this Virago?" Mr le Clare joined in. "I was given the impression that the Praetorians were averse to using it in peacetime."

"We are," Cranston nodded. "But I have no scruples about using it when it may save lives."

"Very good," Mr Plumber said. "We are tasking our vigilance committee with her capture. We would like you to join them."

"Join the vigilance committee?"

"On a strictly temporary basis." Mrs Hopkins interjected. "We know your parents were adamant that you not become involved with all that, but as you said, there are lives at risk."

"Yes," added Mr Plumber. "You would wear the mask only for the purposes of finding the Virago. Once the matter is concluded, you will have no further duties with them."

"And you will be rewarded." Cabot said, looking pointedly at Plumber.

Plumber nodded. "Yes, it has also come to our attention that you are trying to locate a woman by the name of Bella Cane."

"*Della* Caine," Cranston corrected him.

"My apologies. You have your ship captains bringing you newspapers about her despite the fact that she has been pronounced deceased."

"That was a lie invented by Miss Rosamund Syme."

"A lie you propagated. To the police, anyway."

"In the moment, I thought that correcting her would cause more problems than it would solve."

"I see," Plumber looked unsatisfied with this answer. "Should you successfully capture the Virago, the society is prepared to put the matter to rest. We would have the *cognostores* provide you with as much intelligence about her as they are able to find."

Cranston had already requested this last year. The *cognostores*, or the-men-who-know-things, were an organization that could locate prodigious amounts of information in a very short time. His father had once asked them to locate a lost shipment that he had spent weeks trying to track down. The-men-who-know-things took three hours to not only locate the shipment, but provided Father with a complete paper trail. Evidently, someone in Madras had confused two manifests and sent the Walker cargo to Darwin. When they hadn't recognized it, they sent it to Felixstowe. All of that, found in just three hours.

Cranston could imagine the-men-who-know-things handing over Della Caine's current address with a bow on it. At the same time, working with the vigilantes would mean an argument with Vivienne. Despite her intervention in the Syme affair, she wanted him in his office, wanted him home for dinner, wanted him living the life that he was starting to become accustomed to.

"You are free to say 'no'," Mrs Hopkins said. "And, to show that we mean to reward rather than coerce you, this same access to the *cognostores* would be provided to you, should you decide to marry."

That felt like a cup of cold water in Cranston's face. "Pardon?"

"We are concerned that there has been no progress towards the next generation of your family." The old woman said, hardly pausing her knitting. "We understand that your transition back to civilian life has been trying, but we must consider the future. Especially considering that your legacy may be just what you need to settle back into the life you were born to. Should you wish to leave this Virago business in others' hands, we would be happy to see your talents applied to the Walker family business; in particular, children to carry on the family name."

"If you applied yourself to that," Cabot took over. "The society would happily devote resources to your investigation of Della Caine, provided it did not become an impediment to family life."

"I see." Cranston said.

"May I ask," Mr Gates leapt in again. "What is so special about this Miss Caine?"

Cranston had prepared a full proposal for this when he had made his initial request. "Mr Gates," he began. "Are you familiar with Extradimensional Affective Disorder?"

"Oh, yes, I have heard of it. They say it afflicts those who have been too close to one of those pocket things."

"Precisely. Dimensional pockets were one of many dangers on the battlefield. I saw quite a few men struck down by them. Last year, when I was for lack of a better word 'introduced' to Miss Caine, I was informed that she had the most acute case of it that anyone had ever seen. When I finally came into contact with her, I was convinced."

"How was that?" Mr Gates prodded.

"I hesitate to give a full report," Cranston said with practiced reluctance. "As the details are so strange. Suffice it to say, though, that Miss Caine's exposure to the pocket affects her physically in ways that one might expect to see in PT Barnum's freak show."

"Hmmpf," Mr Gates looked unsatisfied.

"Agreed." Cranston said, deliberately misinterpreting his noise. "I believe that if Miss Caine could be studied, it may forward our understanding of the disease and perhaps unlock a cure."

"So you say," Plumber cut in. "But Miss Caine is listed as a patient in some secure hospital; or *was* until her reported death."

"It is my belief," Cranston had prepared a script for this point, as well. "That the hospital where she was being cared for was more of a prison than a medical research facility. Asylums, after all, are not renowned for making their patients better. The Syme Retreat, on the other hand, has been the source of nearly every advancement regarding this condition to date."

"This implies," Cabot said, addressing the table more than Cranston himself. "That if we could locate Miss Caine, you would be satisfied to see her remanded to the care of Dr William Syme? That your part in the hunt would be concluded?"

"I believe so, yes." Cranston nodded.

Cabot gave the others a significant look and fell silent.

"Alright," Plumber said. "Well, Mr Walker, the choices are laid out for you. How would you like to proceed?"

Cranston knew the answer. He had landed on it while mentally reading through the project proposal script in his mind. Vivienne would understand in time.

Chapter 9:
How we got these masks

August 9th, 1921. Silkhaven.

The Saint Lawrence Vigilance Committee was barracked in a small castle. Long ago, mad old Ezechiel Duquette had poured the better part of his fortune into the construction of five such buildings. Each would have been the size of a city block, stone and mortar, with wooden roofs, turrets on the corners, and a small courtyard at their centers.

The old man had lost his mind. That was the official story after his son and daughter got a court order to have the construction halted. Two had been built by then. The construction company and stone supplier were both old friends of Duquette and there was a persistent rumor that the old man was divesting himself of his fortune to keep it out of his children's hands. Which was just as well, since the son was murdered, supposedly, by his homosexual lover and the daughter married a Hungarian Count, then flitted off to Europe, all before the court reached its decision.

What ultimately happened with the money had not been preserved in the city's lore, but the remaining castles were never completed. The city exercised eminent domain on the last three lots and one of the castles was purchased, then demolished. However, the Rose and Chain had secured the remaining castle, using it as a widows and orphans home before St Rita of Cascia's Sanctuary for the Unfortunate was opened. Now, the better part of the castle was used as an archive with the vigilance committee occupying the rest.

Williamson parked in front of the curious, two-story castle and went to open Cranston's door for him.

"Come along," the heir told the driver. "You deserve a homecoming, same as anyone."

"A homecoming?" Williamson said, feigning innocence. "I'm sure I don't know what you mean."

"Of course, not."

Cranston knocked on the great double doors and found one open almost immediately. Standing there was El Tiburon, unmasked, but wearing a red coat reminiscent of the English Army before the Jacobite Restoration.

"Captain Walker!" He exclaimed. "Welcome to the Prosecution!"

They shook hands. "Good to see you, Tiburon. This is my driver, Williamson."

Tiburon startled. "Not *Patrick* Williamson?"

"The same," the driver said as Tiburon gaped.

"Come in, come in, come in!" The vigilante said, ushering them into the castle—the Prosecution—hurriedly.

They doffed their hats in the vestibule, then proceeded through to the entry hall. It was an old-fashioned kind of hall that doubled as a common area for residents. It was lined with bookshelves, and numerous chairs and sofas were scattered about, none of them matching the others. A circular fireplace was set in the middle of the room with a chimney that disappeared into the ceiling. Reading chairs had been arranged around the stone fireplace and an elderly woman was setting its low edge like a dinner table, with the assistance of the Shiek—Tiburon's mute partner in crime-fighting.

Preparing the table was put on hold when they saw Cranston and Williamson enter. Cranston knew Tiburon and the Sheik from his adventure in Montague the year before. The old woman he knew from his parents' war stories of their days in this very committee.

"Ace!" The woman declared, approaching Williamson with spread arms.

"Red!" He hugged her. "What are you doing still kicking around here?"

"What else am I going to do? Join a knitting bee?" She gave him an affectionate punch in the shoulder. "How's that hip of yours?"

"It's alright," Williamson said. "So long as I don't try to run."

The woman—none other than the legendary Red Widow—turned to Cranston. "This is the Boy Captain, eh?"

"Sure is." The driver said.

Red Widow took a step towards Cranston. "You've got your mother's eyes, but that jaw is all your father. You know what that means?"

"I couldn't begin to guess." Cranston answered.

"Nothing but trouble." She pinched his cheek. "Come on, you two. I got toast sandwiches, clam chowder, fried tomatoes, and spinach. Tiburon, get us another chair."

As the company approached their makeshift lunch table, Tiburon found another reading chair and heaved it up on his back for the trek across the hall. Cranston and Williamson took their seats while Red Widow and the Sheik finished setting.

Cranston did a quick count of the chairs. "Are we expecting one more?" He asked as Tiburon put the sixth chair down.

"Your partner." Tiburon said.

"Where's he?" Cranston asked.

"*She*"—Red Widow corrected—"is in the courtyard. Call her in, why don't you? But don't get too close. That sword she's swinging is blunt, but it's the heaviest thing I've carried all week."

Cranston rose and straightened his suit. There were windows looking out on the courtyard and he took a peek to get a lay of the land before venturing out. He could make out a human figure, bare-armed, but in a daringly short skirt. Beyond that, he couldn't see much; the aged window panes warped so.

The door to the courtyard was as heavy as one would expect in a castle. Cranston heaved it open to see a woman wearing a bright blue corset as a shirt with the straps of a pale yellow chemise rising from its upper edge. She wore a skirt of the same color—possibly the lower part of the chemise—which barely reached her knees. Preserving some modesty were a pair of tall stockings of dingy white rising from a pair of tall, brown, leather boots.

Odile de la Porte.

The grand woman was fighting a wooden dummy using a thick, curved sword at a snail's pace. The supposedly blunt sword made contact and the nearly-silver-haired woman adjusted her shoulders to follow through, drawing the edge along the dummy's midsection. When the blade reached the other side, she bent her wrist to bring the sword to full extension before drawing it back through the air in a defensive motion. As her hand approached the line of her hip, she flexed her arm, drew back her elbow, rotated her wrist and thrust into the dummy's heart. All at a tenth the speed one might expect.

"He never stood a chance." Cranston announced himself, though it couldn't have surprised the woman.

"Moving at the slow speed a-trains ou muscle." She replied, pronouncing 'muscle' as 'miskel'. "Ou muscle remembah."

"Yes, back in my fencing days, we did the same when practicing an exhibition fight."

Odile scoffed. "Sa se sport!" She rapped a knuckle on her blade. "Sa *a* se killing."

"You're a corsair." It came out more accusatory than he had intended.

She scowled thoughtfully. "Etais," she said, finally.

"You *were?*"

"Wi, I *were* korsé. Mennon...today, I vijilan."

Cranston knew this gambit. The Rose & Chain had pulled it on his father long ago. During a particularly turbulent time in the island's history, gangs had been rampant. The society had convinced Cranston's grandparents that young James Walker needed a bodyguard. They selected a pretty Russian immigrant—a refugee of the Anarchist Rebellion—ostensibly because she could pose as James' escort to society functions. And that was how Cranston's parents had met.

Mrs Hopkins had shown their hand at this morning's meeting. The guilelessness of it was almost insulting, but Cranston had to applaud their taste.

"How did you wash up in Silkhaven?" Cranston asked, approaching.

She stared at him, evidently parsing what the question meant, then said: "I got the problem. The Woz et Chain got me la."

"It must have been some problem."

"Wi, it's une histoire the a'venture et vyolans. Buy me drink, petèt I tell."

It took Cranston a moment to parse that and he wondered what his mother's English had been like in the 1870s. "Well, lunch is ready now."

"*Now,*" Odile replied, remembering the word.

"But I can certainly arrange drinks for us later."

"Men of Silkhaven, a'e ou good drinkuhs?"

"I think so." Cranston said confidently. He held out his arm and Odile took it while stabbing her sword into the courtyard grass. She was nearly as tall as he was, which the Lothario in him found intriguing.

They went in to lunch.

May 13th, 1917. 100 nautical miles west of the Crescent Isles.

Clothing had always been more impediment than boon in warfare. Bits of cloth getting into sword wounds were more likely to encourage infection than healing. Armor was another matter, but it had suffered a similar fate after the invention of the gun. The modern military uniform was meant to help soldiers and sailors identify their own, not protect them from machine guns or mortars.

The corsairs of the Caribbean Confederacy had staunchly resisted that particular form of modernization. They were a people of liberty and took no small pride in the bespoke nature of their wardrobes, especially aboard fighting ships.

The Caribbean Confederacy could not be said to have a navy, but their power in the Atlantic was second only to the Virginians. Indeed, the ships built in Venezuela were heavily inspired by Virginian designs, though they had never succeeded in reverse engineering Virginian propulsion systems. Nearly every Caribbean spent some time at sea, and three-quarters of their economy was maritime-based. They had monopolies on several agricultural products that sold for luxury prices in Europe and North America. Many of their major ports enjoyed reputations as getaways for the rich and powerful. And that was to say nothing of the corsairs.

For over a century, Caribbean corsairs had been the freelances of every Atlantic war. More than a few times, they had been paid in anticipation of hostilities that never broke out. They were regularly on the payroll of several European countries for free access to Mexico and had been paid well to stay out of the French "interventions".

The Great War had seemed like it might pass them by, though. There were no European holdings left in the Americas, apart from Suriname, and Paramaribo wasn't going to cause anyone any grief. With the Central Powers having little to no presence in the Atlantic, the most the Caribbean could hope for was a blockade of the Strait of Gibraltar.

Then, in 1916, Spain was threatened by the Entente for harboring German soldiers in Africa. While negotiating with the Entente, they secretly allied with the Liberian Caliphate, planning to oust other European powers from North and Central Africa. While an invasion of

Spain was manageable by the Entente, their colonial armies could not resist an offensive from gold-rich Liberia.

And so the corsairs were called in.

Captain Odile de la Porte leapt from the boarding plank as soon as she saw the Liberian start swinging his sledgehammer. In midair, she drew her cutlass in a reverse grip. Landing behind the Liberian, she stabbed backwards, felt the blade sink deep and then whirled to face him, tearing the sword out as she went. He went down, the hammer thunking against the patrol ship's deck.

His face was shocked, mouth agape and silent. She knew that look. It wasn't the blood loss that would kill him, it was the surrender. Men of heart took wounds twice as deep and kept fighting, sometimes even reaching safety before they truly did not have the blood anymore. This one, though, he looked bitter and offended, but also sad; sad that his life had ended so abruptly, but never believing that it wasn't over. In the face of trauma, he was giving up.

Footsteps behind her, she turned again, shifting her sword to her right hand and raising it defensively as another sailor came at her with a pistol raised above his head. In the moment he swung the pistol down like a sap, she saw his face register the sword; the desire to withdraw. But her sword flew up to block, not the gun, but the arm. Between the two of them, they had enough force for the cutlass to break through the bones of his forearm, though not all the flesh around it.

She followed through on the swing and his hand flopped back and hit his elbow, still connected by a strip of muscle and skin. He stumbled, fell on his ass, and wailed, clutching his mostly severed arm to his chest. This one wasn't giving up. The pain was a surprise, but he would recover himself. She moved in and he looked up at her like an actor who had forgotten they were in a play watching the curtain fall.

What a sight she must have been for this good Muslim sailor. Odile towered above him in thigh-high leather boots and a red coat that buttoned beneath her breasts, then swept back sharply, leaving her legs unencumbered, topped with a French cocked hat; like the tragic highwayman. Under the coat, she wore what more progressive nations would see as a swimming costume: a bodysuit with short legs that didn't reach her boots, leaving a saucy strip of flesh exposed. The bodysuit had wide, gold lapels where Odile had sewn in a dozen coins from around the world. Her sun-bleached hair was braided and pinned into a shelf for the hat to rest on.

This was the vision he took with him as her blood-wet cutlass stabbed into his chest; koudeta gras.

"Ou byen, Kapitèn?" One of her men called.

"Wi," she replied and surveyed the ship.

Her corsairs were massacring the Liberians. Credit to the enemy, they did not surrender. Perhaps they thought it was useless, knowing corsair ships did not have brigs, but they didn't even try for peace; preferring to die on their feet. And die they would. There wasn't a sword among them. They weren't prepared to fight this way.

The Liberian ship had four guns, but only one covered their stern. Like her own ship, this patrol boat was built to outmaneuver opponents. Shooting from the bow made them a smaller target, but lacking broadside guns made them vulnerable to boarding. That aft gun was not an armored turret, more a mounted cannon and it required four men to operate it effectively. Her snipers had harried the gunners while her own port gun destroyed their propellers. Once that was done, it was simple to come alongside.

Like most navy ships, the crew only had small arms and not enough ammunition to reload each pistol twice, needing the space and weight for provisions. One of the benefits of being a raider was that you could embark with more bullets than bread and restock your bread later. The men on her ship fought all the better knowing that losing a fight could mean starvation for them later.

Odile hadn't been called to the boarding until the Liberian bullets were exhausted. Now, it was just a matter of cleaning up. Finally, the Muslims began to surrender, every bold heart among them already pierced. The captain was brought to Odile. He was an old sea dog, the salt having carved deep lines into his face. Fat and dignified, he was no fighting man, but he looked like someone Odile would want with her in a storm.

One of her officers held the Liberian captain by her side as the surrendering sailors were brought out onto the deck and arranged in lines. Meanwhile, the Caribbean raiders began hauling food and coal back to their own ship. There was a lull as the raiders opened a deck hatch to remove a very large crate.

"Kisa sa ye?" Odile called to the men hoisting the crate up. They were not completely sure, but they thought it was tins of food. She ordered them to wait, then turned to the Liberian captain. "Box of food, wi?" She pointed at the half-raised crate.

"Yes." He replied.

"I give box of food you." Odile continued in her pidgin English. "You give coin me."

"How much?" Asked the other captain, then added: "We no treasure ship."

"No ransom, one coin. Liberia coin. Good coin: I no need penny."

The old captain eyed the coins stitched into her lapels and understood. Those were trophies. Perhaps it was pride that motivated him then, but he reached into his coat and removed a large, gold coin. It was nearly two inches wide and stamped with the initials of the sitting caliph in Roman letters calligraphed into abstraction so deeply they were nigh impossible to recognize.

Liberians were not the strictest Muslims; they let their women show their faces, they prayed 'in their hearts', and Odile had found pork rations on their ships in the past. However, they held with the prohibition on creating images of humans and animals. The stamp meant it was pure gold as well. Controlling every gold mine from Senegal to the old Sokoto Caliphate, they had the metal and they were pious enough not to put the caliph's initials on a false coin.

"Good good coin." Odile told the old captain. "I give two box of food."

She relayed the orders to her chief raider. They would let the Liberians float and try to get themselves rescued. Then, she returned to her own ship: *Favor Fortunae.*

August 9th, 1921. Silkhaven.

"Where do we start?" Tiburon asked.

Lunch was done and the six of them were sat around the cold fire pit. The vigilance committee was larger than this, but it was a mostly volunteer outfit. The rest of the vigilantes were likely at work. How Tiburon and the Sheik could afford to be here, Cranston didn't know.

"We canvas." Cranston told them. "The Virago had a well-made costume, so she has someone backing her, maybe another committee. Now, I don't expect any of them to surrender one of their own, but I want to turn the rumor mill. We'll start with the committees that are too straight-laced to back an unlicensed vigilante and work our way down the scruple tree."

"Silkhaven's Best and the White Angels," Red Widow said. "Silkhaven's Best might as well be the Vigilante Registration Office and if the White Angels heard someone was poisoning beer, they'd ask how they could help."

"They still might not tell us anything." Tiburon opined. He leaned forward to address Red Widow. "Remember Mad Cap Mark? The Seawatch told the registration office that he wasn't on their roster anymore, then left it at that; even after he almost killed Tempest."

The matron nodded.

Tiburon turned back to Cranston. "We're going to need something serious to even rattle their cages."

"Oh, we aren't going to turn her over to the police." Cranston told him. "We want her help."

Tiburon sat back in his chair. "Is that so?"

"The Rose & Chain has been investigating something Saint Moon calls its 'vaccine project' for two years now."

"They're making medicine, now?"

"That's what the few internal memoranda we've gotten say. It's certainly chemical, though that's no surprise for a food company." Cranston turned his head, addressing the room. Odile was sat sideways with one knee over her chair's arm and an elbow propping her up on the other. Her look was studying him. "Given Edward Blake's public defenses of eugenics, we suspect that there is something nefarious going on. The Walker Company recently contracted with Saint Moon as a way of getting access to their goods. However, as far as we can tell, the 'vaccine project' is still in development. If this masked woman knows enough about it to start burning trucks, we would like to know what she knows."

"How much of that are we sharing?" Tiburon asked.

"We are investigating Saint Moon," Cranston raised one finger, then a second. "And we're in a position to bring them down for good and all, if they're up to something."

The Sheik nodded approvingly.

"If they seem like they're stonewalling, drop the word 'vaccine,'" Cranston continued. "But nothing else until we can set up a formal meeting."

"If you're going to go knocking and claiming to be a friend," Red Widow said. "You're going to need a mask. You got something in mind?"

He thought for a moment. One of Silkhaven's most renowned

vigilantes had been a man who went by 'The Raven'. In a newspaper interview that Cranston had read as a boy, the Raven had said he chose that moniker because, growing up, he had been terrified of the birds. That had stuck with Cranston for reasons he could only guess.

"When I was a boy," Cranston began. "My father was afraid I might be the target of kidnappers. Any time we were out in public and had a free moment, he would ask me what I would do if he told me suddenly to run. Together we would strategize. There was never any telling where the danger might be coming from, so we went over the same places again and again.

"If I were fleeing someone, the general plan was, first, to make myself hard to see and, second, to get somewhere safe; a police station, one of the company's buildings, a church. We discussed routes through buildings I could take to get a distance advantage. If I was caught by shop employees or the like, that was preferable to getting caught by kidnappers. Banks, especially, he said, could put a human shield between me and the nefarious adults. A child causing a disturbance there would not simply be handed over to someone claiming to be a parent.

"If I could get out of sight, I could exchange clothes with a bootblack or a newsie; just swap hats and coats, then walk calmly away. If there were any women about, I could attach myself to one of them. Most people, seeing a child struggle against a grown man, would assume that he was my father and keep out of it. That same man harassing a woman and child would inspire intervention. In a truly desperate situation, I could go into a general store and start breaking bottles. That would get the police involved for sure and my father could pay for the damage later.

"To him, I think, this was a time of bonding. Just father and son discussing daring adventure. It terrified *me*. I had nightmares about the scenarios we discussed. In them, there was a man chasing me and all of the newsies were his agents or every shop was empty. It was always the same man behind me. He had three long, red scars across his face. I knew, in the way one knows things in dreams, that his name was 'the Stalker.'"

When it was clear that Cranston was done, Red Widow said: "I'll get my sewing things."

Chapter 10:
The Vigilantes of Silkhaven

August 10th, 1921. Silkhaven.

Cranston arrived at the Prosecution first thing the next morning to find Red Widow in the castle's hall putting the finishing touches on his costume. The mask was a black balaclava that she had stitched three diagonal, tapering stripes onto, reminiscent of the three-scarred man from Cranston's childhood nightmares. The Widow had also provided him with a large fedora that fit over the balaclava. With this, he wore a matching shirt without a collar—the sleeves rolled up to his elbows like a sportsman—and brown driving gloves. He wore golf pants in dark grey under brown cavalry boots. To unite the ensemble, Red Widow had sewn him a dark grey vest with tan pinstripes.

Odile came down the stairs in black thigh-high boots and a gold-yellow, underbust corset over a black swimming costume or leotard with broad, gold-yellow lapels bedecked with exotic coins, including a Liberian L$10 coin, which was impressively not the most eye-catching thing about her appearance. Her right arm was tattooed to the elbow with a grand image of a draconic sea monster sinking a fully rigged ship. There was a coquettish strip of bare skin between the legs of her swimming costume and boots; where the dark green lines of another tattoo were visible. The lapels of the swimming costume provided a generous view of her décolletage and a tantalizing hint at yet another tattoo high on her left breast. Her silvery-blonde hair was braided and pinned at the top of her neck, where another tattoo still disappeared down the back of her leotard. She carried a red coat and a tricorn hat as she descended the stairs.

"No mask?" He asked as she appeared.

"La," she said, indicating the black hat. She reached a chair, where she could deposit the coat and removed a black domino mask from inside the hat. Tying it on, she said: "*Now*, I am Odile. I am Fortuna!"

With his own mask in place, Cranston affected a gruff, American accent. "And I, the Stalker." He held out an arm to her. Her coat on, she took it heartily. "Our chariot awaits."

The Walker Corporation had a number of subsidiaries, one of which acquired luxury goods and then resold them after the manufacturer's stock was gone. They took losses on about half the items they purchased, but the other half more than made up for it. Cranston, needing a car that could not readily be traced back to him, had asked what the subsidiary had available. What they provided him was a very recently acquired "torpedo" car called a Farman A6B. Painted in dark blue and silver, the only complaint Cranston could possibly levy was that the French import had the wheel on the wrong side.

Stalker helped Fortuna into her seat before returning to the sidewalk to get in the driver's seat.

Silkhaven was divided into six districts. Their job that day was to interview the vigilance committees in Chateau de Cygne; the most populous and central of the districts. Tiburon and the Sheik were headed across the East River to Broadwater; a strange combination of low-rent warehouses, working-class homes, and palatial retirement homes. Those two were going to talk with the White Angels, spry retirees that mostly tattled on bad nurses and maybe helped those who were ready to pass before nature's time; the Night Watch that patrolled the docks; and the recently formed Battle Boys who had yet to distinguish themselves.

Stalker and Fortuna were on their way to meet with Silkhaven's Finest, the Tick-Tocks, and the League of Prodigal Daughters.

Silkhaven's Finest were headquartered on the top three floors of the Levesque Building. Fifty years ago, they boasted of ushering in a new age of 'public trust' by not wearing masks. Led by Henry Levesque, that first generation had armed themselves with gadgets produced by his company. The experiment had ended in disaster when the Black Dog gang shot up a Levesque family picnic. The current squad of vigilantes had an obscure relationship with the family, who had mostly emigrated to the mainland.

These days, their version of 'public trust' was in policing the other vigilance committees; not in itself a bad thing, but it had the reek of cowardice about it. As if they wanted to put someone in their place, but they had decided that proper villains were too dangerous.

Inside the Levesque building, after presenting their credentials—expedited by the Rose & Chain's connections—Stalker and Fortuna were shown to the VC elevator. On the eighth floor, they were greeted by a trio of fellow vigilantes in purple costumes with the same stylized white eagle emblazoned somewhere conspicuous. At the lead was Strong John Blonde, who wore work trousers, a purple shirt with the eagle stretched wide across his broad chest, and what looked like the bottom half of a knight's helmet to guard his neck and hide the lower part of his face. Flanking him were Cheetah—a wiry man in a purple leotard and masked hood, the white eagle down one leg—and Oracle—a woman in a knee-length purple dress over matching stockings and a domino mask, her eagle across her waist.

"Hmm," Strong John Blonde said, not moving to shake hands. "Newcomers."

"Of a sort," Stalker replied. Credentials were presented and introductions made. "Is there somewhere we can talk?"

"Yeah, I had a feeling this wasn't a social call." Strong John said.

"Strictly business, I'm afraid."

"Oracle, you're with me."

Strong John led them from the sparse reception room into a hallway. Cheetah disappeared into a room where a radio was playing, leaving the rest. The quartet ended up in a conference room on a corner of the building which must have had a magnificent view when it was built, though now only looked out on the windows of newer, taller buildings. Oracle took a seat where a notepad was waiting.

"What's your business?" Strong John asked.

"We are investigating the Masked Virago." Stalker said.

"Alright,"

"Specifically, we want to hear out her grievances; see if they have any merit."

Strong John took a moment to think about that. While nothing was being said, Oracle nervously tapped her pen on the paper.

"What makes you think the Virago's grievances might have any merit?" Strong John asked.

"She's in earnest." Stalker shrugged. "Plus, she's organized. That's not a woman throwing a fit. Maybe she's a mad T-totaler, but maybe she knows something that the public should know as well."

Strong John considered this before saying: "She's not one of ours."

"Of course not."

"We are investigating, ourselves," he continued. "But if her grievances have any merit, she can tell them to a judge." The man was using as many of Stalker's own words as he could, which was interesting. "The Virago could erode public trust in the vigilante system."

"I agree." Stalker replied.

"I say that only because you're new."

"I have lived in Silkhaven for some time."

Strong John took a moment to think about that. "You're new to the mask."

He was trying to get Stalker to say something without asking for it. It was a good tactic. It only worked when the subject wanted to talk, but still good. He was going off topic to try to make Stalker volunteer something to get the conversation back on topic.

"Are you familiar with the Praetorian Guard?"

Strong John stiffened. Even Oracle was taken aback and her pen was silent for a moment.

"Yeah," Strong John said.

"Well, the army decided they didn't want our services anymore. It occurred to me that a vigilance committee might have use for them. This Virago business convinced me it was time. Would you mind being questioned under hypnosis?"

Strong John shook his head. "No, that's not going to happen. It's time for you to go."

Stalker didn't argue. Oracle led them out and Stalker and Fortuna rode the elevator down in silence. As soon as they were out of the building, Fortuna turned to Stalker.

"You did hear that woman *tat tat tat* her pen?"

"Yeah," he replied. "It was code."

"You know?"

"The code? No. But she was giving him instructions." They reached the car and both walked out into the street. "The woman is the brains of that outfit." He opened her door.

"Ben sûr." Fortuna said, stepping between him and her seat. "She boss. I know—" she snapped her fingers, meaning 'instantly'.

"How did you guess?"

"I know her...genre."

"Her kind?"

"No," she smirked. "She no kind."

"Alright," Cranston gave her a devilish look before remembering his mask. "What *sort* of woman is she?"

Fortuna reached behind her and flipped the back of her coat up, then slowly bent her way into the seat, projecting the cleft of her bosom into the air between them while keeping her eyes locked on his. Only once she was seated did she swing her legs into the car.

"Oh, that sort." He shut the door.

As Stalker managed to pull into traffic from the right side of the car, he saw Fortuna grinning, holding in a laugh. "What's funny?"

"Ou," she said, drawing a circle around her face in the air.

"I'm wearing a mask." He said.

"I see." Then, remembering: "I *can* see."

"So, compliments are funny to you?"

"Konpliman? I wear corset. Tout femmes look good in corset."

"Pas tout," he replied. "Il y a des nuances."

She was quiet for a moment. "Ill ah day?"

He knew that the Caribbean spoke some descendant of French, but he couldn't tell how much actual French she spoke. It seemed she was stitching together a creole of her French and English that approximated her thoughts. Somehow 'il y a' was not in her vocabulary. He switched back to English.

"There are nuances. Nuances exist." He tried both to see what stuck.

"Nuans egziste!" She replied. "Ki nuans?"

"Size, mostly." He glanced at her face and didn't see comprehension. "Grand et petit."

"Ah!" She nodded. "*Size*." She repeated, memorizing.

"Tout grande siens...look good in a corset." He used words that he was confident she knew. "Petite siens disparaître." He didn't inflect the verb. If 'il y a' had not descended into her form of French, he doubted that the conjugations had survived; not intact, anyway.

Fortuna nodded. "Pitit sens disparèt nan yon korse. Wi. In..." she paused to produce a fair approximation of a North American accent. "... Caribbean...femme...boom boom."

Stalker chuckled. "C'est une bonne publicité."

"Wi, se rezon...rich...homme...vakans nan...Havana."

Stalker processed that. "Vacances à La Havane?"

"Wi, Lahavan." Then, something struck her. "Silk-havan!"

"Oui, refuge pour le...soie." He ventured.

"Swa? Silk?"

"Oui."

"Refij pou swa! Where swa...silk be?"

"Ooh...um..." This was not the time for a history lesson. He searched for the simplest, short answer. "In the depots of my family."

"Fanmi ou?"

"Maybe," he laughed.

"Papa, manman; fanmi."

"Ah, oui."

"I think many femme prefer ou."

He laughed. "It helps. Ça aide."

"Ou femme in picnic, ou madanm?" She asked.

"At the picnic? Rebecca? No. Rebecca is une bonne amie."

"Ami? Wi, yon bòn zanmi. Ou give silk her?"

"Sometimes...when she is kind."

It was her turn to laugh. "When she no kind?"

"I give her leather." When she didn't immediately react, he repeated: "I give cuir."

"Kwi!" Now, she cackled. "Wi! When I ship captain, I give kwi on no kind man." Then she mimed cracking a whip. "Wicha!"

"Oh! That..." That had not been what he meant. If Pearl wanted that sort of treatment, she needed to be very kind indeed. He started thinking how to explain, then decided that detailing his sexual preferences was not on the day's order. "Well...so, where are you from? Where is your home?"

Fortuna breathed out a long, pleased breath. He had backed off the topic and she seemed to be taking that as a victory. "Homme? No homme me, no now."

"Ah, pa homme. *Home.* Uh...where were you a baby?"

"Mwen bebe..." she said quietly. "Vil natal?"

"Oui! Ou es ton ville natale?"

"Fort-de-libète, Matinik."

Stalker did a quick mental inventory of the Caribbean islands. "Martinique. Okay."

"No Martinique," she corrected him, growling the 'r'. "Matinik."

"Matinik." He repeated.

"Wi, we no French, now."

Their next stop was the Tick-Tocks, who had offices in old city hall. When the legislative offices had moved, the building had been largely redone into a petty court; civil suits, speeding tickets, spitting on the sidewalk, and the like. However, one wing had been bought up by an anonymous benefactor and transferred to the vigilance committee that renamed themselves after the long-defunct clock atop the wing. The rumor was that most of the Tick-Tocks were lawyers or policemen since they operated more like a detective agency than a vigilance committee.

When Stalker and Fortuna arrived, they only got as far as an unmasked secretary.

"You are already investigating this Virago?" The secretary asked when the matter had been explained.

"Yes, we are collecting information from other committees." Stalker told him.

"We are not investigating the Virago, so we have no information."

"You're certain?"

The secretary gave him a withering look. "*If* we have any relevant information, it is part of a separate investigation. Here," he handed Stalker a form. "Fill this out. If someone finds out something relevant, they will send it to you once their case is closed."

"This is urgent." Stalker added.

The secretary sniggered through his nose. "Everything we do is urgent. Now, you can fill out the form and leave or you can just leave." He pushed the paper an inch closer to Stalker. "Next!" The secretary called to the line of people behind Stalker and an older woman shoved past Stalker. She too was given a form.

The last of the Chateau de Cygne committees was the League of Prodigal Daughters. Their offices were a block away from the border with Dockside, close enough to the North River that you could smell it. It was not a storied building, just a shop front with the window full of notices regarding missing persons. Entering the building, Stalker was briefly overcome by the thought that he had walked into the temple of a cult of which Vivienne was high priestess or possibly god.

The ladies of the LPD were dressed in an ad hoc uniform of brown knickerbockers with matching jackets, white shirts, masked by white veils held in place by variously, but neutrally colored cloche hats. A large poster hung on one wall was covered in captioned illustrations of women in full skirts variously kicking, throwing, and using parasols as weapons against British policemen with the word 'Suffrajitsu' written across the top. The opposite wall sported a gun rack.

A woman, whom Stalker couldn't help but think of as a reverend sister, pushed through the swinging door in the hip-high partition that divided the room. She folded her hands low in front of her and said "How may we help you?" in a sweet voice. Meanwhile, another Sister with a pair of pistols strapped to her hips moved to sit on the partition, one foot on top.

Stalker and Fortuna provided their credentials to the sweet sister, while the armed sister pinched a dose of snuff out of a brass box and snorted it under her veil. Fortuna gazed at that one with an animal intensity that may have been territorial or sexual or both.

Stalker explained their business; that they were trying to contact the Masked Virago in hopes of bringing her grievances against Saint Moon into a more official channel.

"Do you suspect the Virago is one of us?" The sweet sister asked.

"'Suspect' is putting it strongly." Stalker said in his rough, American accent. "We acknowledge the possibility that you know how to get a meeting."

"I would deny it outright, but that would not be convincing."

"Would someone in charge be willing to submit to questioning under hypnosis?"

"Hypnosis? I'm not sure." She turned to look behind her, then looked back at Stalker. "Are you the hypnotist?"

"Yes, ma'am."

"I'll do it." A baritone woman's voice called from further in.

The sweet sister moved aside as a six-foot-tall woman with the gait of a grandmother came up to the partition. "Let them in, Petunia. We'll conduct this in my office. I have no more to hide than he does."

Stalker turned to Fortuna. "If I don't come back in thirty minutes..."

"Jeanne de Clisson," Fortuna said and winked at him.

He wasn't sure what that meant, but he took it as a good sign. He followed the tall woman he now thought of as the reverend mother down the aisle between a few desks. They turned and walked past a door marked only with a streak of blue paint before entering the reverend mother's office.

"Have a seat." The reverend mother said, taking a place behind her small desk. "What do you use for your hypnotism?"

"Only my voice," Stalker replied.

"*The* Voice?"

"Yes, ma'am."

"You were a Praetorian, then?"

"Yes, ma'am."

"I had a son in the Praetorian Guard. He died in Spain."

"The Navarre Campaign?"

"Yes, I suppose. It was in the mountains."

Stalker nodded. He had been there, before the fighting started. This woman's son might have been his replacement.

"I am sorry for your loss."

"Thank you. How does it work?"

Stalker began adjusting the muscles in his throat. "You'd need a doctor to explain the exact mechanism, but there is a timbre that confuses higher thinking. It requires the subject's attention. The greater the attention, the easier it is for the Voice to do its work."

"You mastered something you don't understand?" The reverend mother asked from behind her white veil.

"Most folks can't. You gotta be born with a certain kind of voice, a certain musculature."

"Does it run in families?"

"Not that I know of. It's just a roll of nature's dice."

The reverend mother inhaled sharply. "God does not play dice."

"The cards we are dealt, then."

The reverend mother was silent, her head slumping a little. "When do we begin?"

"When I'm sure you're listening."

"I *am* listening."

"You're thinking about your son. You're wondering 'why him?'"

The reverend mother raised her head high enough that he could make out the shape of her nose through the veil. "You are perceptive."

"I had to be."

"Yes, I can see that."

"I was in Ixtassou, on the Spanish border, just before Spain declared war. I was the only Guardsman there. Some artillery had been sabotaged, and they had a trio of suspects: American soldiers with Spanish surnames. The commander ordered me to interrogate them with the Voice. I told him what they drilled into us every day at the academy: the Voice is for the enemy. The men he had rounded up were Puerto Rican. I couldn't imagine they had any sympathy for the Spanish cause and I refused. He had me arrested and shipped north for a court-martial."

She was holding her breath.

"I don't know who replaced me." Stalker continued, dropping into the Voice. "<u>Do you know who the Masked Virago is?</u>"

He watched the reverend mother's body relax. "No," she replied.

"Is it possible that any of your vigilantes are the Virago?"

"Yes, but I suspect no one."

"What sins has Saint Moon committed?"

"I don't know."

"What have you heard about Saint Moon?"

"They make food. I like their tomatoes."

"Thank you." Stalker said, breaking the spell.

The reverend mother braced herself against the desk and made a sound like she might vomit.

"I apologize for the side effects." He said. "They're unavoidable, sorry to say."

She breathed heavily for a few moments, collecting herself. "My son came home," she said, her voice cracking. "Before he was sent to Europe. We asked him to show us the Voice, like it was a party trick. He refused. 'The Voice is for the enemy.' He said that, too; like it was the Pledge of Allegiance or the Lord's Prayer. We quarreled. He was still angry with us when he left."

Stalker let that hang for a moment, uncertain if she was finished. "There were times, over there, I thought he wasn't coming home." Stalker told her. "In those moments, I would have given anything to be with my family. I watched men die—ours, theirs—so many of them called out for their mothers. He forgave you."

The reverend mother, still bracing against the desk, said: "You are excused."

"Thank you, ma'am,"

Stalker got up and returned to the main room. Part of him expected to find Fortuna and the armed sister locked in combat. Instead, he found his partner getting a tour of the gun rack. He would have let her continue—he imagined she was starving for company—but he had the feeling their welcome was wearing fast.

On top of that, they had the VC's in Dockside to talk with before dinner. He had plans that Vivienne would not forgive him for missing.

PART 3
The Blakes

Chapter 11:
Blake Congress

Gabrielle put the water on the stove before she sliced the lemons. The supposedly authoritative book sat on the counter—held open by a tin of nuts—was too sparing with its directions and she was not at all confident that she was doing this right. Taking up a slice of lemon and a sugar cube, she began rubbing them together over a punch bowl and letting the slowly dissolving sugar drip down. When the cube was spent, she wasn't sure what to do with the lemon.

According to the single-paragraph recipe, "a small portion of juice" went into the final drink, so she decided to squeeze the lemon and discard the rest. She did this again with the other slices. The cook, silently disapproving, gathered the rinds and put them in a small bowl for some later use. Gabrielle had no idea how much sugar to put in, but six cubes seemed like plenty.

The cook had acquired a bottle of whiskey that afternoon. Gabrielle had heard that alcohol was illegal in America, but apparently not in Silkhaven, which she found confusing. Also confusing was the recipe calling for "pure whiskey", which the cook had never heard of and supposed that meant "single malt". Gabrielle was only more confused by that. Why was European alcohol so complicated?

Lacking any reasonable way to measure the water in the kettle, Gabrielle poured the whole bottle of whiskey into the bowl, only to find herself certain that the kettle was more than one-third the size of the bottle. The recipe book called for boiling water to be added, but at the beginning of the chapter, it said to use tea instead. They had a proper tea service, but the receptacles were too small to reasonably brew for a bowl this size. Already feeling overwhelmed, she could only hope that Father's guests would forgive her imperfect bar-tending skills.

Once the water was boiling, she poured the kettle into the bowl until it was almost full. Then, she had to wait for it to cool before she lifted it onto the trolley. She loaded the trolley with glasses and then pushed it carefully through the kitchen door and into the living room, where Father was delivering a speech to an audience of two.

One of the men, Mr Farrar, was the governor of the island and the other, Mr Syme, was from Boston and was going to "help with the Virago problem". She brought the trolley to a gentle halt, careful not to spill the very full punch bowl and was about to start serving, when she realized that she had forgotten the ladle. Gabrielle bowed apologetically, then dashed back into the kitchen and returned as quickly as possible.

"I believe," Father was saying. "That the term 'race' must be stricken from all documents by serious eugenicists. The rabble too closely associate it with words like 'white' and 'black' and not enough with 'human', for it is the human race that we are concerned with."

Gabrielle served Gov Farrar first, supposing him to be the most 'senior' in the room. He didn't acknowledge her, but sipped the drink right away, not waiting for his host. Mr Syme said 'thank you' when she brought him his drink. Father's drink she placed by his chair, though he was standing for his speech.

"It is also a mistake to think of eugenics as a new phenomenon." Father went on. "It is well-known that all of humanity sprang from somewhere in Africa. We were first all black men. Now, there are some vulgar individuals who would say this makes the negro unevolved, but when we look at the causes of European evolution, namely the success of those accidental children born with fairer skin in the cloudy climes of Germania, it is ridiculous to regard the negro as innately inferior.

"Indeed, the negro is ideally evolved *for his region*. Yes, in one sense, the common negro is less fit than the common aryan in colder regions, but the same may be said of us were we in Africa. Moreover, the negro may be said to be more fit in Africa than the aryan in England. After all, look at the rough living of the African negro. They suffice with homes and agriculture we regard as primitive, but not, I say, for lack of industry. No! The aryan had need of innovation in hearths and homes because he was so unfit for the climate in which he lived, where the negro was and remains in perfect balance with his environment.

"So, as I say, eugenics is no novelty. Humanity has been practicing a form of it for all history. The most successful hunters were those most fit to their environment and through their success became the most desirable to the women of the tribe. Thus, they passed on their genes in greater numbers until those genes which made him so fit were the only ones to be seen.

"On the other side of this self-same coin, we find the truly unfit. Imagine yourself some prehistorical Norwegian woman. Would you allow yourself to be rutted upon by an idiot or a layabout? Of course not! This is how Africa cultivated the mighty negro and Asia the cunning oriental and Europe its balance of the two. Those with the bodies and minds best suited to tame those climes were most desired and procreated most prolifically.

"How then, you might ask, are we still cursed by idiots, bums, and whores? I believe that it is the latter of these that is most to blame. After all, a slattern does not distinguish between her lovers, except by their ability to pay. Even the most anti-social or feeble men might scrape together enough money for an hour's pleasure. How often does such a union unluckily produce...?"

Mr Syme cleared his throat and gave a look towards Gabrielle, who was standing at the cart, waiting to refill glasses. Evidently, he regarded the discussion inappropriate for her.

"Baby," Edward Blake said, as if noticing his daughter for the first time. "You're hardly dressed. Run along and get yourself ready. The Walkers will be here soon." He said, affectionately.

"Yes, Father," she bowed and left, but her father's voice carried as far as the upper stairs.

"As I was saying, the worst of human traits have been—in my opinion—preserved by loose women."

Gabrielle let herself into the ladies' dressing room where Mother was already at work. She was not unfamiliar with hearing men lay the follies of the world at the feet of women, but it somehow sounded much more dire when said with such an air of positivity; as if it needed no evidence.

Either the house had been a hasty purchase or Edward Blake had sentimental tastes. #68 Rue d'Acer, like most of the houses in this part of the city, looked more like a courthouse than a home; a two-story brick box, three windows wide, with a round faux-tower on one side of the rear. They had passed dozens of nearly identical structures on their way in.

Williamson had the night off, so Cranston was driving the Bentley. The faux-towers were baffling. He supposed they were designed to be private rooms—company staying towards the facade—and perhaps the round design was meant to capture more daylight. But the reused design made no adjustments for the compass. His best guess was that there had been some very impressive house built with an eye for those details that had simply been copied, as such things tended to be.

It was hard to imagine a captain of industry—even the food distribution one—living in such a home. It was certainly plenty spacious for a family of four, especially with the children of an age that they may move out at any time. It was only that the house was easily fifty years old and, despite being in excellent repair, looked every single day of those intervening decades.

Exposed brick, for goodness' sake!

Cranston had to park on the road, which he disliked, but they weren't planning on staying long. He killed the engine, got out, and circled around to open Vivienne's door. He wouldn't have bothered opening her door for her before Mother and Father passed, given the nature of this visit. Heirs could get away with such breaches of formality, but the Walker siblings were running the company now. When they called on a home to pick up their respective dates for a social evening, they walked arm-in-arm up the porch in black tie. The floorboards announced them better than anything could, but Cranston knocked anyway.

After a moment, a man in livery opened the door for them. "How may I assist you?" He asked.

That was another thing that didn't belong in a house like this: staff.

Cranston was caught off guard for a moment, expecting to be greeted by the man of the house, but he recovered himself and fished a card from his coat. It was pure luck that he still had some in there. The butler read the card and his expression brightened a hue.

"Mr Walker," the butler said. "It is a pleasure to have you. Please come in and I shall announce you. Might the lady be your sister?"

"I am." Vivienne said.

"Very good, ma'am." The butler said, reaching awkwardly past them in the small vestibule to shut the door. "Just one moment and I will let..."

He was cut off by Edward Blake opening a door and entering the hall. "No need for any of that, Fillmore."

"Yes, sir." The butler replied.

There was a staircase up to the second floor only a few feet ahead of them. Edward grabbed the bannister and leaned over to shout up the stairs. "Gabrielle, Michael, the Walkers are here. Don't keep them waiting." He turned back to the guests. "They'll be a few minutes yet. Do come through."

Cranston and Vivienne left their hats with the butler, who was clearly used to a larger house to manage and was struggling a little with the confined space. Struggling admirably, though. Cranston recognized quality butling when he saw it.

They followed Edward into a parlor where two other men sat with aperitifs. Evidently, Mr and Mrs Blake were entertaining in the planned absence of their children. One man, Cranston recognized immediately: he was half bald with long mutton chops and a mustache, all gone pure white, and the sort of belly one could only get with age or concerted effort.

"Governor Farrar," Cranston said.

The old gentleman rose and swapped his glass to his left hand so he could shake. "Master Walker," then he turned to Vivienne and gave a small bow. "Miss Walker. Edward said nothing."

"We aren't staying." Cranston told him. "We have merely come to abscond with the children."

"Ah, very good!" Farrar proclaimed. "It shan't be too long afore we all hang up our hats and the next generation step in. Knowing people, that's the important thing. It's good of you to extend the hand of friendship. Good and clever. Yes." He seemed to realize that he was becoming confused and bowed out before he embarrassed himself.

Cranston had not been in the country for the election, but what he understood was that Farrar had won on a platform of 'reconstruction'. Reconstruction before the war had ended and in a place that the war had not touched. People had expected tax breaks and a few public projects, but instead Farrar had attempted to divert wartime aid funds to companies owned by his friends. The American half of the Civil Chamber had roundly opposed any alteration to the wartime budget and the Canadian Conservatives had given them the majority out of partisan spirit.

Apparently, when the Liberals realized that Farrar was taking them nowhere, they had turned on him as well. Cranston had seen a lot of talk in the papers about Liberals jockeying to be the new leader, even as Farrar had seemingly resigned himself to being a figurehead and allowing the Liberal senators to do the real work.

"And this," Edward said, gesturing to the second man, who looked like a shaved gorilla stuffed into a Douglas & Cheney suit. He was fully bald, though Cranston suspected it was partly his barber's doing in order to heighten the intimidation of his broad frame. He was a hand shorter than Cranston, but seemed to project a force that made Cranston want to take a step back as he approached.

"This is Benjamin Syme." Edward's voice rang like a dread bell. Cranston felt his body flood with fighting hormones. "Mr Syme, this is Cranston Walker and his formidable sister, Vivienne."

"Cranston Walker," Benjamin Syme repeated, his voice cigarette deep, and extended a hand. "I heard about what you did when my niece was kidnapped last year."

"Yes," Cranston replied, resisting the urge to punch the gorilla in the face. "I heard about what you did, as well."

Benjamin's hand tightened menacingly before he ended the shake.

"Congratulations to your brother," Cranston continued. "Maryland state senator. Won by a landslide, I hear."

"Federal senator," Benjamin corrected him. "Representing Massachusetts."

"Silly me. And the landslide?"

"That you got right. The other guy had essentially conceded weeks before the polls opened. It's kinda hard to get elected when you're being investigated for an international kidnapping conspiracy, no matter how big your church."

"Of course. So, what brings you to Silkhaven?"

"My invitation." Edward retook his hosting duties. "Did you see? The papers are calling that woman from Saturday 'The Masked Virago'. Well, I can't have her returning for another try. The police do not fill me with confidence, so I called my old friend, here."

"My Atlantic Network provides security for these types of operations all the time." Syme said in a practiced intonation. "I've got my boys guarding the factory, already. My best team of hunters are on their way. They had some business elsewhere, but they'll be along in a couple of days."

"Oh!" Edward exclaimed, looking over Cranston's shoulder. "Gentlemen!" Edward moved around Cranston, cuing him and Vivienne to turn. "May I present my daughter?"

Edward hooked his arm into Gabrielle's and led her a few steps into the parlor. She was wearing a draping, white gown that hung across her small frame on a pair of thin straps. It was very good silk; Cranston recognized the weight and weave immediately. It was one they frequently pushed on clients that came into the office hoping for something cheaper because even the uninitiated could see where the extra money was going.

Gabrielle's hair was done up with a pair of above-averagely dangerous-looking pins. Evidently, she was not intending to wear a hat.

"Gentlemen," Gabrielle curtsied. "Mr Walker," turning to him, she again curtsied, but deeper and this time turning her chin up dramatically. "I want to say thank you, once more," she reached out and took one of his hands between both of hers. "Your valor in dealing with that anarchist is a true inspiration. I look forward to spending this evening in the company of your gallantry and"—her eyebrows rose as she said—"boldness."

Cranston had a list of things to do with women who talked like that and none of them were appropriate when said woman's father was in the room.

"That's flattering of you to say, but I hope you won't be disappointed if there are fewer bombs."

The room laughed, except for Gabrielle. She just kept looking at him like she might try to eat him. After a day with Odile, he had been looking forward to the company of an ingenue, but that was not what he was getting.

"Miss Walker," a low, tired voice said from the doorway. Michael stood there, holding a carnation in a way that communicated very clearly that the flower had not been his idea.

"Thank you," she said, trying to make up for his lack of grace as he begrudgingly pinned the bloom to her dress.

"With the formalities out of the way," Cranston said. "The city awaits!"

Chapter 12:
The Soppingest of Wet Blankets

August 10th, 1921. Silkhaven.

They were headed for a Silkhaven staple, The New Barn. Once a municipal stable, it eventually moonlighted as a "traditional" dance hall. That was how Vivienne remembered it from her childhood; a working-class dance hall. She remembered her parents once dressing as farmers to go enjoy an evening at 'The Barn', but she had been too young to ever visit. It burned down when she was twelve and nearly took the entire block with it. New owners had rebuilt it as a luxury dance hall, but it had never been especially popular. When the war started, it was shuttered.

Only recently had the building been reopened as 'The New Barn'. It was not a luxurious-looking building, but whoever was running it now had figured out how to keep prices up and the crowds coming in. There was a large sign above the door—white paint on weathered boards—reading 'No Dances Barred'. With the moral panic over so-called "animal dances", appealing to popular taboos had been all the New Barn needed to get people in.

Not Vivienne, of course, not yet. Having to learn a half dozen scandalous dances sounded like a lot of effort for something she could already secure with almost none. She had been a little worried about making a fool of herself in front of Michael Blake, a good ten years her junior, but he had quickly smothered those nerves by being the soppingest wet blanket she had ever seen. At least her menstruation had been brief this month, or else this would be intolerable.

Meanwhile, Gabrielle was in the front seat of the Bentley asking Cranston questions about the city. At the picnic, the girl had talked as if she owed Vivienne a life debt and, tonight, she had not even bothered to say 'hello'. Vivienne did not know why she cared about the snub, but she did and it was such a novel feeling that she had decided to go on feeling it just to see where it would lead her. If nothing else, she might discover why she was feeling it in the first place.

"Is it a twin thing?" Vivienne asked as Michael stared out the window.

"Pardon?" He said, turning to almost look at her.

"Do the two of you have a single reserve of energy and your sister happens to be monopolizing it at the moment?"

"I'm sorry." Michael said, eyes on the upholstery between them. "I don't understand."

"I understand that I am not as young a date as you would prefer," she explained. "But your nigh-utter silence this entire trip is bordering on the insulting."

"Oh...I apologize. This was all her idea." Probably referring to Gabrielle. "I'm not in the mood."

"When you are in the mood, do you like exciting women? Or are you the sort to make a love connection in the library?"

"Please," he sounded exhausted. "I already apologized."

"Alright, I will be more direct. You are about to be seen in public with me. I have a reputation for stepping out with exciting men; matadors, actors, even the occasional musician if he knows how to wash. Like it or not, you are about to be compared with all of them in the gossip pages. Women love gossip pages, even the dowdy girls. If you spend the evening looking like your puppy just died, it will look much worse for you than for me. So, for your own sake, do buck up. You can look serious and we can talk like business partners, but you are going to need to iron that frown."

"Yes, ma'am." He said, then turned back to the window, countenance unchanged.

Vivienne gave herself permission to dance with someone else, but only if it was someone she knew. There was teaching the boy a lesson and then there was cruelty. Not that she held out much hope of seeing anyone she knew. Pulling up to the New Barn, Vivienne noted that the small crowd making their way inside were decidedly more youthful than what could graciously be called her set. They were not quite young enough to be her friends' children, of course, rather the generation situated between them.

Cranston parked near the entrance, which had a small, poorly organized line in front of it. The crowd was cycling through whatever entrance procedure the place had quickly enough that forming an orderly line was unnecessary. The crowd collectively paused when the Bentley pulled up, staring with a mixture of fascination and fear. No doubt a few of them worried someone's father was about to step out and make a scene. Instead, it was Cranston, putting on his Homburg and adjusting his coat for a moment.

Vivienne watched a few of the youngsters in the crowd recognize him with interest, but not excitement. She thought he was drinking it up for a moment, but then he knocked on Michael's window.

"Come on, old boy," Cranston said. "We have ladies to escort."

Michael tiredly opened his door.

"Around the front," Cranston told him. "Brothers and sisters, tonight."

"Poo," Gabrielle whined quietly from the front seat. That gratified Vivienne and she let the feeling stand, despite knowing it was petty. She hoped it would illuminate why she was feeling petty.

Still, she did not let the feeling show as Cranston opened her door. She was met by a palpable phalanx of gazes. Her outfit had one of the Japanese-inspired robes that was somewhat diaphanous over a boxy dress that was more frill than fabric. It was the very knife's point of fashion.

The girls crowded about the New Barn's entrance were also on *la mode du jour*'s knife, but not the sharp part. They looked on this older woman, with her tailored garments imported from Paris, and some eyes scowled into points while others were wide-eyed with wonderment.

All-in-all, this was the most mixed reception Vivienne could remember having.

She took Cranston's arm and he led the quartet into the crowd. He locked himself onto a straight line for the door and let the members of the crowd decide whether they wanted to be in his way or not. Vivienne was impressed by the elegance of the thing. Several young men tipped their hats and made a show of making way and Cranston reciprocated with a lift of his own; the elder statesman of the nightclub scene being gracious to the newcomers.

The man on the door was a pimply kid in a crisp, red uniform standing at a lectern with a guest book open in front of him. "Names?" He said bluntly when Cranston got to him. Cranston seemed to hesitate, then fetched another of those cards from his coat pocket. The doorman looked at it for several seconds. "I don't think you're on our list." He said finally.

"It's our first time." Cranston replied like he was forgiving the boy.

"Yeah, maybe," he rubbed his neck. "Just the two of you?"

"No," Cranston drawled. "We're a foursome." Then he gestured to the Blake twins.

"Ah, yeah," sweat appeared on the doorman's brow. "Listen, we don't like to advertise it. You know, people are real sensitive these days, but...well...colored folks don't usually come in through the front if you know what I mean."

Vivienne felt herself begin to flush. Whatever pettiness she felt towards Gabrielle did not extend so far as to allow the girl to suffer indignities, certainly not in public.

"Is this a policy of the establishment?" Vivienne asked, her voice sharp.

"Oh dear," Cranston said.

"Uh...yeah, I guess." The doorman's mouth got halfway to a smile and then seemed to second-guess itself.

"And the owner, is he in?"

"Mr Knapp? Sure, but he's going to tell you the same thing."

"Would that be Arnold Knapp?" Vivienne asked.

"He a friend of yours?"

"It has been a while."

"Since you pushed him off that boat?" Cranston added.

The doorman looked at her shocked.

"He was getting fresh." She told the kid. To Cranston, she said: "No, he and I attended a few of the same meetings regarding liquor austerity during the war."

Someone shouted from the crowd behind them. "What's going on?" The youths had been at a standstill for a minute now and were getting restless.

"Sorry!" The doorman shouted. "They were just leaving." He turned back to Cranston. "Don't make a scene, yeah?"

"I beg your pardon." Cranston laughed. He had not once been denied entrance to a club of any sort.

"Listen..." the doorman started, but then saw Vivienne let go of

Cranston's arm and began walking into the club on her own. "Hey, you can't..." he held out an arm to block her path.

Vivienne looked down at the kid's splayed hand and followed the line of his arm up to his eyes. "What *exactly* do you think you are going to do with that hand?"

"I gotta stop you." He said like she was being ridiculous.

"You truly do not." Cranston said, taking off his hat. "Michael, would you take this, please?"

"What are you doing?" The doorman asked as Cranston took off his coat.

"I am preparing..." Cranston handed the coat to Michael and began rolling up his sleeves. "...for the moment you lay an unwanted hand on my sister. You know how it is."

"Hey, fella, I don't want any trouble."

Another voice shouted from the growing crowd. "Let us in!"

"Yeah!" Came another. "You open or not?"

Vivienne took hold of the doorman's thumb between two fingers like it was a dirty dish rag and moved it out of her way. "I am going to speak with Arnie. If you so much as sniff in resistance, I will get your name and from there I will get your mother's name and address. Tomorrow morning, I will put on my best tea dress and pay her a visit. She and I will sit and talk and come to the conclusion that it really is best for you to come work for me. Arnie will have fired you by this time, of course. In my employ, you will arrive at my office at 9am sharp. You will polish my shoes, then the shoes of my secretary. In fact, you will polish the shoes of every secretary on the floor. Once that is finished, you will spend the rest of the work day as my own personal footstool. Is that clear?"

The doorman slowly withdrew, while simultaneously looking Vivienne over. She could not tell if he was determining how expensive her dress was—and by extension the weight of her threat—or if he was thinking that he would like very much to be her footstool, please and thank you, mistress.

"Fish or cut bait!" Someone shouted.

The club's door opened then and an older man in a black suit, but with the red waistcoat of an employee, stepped out. "John," he addressed the doorman. "What's the hold-up?"

The doorman stepped closer so that he could whisper: "This lady is trying to bring coloreds in."

The adult employee turned to Vivienne with a calm, professional gaze and then recognized her. "Oh, Miss Vivienne Walker, I presume?"

"Correct," she nodded.

"I gave him my card." Cranston added, rolling his sleeves back down.

"Mr Walker!" The adult said. "You both have my sincerest apologies." He silently waved the doorman back to his post. "I understand you have guests."

"Yes," Vivienne said. "May I introduce Michael and Gabrielle Blake of the Manhattan Blakes."

"Of course!" The man said, almost giddy with nerves. "Is it just the four of you?"

"Indeed,"

"Splendid, I have a four-top with a bird's-eye view of the dance floor ready and waiting. Let me show you there, myself."

It was a very nice table. The manager that had rescued them, Gagnon, also took the liberty of telling a passing waitress—in the skirt version of the red uniform—to bring four of the club's signature cocktails to the table. No sooner had the Walkers and Blakes sat than drinks equal parts sour apple juice and a very floral gin were being set before them.

Vivienne was giving hers an exploratory sip when Cranston leaned in. "That was a bit much with the boy on the door, wasn't it?" He said.

"Polite women get sat by the kitchen." She replied, then gestured at their commanding view of the club.

The New Barn's owners had gone all out with the interior. They had taken advantage of the high ceiling to install balcony seating for the upper class experience, while leaving the first floor completely open for dancing. Cleverly, the bandstand was a large round in the center of the dance floor. From their table, Vivienne could see the trap door leading to the basement, presumably where the musicians could prepare. Also likely where the kitchen and other such things were.

The wallpaintings—cheeky burlesques on the Greek tableaus of older clubs showing nymphs and satyrs doing the Bunny Hug, Turkey Trot, and Grizzly Bear—started a foot off the floor and reached to the ceiling. Most clubs did not bother decorating anything below the four-foot line; it was an extra expense for something the dancers would rarely, if ever, see. And there *were* dancers. The negro band was in high spirits and the crowd was just about shoulder to shoulder. The only time Vivienne could see the floorboards was when some couple dared to do a lift.

It was hard to imagine that such a tightly packed crowd could radiate so much energy, but it did not take long for Vivienne to feel tempted to the floor. Gabrielle gave in immediately.

"Michael," she tittered. "Order me something. You know what I like." Then she circled around to where Cranston sat watching the dance. "Mr Walker, I must insist that you ask me to dance."

Cranston said one of those lines other women found charming and then led the girl to the stairs and down onto the floor. Vivienne watched them go, then took her cigarette case from her bag. She tapped it on the table in a vain attempt to get Michael's attention before opening it and withdrawing one. Vivienne held the unlit cigarette in Michael's peripheral vision and waited for him to take the hint.

When he continued to sit, glumly mute, she said loudly: "What did they teach you in Hong Kong?"

This brought him far enough out of his reverie that he turned to look at her. "Business, mostly," he said. "There were languages, of course. Some literature." He trailed off and looked at the table.

"No graces?"

"Pardon?"

Vivienne used her thumb to make her still unlit cigarette bounce in between them.

"Oh," he said, apparently noticing it. "No, thank you. I have my own."

"Light it." She said.

It took him a moment, but Michael eventually fumbled for his lighter. Once it was open, he was elegant enough in bringing the flame to the tip. She had seen inexperienced young men burn half the cigarette off, so Michael was not a complete beginner. Vivienne took a puff to start the burn, then leaned back and sucked air through her teeth to chase the smoke and activate the flavor.

"You know," she let the smoke escape her mouth. "Most women are going to be less patient than I am."

"I'm sorry," Michael said, eyes back on the table. "I'm not very good company of late."

It then occurred to her that he had not been looking at other women. She could understand a boy of twenty-two, twenty-three, being disappointed that he had to escort a woman over thirty, but there were so many young women here and in party dresses, many seemingly unspoken for. Perhaps he was a fairy, but they were supposed to be fabulous company. There was only one reasonable conclusion.

"What is her name?" Vivienne asked.

"Whose?"

"The girl you are pining for."

"I'm not sure..."

"Come along!" Vivienne said, leaning in and propping an elbow on the table. "You—a young, strapping, wealthy man of good breeding and reputable education—have been sulking all evening as if a black cloud had descended upon you. It is not a death in the family, or else there would be signs of it in your sister. You might feel burdened that you must escort an older woman around, but darling"—she leaned back and gestured at her trim, fashionable frame wrapped coquettishly in tight silk—"my burden is light." She leaned back in, pointing her ash-tipped cigarette at him like a gangster's pistol. "So, that leaves one thing: you are lovesick. So, if you are not going to be charming, the very least you can do is regale me with tales of young love."

Michael looked stunned and she wasn't surprised, but then she watched as something broke and his eyes turned wistful.

"Thursday." He said and if he had held the last vowel for a second longer, it would have been a moan.

"You want to tell me tomorrow?"

"No," he furrowed his brow. "Her name is Thursday."

"That raises several questions," Vivienne said. "But I would need to ask her mother."

Michael continued, undaunted. "She's a reporter for the Journal."

A sudden spasm racked Vivienne's body. It was not a feeling she was accustomed to. It had shot up from the depths of her ancestral, millennia-old survival instincts. It was a spasm that her caveman forebears had used to get themselves out of the range of a tiger's swipe and it almost knocked her from her chair.

"I'm told it's a very respected paper." Michael added in a tone of reassurance.

Vivienne needed a moment to steady herself against the table. "You have taken up with a journalist?"

"Why not?" Michael's face started to contort as if he might cry. "She's clever, educated, articulate."

"She is a journalist!" Vivienne growled just under the din of the band. "A man of your standing would be better off wooing a seamstress or...another man. *Those* men know...well, not how to keep their mouths shut, but certainly how to stay quiet."

Michael's face went red. "I am not a homosexual." He whispered.

"No, there is something to be done with a homosexual. We marry him off to a lady homosexual, attend their wonderful parties, remark on how sad it is that they never had any children and how good it is that they each have a friend close enough to help them clean up after the rest of us go home. A company heir stepping out with a journalist? You might as well have challenged her to a duel because one of you will be destroyed by it."

"You sound like my mother." Michael spat.

"Your mother sounds like a woman who knows how to avoid a scandal. Listen, I do not say a word of this to be cruel. A day will come when either she will use her intimate knowledge to write a story that ends your family's salad days for good or else a day will come when her employer decides she is holding back on him and ends her career as a woman of letters. Do you see?"

Michael looked like he wanted to slap her. "I'll buy her a paper. I'll start a paper or, better yet, a magazine. Why shouldn't I? This is what the new generation does, isn't it? We find solutions to the problems our elders thought insurmountable."

Vivienne stifled a chuckle. "Start a new business to keep your lover happy? La, tres original!" Then they sat in tense—not silence for the band was still banging on—but a dearth of conversation.

In that lull, it occurred to Vivienne that the scandal might be Saint Moon's vaccine project, or whatever eugenicist plot it was hiding. Having a nosy girl up close to the family like this could make Vivienne's own job that much easier. She did not relish sacrificing this boy on a pyre of gossip rags, but it may be for the greater good. That being the case, she decided, she had been hasty to deter him.

"She must be *very* pretty." Vivienne said at last.

Michael took a breath that melted the indignation from his face. "She is."

"Well, go on then." She sipped her drink. "Wax poetic."

Chapter 13:
Summer and Queen

August 10th, 1921. Silkhaven.

Ed Grace couldn't believe that he was here. Silkhaven. The Jewel of the Atlantic. He'd left Brockton because he didn't want to take over his pa's grocery store, nor did he want to make shoes like his friends from school. Back then, he'd thought Boston was going to be real big city excitement. It had its moments for sure, but every fourth person you met was a negro and every third person you met was a mick. Alright, it was hard to get lonely in a city with so many Catholic girls, but their drunk and good-for-nothing brothers made them more trouble than they were worth.

Mostly.

But Silkhaven! Brother, just look at those lights! Driving through downtown, he bet you couldn't tell when the sun set it was so bright. All the men were in tony suits, even the coloreds, and the girls? Oh boy, were there plenty and genuine flappers every one! They'd been driving around all evening and he hadn't seen one with hair past her shoulders, yet.

Ed couldn't wait to get this last bunch of crates dropped off so he could polish up and hit the town. When he had gotten hired by the Atlantic Network, Ed knew he'd done good, but he couldn't have guessed it would be this good.

He was riding shotgun on a Saint Moon truck, double revolvers strapped to his thighs like a gunslinger out of a story magazine just daring that Virago dame to make a move on them. The Network had installed a wireless telephone in the cab, so they could call in reinforcements. Mr Syme had also changed the delivery schedule to nights; less traffic meant other trucks could come to aid you faster and the radios worked better when it was dark. Yes, sir, they were ready for this Virago to make her move. That was not to say that Ed was excited about shooting a woman, of course. He figured she'd catch the street lights glinting off his Single Action Armies and surrender or run.

Then, the world got really loud all of a sudden. There was an awful sound of rending metal. The Saint Moon driver screamed bloody murder and the tires screeched. For just a second, Ed saw the woman in red kneeling on the hood; head-to-toe leather and a broad-brimmed hat the same color as her boots, just before the windshield was painted black with oil gushing from the engine she'd just speared.

Ed was about to leap out of the truck when his knee bumped the telephone box. He remembered to call for backup. Picking up the receiver, he switched on the transmitter.

"Truck twelve! Truck twelve! Virago attacking! Virago attacking!" He looked at the driver. "Hey, where are we?"

"It's...we're..." The driver stammered, hearing boots on the cab's roof.

"Where are we?"

"Summer and Queen!" He shouted, fumbling with his door handle. "I ain't burning! I won't!"

"Summer and Queen," Ed shouted into the phone before whipping his guns out and kicking the door open before leaping down onto the street. He wheeled around and saw the Virago on top of the truck.

"Hands up!" He shouted.

She saw the pistols and did a wild sort of sideways leap off the truck. She landed on the driver, just as he was making a break for it. The two of them got tangled up with the driver screaming his head off. Ed jumped onto the truck, planting one foot on the running board, then the other on the wheel guard, pushing himself up onto the hood where a long metal pole was gouged into the engine.

He was one foot off the metal, starting to jump down to the street when there was a flash of red coming at him. The Virago was inside his guard before he saw her and she punched him in the gut. He doubled up and landed on the driver's side wheel well. Bright pain shot through him as his coccyx impacted against the metal. Ed rolled and fell limply to the ground, losing his grip on his guns. The pain made him feel sick.

Before he could recover himself, the Virago was climbing on top of him, knees pinning his arms to the pavement.

The moment was something he'd never imagined. A woman all in leather, spreading her legs wantonly to hold him in place. He'd never imagined something like this and his mind had already given up on thinking of a way to react. All he could see of her face were her eyes, black makeup all around them like a harem girl. She started talking, but it was strange and dreamy somehow.

Then, she was gone in a blur of red. Fighting through a sudden dizziness—he must have hit his head—Ed got to his knees. The driver had found his courage and was wrestling with the woman. As Ed picked up his guns, the Virago got on top of the driver, pressing her knees to his ears. She must not have weighed much because the driver rolled her onto her back, then reared up on his knees. Somehow, she held on that whole time and slid her thighs down his ears until he was getting a face full of cunt.

Even as the driver was rising up on his knees, carrying her with him, she whipped her head back, bending her whole torso like a scorpion's tail and pushing her knees down into his shoulders. This shift in weight threw the driver off balance and he fell backwards. The Virago's sinuous body pushed him skull first into the pavement. There was an almighty crack as he landed and his body went unnaturally stiff.

The Virago kicked her legs wide and rolled backwards off the driver until she landed on all fours like a prowling tiger.

"Don't move!" Ed shouted, training both pistols on her, now that he had a clear shot.

She didn't. Without her hat, Ed saw that she was really covered head-to-toe. Most of it was red leather, but she also wore a thin red coat of something soft-looking. He couldn't believe it hadn't torn in the scuffle. At this point, he didn't know what to do. He didn't have handcuffs or anything. Help was coming, though. The thing to do was keep her from running, which meant he needed to get a hand on her.

Ed approached, keeping both pistols raised. "Stand up slow like." He told her. "Nothing funny, alright?" She stood. "Hands up." She obeyed.

Ed needed a hand-free, so he holstered his left gun. Well, he tried. He missed the first time, his hands shaking fiercely from the excitement of the moment. It was just a second that he looked down, but the moment he did, Ed felt the Virago grab his right wrist and push his gun wide. Then she kicked at his left gun, catching the hammer and his knuckles with her boot heel.

A shot rang out and Ed jumped, dropping the gun. There was a sudden heat in his foot, but he had no time to examine it. He grabbed for her left arm, but she tried another kick. He got his arm around her leg right as her knee was colliding with his ribs. Ed toppled and his own head hit the pavement, but he clung for dear life to that leg.

They landed on their sides and his gun was again pointed right at her.

"Wait!" She said and it sounded like two women talking at the same time. "<u>Don't shoot!</u>"

He felt another wave of dizziness. He didn't shoot and the Virago leapt away from him. Now, Ed could see that he had shot himself in the foot. It hurt. His ribs hurt. His ass hurt. His head hurt. But he had to stop her. Ed pulled himself up on his knees and crawled to his second gun.

The world spun as he got to his feet and searched for the Virago. It took a moment, but he spotted her on top of the truck, pouring something flammable onto the crates.

"Stop!" He shouted, lifting both pistols. But he couldn't quite bring himself to shoot. He should, he knew. He had to stop her.

Then, he was being painted in headlights. Ed looked over to see a car pull up, not one of the other Saint Moon trucks. A pair of vigilantes came running out, both sort of dressed like pirates. The man had an old-fashioned soldier's coat on, but the woman was dressed in something more modern. Ed caught a line of exposed skin on her leg, which made him want to sigh, and that was before he saw her bosom nearly burst out of the top of her shirt.

The man ran for the truck and the woman looked at Ed. "Guns down!" She said.

They were here to help the Virago. Ed was outnumbered, but none of them had drawn on him. Not yet. Dizzy and hurting, he knew he was an easy target. To hell with that!

Ed fired twice from each gun on the lady pirate. She bent over and Ed turned for the man in the old army coat. He dove behind the truck just as the Virago dropped her match, and a bonfire lit up. Ed fired again. He saw the Virago leap and fall behind the truck.

Before he could make another move, something touched his neck. He whipped around and someone's hand smashed into his arm. The lady pirate was on him with an honest-to-God pirate sword drawn.

"Guns down!" She shouted as the sword's tip poked at his chest.

For a second, he thought he was about to die, but then an idea pierced through the confusion of the moment: if she wanted him dead, she would have done it. Shakily, he slid his guns back into their holsters, then raised his hands.

"Tiburon!" The lady pirate shouted. "¿Estás bien?"

"Si!" A man's voice called back. "La Virago desapareció."

"¿Cómo?"

"No sé. Ella desvaneció. ¿Te dispararon?"

"No, este bastardo no puede dar su culo con un zurullo."

Black spots appeared in Ed's vision. The next thing he knew, he was lying on his back on the sidewalk. Over the next few hours—as the police came and his supervisor came and he tried to answer the same questions again and again—his mind kept going back to that image of the Virago pinning him to the street. Fellows kept saying he hit his head and Ed agreed, letting his mind drift to spend another few moments uninterrupted as he thought about her eyes staring down at him, the shadows of the streetlights under her bosom, the stitches in the leather between her legs just inches from his face as her knees dug into his arms.

It was just one moment on one night, a night most people eventually forgot about; but Ed would never stop trying to get back to it.

Chapter 14:
No Dancers Barred

August 10th, 1921. Silkhaven.

Context meant a great deal. A man going shirtless on the beach meant something different than a man going shirtless in a department store. Likewise, a few yards of 42lbs, white silk georgette were unassuming and a pleasant little surprise when stretched across a mattress; but drape it across a dusky-hued woman who was clearly not wearing a corset and it became electrifying.

The worst thing about having a well-dressed woman on your arm was that you hardly got to enjoy the view. You only really got a look when you turned to speak to her, which may have been the point. And what a look it was, Cranston being so much taller than Gabrielle. Looking down into her face, he put her small but not insignificant bosom in the near periphery of his vision. The dress shifted a great deal as she walked, and while there was little cleft on display, on the occasions when gravity and light conspired so, he could see the distinct edges of tall, erect nipples.

Cranston had to remind himself that he had very good reason not to be seduced by the young woman's charms. Under the best of circumstances, it was bad form to bed a business partner's daughter, no matter how brightly her eyes shone when she looked at you and especially at the beginning of the partnership. (After some years of close acquaintance, marriage became a distinct option, but not much less.) Gabrielle's eyes were so deep a brown that they were nearly black, yet they seemed to burn when she looked at him; the paradox was intoxicating. Of course, the effect was aided by her pale pink eyeliner, which would have looked childish if not for the swarth of her skin. On her, it looked like the touch of some vernal goddess.

Goddess-like did seem to be the goal. The dress looked like a happy accident from a lazy couturier. The white silk was almost shapeless and seemed to strain against the silvery chains it had in lieu of proper straps; like the spare cloth brought to Botticelli's Venus hastily transformed into evening wear. It fell almost to her knees and the way it expanded as she strode alongside him betrayed the cleverness of its design. When she stood still, it appeared half as voluminous as it became when she extended a pale, slender leg.

Stores called it 'Greek' because they couldn't call it 'hedonistic'. Gabrielle, with her feline eyes and wide-set cheekbones, had made a further attempt at a Grecian mode with a gold laurel crown pinned into her thick, black hair; blacker than the tresses of any true love along the River Clyde.

Her black and white pumps somewhat spoiled the effect, but made it clear that whatever seduction she might have planned, it would wait until after they danced.

They ventured down the stairs and onto the crowded dance floor. Up close, he found something that shook his usual confidence with the fairer sex; namely, that the dance du moment was completely unfamiliar to him. There had been dancing during the war—quite a lot of it; at every opportunity, really—but never of the fashionable sort. The soldiers, nurses, engineers, and lonely civilians had wanted nothing more than the sensation of safety that came from human touch. Far from the front lines, the jazz "cats" had been hard at work inventing novel steps for their novel tunes and, for a moment, Cranston felt that he was too old for this.

He glanced down at Gabrielle and was relieved to see the same sudden hesitance wash over her.

"We didn't dance like this in France." He said with an air of apology.

"Nor in Hong Kong." She giggled. "The old majors were never more adventurous than a waltz."

"I'm surprised your mother let you go dancing with old Englishmen."

"A requirement of the ladies' salon," she answered. "We had to test our deportment with the only people who would know the difference."

They lapsed into quiet observation for a moment. Finally,

Cranston said: "Shall we make a go of it? Everyone seems to be in their own world, so I shouldn't think we'll embarrass ourselves too much."

"I was beginning to think you'd never ask."

The dance was from an entirely new logic. It was heavy on kicks, which made couples face each other a foot apart, rather than touch for much of the time. The core step was a back step followed by a little walk forward, then a kick with a back step to switch feet. There was a move where one squatted down with hands on knees and flailed their legs out to the side. Cranston wasn't ready to attempt that, but the back step kick he could about manage. Along with these dangerous kicks, the men swung their arms to the sides while the ladies raised both hands, wiggling them like the most desperate of taxi hails.

One man was doing a kicking walk and turning his upraised palms in circles like he was polishing glass. His partner did a similar kicking walk while holding herself across the chest like there was a chill in the feverish air. Walking this way, they would pass each other, jump to turn around and repeat the move.

Well-practiced couples did synchronized sidesteps while alternating between claps and hip slaps. It seemed to be the fashion for couples to create little routines for themselves. Or perhaps there was simply so much variety among the fashionable dances that a dozen well-schooled dancers could all do different steps at the same time.

As consternating as learning an entire new school of dance was, Cranston immediately saw the appeal. These dances solved that ancient problem of not enjoying your escort's finery. The daring dresses of the flappers invited a leer and the dances put enough distance between you and your girl that you could really take in the vision.

After one frenetic dance—Cranston being certain that he was waving his arms wrong—the music slowed to something close enough to a tango that Cranston found a fresh confidence. He grabbed Gabrielle's hand and pulled her into him, guiding her hand up over his shoulder, while snaking his other arm up her back and sliding his right leg between hers. She responded by looping both arms around his neck and lifting her left knee to the height of his waist, thus signaling that she knew what they were doing.

What followed was a double-time tango with kicking flourishes borrowed from the jazzers about them. A minute of this and Cranston noticed that they were drawing attention. It was no surprise, an old dance like this coming out, but *tabarnak* did he not care. The only thing

finer than the feel of that silk under his hand was the lithe figure of
Gabrielle's trim body beneath it. Golly, but her hands and arms were
softer than the fabric. He couldn't help but imagine how her halved-
mango-sized breasts would feel in his palms. And on the dance floor,
there was no danger of the two of them falling into the heat of passion,
so he could indulge his imagination without qualm. Passion was, after
all, the fuel of the tango.

Gabrielle slid her cloud-soft hands into his then dropped into
splits on the floor before pushing herself back up, sliding her chest
along his legs, over the erection he was suddenly self-conscious about,
and up his stomach until they were within kissing distance.

"People are staring." She said over the music.

"Of course they are," Cranston abruptly spun her out—sending
her dress spiraling—then pulled her back in. "You're the most beautiful
woman on the dance floor."

They pressed their cheeks together and walked a few steps, the
crowd making way for them. "Do people here usually give the evil eye
to beautiful women?"

"That's jealousy, doll." He dropped a hand to her leg, pulling it
to his side, then dragging her other foot along the floor. "It's as old as
Egypt."

Cranston moved his hand to her derriere and hoisted her up.
Gabrielle kicked that leg up while bringing her other knee up to rest
on his hip, arms wrapped around his neck. "And what would it take to
make you jealous?"

"Why would you want to do a thing like that?" Cranston said
easily. The girl weighed nothing.

"Maybe I want to see what you're willing to do to stay on my
dance card." She said while he spun before letting her back down to the
ground. They resumed a classic tango posture and stepped with those
sinking moves that Valentino had made famous last spring.

"Well, I think I'll start by minding my manners and see how far
that gets me."

"You beast!" Gabrielle exclaimed. In response, Cranston lifted
her off the floor and turned in a half circle, then bent to set her down.
Gabrielle knelt drawing him down like one of Waterhouse's sirens. She
said: "I absolutely insist that you forget your manners entirely."

He brought her back up. Holding hands, he pushed her away and
resumed the jazzy kicks. "But, darling, haven't you heard?" He pulled

her in close. "Manners maketh man." Then stepped away with a flourish.

"And what if I want to unmake you?" She asked the next time he brought her close.

"You wouldn't be the first to try." He spun her out and let her go, expecting another round of kicks.

Instead, Gabrielle stepped backwards until she was against his chest. Her arms flew up around his neck. "But those other girls weren't oriental."

"You suppose that gives you an advantage?" He asked as she began to curl up and down, arms dancing around his head.

"Don't you read novels?" She spun, but returned her arms to his neck. "Oriental women are all temptresses, witches even."

He put his hands on her hips. "You are nothing if not hypnotic in that dress."

"Just imagine me out of it." She spun herself away and stopped with a flourish, elbows on hips and hands out. "Please."

Cranston returned Gabrielle, her virtue intact if just barely, to the table where Michael was going on about some girl. His words were an ode worthy of DH Lawrence, but his eyes were mournful. Vivienne took one look at Cranston and handed him a napkin for the sweat.

"Are you boring Vivienne?" Gabrielle asked abruptly, taking up her own napkin and gently dabbing at her brow.

Michael immediately hushed up and Cranston thought it odd. One expected siblings, twins especially, to be gentler than that with each other in public. Perhaps oriental families were coarser in some ways.

A plate of toast, meats, cheeses, and fruit had been brought along with a round of drinks. Vivienne had gotten Cranston a proper glass of whiskey, which he tested, then—finding it satisfactory—downed the whole thing.

"Won't you dance?" Cranston asked Vivienne.

"I am afraid my Jack is hung up on another Jill." She replied quietly. "Though, I do not think my dress would weather *that*"—she gestured at the wild jazz dancers—"very well."

Gabrielle was nibbling at the charcuterie, ignoring the silent Michael. She really knew how to turn it off and on.

"I wonder," Vivienne said conspiratorially. "If you can think of a way to get his mind off the girl?"

"Oh dear," Gabrielle said, a finger at one eye. "I think I need to freshen up."

"I am not surprised." Vivienne said. "Come along, let's find the powder room." She gave Cranston a nudge and he stood to help her with her chair.

Gabrielle waited for him to get her chair as well, since Michael was evidently not going to do the honors. As the ladies went off together, Cranston took Gabrielle's former seat.

"Lady troubles?" Cranston asked lightly, reaching for the platter and assembling himself a sandwich.

"I should apologize," Michael replied. "I didn't mean to put a damper on the evening. I just can't get myself free of this mood."

"Would you take offense if I offered to assist you with that?"

"How?"

"Tell me, how long have you known this girl?"

"I just met her last week, but she's cast her spell on me. That's all there is to it."

"Last week?"

"Yes, at the picnic."

"Not the journalist!"

"I know! Your sister already chided me for it."

"She's one to talk! I won't tell tales, but my sister likes them exciting and excitement always means a bit of danger. I had a run-in with your girl reporter. She's pretty, no question, but I'll tell you this: those things which are truly irreplaceable in a woman do not become evident until after long weeks, even months. I don't mean to belittle your feelings, of course, but whatever charms your journalist has shown, they can be equalled."

"I can't imagine how." Michael replied forlornly.

"You've never seen a mermaid."

"What?"

"When the ladies are ready to leave," Cranston grinned. "You and I shall seek gentlemanly entertainments on our own. What do you say?"

"I suppose," Michael said, his face still downcast.

They didn't last much longer at the New Barn. Gabrielle had mottled her makeup with sweat and spent the next half hour behind a fan she produced from her little purse. They finished up the charcuterie and then took their leave.

To Cranston's surprise, Gabrielle insisted on sitting in the back with Vivienne. She gave him an address at the edge of the Royalty district. It was on the last commercial block, just before the businesses turned into houses. It was, by the time they arrived, the least lively place in the city. He ushered the ladies out in front of a dark and signless storefront. Gabrielle immediately went to the front door and produced a key from her bag.

"We will take it from here." Vivienne told him.

He had no doubts about her abilities, so he bade them good night, then returned to the car. He turned around and headed right back into downtown, bound for the Mermaid Club.

Chapter 15:
Qipao

In the Old Barn's powder room, Vivienne watched Gabrielle's priorities change the minute she looked in a mirror. By some miracle, she was not half as sweaty as she ought to have been after an hour on a crowded dance floor, but the few beads that she had mustered were making streaks in her foundation, which was a few shades lighter than her skin. She repaired the damage as best she could, but the three cosmetics she had packed in her little purse were insufficient to complete the job.

Vivienne was no expert, but there seemed to have been a shadow she used to enhance the European qualities of her face that was missing. It was discomforting, but Vivienne could hardly blame her for obscuring her race, given the trouble they had had at the door.

Sweat-mottled, Gabrielle was suddenly the picture of sisterhood as she asked Vivienne to assist her with the repairs. When their utmost combined effort produced a presentable facade, though one lacking some of the shape, Gabrielle had become briefly despondent. After a moment, she recovered herself and began wondering aloud how long they might stay at the club.

"I hadn't wanted to mention it before," Gabrielle had said as they left the powder room; arm-in-arm, as if Gabrielle had not been ignoring Vivienne all night. "But I was hoping you and I could finish off the night with a dress fitting. You would look darling in a qipao, don't you think?"

"A what?" Vivienne had asked.

"A Chinese dress." Gabrielle had then reminded her about the personal seamstress she and her mother had brought with them from Hong Kong. "Papa had to pull some strings to get her into the country. He set her up in a little shop. It's perfect, too; everything a lady could want in a place of her own."

Hiding behind her fan, Gabrielle had utterly ignored the boys and kept all her conversation to little comments made close to Vivienne's ear. The near-mania she had held for Cranston was apparently a side-effect of the shadow on her cheeks. With the shadow faded, Cranston became far less interesting than Vivienne herself.

On the drive out to the seamstress' shop, Vivienne tried to remember if this was simply what girls of twenty were like. There were endless newspaper pieces about the silliness of young women and Vivienne had bristled at them all, but watching Gabrielle's affections shift with the quality of her makeup, she began to see their point. The fickleness took the sting out of being ignored, at least. It was no longer an affront, going from childhood hero to chopped liver. The girl was simply a ship on the sea—the old kind—in want of a rudder and subject to the prevailing winds.

The seamstress' shop itself was nothing special. It had a wide front window, like any regular sort of shop—though with curtains drawn across them—but no sign, like a more luxurious boutique. It was one in a row of businesses with a second floor to the building. Depending on the success of the store, that upper floor would either be an apartment for the proprietor or storage for the business.

They said goodbye to their respective brothers and went in. No bell tinkled as Gabrielle opened the door. The younger woman did not usher Vivienne in, nor exactly invite her, only went in and left the door open, presuming Vivienne would follow. As Vivienne found herself miffed by this, she suddenly wondered: *Have I gotten old?* She was surrounded so often by men her father's age—men that looked on her as a child—that she always thought of herself as 'young', even as the few other women in her world made comments about her being unwed.

Yet, here she was, disapproving of a decidedly young woman being fickle with her attentions and not caring much about formality. Lolita Walker certainly would not have stood for the childish behavior Gabrielle was putting on display. It was not something Vivienne had been prepared to encounter. Being *older* was one thing, but being *old* was quite another and the prospect of the latter made Vivienne dizzy.

"Isn't it darling?" Gabrielle interrupted by turning on a light.

"Positively," Vivienne answered too quickly. She was over-correcting and she knew it. She resolved to be quiet and pleasant until she could find the time for real introspection.

The store front area was halfway to presentable. The floors were clean, but there were loose tiles. A long, scuffed-up counter dominated the room. It would need to go if they intended to turn this place into a dress shop. There was a single dress form in one corner, by the curtains, itself covered with a sheet. Vivienne suspected that the place had been a pharmacy most recently, but the old-fashioned kind; no soda or sandwiches, just pills and maybe a jar of sweets.

Vivienne followed Gabrielle into the back room. Twice the size of the front, it was a used space. Fabric was everywhere; bolts of it sat in neat stacks on shelves, scraps littered the parts of the floor that were not walked on, swatches were piled on a table, large pieces were folded and laid all around, and two incomplete Chinese dresses hung on dress forms in the center of the room, glittering with pins. There were stools of various heights set at random places and one ancient but comfortable-looking high-backed chair in a corner. There was also a large cushion sitting on a very wide platform surrounded by ephemera; folded fabric pieces, little balls bristling with pins, a long-necked and many-hinged lamp, a few spools of thread, a box of sewing needles. There was a table with a sewing machine where fabric was piled, but conspicuously devoid of bobbins.

It was a workshop. There was a thickness to the air that came from humans spending time in these confines; not an odor, per se, more the pleasantly haunted quality of a room well attended.

Gabrielle moved about the place with an ease that Vivienne had not realized was missing from her before. A small kitchen had been arranged around an industrial-grade sink. A wood stove had been installed—the chimney pipe looking too pristine to be from the previous owner—and a squat, ceramic kettle hung from a hook that dangled from the ceiling.

"Tea?" Gabrielle asked, throwing a log into the stove and lighting it with a long-stemmed match.

"Please," Vivienne replied, standing near the entrance and not knowing where to go.

With the stove nearer to her and the sink beside it, there was a cabinet on the far side of the sink. From inside, Gabrielle took a red, lacquered box. "Any preference?"

"Something gentle," she shrugged. "I plan on sleeping at some point tonight."

From the red box, Gabrielle withdrew a short cylinder and set it to one side. She put water in the kettle and set it on the stove. "Just a moment," she smiled. "I need to rouse Bo Myeong. She will measure you for the qipao. Do you mind if I freshen up while I'm at it?"

"By all means," Vivienne replied, deciding it was no business of hers how bad the girl was at hospitality. Vivienne herself was no famed hostess.

Gabrielle disappeared through another door and her footfalls described a flight of stairs to the apartments above. Vivienne politely entertained herself with the room. It was bad form to listen to the clomping and scuttling of the upstairs. Giving the stove as wide a berth as possible, she examined the kettle. It was brown and adorned with faint reliefs of some kind of four-legged animal; a fox was her best guess, but there were not enough details to be sure.

She sniffed the tea and was satisfied, though she did not recognize it. Closer inspection of the sewing machine made her starkly aware of how little she knew about these things. The in-production dresses were of medium-grade silk, but not ones Walker imported and if Walker did not import them, you could not get them in North America. On a nearby table was a pile of cheap fabric squares with exquisite, embroidered designs on them of flowers, birds, and circles filled with angular lines.

After a respectably short interval, Gabrielle reappeared and Vivienne nearly did not recognize her. Her face glistened with water, her hair was in a simple bun, and she had changed into pajamas. Sans makeup, she was a new woman. Her natural face was rounder, with her wide-set cheekbones hardly noticeable. This had the effect of making her jawline look sharper by contrast. Vivienne had spotted the trick with her eye makeup on their first meeting, but was still surprised at how narrow they appeared without shadow. Not every trace of her father's European blood was gone, of course. The bridge of her nose was still higher than her mother's and her forehead longer.

She beamed at Vivienne when she walked in. "I'm dreadfully sorry for keeping you waiting." She said, taking a few rapid steps closer. For a moment, Vivienne thought she was looking for a hug. "Here," Gabrielle course corrected, and arrived at the ancient chair, which she cleared of sewing detritus. "Have a seat, please. I don't know where my head was, not offering you a seat earlier. I suppose I was just so flustered after the club. I don't think I have ever been in such a sweat and certainly not from dancing. Jazz dancing, isn't it remarkable?"

The tea caught her attention then and she pranced over to it.

"I did not see much of it." Vivienne said, now that Gabrielle had stopped longer than a breath. She crossed to the chair, not wanting to look ungracious in any way. "Your brother was regaling me with odes to his auburn-haired lady."

"It's just awful, isn't it?" Gabrielle said, handling the kettle with a thick cloth to protect her hand. "The poor lamb is absolutely inconsolable, positively despairing, over this woman. And yes, I suppose it is horribly romantic of him, and the girl was very pretty—really, her eyebrows are magnificent, though I doubt Michael noticed..."

"He did not mention them." Vivienne managed to slip in.

"But it's doing no favors to the family." She continued preparing the tea with an increasing number of foreign utensils. "Mother is in a rage over the whole thing and his every frown only reminds her of what she considers his darkest moment. Meanwhile, Father, for all that he loves Michael, really hasn't any patience for this mood that Michael is in. Which is not to say that Father isn't a romantic, himself, but he's...well, to put it in novel terms: Father is the swashbuckling sort of romantic, all dash and flourish. I have to imagine that if Father were in Michael's place, he would be creeping out of the house and then running through the streets calling her name.

"Michael's more poetic, you might say. He has a gentle temperament that Mother took great pains to cultivate." The tea was left to steep, Vivienne supposed, as Gabrielle turned back to face her. "You didn't see him at his best tonight. I want you to know that and please forgive any lapses in decorum. He really is lovely."

Before she could launch into another speech, the stairway door opened and the woman Vivienne presumed to be Bo Myeong entered. She too was in pajamas and of no lesser quality than Gabrielle's. The girl treated her staff well, at least.

"가브리엘, 말이 너무 많아." The new woman said, then turned to Vivienne and bowed. "안녕하셔요."

"Vivienne, meet Bo Myeong," Gabrielle said, as Vivienne stood. Then, she turned to the seamstress and presumably repeated the introduction. "그녀를 초대했으면 안에 들어와 앉기라도 하게 했어야지."

Bo Myeong was more characteristically Oriental, every feature soft and round. The two young women were about the same height and figure and so forth and, just for a moment, she understood why it was sometimes said that all Orientals looked alike. However, she banished that thought. It was only very tiresome chauvinists who voiced such things and Vivienne refused to entertain sympathies for such as them. She immediately began looking for the features that separated the two.

Coming closer to curtsy before Bo Myeong, Vivienne took note of her rounder jawline and larger eyes. That was interesting. Perhaps Bo Myeong had some European blood in her as well.

Bo Myeong turned to Gabrielle. "성미 나쁜 여주인이어서 미안해. 그 동안에 분이 열어지고 있어서 비비엔이 날 바루 볼까봐 걱정했어."

"오히려 그렇게 어색하게 하고 있으며는 비이엔느가 더 눈치를 빨리 챌것 같네." Gabrielle replied. "Are you ready to be measured?"

"Ah, yes," Vivienne replied. "Down to my corset, then?"

"Oh," Gabrielle blushed. "We do not wear corsets. I'm afraid that it would show through the cheongsam."

There was a heavy silence as Vivienne waited for her to say more, but she did not. "Down to my skin it is, then."

"어디 서양의 참한 몸 좀 볼까." Bo Myeong said.

"애, 착하게 굴어라." Gabrielle said with the universal posture of a lady commanding her servant.

Bo Myeong crossed to what appeared to be the main workstation and began preparing a bolt of cloth. Gabrielle found a folding screen for Vivienne to disrobe behind, not that it would matter, since the measuring would happen in the open. Still, Vivienne took her up on it.

"I must confess," Gabrielle said from the other side of the screen. "I had a secondary motive for inviting you here. I was very much hoping I might ask a favor of you."

"이야기 하나 하려고 그만치 길게 말하구, 놀랍네." Bo Myeong said.

Gabrielle did not reply, only continued: "It's about Michael. Now that you have seen the distress he is in, I had hoped—and still do, of course—that you might see your way to helping with a bit of intrigue."

"내가 그 남자애랑 자게 두어." Bo Myeong's flat tone baffled Vivienne. The woman might have been complaining or asking a question, anything really. It sounded like a schoolgirl doing a recitation as quickly as her mouth would let her. "나와 하룻밤이면 그 서양 여자애에 대해서 까맣게 잊을 테니."

"Is everything alright?" Vivienne asked.

"Oh, yes," Gabrielle replied. "Bo Myeong likes to talk her decisions out. She is trying to decide which fabric is best." Then, she added: "오라버니랑 자기 시작하면, 어머니는 지금보다 더 너를 통제하려 할 거네."

"시어머니는 다 그래."

"Would you prefer vermilion or cerulean?" Gabrielle asked.

Vivienne thought for a moment. "Cerulean, I have enough red in my closet."

"다른 시댁 어머니들은 암살범들을 알고있지는 않지." Gabrielle relayed to the seamstress. "I have a plan," she picked up her previous thread. "I know that I can get in contact with the girl Michael is pining for, and if she is half as smitten as he is, I have no doubt that I can arrange a meeting for them. The trouble is getting him away from Mother. If she thought he was courting a woman she found more acceptable, that would tie the whole thing up with a ribbon."

Vivienne stepped out from behind the screen in nought but her half slip. If the seamstress needed her inseam, it was acquirable without completely exposing herself.

"망할, 모양 참한 젖이네." Bo Myeong commented. "젖꼭지가 분처럼 연분홍이라 보이지 않겠어."

Gabrielle translated: "You are slimmer than she thought you would be."

"Yes," Vivienne replied. "The current fashion has turned very much in my favor."

The seamstress gestured Vivienne into the center of the room. She began with the usual tape measure and Vivienne stretched her arms out. She was no good with a sewing machine but knew how to be measured.

"So, you would like me to find a respectable young woman for Michael to pretend with?" Vivienne asked. "It will take some time, I am afraid."

"Actually," Gabrielle said, hands toying with each other over her stomach. "I thought you might do it."

"Me?"

"Yes, you see, my plan is to arrange the meeting somewhere private. Michael and his girl could go about their business and then you and I could pass the intervening hours together."

Vivienne could not help herself. "Should I bring Cranston along?"

"Oh," Gabrielle looked wounded. "I suppose."

"오늘 밤에 한 행동을 보아 물어보는 거지." Bo Myeong seemed to

have finished the general measurements. "나중에 설명해 줄 테니."

"You may put your arms down." Gabrielle said, looking cross. "If you like, of course, Cranston may join us. My thought had been that we might have the chance to speak frankly, though."

"He did not do anything, did he?" Vivienne asked. "It is just that you seemed very keen on him before."

"그는 참으로 잘났어." The seamstress tapped on Vivienne's arm and Vivienne raised her arms above her head. Bo Myeong had a cheap piece of fabric that she wrapped around Vivienne's torso, then began carefully pinning it.

"Cranston was charming." Gabrielle said. "I suppose I should apologize for this evening. It was just so exciting to go out dancing. I sort of lost myself in it."

"It is quite alright." Vivienne lied. She wanted to scold the girl for ignoring her all evening and then trying to ask for a favor, but it was both too much effort and made her feel too old to contemplate. "I just fear that it might not be believable."

"You're not so much older than Michael."

It stung a little how quickly she had gotten that. "Then, I suppose the deception will depend on what mood Michael returns home in."

"My only fear on that point is that he may be too happy. Thinking of that, where is Cranston taking Michael?"

That afternoon, Vivienne would have been sparing with the details, but after seeing Gabrielle slather herself across Cranston on the dance floor, she decided the young lady needed no sheltering.

"It is the Mermaid Club, I believe." Vivienne answered. "A gentlemen's club, but I have visited a few times. It is a spectacle. There is music, of course, but they have women dressed as mermaids swimming in a tank beneath the stage. Of course, knowing Cranston, Michael will not get within ten feet of the stage. He will be whisked up to one of the box seats where he can be entertained by a mermaid of his own."

Gabrielle frowned. "Michael isn't one for music."

"That is alright," Vivienne said. "The women in the private boxes do stripteases."

Gabrielle looked at her blankly.

"They do a dance where they take all their clothes off."

"Oh my, Mother wouldn't approve of that, either."

"No mother would. But I dare say your intrigue might be moot once Cranston's through with Michael."

Gabrielle looked stunned and Vivienne felt she had won some small victory. It felt good, but then she felt guilty for feeling she had won something by...well, she was not sure what she had just done. Offend the girl's sensibilities, perhaps. It had been petty. That meant it was time to stop letting that feeling take its course. For the rest of the evening, she would be a perfect guest.

PART 4
The Suspects

Chapter 16:
Jiggling and Quaking

The last time Cranston saw Michael, he was being absconded with by his very drunk father, possibly to an actual brothel. The Mermaid Club, being the city's finest look-don't-touch club, catered to all the local elite, so it was no surprise that Governor Farrar brought the elder Blake and Benjamin Syme there to take in the sights. Still, Edward was unpredictably pleased to see his son receiving a lap dance two boxes over.

Edward had insisted that Cranston join them, as they were on their way out, but Cranston had successfully begged out to the relief of everyone, perhaps save Michael. The Walkers had not supported Farrar in the last election and Cranston had his own score to settle with Syme. Watching them go, all Cranston could think was how grateful he was that his own father had not been the kind to take his teenage son to a brothel to be ushered into the secrets of the feminine.

Now, Cranston was stirring to wakefulness in Pearl's bed. He smelled her brewing coffee in her little kitchen and pulled himself up to a sitting position.

"Do you have milk?" He called.

"*Yes,*" she said, recalling two weeks ago when he had gallantly gone to the grocer's in one of her bathrobes to buy them a jug. "Good mornin', by the way."

"Good morning to you." He replied.

He sat in pleasant anticipation while she finished preparing the coffee. What was to follow was one of the great visions of the city. Pearl was always so cheerful the morning after she had had her nethers licked into a frothing cascade. With the coffee ready, she bounded cheerfully back to the bed; stark naked and jiggling with every cheerful step. There were few things in the world so splendid as Pearl's jiggling.

She served him his coffee in a beer stein because it was funny and prevented spillage.

"Cheers," he said and they tapped cups.

Pearl threw back a hefty glug of her drink, set the stein on the bedside table, and, with eyes like a prowling tiger, moved in to set her mouth on one of Cranston's nipples. She was always as ravenous as she was well-ravaged.

Finding himself distracted and wanting to clear his mind the better to enjoy what was to come, Cranston said: "I have a question. What would you say if I asked you to marry me?"

Pearl's head shot up like a spooked deer. "Are you proposing to me? *Now?*"

"No, I am asking what you would think if I *were* proposing."

A smile cracked her face and he thought that she was about to laugh at him. Instead, she scurried off the bed and ran—jiggling, jiggling, jiggling—to her little bookshelf. She pulled the largest tome off the shelf and began frantically flipping through it. Cranston couldn't see what the book was, but based on its size, it was either a dictionary or the complete works of Shakespeare.

"Ah ha!" She said triumphantly. "Okay, ask me again."

Cranston laughed. "What would you think if I asked you to marry me?"

"No, my lord," Pearl read in a fancy voice. "Unless I might have another for working days. Your Grace is too costly to wear every day."

Now, they laughed together. "More women should use Shakespeare in their proposal rejections." He said, as she climbed back onto the bed.

"I've never gotten to use Shakespeare in a real conversation before." She picked up her stein of coffee and cuddled up under his arm.

"You did it with aplomb."

A sip later, she asked: "What do you think happened with that kid you were with?"

"I'm not sure I want to know." He replied. "It sounded like he was being taken to a brothel."

"With his dad?"

Cranston shrugged. "That's not the strangest thing you've heard of a family doing together."

Pearl shivered. "That's true."

The block of apartments that Pearl lived in was designated for women only. As far as Cranston knew, the other five women that shared her staircase were all sex workers of the look-don't-touch variety. While they were obviously allowed to bring men home, male callers were not free to come and go without invitations. To enforce this, the sex workers' union paid a rotation of their older, mostly retired members to mind the door. There was always a woman in her 50's or 60's posted just inside the vestibule, armed with a gun and Silkhaven's unforgiving trespass laws.

It was one such matron that interrupted them with an impatient rap on the door.

"Rebecca, you up?" The older woman called.

"Yeah, what's happenin'?" Pearl replied.

"There's a lady here to see you."

"Mierda," she peeped.

"What's wrong?" Cranston whispered.

Pearl turned to him with terror in her face. "There's a chance that's your sister."

"Not again." He said and began looking around for his trousers.

"One second!" Pearl called, dashing to get her frumpy dressing gown.

"Hey, Rebecca," a younger woman's voice called. "It's Thursday."

"Oh, thank goodness." Pearl relaxed.

"What day did you think it was?" Cranston asked, still in a whisper.

Pearl leaned over and smacked him on the back of his head. "That's her name."

"Wait, the journalist?"

"Yeah, get dressed."

Cranston hurriedly pulled on his shirt as Pearl answered the door. The tall, brunette reporter barged in, looking like she had been crying.

"Hey," Pearl said, pulling her into a hug. "What's wrong?"

Thursday just cried for a few moments while Cranston, staying out of her eye-line, buttoned his shirt as quietly as he could.

"Oh, it's awful." Thursday bawled. "Yesterday, I went into work and Percy told me that he had to fire me."

"What? Why?"

"I did something stupid. It was so stupid. Remember at the picnic?"

"When you were planning on seducing the Blake kid?"

Thursday sobbed again. "Yeah! Now, his mom is threatening to sue the paper."

"For what? You can't sue someone for having sex."

"She's rich, Rebecca!" Thursday cried in frustration. "They can do whatever they want." She turned and stamped both her feet and then caught sight of Cranston. She screamed. "What's he doing here?"

"Me." Pearl told her. "You knew about us."

"Fuck!" Thursday sobbed.

Cranston restrained himself from commenting.

"He's one of them!" Thursday waved an angry finger at him. "You people won't stop until we're all dead!"

Pearl grabbed Thursday, lest she lunge at Cranston. Cranston, for his part, was trying to keep Pearl's dining table between him and the sobbing journalist.

"Be assured," he said calmly. "I have no ill will towards you."

"Then why are you in business with Saint Moon?"

"What do you know about Saint Moon?"

"I ain't telling you shit!" Thursday pulled herself free of Pearl and stomped off to the other side of the apartment.

There was a knock at the door. "Rebecca?" The matron called. "You got trouble?"

"No, my friend's just upset."

"Mind if I look for myself?"

"Sure,"

The old woman burst in, gun drawn. Thursday threw her hands up, plastered herself against the wall and began weeping again. She slid to the floor. The matron then swung the gun towards Cranston.

"You causin' trouble?" She asked.

"No, ma'am."

"He isn't." Pearl added.

"What's her problem?" The matron lowered her gun and turned back to Thursday.

"She got fired." Pearl said.

"Is that all?"

"Please..." Thursday eked out.

"Wait a second." The matron said, holstering her gun. "I've seen that look. Did someone attack you, girl? Who was it?"

Thursday gulped air, trying to control herself. "I was...there were two men...they were in my apartment this morning."

"What?" Pearl knelt to put an arm on Thursday's shoulder.

"After I got fired," Thursday pressed on. "I stayed with my mom. I went home this morning and these two men were ripping it all up."

"Did you know 'em?" The matron asked.

"Were they wearing masks?" Cranston added.

"Fuck you!" Thursday said to Cranston. Quieter, to the women gathering closer, she said: "They were oriental. I just know that Blake bitch sent them."

"Blake who?" The matron asked. "What's she got against you?"

"No," Thursday replied. "I'm not saying another thing with him here!"

"I'll take my leave, then."

Pearl got up and helped him gather his things while the matron rubbed Thursday's back. She stepped out into the hallway with him and shut the door.

"What's goin' on?" Pearl whispered harshly. "You were talkin' like maybe you knew somethin.'"

"I don't, but I'm trying to find out." Cranston replied.

"About what?"

"There are suspicions of foul deeds at Saint Moon."

"Then why are you in business with them?"

"Because it gives us better access to find out what's rotten in the state of Denmark."

She squinted at him for a second, then shook her head. "Of course, you're playing Robin Hood."

Cranston was having a hushed conversation, half-dressed, in a hallway; he was not comfortable. As such, he said: "Would you like me to get you a Maid Marian costume?"

Pearl rolled her eyes. "Of course, but now ain't the time."

He leaned in and kissed her on the cheek. "Good luck."

"You too." She replied.

Chapter 17:
The Stalker Unmasked

August 11th, 1921. Silkhaven.

With her period over, Vivienne was back in the office and back in trousers. Days off for menstruation were a privilege she extended to all of her female employees, though they rarely took them. She assumed it was the embarrassment of others knowing so intimate a detail. There was no escaping that for Vivienne. If she had to come into work while bleeding, she had to wear a dress; as dead a giveaway as not coming in at all. More so, in fact, as she could decide to be absent from the office for any reason she liked.

Still, the work did pile up. She was reading through a report from a long-delayed ship. It was a client's ship, registered in Madagascar. They had been briefly accosted by Caribbean corsairs. Since 1918, Liberia had been offering bounties on French ships as revenge for their loss at the Battle of Lake Chad. However, no sooner had the skirmish commenced than a dimensional pocket had appeared. Avoiding the pocket had sent the ship into Brazilian waters, where the local colonel had them impounded. The ship had become something of a bargaining chip between the Brazilian oligarch and the Caribbean Confederacy.

Ultimately, the corsairs had declared the ship "untouchable", thus removing it from the negotiations. The Brazilians were forced to release the ship. Their partnership with France in the Great War had opened several lucrative doors in Europe and they could not risk those closing for one shipment of coffee, cloves, and cobalt.

She set down the report. There was nothing more to be done with it apart from noting the proverbial temperature of the water. Next was a report on a ship that had suffered from an outbreak of diphtheria. She had only gotten through the first paragraph when her secretary, Esme, knocked on the door.

"Miss Walker?" Esme asked.

"Yes, Esme?"

"There's a woman to see you."

"Did you get a name?" It was not like Esme to miss such a detail.

"Yes...she says her name is Oracle."

Vivienne tried to remember any girlhood chums of hers that had gone by that nickname. There were none. "Send her in."

Esme opened the door. In walked a woman no more than 5'6", with a trimly athletic figure and a bright blonde bob. She was a fairy princess without the wings. Women like her were the reason for the word 'darling'. Less adorable was her purple domino mask and the knee-length dress that went with it. The white eagle design stretched across her waist identified her as a member of Silkhaven's Finest.

A *vigilante*, Vivienne thought. *Wonderful.* She rose and offered Miss Oracle a seat.

"What can I do for you...Oracle?" Vivienne said, feeling silly.

The darling woman took a notepad and paper from her purse— needless to say: purple—and assumed the posture of a stenographer. "I am here on behalf of Silkhaven's Finest Vigilance Committee. We are investigating the Masked Virago; the woman who molested the Saint Moon production facility, reportedly while you were present."

"I remember, yes."

"New information is thin on the ground, I am sorry to say; so we are casting a wide net."

"Understandably," Vivienne was still deciding how she felt about this interview.

"I would like you to tell me what you know about the St Lawrence Vigilance Committee."

Now, that was an interesting question. The St Lawrence VC operated under the supervision of the Rose & Chain, which created a near connection with Vivienne. However, there was no way for Oracle to know that. If she had known about that connection, she would have gone to speak with Mr Cabot or someone of his stature.

"Very little." Vivienne answered.

Oracle cocked her head a little. "Are you sure?"

Ah, Vivienne thought. *We are not going to be friendly.* She took a breath, then said: "How about you tell me what you think I know and we can go from there?"

Oracle made a note. "I think you know that your parents were members." If this had been a duel, the pixie would have just drawn first blood. "I think you also know that nearly every current member attends mass at Cathédrale la Pucelle—as do you—which would explain why, last year, you employed the Sheik and El Tiburon to help your brother foil a kidnapping. A mission which left eleven people dead, including three boys under the age of sixteen." She was not consulting notes. Oracle had this memorized.

The darling vigilante had the advantage of Vivienne. As the mysterious Aurelia might say: here was a woman worth killing. To her consternation, however, Vivienne found herself without a weapon; only the armor of being unsurprised by any of this.

"You forgot my uncle, Petro." Vivienne replied like a disappointed schoolteacher. "He was in the St Lawrence VC before Father was."

Oracle made a note, then looked up. "And your brother?"

"That was before he was even born."

Oracle wrinkled her mouth, which was tiny. Really the smallest mouth Vivienne had ever seen. Heavens, she was perfect and Vivienne just wanted to hug her until she suffocated.

"On Tuesday," Oracle said, still from memory. "Two new vigilantes were registered with the St Lawrence VC, curiously without a judge's review, and the very next day, they turned up at our offices asking about the Masked Virago, a woman, let's remember, that your brother was in a fistfight with last Friday."

Vivienne suddenly was not sure who to murder first; Oracle or Cranston. Still, she could not let this stranger know she was anything but Cranston's nearest ally.

"And?" Vivienne said, finally; as if she had been waiting for Oracle to go on instead of fuming over the idea that Cranston had joined a vigilance committee.

"It would seem that your brother is now going around calling himself..." Now, she checked her notes. "The Stalker."

Good gracious, that was a strong move; reading the name like it was not worth memorizing. It was exactly the sort of thing Vivienne herself would do with an uppity client. Women as pretty as Oracle were not supposed to be this cunning; it unbalanced the universe.

"If that is the case—and I could not say one way or the other—then my brother does not know who the Masked Virago is. By association, I do not know who the Masked Virago is. So," Vivienne leaned forward, putting one elbow on her desk and resting her chin in that hand. "What are you doing in my office?"

The corner of the darling pixie's tiny little mouth crooked up. She wanted a fight and Vivienne was happy to give it to her.

Oracle said: "You are in business with Saint Moon. In fact, that partnership is what allowed Saint Moon to import here. Which is to say, you brought them. Now, this Virago is burning trucks in our streets. You brought that, too. Atlantic Network agents are protecting the trucks, one of whom has already been injured, and a man who may be your brother is hunting the Virago because he wants to know 'if her grievances have merit.'" This last part she quoted in a mocking tone. "This is starting to look an awful lot like a war and we can't tell what side you're on."

"What side are you on?" Vivienne asked, shifting the defensive line.

"Silkhaven's." Oracle replied, losing a measure of ferocity. "We are trying to keep this city safe. We are trying to maintain the peace."

"Peace *is* good for business." Vivienne told her.

"So is war."

"Yes," Vivienne drawled the way Cranston would. "It is wise to be in a position to profit from either."

"You're saying you're ready for a war, then?"

"*Always*, darling."

"Silkhaven's Finest won't let this city fall into chaos. If you're on the wrong side, our next conversation won't be this convivial."

"Mm...that is a good line to exit on," Vivienne said. "But I am afraid that I am going to have to deny you." She rose. "This city is called 'Silkhaven' because several generations of very rich people demanded that luxuries be brought to them from around the world. Those luxuries arrived on Walker ships." She crossed around to sit on the front of her desk. "With those luxuries came artisans who opened shops which drew mainland customers who needed hotels and entertainment which created demand for musicians and actors and sex workers who attracted more visitors who all spent money. Without the Walker Corporation, Silkhaven would be Lexington. Well, really, Silkhaven would be 'Marieville'.

"So, while you are nobly trying to protect the city." Vivienne leaned in until the two women were nearly nose-to-nose. "La ville, c'est moi."

"That was good," Oracle said. "But I prefer Lillian Gish."

Vivienne straightened. "And I prefer quiet. The door is where you left it."

Oracle stood. "It's not an idle threat. If you bring a war to this city, you won't be safe."

"And if we both insist on having the last word, we will be here all day. Toodle-loo."

Vivienne watched the vigilante sashay out of the room. It was a shame that Oracle knew so much about her family. It would be a delicious revenge, sicking Cranston on her. With how mortified Rebecca had been, she could just imagine the shame of that pixie's perfect, smooth, little face when Vivienne caught her *in flagrante delicto* in the penthouse.

Which reminded her...

Vivienne phoned the hotel and found that Cranston had not returned. That much was unsurprising. He had likely spent the night with Rebecca, after his visit to the Mermaid Club. She did not have Rebecca's number, nor was she even sure Rebecca had a phone. There were a million places that Cranston could be, but only one which would make her incandescently angry.

Vivienne did not knock on the great door of the Prosecution, she just shoved it open and walked in. It was as she remembered it from last year. It looked like an old-fashioned gentlemen's club, back when those had been places to escape one's family. There were a surprising number of books and several comfortable chairs arranged near a dead fire pit. There was also a gentleman's dress mannequin—the support post off-center to accommodate trousers—which was naked save for a kind of full-faced hood with eye holes and three red strips of cloth sewn diagonally across the face.

A wave of memory crashed in Vivienne's mind. 'The Stalker', Oracle had said. 'The three-scarred man'. It was a recurring nightmare from Cranston's boyhood. To her own shame, Vivienne could only now remember it because she had teased him for it.

Nightmares at age 10? La, so childish!

The mask she was looking at, pulled over a mannequin's head, was not so different from one she had made for herself once to torment her little brother with.

Still, she reminded herself, that ancient guilt was no reason not to be furious with him about joining a vigilance committee. Instead of calling out like an ingenue in Dracula's castle, Vivienne listened for the audible signs of residence. There were distant voices, but before she could determine their direction, a door opened to her right. It was the old housekeeper, Red Widow, as she had always been called.

"Vivienne?" Red Widow said brightly. "Oh," she added a moment later. "Come to read him the riot act?"

"Indeed,"

"I'll clear the courtyard for you." The old woman made for a heavy, wooden door on the far side of the room. "Everyone inside, except you, Mr Walker."

Vivienne stood ready as five people she did not recognize filed into the room, only to be further dispersed by Red Widow. The path clear, Vivienne tilted her chin up and marched into the courtyard. It was a charming space; very green, which kept it from looking like a prison yard. There was a battered-looking log propped up in the ground for reasons she did not care about.

Cranston saw her emerge and responded by assuming the straight posture of the vindicated. "Cabot sent me." He called to her before she could get a word in.

That made Vivienne halt for a moment. The chairman of their company's board and an elder in the Rose & Chain was not one to be refused lightly. She cast her mind about for some way to still be angry at him.

"Why did you not tell me?" She demanded, resuming her forward march.

He leaned caddishly against the log. "When do I ever tell you what I'm doing?"

"Father would be fuming."

"No, Father would be negotiating a different deal."

"So, why not you?"

Cranston looked at the ground. "I...I don't have much to offer. Not the society."

She wanted to tell him that was ridiculous, but she knew it wasn't. His chief value to the company was entertaining clients and more than a couple of them refused his company because of his service in the Praetorian Guard. Some of their clients refused to have him in the room during negotiations for the same reason. Older men were less prejudiced, but as more and more members of their own generation took up leadership, Cranston was becoming more and more of a liability.

Vivienne's hope was that he would eventually develop a reputation for being trustworthy, but that was in the future.

"Still," Vivienne was clutching at her anger. "*Joining* a vigilance committee?"

"Temporarily," he replied. "Only until we catch the Virago. How did *you* find out?"

"I had a visit from one of Silkhaven's Finest."

"The girl?"

"Yes, how did you guess?"

"She's the brains over there. She hides behind the big guy, but I caught him taking orders from her."

"What do you think of her?"

"I just told you."

"No, I mean...forget I said anything."

"Hold on," Cranston straightened and scrutinized her face. "Did she embarrass you? Is this like Milly Gardner?"

"Milly Gardner?"

"Yes, you tried to get me to seduce her so I could pass along embarrassing details to you after she convinced that haberdasher to stop seeing you."

"Oh, no. I did. It sounds so sordid when you say it." She clapped her tongue like the word had a bad taste. "Wait, stop. I am here to be angry at you. Why is it so hard to be angry at you?"

"I don't know. You've never had any difficulty with it before."

Vivienne started to pace. "Mother and Father were very clear on this."

"I know."

"It is dangerous!"

"The Blakes are dangerous!"

"Not to us."

"Vivienne,"

"Yes, I know." She went to him. It felt wrong to just stand there, but she was not sure what else to do. She set both hands on his shoulders and that felt alright. "Be careful." Was all she could manage.

"I will."

"You usually are not."

"I was careful enough to survive France."

"You had an army, then."

"And I was against an army." He grabbed her wrists, but did not move them, only returned the touch. Golly, but his eyes were so blue. "One especially lithe woman is not going to be my match."

"I was more concerned with the dynamite." She released him.

"That's fair." He said and they lapsed into silence. "You know, they have one of Mother's old costumes, here. You could come along, if you wanted."

"Come along where?"

"We got a lead, yesterday, talking to the Silver Sabres. It's probably nothing, but it's the best we've gotten, so far. They say that a woman recently set up a fortune telling business in Royalty and has gathered an almost cultish clientele."

"And you think she is the Virago?"

"Not really, but we have to look into it."

"I think I will go back to work." Vivienne said. "That woman from Silkhaven's Finest deduced it was you under that mask."

"Did she?" Cranston looked thoughtful. "Interesting."

"She seems to think there is a war coming. And she knew about Mother and Father. I think she would see through it pretty quickly if I started going around in one of Mother's old costumes. And then she might become a real nuisance."

"I can see that."

"It really might be a good idea to seduce her."

"To make her more sympathetic to our cause?"

Vivienne shrugged.

"I would need to know who she is, first." Cranston said with a grin, but not one of intent. He was using this as a reason to erase that possibility from the list.

"I will see what I can find out." Vivienne grinned back. "Be safe. I am going back to the office."

One more round of goodbyes and she was off. Vivienne began to think through how she would unmask Oracle, then recoiled wondering why she was so serious about the idea of Cranston seducing her. It was not like her. Nor had she felt herself last night, nursing her pride against Gabrielle's fickle attentions. Something was wrong with her and she could not quite determine what.

She decided that she would try finding a competent man to bed

her and see if that fixed things. It was too bad Tiburon had not been at
the Prosecution. He was a hell of a swordsman.

Chapter 18:
The Fortune Teller

August 11th, 1921. Silkhaven.

The Farman Torpedo pulled to a stop beside a sign that read "Titania's Grove". On a street of shops and tea houses, it was the perfect place to make money telling women what they wanted to hear. This wasn't Highland Ave, of course, where the department stores had long ago swallowed up any hobby businesses and were kept at bay only by the haughty gazes and upturned noses of the boutiques. Royalty was a working-class district. The tailors, haberdashers, and cobblers here had likely given up on appearing in any magazine and had contented themselves to copy the more noteworthy members of their industry at a quarter the price.

Titania's Grove wasn't even on the street. It was a basement operation, with stairs leading down into a narrow, concrete trough where one could access the front door. Peering over the wrought-iron railing that kept pedestrians from falling in, Stalker saw that someone had tried to make the entry area more attractive with potted plants. They must have been the hearty sort for how little sunlight they would get down there.

The stairs were about a yard across and the space between them and the door another yard. It was a tight spot.

"Bad fight place." Fortuna said.

"D'accord." Stalker agreed.

"Ou premye." She gestured towards the stairs.

"Naturally." He moved to the stairs ahead of her and began the descent.

The shop had a large window, as was tradition, but it was completely curtained off; no way to tell who or what was inside. Fortuna stopped on the stairs and drew her pistol, training it towards the door. Stalker opted not to draw himself, better that he look ready for a conversation. Still, he did not stand in front of the door when he knocked, lest someone inside shoot through it.

"Come in," called a woman's voice. It was full, womanly, rather like Belle Baker.

Stalker opened the door, still not standing in the doorway and letting Fortuna squint to see inside. Stepping back, Stalker could hardly see anything inside, but there was a luxurious scent of cloves and cinnamon wafting slowly out.

"Hello?" The woman inside called again. "What are you hiding for?"

Stalker stepped in, one hand resting on his pistol like a sheriff in a cowboy film. "My apologies for the caution," he said in that gruff impression of an American he did while wearing the mask. "There was a small chance we were going to be real unwelcome."

"Isn't that true most places?" The woman in the darkness said.

"Some more than others," he replied.

"Well, come in and have some tea. I've got mint, camellia, and pine if you're feeling adventurous."

"Camellia, please," Stalker replied, thinking mint might spoil his image and briefly forgetting that he was wearing a mask.

Fortuna followed him and closed the door. This allowed their eyes to start adjusting. It was not merely a dim room; it was mostly unlit. There were a few lamps towards the back of the room, but none close to the door. In the patch of light, about twenty feet ahead, Stalker saw a table with a multi-colored cloth over it, resembling something Caribbean; though Fortuna would probably say it was a cheap fake, as locals were wont to say of anything *resembling* but not *of* their country. The table had the usual fortune-telling ephemera: a deck of cards, a crystal ball, a velvet sack containing coins or bones or runes.

He began moving towards the table, but Fortuna remained by the door. He imagined that corsairs had room-clearing methods similar to trench clearing and keeping someone at the door was standard procedure. Stalker was moving slowly and, as his eyes adjusted, he froze. All around him were beds; stacked, wooden bunks three high.

Those nearest him were all full.

"First time?" The woman's voice came as her form appeared between him and the table.

"Not exactly," he said, trying to get an idea of how many beds there were. He imagined one only took a bottom bunk if all the upper ones were full.

"I ask only on account of most people have found their way to a chair by now." She continued cheerily, making no effort to be quiet around the sleepers.

Stalker turned to observe the woman. She was tall and dark-skinned. Backlit as she was, all he could make out were the whites of her eyes, as well as her teeth when she spoke.

"Come sit down." She said.

He followed her to the table and the better light, but he did not sit down. In the light, he saw that she wasn't a negress, or not entirely. Her hair curled too broadly and there was more of the Turk about her. She was on the thin side and had a scholarly air. Her clothes were modest: a white blouse and a long, brown skirt. Not quite a working woman's outfit, though, not with the little crystal earrings or the short string of pearls around her neck. And there was a very colorful kerchief holding her curly, black hair in place. She fetched the tea tray, then sat in a high-backed chair, the wood carved ornately, but not carefully. She gestured to a more modest chair opposite.

"Come on, it's not all that bad."

"The last time I talked with a fortune teller surrounded by people sleeping, it did not go well."

"Not well for you or not well for them?"

"For them," he growled softly.

"You're talking about the old lady in that house way out in the sticks?"

"That was her."

This fortune teller narrowed her eyes, but kept her voice playful. "Says you. What was their name?"

"Barnaby,"

She drew a long breath that seemed to inflate her. "When was this?"

"Last September."

"So, it was you." She propped her elbows on the table, folded her hands, and rested her chin on top of them. "You killed all her sons."

Stalker put his hands on the back of the nearest chair and leaned in towards the fortune teller. "They shot first."

"Oh, I believe it. Well, it seems I owe you a debt of gratitude." She picked her chin up, then grabbed the deck of cards. "How about a free reading by way of thanks?"

"Thanks?"

"Without boring you with the details, that old witch had something that belonged to me. Now, it's back where it belongs. But where are my manners?" She extended her free hand. "Call me Miss Naomi." They shook.

"Stalker."

"Is your friend coming?" She looked at Fortuna.

"I don't think so."

"Are you gonna sit already?" Stalker relented and sat as Miss Naomi poured him tea. "Sugar?"

"Please," he said.

She dropped a sugar cube in with a pair of tongs and slid it to him. "So, what brings you to my shop? You didn't enter like someone looking to get their fortune told, but I bet I can still help."

"I am looking for a woman. Someone told me it might be you."

"Might it be?"

"No, wrong eyes."

"Ooh, mysterious. But watch it, buster, that's *my* job." She grinned amiably. "So, what do you know about this woman?"

"She has a vendetta against the Saint Moon company. She's been burning their trucks all week."

"What?" Miss Naomi blurted, surprise shaking her poise.

"You don't read the papers?"

"Ah, not me. The newspapers just tell you all the troubles in the world and I've got people telling me the troubles of the neighborhood all day. There's only so much trouble a girl can take."

"Well, there is a woman burning trucks and I would like to know exactly why."

Miss Naomi, shuffling her tarot cards, said: "Let's see what we can find out." The first card was the Knight of Coins. "That's good news. You have the resources to find this woman." Next, she dealt out the Five of Wands and scowled. Next came the Two of Swords and the Page of Cups. "But she's not who you really want. There's someone else you're trying to find."

Stalker looked towards Fortuna, wondering if she was listening. He hadn't said anything to the vigilance committee about Della Caine. If Fortuna pressed him, he wasn't sure what he would say.

As he looked, Stalker saw the lamplight reflecting off a nearby bed frame. It was brass. He was sure it had been wood before. He was thrown back to the Barnaby house and how it had transformed luxuriously around him while the matriarch read her cards. Part of him wanted to bolt, but he had more to gain by staying, for the time being. There was a chance that Miss Naomi might really know something.

"Who?" Stalker said, pulling his attention back. "Who is it I'm really after?"

Miss Naomi dealt again: the queen of cups, the devil, and the tower. "A woman that will destroy you." The pearls around her neck had multiplied into several dangling loops. Her earrings as well had sprung a chain and peacock feathers. The kerchief was now a web of shiny beads. "You need to stop chasing her."

Stalker leaned and hushed his voice to a whisper. "I have to find her. She...she could cure thousands."

"No," Miss Naomi said, putting her cards down. "Not if you go looking for her. Please, listen. You will burn everything you have finding this woman. What you have, what you have been given, is worth far more and to far more people. There is a war coming to this city."

Stalker recoiled.

"A war for the heart of the city." Miss Naomi continued, her words speeding up. "The royal family is gathering, returning their crowns to the rightful bearers. But the pretenders won't go quietly. It will be war and we need people like you if we are going to win. Someone with your influence could do so much to prevent disaster."

"What is this?" Stalker growled. "You're the second woman today who has told me about a war coming. Well, I already fought one war and I'm still suffering from it. This woman you say will destroy me, she is the key to that war ending for me. So, you'll forgive me if I'm not volunteering for another."

"You don't understand." Miss Naomi grabbed him by the arm. "The city is in danger! We need..." She cut herself off at the sound of Fortuna charging through the aisle of stacked, brass beds.

Fortuna drew her sword. Miss Naomi leapt to her feet, knocking her chair over. Fortuna halted, her cutlass' point an inch from Miss Naomi's throat.

"Please," the fortune teller said, raising her hands. "I don't want to hurt anyone. I just want to explain." She was now wearing a voluminous, red dress.

Lowering her sword, Fortuna stepped closer and wagged a finger at Miss Naomi. "No touch or no talk." Fortuna pressed a menacing finger to Miss Naomi's lips.

The fortune teller suddenly wrapped her lips around that finger and sucked. Fortuna pulled her hand back and brought her sword up. As she did, Miss Naomi's lips moved, but no voice came from her mouth.

Instead, the sleepers all around them commanded in unison: "Sleep!"

Fortuna fainted instantly, her sword clanging to the floor.

Stalker lunged to catch her, dropping to one knee as he did. He watched her long enough to confirm she was still breathing, then rested her on the floor. "What did you do?" He bellowed as he flew up at Miss Naomi, grabbing for her.

She grabbed his wrist as he came and held out her tongue, drawing it across his palm. He watched the fortune teller's lips move silently.

The chorus of sleepers called out: "Dream with me!"

Everything went black.

Interlude:
The Crown of the Princess

May 13th, 1867. Barnaby Hill, KCI.

Smoke was seeping into the kitchen under the door. Sucking in breaths between sobs, 12-year-old Esther Barnaby pulled a short stack of towels out of a cabinet and ran with them over to the irregular stream of white carbon. Her mother had told her to stay there and keep a knife close. So, she threw the towels down—assuming she wouldn't get in trouble for dirtying them, under the circumstances—and grabbed the big carving knife from the center counter.

Placing the knife on the floor in front of her, Esther began stuffing the towels under the door. She couldn't say exactly why she was doing it, beyond a general sense that keeping the smoke out was a good thing.

The house had been all commotion this evening. Mother hadn't barely gotten started on dinner before the shouting in the front yard. That was when Mother had told Esther to stay hidden. The gunshots had come later and several glass things broke. One of them must have been a lantern, which had started the fire. Since then, there had been running footsteps all around the house. No one had come to the kitchen, though, which Esther supposed Mother had known and that's why she'd told Esther to stay there.

Mother was a great one for knowing things.

With the kitchen door all blocked up, Esther clutched her carving knife and crawled back behind the center counter and beside the stove. It was a good spot to hide because she could see the top of the door if it opened, but you'd have to be a giant to see over the top of the counter.

Knees to her chest, knife pointed out, Esther listened to the commotion. Upstairs, she heard her brother, Jeremiah, shouting something. It was louder than the fire in the next room that was getting louder by the second. She knew Mother was on the near side of the house, just from the distinct sound of her boots on the wood. If she was saying anything, though, it was too quiet to carry. And then there were the strange steps. They weren't running like most of the footfalls she'd been hearing, but they had a deliberation, like whoever they belonged to knew where they were going.

Just above the kitchen, in one of the guest rooms, Esther heard Mother run around the old bed to the window. The strange steps followed her there and she heard a few notes of talking, but not many that could break through the sound of the fire. Then, she heard a mighty clang and something very heavy hit the floor. In her terrified state, Esther thought whatever it was might break through the floor and land in the kitchen in front of her. The house proved sturdier than that, though.

Mother's feet raced out of the guest room and down the hall to the stairs. They hesitated in the sitting room, but Esther was on her feet and ready when Mother burst through the kitchen door, scattering the towels.

"Come on, Esther!" Mother shouted. She was crying and holding out her hand as smoke poured in from behind her. "Bring your knife!"

Esther took her hand and the two of them ran out of the kitchen, out of the house, through the back door. It was half an afternoon outside as the light of the burning house illuminated the night. They kept running through the yard, even as it began to slope down into the forest. But Mother stopped them at the edge of the trees, so that she could lean against one.

Only now did Esther see that her mother was bleeding. It looked black in the distant firelight. Mother bled blue. Esther had seen it a dozen times in kitchen accidents. Any time Mother got a cut, they had to carefully clean up every drop of it and then the rags had to be burned. Looking at her now, Esther knew that Mother's entire dress would need to be burned.

"Esther, honey," Mother said. "You need to listen carefully." She sank down to sit on the ground, back to the big tree. "There's a man come to take the crown from me. He's the Prince, but he wants the Princess, too."

Esther knew a little about the Princess. Mother mentioned her from time to time, but never explained much. All Esther knew was that the Princess talked to Mother in her head.

"That man," Mother continued, sucking in her breaths and trying not to cry. "He hurt me real bad and I ain't gonna make it, you understand?"

This hit Esther like a hammer and she started to cry too.

"Baby, no. This ain't the time to cry."

Esther squeezed her face shut for a moment to stop herself from crying.

"That's a good girl. If I die like this, the Princess will pass to the Anointed. That's Jeremiah, but I don't want him to have her. I want you to have her. The Princess should stay with a woman, right? So, you gotta take her before I go. You understand. It's gonna be hard for you, honey, but you have to do it. Can you do it?"

"Yes, ma'am." Esther squeaked dutifully.

"This will be the hardest thing you've ever done," Mother added. "So, you gotta promise me and God, both. Can you make that promise?"

"Yes, ma'am." Esther nodded.

"Say it."

"I promise."

"Promise you'll take the Princess, no matter what it takes."

"I promise. I promise to you and God that I'll take the Princess, no matter what."

"Good girl," Mother said. She was starting to cry now. "The way you take the Princess is you gotta stab me and drink the aqua vitae. Are you ready?"

"What?" Esther blurted.

Mother grabbed her arm, the one still holding the knife. "You made me a promise. Don't let go of that knife." Guiding Esther's hand, Mother cut open her dress and chemise, exposing her left breast to the night air. "It has to be you that does it. You gotta put that knife in me and drink the aqua vitae."

Behind them, there was a thud. Esther looked back to see a strange man lying on the ground between them and the house, like he'd fallen from the sky or jumped from the second floor. He started to get up on his hands and knees. Silhouetted by the fire of the house, Esther couldn't make out one detail of his face.

"Elizabeth!" He shouted. "Come on, now. See reason. There is still a chance for you."

"That's him!" Mother shouted. "He's going to take the Princess! Do it, now!"

"No!" The man shouted and began crawling towards them.

"Now, Esther! You promised!"

Mother was holding Esther's arm with the knife's tip poised above her own heart. As the shadowy apparition bore down on them, fear overwhelmed Esther.

"Do it or he'll kill you, too!"

Barely knowing what she was doing, she gave in to her mother's guidance. She leaned forward and pressed the knife into her mother's flesh. It sank, wet and firm, like cutting into raw chicken. Esther sobbed. There was unrelenting bone for a second, before the pressure bent the blade along the curve of a rib and the knife sank even deeper.

Blue blood was running down Mother's skin.

"Drink!" Mother wheezed, her eyes wide.

Barely able to keep her eyes open for the tears, Esther let Mother pull her face close to the knife. She felt the warmth of the liquid against her mouth and she opened her lips to let it in. It didn't taste of copper like blood ought to. It was some other, strange metal. Just as bitter. The blood began gushing out despite the knife being in the wound and Esther pressed her face into her mother's dying body—honoring her promise to Mother and God—and sucked at it like it was ripe fruit.

Suddenly, Esther was transported. She was flying through a snowy desert of palm trees. An ocean cast its waves against a coast of wrecked ships and the sea foam became a milk river that ran up a mountain to a pool where kitten-headed mermaids splashed around and sang songs about the Second Coming; the lyrics spelling themselves in the air for a moment before they turned into butterflies.

Up ahead, Esther saw a pair of gates. One of them grew like hair out of a great wall, but the strands wove themselves tight together until they were hard as rock. The other grew like long teeth from the side of that same wall that Esther knew without knowing extended all the way around the world. The Princess was waiting there, a dark-skinned girl about Esther's age, and the girl pushed the toothy gate open with one hand while reaching out to Esther. Mid-flight, Esther caught the Princess' hand and the two took to the air together.

For a moment, then, Esther saw the strange man's face illuminated in silvery light. He was a normal-looking sort of man. There was nothing about him to remember. The light surprised him, and he was knocked back, and Esther was back in her yard.

"He can't hurt you." The Princess told Esther inside her head. "You got your boon and he didn't. He only got a half measure."

Esther watched the man try to stand, but he was suddenly feeble. Jeremiah, then, came running around the house with a hunting rifle in one hand. Her big brother called out her name before seeing the man on the ground.

"Look away, Esther!" Jeremiah shouted as he came to a stop beside the man, lining up his gun. "Look away!"

September 20th, 1920. Swing B Ranch, KCI.

Her family was gone. Esther stood at the foot of Shem's grave, her only blood son. They'd laid him beside his three boys. His daughter, Lydia, had run off and they hadn't even known where to reach her to tell her about her pa. When Jeremiah had heard they were dead, he'd barely understood, but he'd flown into a rage that his heart couldn't handle.

They'd buried him way over by Father and Mother, near the old house.

All in one day. Those two men had come spoiling for a fight and she'd commanded peace. They had taken her granddaughter and when Shem went looking for her, they'd gunned him down and his cousin and their boys. Only two of them had escaped, the youngest, Luke and Ezra. They were Esther's sister's grandsons. They had gone away, too.

Ruth had gathered up her two girls and their kids and they'd all piled into a truck, just as soon as the graves were full. Esther hadn't asked where they were going. It didn't matter. The farm was as good as dead, now. It was just her and Zillah, now. Just a couple of widows.

Zillah had married Jeremiah's son, Buck. Buck had helped Shem look for Lydia and he was buried two graves away. Zillah was young, might remarry. If Esther had been her age, maybe they could have kept the farm running for a while; but the best they could do now was sell the herd and move into town, she supposed. Shem's wife, Mary, had run off years ago.

It was all gone. Even the Princess had been silent since that dark day. Not enough sleepers around to wake her up.

When Esther heard the footsteps approaching, she knew who it was: the old Jew. He'd been skulking around their property for weeks and now there was no one to keep him at bay.

"I come to offer my condolences, me." The old Jew called.

"You come to gloat." Esther replied.

"No, ma'am. No. This bloodshed, I take no joy from it."

"It was you that sent the killers to my house."

"Now, that's true, but I didn't send them for killing. I sent them 'cause they was looking for someone who needed to be found, her. Who am I if I'm not the man who finds lost things, yeah? I could not see this coming. No, ma'am."

"And if you had?"

"Maybe I do things different, maybe not. It was him"—he pointed at the grave of Buck's son, Leroy—"that fired the first shot."

"So, they deserved it?"

"No. No, it's just tragedy. None of those men wanted that fight. They wanted to make the others back down. Just stubborn men all around and then one boy, he got too nervous. Tragedy."

Despite herself, Esther did feel soothed by that, but she wouldn't let it stand. "But there's more blood to spill, isn't there."

"Doesn't have to be." The old Jew said, quietly. "You can give up the crown anytime. Bless the girl, send her on her way. It's all peace, that."

"I have a granddaughter, still." Esther told him. "She is my Anointed, now. I'd rather know that traitorous slip had the Princess than whatever hebe bitch you have in mind."

The old Jew let out a long sigh. "So long you have had the crown, you, but no understanding of its mysteries. There is no Anointed in your line. The royalty is not in you. Now, please...that spirit in you what you call 'the Princess', she got one thousand faces. If we got to take it from you by blood, we get her blood face. That's just what we are trying to prevent. It will be another generation before we can make all the crowns gold, again."

"I don't care." Esther said. "I'm going to get a gun. You better git. It's kike season."

Esther marched into the house. There were guns propped up all around the living room. One of Ruth's girls had thought they'd bury them with their men like some kind of pagan rite. Esther had told her 'no'. They'd sell the guns, along with the cattle. A widow needed something to live on and it wasn't Christian to bury things with the dead, save their Sunday clothes, but that was for modesty.

When she entered the living room, Esther found Zillah asleep on one of the couches. The Princess was there, stroking her hair. She had gotten old right along with Esther.

"What is this?" Esther demanded.

"Good manners." The old Princess replied. "Before I go, I wanted you to know that I'm not angry at you. Not like Sire is. It's okay that you never asked about my mysteries. I had them whether you knew about them or not."

"You coulda told me."

"Not unless you asked. Those are the rules."

"Rules!" Esther stamped her foot and winced at the pain that radiated up her leg.

"Esther," the old Princess said softly. "Don't trouble yourself. It's too late."

That was when Esther felt the knife enter her back. It was cold for one brief moment, then very hot; like a wasp sting. Dizziness swept over her and she felt her knees give way. A pair of arms caught her and lowered her gently to the floor. As she descended, the cold returned like a slap. The Princess changed right before her eyes; younger, swarthier, with a thick mane of ring-curly hair.

Esther didn't feel herself reach the ground.

Chapter 19:
Sins of the City

Then. Elsewhere.

A cold rush of water was the next thing Cranston sensed, followed by a banal warmth. He sat up and discovered that he was sitting—nude—on some paradisiacal beach. The sand was white, the sea crystal blue, the sky clear. The beach extended for miles in either direction before ending in rocky, well-foliaged coast. Up the beach was a forest of palm trees and a rustic, but well-made cottage with a thick, brown grass roof.

In front of the cottage were a pair of upholstered fainting couches that looked like they each cost double what that cottage would, including labor. The couches were set at angles on either side of a blackened pile of wood, above which hung a black pot suspended from a tripod.

Waves were rolling in and out around him. Despite the strangeness of the situation, Cranston felt no particular need to get up. He could stay here until hunger or thirst set in. It was a nice thought. Then, to his right, a dozen yards away, Miss Naomi's head rose out of the water; all those curls plastered flat by the sea. She walked up onto the beach, also nude, with a wooden trap full of fish slung over one shoulder.

"Be a darling," she called to him in an Atlantic accent. "Start a fire for us."

Cranston had a broken continuity of memory. Dreams were disorienting like that. They made you forget that they were not really happening. In that moment, though, he was fully aware that he was lying on the floor of *Titania's Grove* and there was no fogginess separating this moment from the ones he had spent awake. It occurred to him to resume hostilities, but the fire of adrenaline was gone and, besides, there was no telling what powers Miss Naomi could wield in this place; assuming of course that this was really her in this dream. Nothing about this felt like a dream he would have. It was best to talk pleasantly until he had a better sense of the rules of this new game.

"If we're dreaming," he called out, dropping his Stalker voice. "Can't a fire just be there?"

She grinned at him. "So, make it!"

Cranston looked at the dark fire pit and imagined a fire burning in it. Sure enough, the fire appeared.

"Convenient," he remarked.

"Yes," she called back. "But you will find that there is more pleasure in doing than imagining."

"Tell that to pomegranates." Cranston stood and imagined himself a pair of linen pants and one of those loose white shirts one always saw in photographs of the French Riviera.

"You're no fun!" Miss Naomi teased.

"Not yet, I'm afraid." He began walking up the beach towards the unnaturally pristine couches. "Perhaps you can convince me I should be."

"Things were rather heated, just now, weren't they? But I dare say it's no fault of mine. Your lady friend tried to stab me."

"She's a woman who prefers doing, too. Where is she, by the way?"

Miss Naomi paused. "Odile is swimming. I gave her a private little lagoon."

"And the others from your shop?"

"They are scattered around."

"Swimming?"

"Copulating, mostly."

"That would certainly explain your popularity."

"The stresses of working life, darling. Not everyone is terribly creative about how to shed them, nor am I the sort to tell them how they should."

They had arrived at the fire pit and Miss Naomi began unfolding a little table on which she could clean the fish. "Ever done this?" She asked, holding up a slender knife.

"I'm afraid not."

"You can try. You won't fail, unless you can't imagine yourself succeeding."

"I'm sure I heard a lecturer once say that was true of anything."

"Yes, but I'm not lying to get your money."

"I'll watch you work, if you don't mind."

"Not at all."

Naomi's hair was tied back in a single, great, waterlogged lock. She seemed more filled out here than she had. Though Cranston couldn't be sure if that was part of the dream or not. Her breasts were small for her frame, but nicely shaped, and there was a charming fold to her belly as she bent over the fish. It was unnerving when you saw skinny, malnourished girls at the beach pick up a seashell and it was like their stomachs got even tighter.

Once Naomi had filleted three of them, she took a ceramic jar out of thin air and set it beside the fillets. She pinched brown powder out of it and patted a generous coating onto the pink side of the fish. "I'm going to assert myself a bit more here," she said. "You are about to taste a memory of mine. Isn't that delightful?"

"In theory, I suppose." Cranston answered.

"Allspice, they call it. Have you had it before?"

"Likely, but I don't interrogate the chefs very often."

"Well, you'll taste it the way I remember it." Next, she spitted the fillets. "You turn that." She indicated a handle on the end of the cooking stick. "Make yourself useful."

"Yes, ma'am," he began to turn the spit, which was near enough that he could sit on the couch as he did it. "Is this where you grew up?"

"This is nowhere. It's like the places I loved most, but without anything I didn't. You can walk the beach forever and never find the island's point."

"Endless walks on the beach? That's how you intend to win me over to your crusade?"

"I intended to appeal to the better angels of your nature."

"Alright, appeal on."

Naomi leaned against the arm of her couch and stretched her legs out like Titian's *Venus of Urbino* without the modest hand. Cranston drew his eyes from her feet to her eyes.

"I didn't think those were the angels you were referring to."

Naomi laughed, her belly quivering. "You're too easy."

"And now I say 'you're too beautiful' and take my place on the couch?"

"No, you keep turning the spit. The fish will burn."

"So far, I must say, I find your crusade confusing."

"I'm stalling."

"For what?"

"The fish," she said.

Cranston stood. "The fish will be done when you want them done, but I do believe you are stalling."

"You really aren't any fun." Naomi grimaced and stood. "You know what evil lurks in your city, Cranston Walker, but all that matters to you is finding a woman to...cure you?"

"You share your dream and get inside my head, is that it?"

Naomi shrugged. "Most people rather expect that from a fortune teller."

"Reading me like a book? Making notes in the margins, perhaps?"

"Why won't you fight?" Naomi barked.

"I tried! You brought us here!"

"Not me! The darkness! There are people starving in Silkhaven. There are homeless men, women, and children. And you do nothing."

"Nothing? My company has fostered the strongest labor unions in the country. Agreements we have made with them that have become laws, bettering the lot of every worker."

"It's not enough!" Naomi flourished one arm and the beach vanished, replaced by a smoking room decorated with taxidermic fish. Cranston's clothes were unchanged, but Naomi now wore a simple dress like the one she had in the waking world.

There were plush sofas in a U-shape where several older men sat; Governor Farrar, Mayor Ulster, several businessmen of Cranston's standing and his father's age. They were cheering and braying as a pair of dwarves boxed bare-knuckled in the center. Several young women were about the room in tawdry lingerie, including Pearl. One of the others was distinctly less comfortable and in much simpler underwear. She was perched on the mayor's lap.

This wasn't happening, right now. This had happened last winter, a few days before Christmas. Cranston hadn't been there, but he had heard versions of the story, including one from Pearl, herself. The lady on the mayor's knee was the wife of a junior department head at City Hall. The young man had done something to offend his superiors and his pretty wife had been offered the chance to keep her husband employed. In two versions of this story, she had loved every moment.

In Pearl's, she had not.

The plan, of course, had been to despoil this good wife, but her virtue was saved—on this night, at least—by what happened next. One of the dwarves knocked the other back with particular ferocity. The governor, drunk and mischievous, stuck out his foot and tripped the boxer as he tried to recover from the blow. The small man tripped and fell backwards, his head catching the corner of an oak plinth.

There was an unholy crack as the hardwood punched through his skull. He died instantly, as the story went. There was screaming and chaos, then, before the scene evaporated into the mayor's fishing boat where, under cover of night, the dwarf's body was dumped into the sea. No charges were filed and the other dwarf had supposedly left town.

"What's next?" Cranston growled, grabbing Naomi by the arm. "We tour every misdeed in the city?"

"Just the ones you choose to ignore."

The boat vanished and they were in the lavish gardens around the Vergennes House in New Versailles. Naomi had seen fit to dress them in the appropriate party clothes. Cranston, reflexively tugging at his shirt cuffs, knew what night this was. If Naomi was touring the city's dark secrets, there was only one night this could be. It was the most infamous event that no one talked about.

Richard Cullen, a man of thirty, was dancing with fifteen-year-old Mary Reid alone, under the stars in a secluded part of the gardens. He raped her that night and their families insisted that they marry to avoid a scandal. She had gotten her revenge, donating to charity until Cullen was near bankruptcy, while promoting him as one of the city's most celebrated philanthropists.

Knowing that was coming colored the scene before them. Mary was smiling, mouth agape, looking like she thought herself the luckiest girl in the city.

"Well?" Naomi said, reading his thoughts.

"What would you prefer?" He shouted as Richard and Mary continued their so-far-innocent dance. "Should I have assembled a posse to string him up? Or maybe just hired some street toughs to hold him down while I castrated him with a grapefruit spoon? Is that your crusade?"

Brief tongues of flame leapt from her eyes, leaving soot only just visible on her brown skin. "We will rally the poor! We will gather the workers! We will call your priests who can still hear the voice of the

Lord!"

They were transported to a police station, their previous dress returning. Officers were busy about their paperwork when a door labeled Chief Ephram McManus opened. Silkhaven's chief of police stepped out carrying a box that was as long as his chest was broad. Cranston didn't know what this was. Nor did he know why a spectral crest—like that of a Roman helmet—glittered on his head.

"The standard issue police baton," the chief declared. "Is made of common ash wood. It's a good tree, the ash. Sturdy, reliable, abundant. Mr Brinell gives the ash a hardness of 3.7." He shifted his hands to cradle the box with one arm while the other lifted the lid. From within, he produced a baton of glossy, polished wood, deep red in color. "This baton is made from the wood of an Amazon tree that the tribesmen call Muirapiranga."

Cranston was surprised by how the gruff man pronounced the foreign word, no traces of his native phonology tainting the sound, as if he had heard it dozens of times, but never seen it written.

"The Muirapiranga has more than twice the hardness of the ash." This elicited some cheers from the gathered policemen. "That's right. This ain't a baton. This is a hammer." More cheers. "Coincidentally, in English, we call it 'bloodwood'. Now," he addressed the congregation as they approached exuberance. "Where's that nigger we caught in the department store?"

"I understand." Cranston told Naomi, even as time skipped ahead to when two policemen walked a black man in a cheap suit into the office.

"Do you?" Naomi said.

This recreation was from her, not him. A story she had heard.

"I'm no prophet." Cranston told her. "I can't call down fire to cleanse the evil from this city. I do what I can!"

"You could do more." She said, watching the man being brought before Chief McManus.

"That cure I'm after," Cranston said, dreading what he knew came next. He tried to turn away, but the room spun so that McManus remained near the center of his field of view. "It's not just for me. Have you seen what the pockets do to people? What I'm looking for will help thousands of people return from prisons within their own bodies!"

An almighty crack resonated as the police erupted in cheers. Cranston didn't look. He focused his mind on Naomi. She felt it as her clothes changed: a transparent nightgown in a bright blue, the color of her oneiric ocean. Naomi lost focus on the faux-memory and gazed down at herself. In the loss of concentration, they were whisked from the bloody police station back to the beach where the fish still hung above the heatless fire.

"I do not deny that there is injustice in this city!" Cranston bellowed. "So, by all means, march your family in and root out whatever corruption you can find. But do not try to paint me as a frivolous playboy. What I do, I do for all who share my affliction; from simple housekeepers to soldiers who wanted to see me dead."

When Naomi had no retort, he continued.

"Have you seen?" He asked and she said nothing. "Have you seen?!"

The look in her eyes was resolute and she stood in her risqué gown with defiant stature, but it all betrayed the answer: 'no'. A deep part of Cranston's mind screamed like bars of a prison being wrenched free as he dug up his own memory.

"Behold." He said.

Suddenly, an enormous ball of white, brighter than the tropical sun, but casting no shadow, appeared above the trees. Naomi screamed as Cranston's memory of the pocket—the raw animal fear that knew no object—ripped through her nowhere island. It ran along his nerves like cold fire, awaking every survival instinct that had been passed down from the first humans who lived long enough to procreate.

His body exploded with every chemical it had to protect him. His muscles sang with power, his mind slowed time the better to see the danger, his brain turned off the lights on any thought that did not help him run. It was the disease that he sought to cure. It ate away at him until he was a sobbing mess on the floor. It was the supreme fear that kept him awake on nights when he had been without a bedfellow for too long.

It was familiar.

He knew it, had faced it down, had willed his fingers to hold stable long enough to light a manitaurine cigarette and dispel the worst of it. Naomi had not.

Cranston heard the sleepers all cry out with her. She was not curling up to protect herself, she was not running; she was staring, transfixed by his memory of the pocket and she screamed into its milky void.

Cranston opened his eyes on the dim little shop. His nerves on fire with the message to flee. Echoing off the back of his skull were the whispers of the things that swam inside the pocket: "The krakens!" They said. "The krakens!" And in those simple words was the undeniable sense that they wanted something from him, wanted him to do a thing that would be terrible and maddening to behold; only he had no inkling of what it was.

Every muscle trembled as he scooped up Odile. Her eyes were closed, but she was panting and grasping at the air as he lifted her on legs that shook so much that every step felt like he might fall. He fumbled the door open and nearly fell through. The world outside spun as he took one quaking step after another.

On the street, there were people that his eyes could not focus on. "Saint Lawrence!" He said. "Saint Lawrence...Saint Lawrence...Saint Lawrence..."

As the late afternoon shoppers gasped and recoiled around him, he stumbled towards a shop. The door opened for him, but his foot caught on the frame and he tipped forward, spilling Odile onto the tiles. He landed on his back.

"Saint Lawrence..." he repeated. "Saint Lawrence..."

Chapter 20:
The Woman behind the Screen

August 11th, 1921. Silkhaven.

Vivienne was leaning against the bar in the small dining room, having a glass of wine and deciding what to have for dinner, when the elevator dinged. Fortunately, she had decided to order food before dressing for the night.

"Cranston?" She called down into the living room, only to be greeted by the sight of Williamson and Hornsby, followed by a strange woman in an elaborate pirate costume, carrying Cranston in and depositing him on a couch. "What is this?" Vivienne ran down the stairs. Cranston was dressed as she had seen him earlier that day. No one had taken their shoes off.

"I'm sorry, Miss Walker." Williamson said. "I didn't think you'd want a hospital to see him like this. They talk, you know."

"Saint Lawrence...Saint Lawrence..." Cranston jabbered as his body spasmed. His face was empty.

"Nou saw boul dyab." The strange, blonde woman said. "Li sove m."

"What?" Vivienne asked.

"A dimensional pocket." Williamson said. "Une boule du diable."

Vivienne had only second-hand expertise on the subject from Rosamund Gabriel. She had read Rosamund's book and, after they had been acquainted, had discussed the subject a few times. According to her, the best thing for exposure to one of the strange spheres was oxytocin and Vivienne knew precisely where Cranston liked to get his.

"Thank you, miss." Vivienne told the pirate woman. "You are excused. Hornsby, find a way to apply manitaurine. There are patches?"

"Those are military, ma'am." The old butler said.

"Well, hold a cigarette under his nose. Something."

"Yes, ma'am."

"Williamson," she addressed the driver. "We need to fetch Rebecca."

"I rest." The strange woman said. "La." She pointed at the sofa where Cranston lay.

"No," Vivienne picked up her suit coat from the chair she had left it on. "Come along." She pulled the strange woman with her towards the elevator as Hornsby phoned down to some nether region of the hotel for supplies.

"He save me." The woman said, while she rode the elevator down with Vivienne and Williamson.

"Feel free to write a thank-you note." Vivienne replied.

When Williamson stopped the elevator on the ground floor and opened the gate, Vivienne pushed the woman out. O'Reilly, the night manager, ran across the lobby to meet them.

"O'Reilly," Vivienne ordered. "She does not go back upstairs."

"No, ma'am."

Vivienne and Williamson continued on out through the front door where the car still waited.

The Mermaid Club was only just opening when the car pulled up in front. "Keep it running." Vivienne told Williamson. On the short drive over, he had explained that a shopkeeper had found Cranston. Williamson did not know exactly what Cranston had been doing in that neighborhood, but the woman was with the St Lawrence Vigilance Committee. The shopkeeper had called the VC, who had informed Williamson.

Cranston had said that the board sent him to find the Masked Virago. Of course, they had teamed him with an exotic and exciting woman that could handle herself in a fight. The Rose & Chain had used the same ploy on their father.

Lolita Bakurova had been a poor immigrant that the SLVC had taken in. Then, the Rose & Chain had made her James Walker's bodyguard. She posed as a newcomer to the social scene so that she could accompany James without raising suspicions and the two had fallen in love. In all the years Vivienne had spent as her father's secretary, he had never once shown the slightest bitterness at her mother's subterfuge. It had been one of the city's great marriages, so of course, the board thought it would work again.

In her youth, it had seemed romantic. Now, though, she was furious. Part of her understood that, really, she was afraid of what was happening to Cranston, but fear was an uncomfortable emotion; so, she was finding someone to be angry with. Anger felt like strength. It felt like the opposite of fear.

Vivienne stormed past the man on the door of the club and waved at the first 'mermaid' she saw. She wore a strapless, sleeveless, corset-like thing with shorts covered in shiny, turquoise circles to resemble scales.

"I need to see Re...Pearl." Vivienne said brusquely.

The startled mermaid looked up and over Vivienne's shoulder. The man on the door had followed her in, but was not doing anything yet. He was what they called a goon. Well over six feet tall with hands like he was wearing baseball mitts.

"Yes?" Vivienne demanded of the goon.

"I gotta keep things nice in here." He said with a shrug.

"Alright," she turned back to the mermaid. "Where is Pearl?"

"Oh...um...I don't know."

Vivienne made to push past her when one of the mitts landed on her shoulder. "How about you talk to the owner?" He said. "You look like you wanna talk to the owner."

"I want to talk to Pearl." Vivienne replied, staring at the hand on her shoulder.

"Yeah, sure. Sandy here will go find her and Pearl will meet you in the owner's office. It's this way." The mitt moved to her waist and guided her gently, but irresistibly, through a curtain and into a hidden hallway.

Vivienne had been screamed at by plenty of men over the years, mainly when fuel prices went up or a shipment failed an inspection. They never got what they wanted. None of them had hands this big.

The door to the owner's office was marked with a brass trident and nothing more. The goon opened it and ushered Vivienne inside. The better part of the office was closed off by a folding screen of sturdy, but not especially fine silk. It was a type that they imported, but kept hidden until a client seemed ready to walk out; the company's last chance to get their money. Two chairs sat along the wall facing the screen.

"You can sit if you want." The goon said. "The owner's a nice lady, but private. Fancy lady like you? You understand."

"Thank you, Frank." A voice came from beyond the screen. There was a strangled quality to her voice. Not husky, like one heard from a serial smoker, but like there was something very tight wrapped around her neck. When the door closed, the owner introduced herself: "Forgive the eccentricity, please. My name is Jillian Moll, owner of the Mermaid Club. And you are?"

"Vivienne Walker," she was not sitting.

"It's an honor to have you. I don't think your brother is here."

"No, he is not. He is at home." She forced herself to slow down. This was not a time to demand. This was a time to lay out why she wanted something followed by what it is she wanted. "I assume I can trust you to be discreet?"

"Discretion keeps my club open."

"Cranston is suffering from an affliction of the nerves. It is my understanding that a natural hormone called oxytocin can allay the symptoms."

"A pocket?" Jillian rasped. "He encountered a dimensional pocket? Here in the city?"

"You are familiar?"

"I keep to the city precisely to avoid them. If they've started appearing here, that's concerning."

"I do not have the details. I came only because Cranston's favorite source of oxytocin is your girl, Pearl. I can pay for her time."

"I know you can," Jillian replied. She spoke so slowly that Vivienne began to wonder if it were not a trick of her own mind; the urgency slowing the world to a crawl. "But Pearl is not licensed to work outside of the club."

"I would not be paying her," Vivienne said, negotiating was second nature when she was under pressure. "I would be reimbursing you for lost labor. Pearl would be doing me a personal favor."

"Good, we have a number of high-ranking policemen in tonight." Jillian's words dragged through the air. "All that's left..." She was interrupted by a knock at the door. "Would you mind, Miss Walker?"

Vivienne had felt the urge to open the door anyway, but still resented being asked to do it. When she did, the girl in the fish-scale underwear was there with Rebecca, who wore a revealing pirate costume. Why were there so many pirates today?

"Vivienne?" Rebecca shouted. "This is where I work!"

The other mermaid scampered away.

"Miss Walker would like to borrow you." Jillian said. "It seems your best client is in need of your care."

"What?" Rebecca asked Vivienne, looking no less upset.

"Cranston encountered a pocket." Vivienne explained, trying to speak at a normal speed. "It has shaken him and it is my understanding..."

"Yeah, we all read Miss Syme's book." Rebecca cut her off. "Jillian, you're okay with this?"

"You are not?" Jillian rasped. "I thought you liked Mr Walker."

"He's a peach, but he knows the rules."

"You can say 'no'," Jillian told her. "But you read Miss Syme's book. It might be bad."

"My license?"

"You would be doing me a personal favor." Vivienne interjected.

"More favors," Rebecca scoffed.

"I do not understand..." Vivienne started.

"Because..." she cut herself off. With lips pressed tight together, Rebecca screamed for a second, then composed herself. "I'd like to go."

"Go on." Jillian said lightly. "Miss Walker and I will settle our part later."

For reasons Vivienne could only guess at, there was a small closet by the front door with long, ladies' coats inside. Given their proximity to the door—and Frank—she suspected they had a dark utility, but perhaps mermaids often left with impatiently amorous clients. Rebecca bundled up in one of the coats and made for the car without waiting for Vivienne. Either she recognized it or she recognized Williamson, who waited by the back door.

He opened the door and the two women climbed in. As soon as the door shut, Rebecca asked: "What happened?"

"I do not really know." Vivienne replied, feeling like she was being chastised for something. "I am told he encountered a pocket somewhere near a shop."

"In the city? I thought pockets only happened in the country."

"I do not know. Cranston was trembling and he kept repeating 'Saint Lawrence' over and over."

Rebecca nodded. "Yeah, he gets like that sometimes."

"This has happened before?" Vivienne cried.

Rebecca fixed her with a scalding look. "You and me are gonna talk later, but I wanna be real clear on this: I ain't doing you a favor. I'm doing him a favor."

"If I..."

"Later," Rebecca insisted. She took a deep breath and let it out slowly. "But yeah, this has happened before. Sometimes his head gets busy and it makes him want to fight. If he can't fight, he tries to leave. If he can't leave fast enough, he starts saying something over and over like his mouth has forgotten every other word. After a while, he can write things, but his mouth is stuck."

"And..." Vivienne tested to see if she would get another scolding look. Rebecca kept her gaze forward. "And you have returned him to his senses."

"Yeah," she crossed her arms over her chest.

"He has never told me. A man is entitled to a few secrets, I suppose."

"Or maybe he doesn't trust..." Rebecca cut herself off. "I shouldn't've...I'm sorry. I got too many feelings right now. So, I gotta focus. For him."

"Yes," Vivienne said. "Later."

It would not have occurred to her that Cranston did not trust her. They had never been confidantes, not unless it were some shared intrigue. Of course, in their youth, when one knew that the other had broken a rule, they did not tattle. There had been that much trust.

For almost three years now, there had been a little thought—a question—in the back of her mind. When it began to drift forward, she had always pushed it back. Lock and key. Rebecca's words had not only broken that lock but dragged the question out and demanded her to ask it: Did Cranston really come back from the war?

On Rebecca's orders, the butler and the driver carried Cranston up the stairs to his room. Vivienne disappeared into a room on the first floor of the penthouse. It was a weight off Rebecca's shoulders, not having the sister hovering around her.

The gall on that woman! Then again...what were her options? Still, Rebecca was starting to feel like an employee and she didn't like it. But Cranston was in a bad state, as bad as she'd ever seen.

Rebecca kicked the driver and butler out and wished she was wearing something else. Sure, Cranston liked her costumes, but the sexy pirate captain was not ideal for the situation. It consisted of an underbust corset with high-cut bloomers and matching Spanish chemise: off the shoulders. Around her waist was what the catalogues called a 'fencing skirt'; very short on one side and full length on the other. It left your lead leg unfettered without revealing your sex and was worn with pants in all the illustrations. She had no idea if any real lady fencers actually used them, but they were popular with the mermaids.

Rebecca shimmied off her bloomers, but kept the skirt on. Then she sat on the bed beside Cranston. The terrors seemed to have stopped. He was still, looking exhausted but unable to sleep. She started by singing to him. She wasn't much of a singer—not good enough for the stage at the club—but she could carry a tune.

"La noche es cálida. Ningún pájaro canta. / En mi ventana huelo amaranta." She sang, taking off his gloves; gently, testing his unease. "La brisa toca mi piel como dedos suaves. / Las bocanadas y yo estamos graves." She reached under his shirts and pulled his arms from the sleeves. "Es porque te extraño. No son tus dedos. / No estás aquí para borrar mis miedos." As gently as she could, she slid the light sweater and undershirt over his head.

"Mi valiente perro que aleja las dudas. / Mi fe y mi corazón no son forzudas." She took off his boots and set them quietly on the floor. "Otro pretendiente ha traído un anillo. / Negarse es difícil en veranillo." She undid his belt and slid his trousers off his legs. "¿Cuándo volverás pronto? ¿Prometes volverás pronto? / Quiero creer. ¿Estoy siendo tonto?"

He was down to his trunks and she left those alone for now. Rebecca knelt beside him and leaned down to plant a few little kisses on his chest. Her eyes were turned almost painfully up so she could look at his face, waiting for some reaction. He remained impassive, so she moved to one of his nipples. It was just soft lips on that dark skin, but she felt it harden in a couple of seconds. Now, Cranston responded with a big breath.

She took that for consent and started getting serious. She sucked in his nipple with her whole mouth and gave it a gentle nibble on its way out. Another big breath. Again, she sucked it in, half released, nibbled, released; and a third time. Then, she switched sides. A few little kisses to prime the skin—though the nipple was already hard—then the big kisses and the exciting little bites.

Bending across his body like this put his cock so close, she almost couldn't help touching it. So far, though, it was not reacting.

Rebecca went back to his left nipple and began aggressively

tonguing it with the speed she liked on her own with about double the pressure. As she did, Cranston's left hand rose and rested on her corset. It didn't do anything, just sat there, but it was a good sign. When she shifted to tongue his right nipple, the hand slid down to her ass, covered by the skirt. Still, no action from the hand, but it took a modicum of effort to keep it there and that told her that he was coming around.

She let herself stop worrying about him, then. Worry was the enemy of excitement. Letting her brain get a little more amorous, she pulled the skirt up so she could get a knee between his legs, then pushed his right further out. It really was her pushing; Cranston still hadn't found the energy to do it himself. It made her wonder what it was like in his head just then, but she banished the thought as it would make her worry again.

Putting both knees between his legs, Rebecca slid down the bed so she could kiss his stomach. His muscles tightened reflexively and he let out a sharp breath that almost had voice in it. Her boobs were on his thighs and there was an instant burst of blood into his cock. Now, she was reaching him. It was easy to tell when he was getting excited. Cranston had one of those cocks that doubled in size when he got aroused.

Rebecca continued planting her little kisses on his abdomen, pausing between them, letting the nerves settle so that she could unsettle them again with the next one. Of course, with each kiss, the reaction was a little weaker and a little weaker, until she could draw her tongue along the little gutters where his legs met his pelvis and only get small, voiced sighs from him.

By this time, his cock was at near full strength. In this state, she knew he couldn't reach his complete hardness, but it was pressing against the buttons of his trunks. She decided that now was a good time to take them off. She used teasing little gestures to open the buttons and tugged the cotton down his hips. Cranston raised himself a little to facilitate; another good sign.

Rebecca had to move to one side to get the trunks off his legs. Kneeling more erect herself, she could see that his eyes were still closed. Not sleeping, he was breathing too quickly for that, just...protecting himself maybe? But that was worry creeping back in and worry would steal the moisture building between her legs.

Now, Rebecca threw a leg over Cranston's hips, letting the skirt fly around her. He didn't see it, but it felt grand and feeling grand made her feel sexy. She adjusted herself so that her bare cunt could touch his swollen cock. Hands planted on his chest, she began to slide those lips up and down his shaft. That really got the juice flowing. It worked on Cranston as well.

He turned his head and opened his eyes. There was a vacancy in them and it was like he was focused on something behind her; which wasn't all that strange in the throes of passion, the mind elsewhere.

"Fortuna?" He whispered.

"Si," she said throatily. "Eres afortunado." She took hold of the laces on her corset. "Mirad."

She undid the bow and tugged the black leather loose enough that she felt her belly start to relax. Then, she pulled her chemise up until it was all bunched around her chest. She took his hands and put them on the fabric. Weakly, he pulled at the fabric, while Rebecca leaned down to make it easier on him. He got the chemise free and dropped it on the bed. Her nude breasts were pressed into his ribs now and she looked up at him with her best hungry tiger face. He looked down and offered a faint smile.

Then, Rebecca rose up, arching her back to put her breasts on full display. As she did, she adjusted her hips so that his cock teased the opening of her cunt. Still arched, she reached behind her to pull his shaft up a bit and align it with her opening. She pushed back and felt him enter an inch or so. Balanced on her knees and left hand, she rolled her hips, dipping his cock in her juice and driving it a little deeper and a little deeper until she had taken him to the hilt.

Cranston saw the world around him as flat, paper artifice. It was a strange, unreality that set in with these episodes. Nothing seemed real, just a set for a play he didn't have the script for. The woman deliciously riding him was simultaneously Fortuna and Pearl, which made him think he was dreaming. That was fine. It was a very nice dream.

PART 5
The Clues

Chapter 21:
Frêne and Endeavor

Thaddeus Granger was in Silkhaven because polio was ravaging Anishinaabe and the Atlantic Network paid top dollar for a man with his skills.

As a young man, feeling the pull of adventure, he had hopped on a train to Mishigami to get a job on a fishing boat. It was dangerous work and with more and more young Anishinaabe men going to university to study engineering or banking, they were willing to take on strong white boys even if they didn't speak a word of Ojibwe.

Five years later was the Trespasser Rebellion; German settlers in Ashwaubenon decided they didn't like the government's restrictions on immigration. Anishinaabe, bordering the Federated States of America, only allowed immigration by those who bought $600 worth of property—property that could not later be inherited by non-citizens—which completely excluded the political refugees flooding in from Europe. To the south, though, Nadowessi welcomed the cheap, agricultural labor. They restricted land ownership, but they let the Germans get their foot in the door.

This drew boat after boat of poor, strong-backed Krauts to the Great Lakes. The problem was that Lake Mishigami and Lake Gichigami had banks too massive to be patrolled. With a little organization, thousands of Germans had entered Anishinaabe without permission. "Trespassers", they were called, since the North American Union used English as its language of government (there were a hundred languages in the Union and English was a useful, neutral language).

When the Union started cracking down, the Germans fought back and Thaddeus found himself on one of the many boats targeted by Lake Pirates. Over the next two years, he had learned war up close and bloody. In response to the piracy, Nadowessi expelled all German citizens from its borders and Thaddeus had been offered a substantial salary to infiltrate the remaining trespasser networks. After that, he had become a bounty hunter until the Union adopted the Jurisdiction Reform Bill of 1899 and formed the Aki-Dakoniwewininiwag.

For a few years, it seemed like the bloody years of Thaddeus' life were over. He moved to Opinikaaning and became a gunsmith. There was a pretty doctor there, Memengwaa, who fell in love with him for reasons he couldn't imagine, but wasn't going to argue with. They got married and six months later, the Mexican-Indian War broke out.

Memengwaa volunteered, as female doctors were a rarity, but female prisoners less so, and Thaddeus went along with her. They traveled with an Anishinaabe army division, and by the time they arrived in Apache, he had been commissioned as what English speakers called a Drill-Sergeant. He trained volunteers from all over the Union, as well as the Federated States and Canada and more than once was forced to fight Mexican guerrillas himself.

He and Memengwaa stayed in Apache when the Mexican Revolution kicked off. Thaddeus led a patrol that clashed with Maderistas that wandered too far north. However, Memengwaa got pregnant in 1912 and they decided that they had done their part. Returning to Opinikaaning, Thaddeus accepted a contract from the FS Army as an advisor on the establishment of a joint FS and Union army division. That had only lasted a year, with the FS deciding he was too biased towards the Union's interests. That, however, had gotten him in touch with the Atlantic Network and he accepted contracts from them whenever the family coffers were getting low.

The first polio outbreak in Anishinaabe had been in 1918 and nearly claimed the life of his son, Nimkii. Since then, Memengwaa had been trying to establish a quarantine hospital and Thaddeus was spending the majority of his time living like a monk in Boston so he could send her as much money as possible. Now, he was in Silkhaven, the Jewel of the Atlantic, hunting a woman dressed all in red that had a habit of setting things on fire and then disappearing without a trace; a guerrilla in the city.

In the last attack, some *oshkinawesh* had started shooting wildly on the street, so the Atlantic Network men were forbidden from carrying guns. So far, Thaddeus had been told, the woman-in-red had never carried a gun. None of that bothered Thaddeus, though. He was better with his "tomahawk", as the English speakers called it, than a gun anyway. The hand-axe was Union Army issue and the specifics of the design and where it was worn were a sign of rank.

Being the equivalent of a sergeant, Thaddeus wore his across his chest on a buckled sash. The buckle had two spring-loaded clips that released when he pressed a button at the buckle's center. Reach up, press the button with the right thumb and the axe dropped into your palm. If the clips failed, you could draw the axe out longways.

"You get that off an Indian?" The truck driver asked Thaddeus as they entered Silkhaven proper.

"No," Thaddeus said. "I served in the Union Army."

"Is that so?" The driver was sociable now that there were street lights. "I didn't think they let us pale faces in."

"When there's a war on, they aren't picky."

"Did you get an Indian name?"

"Nope, they call me Thaddeus. Most folks pronounce it 'Shah-dee-ooz', but same thing. My wife's got an Ojibwe nickname for me, but that's just her."

"Oh, yeah? What is it?"

"Private."

Thaddeus had had this conversation dozens of times and was basically reading a script at this point. Most people thought that last part was funny, but the driver took it seriously.

"Just funnin'." Thaddeus replied.

"Oh," the driver forced himself to chuckle. "Sure."

"You married?"

"Yeah, two kids and another on the way."

"How's she feel about you working nights?"

"Not happy, but it's only temporary. Once you catch this Virago broad, we get to go back to daytime deliveries. First time in Silkhaven?"

"Yep,"

"What do you think?"

Thaddeus looked up at the sparsely lit towers that appeared between the nearer buildings from time to time. "I prefer the country."

"You're like my wife." The driver said. "She wants us to move out to Mermaid. Says it's more healthsome for the kids."

"Mermaid? You have a town called 'Mermaid'?"

"Yeah, my wife's from there."

"Ah, so maybe it's not about the kids, then?"

"That's my thought on it, too. Anyway, it's no good right now. We can't afford a new place until I've been in this job awhile. Still, she might go stay with her folks when the baby—" the driver was cut off by a woman in a red getup landing on the hood of the truck. There was an almighty cacophony as she drove a metal spear into the engine and the driver slammed on the brakes. "Shit! Shit! Shit! Shit! Shit!" The driver exclaimed.

Thaddeus braced himself against the dashboard until they came to a stop. That woman had a hell of an arm on her since she kept herself planted on the hood while the truck lurched to a halt. It was like a buffalo hunter out of old stories, always leaping off their horses to kill the beast with one piercing blow to the brain.

The moment the truck settled, the Virago jumped up on the truck's roof. Thaddeus threw his door open and pulled himself halfway up onto the roof when a red leather boot came flying at him. He moved his head out of the way, let go of the truck and pushed off as he grabbed the retreating leg with both hands. The woman landed heavily on the roof with one leg, then tumbled down on top of Thaddeus as he hit the pavement.

It was no harder than falling off a running horse and he'd done that enough. A big breath out before and a big breath in after the moment of impact. Thaddeus sat up and heaved the woman-in-red's leg over his right shoulder, reaching with his left hand for her waist. She was wearing a red silk coat and she pulled some kind of knife from it. As it started to swing, Thaddeus grabbed her hand—half the size of his own—and began squeezing like he wanted to break her fingers.

Rolling, the Virago threw her free leg over his head. She was going to get her leg around his neck and, sitting on the ground, he was going to lose a lot of control if she succeeded. He released her and punched her as solidly as he could in the back. The blow sent her tumbling off of him. This woman had perhaps a third of Thaddeus' mass, but she knew what she was doing. He had seen well-trained, hundred-pound, Apache soldiers take down much larger, amateur, Mexican militiamen. So, he wasn't overly surprised by how fair this fight was turning out to be.

Thaddeus hauled himself up and popped the latch on his

hand-axe. The Virago had recovered herself into a wide, low stance, brandishing that knife. It had a diamond-shaped blade, which was new to him. His driver was nowhere in sight. Not that Thaddeus wanted him complicating the fight, but the guy could use that phone to tell someone what was going on.

Thaddeus feinted a lunge, but the Virago didn't react. That told him nothing, not even which foot her weight was on. He wound up for a swing with the axe, trying to draw her eyes upwards. As he swung, aiming for her knife, he whipped his back leg forward to kick her knee. The Virago leapt straight up, spun, and kicked at him with her back foot. Thaddeus smacked it away with the top of his axe and she landed solidly on her front foot. She immediately unleashed a series of punches in time with retreating steps. It gave her a gap and prevented him from closing it. If he could get her in a bear hug, this would be over, though he imagined she could still headbutt with the best of them.

Thaddeus decided to try 'buffalo fighting'. It was the name Anishinaabe warriors gave to a combat style modeled on the animals. He launched himself at her, arms low like he was going to grab her and creating a false opening in the high part of his guard. He was expecting her to stab, but instead, she jumped to the side, landing one foot on the truck, which she used to propel herself upwards.

Seeing her rise up like that, Thaddeus indeed felt like a buffalo; one that was about to get axed in the neck. He had planned to catch a swing from above, though; it was going to be higher than he'd anticipated, but the tactic was the same. Thaddeus straightened his body and sprang up to his full height. The Virago flipped from the truck, bringing one of her heels down at him like a hammer. He again grabbed her leg, this time using the arc of her momentum coming off the truck to try and swing her down onto the sidewalk. His fingers wrapped around her right calf and her left foot stomped down on his fingers. Then, her left knee bent and plowed him in the forehead.

Thaddeus threw his arms out to catch himself as the sidewalk rushed up to meet him. He felt her scramble off him just before his hands met pavement. His arms absorbed the fall, then pushed his body up and he tucked in his legs to stand back up fast and spinning. Eyes back on the truck, the Virago had her hands on the top of the cargo rails, pulling herself lightly up onto the racks.

He tried to follow her, climbing up the side, but as soon as his eyes rose above the edge, he saw her on the opposite side, dropping her match. Thaddeus let go as the fire went up and he landed on the street, running around to the other side and finding nothing. He quickly retreated a few paces from the truck, getting himself in the open; away from anything she could jump off to attack him again.

Fire is a noisy thing. In winter campaigns, a campfire was an ambusher's best friend. If you stepped lightly, they wouldn't hear you, and the light made them blind until you were already on them. Thaddeus closed the eye nearest the fire and tuned his ears, trying to cut through the crackle of the fire to hear footsteps or the rustling of fabric. Instead, he heard her voice: "I am inv—"

The words swirled his head and Thaddeus felt them like poison in a cut. He let out a battle cry to block it out and the swirling dispersed. Casting his eyes about, he caught sight of her climbing up a drainpipe like it was a ladder. In a flash of red in the firelight, she swung up onto the roof of a nearby building.

He tried to give chase, but the drainpipe wouldn't hold him and the structures of the city were too unfamiliar. By the time he figured out a way to get up on the roof, using a fire escape around the back of the building, the Virago was gone. The residents were flooding the street by then.

Thaddeus stood on the roof and looked down. There was no way she could have jumped from here. The only place she could have been was the streetlight, and while he believed she could have climbed it, he couldn't imagine how she did it without someone seeing. Inside the truck, he certainly would have seen her do it. That meant she had been waiting for them, which meant she knew they had been coming. Whoever this woman was, she knew their schedule.

Saint Moon had a spy in it.

Chapter 22:
A Strapping Pirate

August 12th, 1921. Silkhaven.

Stretched out on a living room couch, Vivienne heard the bell of the elevator, but did not entirely wake up. She knew, in her half-slumber, that Rebecca was leaving. She decided it was not important enough to wake up for and let herself fall back into the darkness.

When she finally did get up—morning light streaming through the penthouse's two-story windows—she thanked herself for staying still and quiet. Her next conversation with Rebecca was going to be a fight. All that anger Rebecca had held back in the car was going to stew, not evaporate. Vivienne could not understand it. It had been an emergency and Rebecca liked Cranston. Really, her anger was entirely misplaced.

Setting the whole thing to the back of her mind, Vivienne went to take a bath. It was a long bath, filled with conjured images of a strapping pirate who was either rescuing her or kidnapping her; she could not decide which. Either way, she ended up in his quarters and he was so very rough with her. Afterwards, she felt much more focused and, importantly, herself.

Once dressed, she checked on Cranston, who was still asleep, and then ordered a breakfast she could eat with her hands to avoid clinking. The kitchen sent her scrambled eggs with sausage, bell peppers, and black pepper rolled into a flatbread. They included a gravy boat full of a sour fruit sauce. The whole thing was curious, but one needed to let the chefs have their fun. Perhaps it would be the next Waldorf Salad.

Vivienne carried the platter, with its usual carafe of orange juice, down to Father's study. Except it was not Father's anymore. She reminded herself of that. Her parents were gone, truly gone; their ghosts did not linger in every fiber of the room. Most of the room was simply old books and older furniture. There were a few items that still held some emblematic power of them and she decided that, this morning she would find those things and set them aside and prepare the rest for disposal.

There were a pair of maids at work in the grand dining room, keeping the place in good order, should it be needed, which it had not during Vivienne's tenure as lady of the house. Vivienne sent them to find any and all boxes on hand for her parents' effects. With her flatbread-rolled omelette in one hand, Vivienne began surveying the study, item by item, seeing which things still bespoke her parents to her and taking distracted bites.

The few tokens she found went to the desk: Mother's pens. Father's bronze Trojan Horse figure. Their shared cigarette box. In the desk itself, she found several stacks of bound letters. The maids brought in the boxes and helped her find ones suitable to the dimensions of these little treasures. It was at this point that Cranston made his appearance.

"How are you feeling?" Vivienne asked as the maids began arranging the yet unused boxes.

"Rested," he said. "And with a certain clarity."

"Strong?"

"Not especially. It's more like some junk has been cleared away, not a renewed sense of purpose."

"I meant: are you feeling strong?"

"Oh, strong enough, I think."

"Good, start packing up these books." She said, gesturing to the shelves. "Set aside anything you want to keep. The rest, I am sure some library would like to have."

He took one of the larger boxes from the maids and started with the high shelf on the far side of the room. Silently, Vivienne dismissed the maids.

"Have your symptoms subsided?" She asked.

He thought for a moment. "Yes,"

Vivienne herself was shaping wads of newspaper for the bronze horse, before covering them with a square of velvet. "How does it feel?"

He looked over his shoulder and she thought for a moment that he would play with the pronoun, but he seemed to lose interest. "That's difficult to say, really. So much of it is a queer sort of detachment. It is as if you are sitting in the backseat of your own mind." He reached up and pulled down a book, glanced at it quickly, then set it in the box. "You're in the backseat and you are too tired to climb over the seat to take the wheel."

"What about in the first moment?" She asked, closing the box on the horse. She wondered for a moment why she was asking this, but unlike her other unaccustomed behavior of the last week, when she examined this, the answer dropped into her hands. For the first time, Vivienne had seen what the condition did to her brother. It was real, now; a real force in his life. There was a part of her that wanted to experience it for herself, just so they would have one more thing to share. "How does it feel when you are looking at the pocket?"

Cranston set another book in the box, then turned around. He took a step to stand behind Mother's old, high-backed reading chair. Resting his elbows on the top, he looked at the floor near her. "Fear," he said. "Strong and pure. It's like no fear you've ever known. It has no object. You aren't afraid of anything; it's just the emotion. When I say it, it doesn't sound as bad as it is; but I have learned that directing fear softens it. Because you aren't afraid of the pocket. You do not imagine that it will hurt you, nor do you wish to run away from it. Indeed, it's rather difficult to run. For some reason, it is enchanting.

"When you are afraid of something, you can run from it or attack it. But when there is no object, nothing to be afraid of, and yet you are afraid, there is..." he took a breath. "...a hopelessness. It is inescapable or it convinces you of such. Yes...yes, I suppose that's it. And the fear is the only thing you can feel. It is your only thought while also being a kind of absence of thought. It is a mental emptiness. And the mind rebels. In the face of that, your mind tries to create an object. It dreams up things inside that ball for you to fear. I guess, for some, the emptiness is never filled in again."

He pushed himself upright. "That's what it feels like." He nodded, still not looking at her, and returned to the bookshelf.

Vivienne tried to imagine all that. Imagining was not something she did much of and she supposed she was not very good at it. What she imagined did not really scare her. It just reminded her of times she had been afraid in her own life. The last time she had been truly frightened had been in 1916. It was when they had not received a letter from Cranston in two months. Her dread had grown steadily every day until a letter did come, and for a few terrible seconds, she was sure that he was dead. Inside the envelope that she tore open were three letters from Cranston and a note from the War Office. It was a short apology that these letters had been delivered to the wrong address.

Vivienne thought about how it had felt, falling to her knees in the living room and clutching the letters to her chest. She remembered the one thing she had wanted in that moment.

As Cranston continued packing books, Vivienne walked up behind him and wrapped her arms around his chest. She pulled her body close to his, resting her head against his neck. He put his hands on her forearms and stood a little straighter.

What she was feeling crystalized in her mind. "We are all the family we have left." She said.

Cranston turned around and pulled his sister into him. "I know."

It felt wonderful being in his arms like that and feeling the soft warmth of his chest. It was entirely different than any other embrace she had experienced. "You need to find a cure." She said.

"Yes,"

"To find your bird woman." She added.

"Yes," he said again.

Vivienne felt like she could fall asleep like this. This was the greatest moment of comfort she had experienced since Cranston had been conscripted. "Fine," she told him. "I will come with you."

"Pardon?"

She released him then. Taking a step back, she smoothed his shirt where her face had been. "As soon as this Saint Moon business is over, we will go find your bird woman *together*." She was not feeling especially forceful just then, but she tried to intone her voice in a way that would brook no argument.

Cranston stared at her like he was formulating said argument, but then his eyes drifted away in surrender. "Alright," he said, looking back at her. "Together." Then, he reached out and took her by the shoulders and planted a kiss on her cheek. "I'll see you later."

"What?" She asked, feeling it was inappropriate for him to leave now. "Where are you going?"

"To finish it." He said, then marched out of the room.

She saw him head back for the living room and, presumably upstairs to change. It occurred to her to follow him, to demand more explanation, but she decided to leave the moment as it was. That promise felt soft, right now, and perhaps if she did follow him, he would take it back while it was still fresh. Best to let it cool—she decided—to let it harden.

Returning to the task at hand, Vivienne began looking through Father's biographies of great explorers and realized that she had no idea what it was she herself had just promised.

Cranston decided that he really ought to visit the Caribbean Confederacy. Odile was lying on a blanket in the Prosecution's courtyard in a pair of sunglasses and a swimming costume that would get her fined on public beaches. Take away a foot of fabric and add rhinestones and the thing would be fit for a showgirl.

His fascination was aided by that dream he had had about the woman who was her but also Pearl. Pushing that out of his mind, he strode out through the doorway into the courtyard. There was a moment of deciding how to position himself. He couldn't stand over her for this conversation; it was too domineering, but he also couldn't sit in the grass wearing these trousers. He was wondering if there was a simpler word than 'déranger' that she would know, but she saved him the trouble by sitting up when she saw him and patting the blanket beside her.

"Hello," he said when he was close enough.

"Bon apremidi." She replied, giving him a smile that he couldn't read with her eyes obscured. It made him self-conscious, as if she knew the dream he had had about her.

"How do you feel?" Cranston asked before sitting. "Comment tu sens-te?"

"Santi? *Feel.*" She repeated. "Good. Ou save me. *Saved.* Ou saved me."

"It would have..." he stopped himself, realizing this was probably too complex a sentence. "It was the gallant thing to do."

"Pa many men saved me." Odile looked away thoughtfully. "Two." She said, finally. "Two men saved me plus ou."

"No surprise. You are a capable woman."

She leaned in a little, still smiling. "I pa t ekri...I no write them... thank you note."

"I am sure you showed your gratitude." He still had the uncomfortable and impossible feeling that she knew about the dream.

"Tonight, I will go out again as the Stalker."

"Bon, I too."

"There is a man named Benjamin Syme; he has information. I need that information."

"We pa return the gypsy la?"

"No," Cranston shook his head. "No good. She is not the Virago."

"I want revenj."

"How? If we return, the same thing happens."

"Se...she get away?"

"In the future, peut être, we can fight her. Today, we pa can fight her."

Odile turned away and Cranston let her ponder. He couldn't imagine that a Corsair of all people did not understand being outgunned. Their ships were famously light on weapons for greater maneuverability and their success over the last century had been down to tactics. They had no tactic to use against Miss Naomi. Then again, it was possible that Odile had spent the hours since their encounter strategizing.

"Wi," she admitted, "in the future."

"Bon. If you want, you can stay. Tu peux rester ici."

"Rest? I pa rest. I come with ou."

"It is dangerous."

Odile guffawed at him, then slapped her knee. "Bon!"

"C'est l'esprit." Cranston said, standing. "Now, I need to talk to a maid."

"M'aide?"

"Uh...femme de ménage...servante."

"Sèvant?"

"Maybe?"

Odile stood as well. "I dress." She gestured at her bare legs, much longer than Cranston had dreamt them.

"All good things, eh?"

"Wi," she patted one of her thighs. "Good."

Chapter 23:
After Hours at the Pink Lady's Slipper

August 12th, 1921. Silkhaven.

On the corner of Beacon St and 3rd Ave, was the Mucha Building. That was a nickname, of course. Despite many efforts, Silkhaven had not yet managed to attract the Czech. The Rothschilds were intent on making him a staple of New York City and had thus far made that city preferable to any other in the Americas.

Silkhaven's 'Mucha Building' had actually been designed by Marcus and Satine Langlois at the St-Amour Architectural Firm. Satine was not an official employee of the company. She had been the city's most feted art nouveau painter back when that had been the fashion. Sadly, her work never got sufficient attention to leave the island before the art world moved on. However, her work with her husband had left marks on the city that were likely to stand for decades to come.

The building at Beacon and 3rd was a three-story affair with faux-Greek columns whose capitals and bases were shaped like the roots and canopy of trees. The stone tree canopy housed a complex structure of gutters that distributed rainfall naturalistically; achieving the goal of drainpipes without the unsightly cataracts of water they produced. The arched windows were adorned with carved, flowering vines. There were several conspicuously flat surfaces where reliefs had once been mounted, but the tenant businesses had asked to have them removed when they became outdated.

On the third floor and roof of the building was the Pink Lady's Slipper café; a favorite among Silkhaven's younger women, according to one of the executive secretaries. Vivienne had insisted on meeting Michael at the café. She could not bear the idea of him turning up at the hotel, clutching a bouquet of flowers and doing his best to look like they were meant for her. The only reason she was indulging in this high school intrigue was the goal of leveraging her friendship with young Gabrielle towards learning something of Saint Moon's clandestine dealings. How she would do that was obscure, but she was old money and old money knew the surprising opportunities that connections can provide.

For Vivienne's part in this façade, she had paid the Pink Lady's Slipper to keep their cook on for the evening and promised that they could host her next birthday party. She was also delivering one of the exclusives she had promised the King Charles Gazette by telling them exactly when and where they could catch her stepping out with the eligible—and much younger—Michael Blake. Of course, with the Pink Lady being on the third floor of its building, their reporter would not see much else until she and Michael departed.

As promised, Michael—tops and tails—was there early. Vivienne was not so indulgent of young love as to let herself be seen waiting for a man to arrive. Being the subject of salacious double-entendres was one thing, but a lady had her dignity.

Her driver—one of Williamson's trainees—parked but did not get out, leaving the honor of Vivienne's door to Michael. The boy fumbled with the latch, looking like he was about to jump out of his skin. It was pitiful. It was the exact reason that Vivienne had preferred older men in her 20's. She unfurled from the car in a black gown with string-thin straps and a square neckline, imported rhinestones sewn into the fabric that flickered in the streetlamp with every swish of the skirt, under a heliotrope silk shawl bearing three black stripes of the same material as the dress. Her blonde hair was done up, pinned, and waxed so tightly it could stop a bullet just so it would all fit under her heliotrope cloche hat.

Michael did not seem to notice, but the reporter hiding across the street would. Too bad that was almost certainly a man. They never knew anything about color.

The boy did offer her his arm, though, and they walked up the exterior stairs to the third floor, where an aproned, negro waiter was waiting to open the door for them. The lavishly floral interior of the café was empty, save for two young women: Gabrielle Blake in a modestly fashionable red evening dress and, presumably, Thursday Johnson in a navy dress cascading with strings of rhinestones held in by a seafoam green sash and matching chemise hiding her décolletage. It was a knee-length dress, as if she expected to go dancing.

Vivienne had been imagining a plucky girl reporter in wide-legged trousers and a fedora with a press ticket in the band. But, of course, Miss Johnson was a society reporter. She had to look the part so well that people did not know they were being interviewed.

Seeing her, Michael immediately disengaged from Vivienne and practically ran to Thursday, tripping over a chair as he went. The lovers embraced, but Thursday's eyes met Vivienne's for a little longer than seemed appropriate for the moment.

"All I've thought about was you." Michael was declaring.

"Good," Thursday replied, taking her attention away from Vivienne. "I got us a room at the hotel next door, but we need to go out the back."

"Oh, my, yes," Michael said, sounding like he was salivating.

"But first, I need to give Miss Walker something. Wait a moment." Thursday picked up a large, leather bag from the floor and crossed to Vivienne. "Miss Walker," she extended a hand. "It's a pleasure."

"Likewise," they shook.

Thursday reached into the bag and produced a large, folded envelope. "I think you should read this. My editor refused to run it," her voice dropped to a whisper. "But you should know who you're in business with."

Vivienne took the envelope and peeked inside. There were several sheets of typewritten paper; thin, cheap, almost brown pulp.

"Alright," Vivienne said.

"Thank you. My card is inside." Thursday then called over her shoulder. "Come along, Michael." She made for the kitchen at a leisurely stroll and Michael chased spaniel-like after her.

Vivienne joined Gabrielle at their lonesome table and the waiter followed with a menu. He stood back and waited for a signal that they were ready to order.

"Good evening," Vivienne said.

"Good evening," Gabrielle replied with a furtive glance at the waiter.

"What is wrong, dear?" Vivienne asked.

"Can we talk?" She replied softly with a quick glance at the waiter.

"Of course," she turned in her chair. "What is your name, please?"

"Moses, ma'am," the waiter replied, giving a small bow with his hands folded in front of him.

"You are not a rat, are you, Moses?"

"No, ma'am, no room for a tail in these trousers."

Vivienne turned back to Gabrielle. "There you are. What is the matter?"

Looking unconvinced, Gabrielle spoke quietly. "I don't like the way Thursday talks to Michael."

"Oh," Vivienne laughed. "Better men than your brother pay good money to be spoken to that way. It does make me wonder who her people are, though. They do not teach you how to do that in college."

"What is that she gave you?" Gabrielle said, changing the subject.

"It appears to be an article she wrote, but I did not get the feeling that it will make salacious reading, so it can wait." She got out her cigarettes only to find that her lighter was empty. Moses was at her elbow in a minute with a flame. "You are a man who knows his trade." She said before getting her cigarette going.

"Thank you, ma'am."

"Do you know what you want?" She asked Gabrielle.

"A green tea," Gabrielle told Moses. "And a sandwich, ham with Swiss."

"Have you ever had that toasted?" Vivienne asked.

"A toast sandwich?"

Vivienne grinned, then turned to Moses. "A green tea for her and peppermint for me. Four ham sandwiches with double Swiss cheese toasted in butter, please."

"We can do those in *pain doré*, if you like, with vanilla and powdered sugar."

"Decadent! I love it. Yes, please."

"I'll be right back." Moses said and disappeared into the kitchen.

"Pandora?"

"*Pain d'oré*, golden bread. It is wonderful for everything but your figure. Now," Vivienne turned in her chair to lean in conspiratorially. If she was going to indulge in this sort of intrigue, she might as well act like a twenty-year-old. "What sort of sister are you? Arranging trysts for your brother?"

Gabrielle sighed. "He has been positively despondent ever since Mother caught him with Thursday. She is furious about the whole thing;

Mother, that is. At first, I thought they only needed to patch things up together. Michael loves Mother dearly, of course, but when I talked to him about it, he could only speak of Thursday and how he feared he would never see her again. Really, I've never seen him in that state before. And twins being twins, you know, it hurt me, nay, wounded me to see him so.

"Mind you, there were girls in Hong Kong and more than one of whom Mother did not approve of, and Michael dropped them instantly. It's no help at all that she is white. Mother is determined to see Michael with an Oriental girl from a good family. Why, she'd rather see him with a Korean than a European duchess. She might deign to let him court a princess, but I suspect, even then, she would want to know how far down the line of succession she was.

"The only reason she agreed to let him dine with you is for the good of the business and that she is confident the two of you would never wed. She imagines that you are pandering to us *children*, showing us the sights as it were, as a way of ingratiating yourself to Father; which she regards as shrewd. If she thought you had real intentions on Michael, she would be paying you a visit to discourage you in no uncertain terms. Not as vehemently as she did with Thursday, of course, but I think she would be willing to sacrifice your contract with the company to ensure that Michael had a suitable wife."

"One moment," Vivienne held up a hand to interrupt. "What did she say to Thursday?"

"Not so much 'say.'" Gabrielle continued as the tea arrived.

"I'm sorry, ma'am." Moses said to Gabrielle. "I just wanted to let you know that those sandwiches will be along in just a few minutes. Chef Antoine is particular about his batter."

"As well he should be," Vivienne said with a reassuring smile. "Thank you," she dismissed him, then to Gabrielle: "Go on."

"I really shouldn't be telling you this, but Mother is very old-fashioned and that's in the way of the east, mind you." Gabrielle sighed the way one does about embarrassing relatives. "It will be no surprise to you that she has gotten in contact with some ladies in Little Beijing; she did so almost as soon as we had gotten off the boat. But I'm sure you understand how important connections are.

"Anyway, she talked to someone down there and hired a couple of toughs to go 'talk' with Thursday. They weren't supposed to hurt her or anything, just make a little mess so that she understood how out of bounds Michael was. Her leg was not part of Mother's plan, though it doesn't seem to be bothering her now, so it couldn't have been so terrible.

"You can imagine, I'm sure, that Thursday was not happy to see me yesterday. It took a great deal of explaining about Mother's intent and apologizing for her leg. I even promised to reimburse her for her hospital visit as soon as she gives me a receipt. Which, I understand, may seem tactless, but one must always temper kindness with wisdom. Admittedly, it will take a little doing to get that money, but I'm sure I can manage it. Father has always been very generous with me, and while I have no intention of telling him what the money is for, I am certain that if he knew, he would agree that it needs to be paid."

"Your mother hired men to ransack Thursday's apartment?" Vivienne asked when Gabrielle took a breath.

"Yes. Like I said, she's old-fashioned. I'm sure your parents would have done the same if you'd stepped out with an unsuitable young man."

Vivienne's mind flashed to her own mother's silvery vigilante costume, hung so carefully in the family museum. "I suppose you are right. *But*," she said pointedly, seeing Gabrielle taking in another deep breath to fuel her next speech. "I was trying to ask about your own romantic prospects. I know it has not been very long, but you had such a collection already at the picnic."

"Fresh meat," Gabrielle shrugged with a mild grin. "Blood in the water and the sharks come sniffing." She went silent.

"Oh," Vivienne replied, equally surprised at the pragmatism and brevity of the statement. "So, what is it you like in a man? You were certainly taken with Cranston."

"Ah," she exhaled embarrassment once again. "I really must apologize for that. I was caught up in the romance of the evening more than anything else."

Moses reappeared with two plates of steaming sandwiches, white and aromatic cheese oozing over the crusts and a fine layer of powdered sugar on top. The chef had even included a little dish of strawberry jam.

"Thank you," Vivienne said, eyeing her plate.

"Yes, thank you," Gabrielle said as well.

Moses left a little bell on the table. "I'll be in the kitchen, so you ladies can have your privacy. Just give this a ring and I'll come running."

"Very good of you, thanks," Vivienne said.

As Moses departed, Gabrielle began anew, not yet touching the piping hot sandwich. "I don't know how many novels you read, but I have read so many that involve a young woman going out on the town with a man of means and they are always such spirited adventures. I suppose I was trying to play it all out for myself; with Cranston, I mean. I do hope I didn't cause you any embarrassment."

"Not at all," Vivienne replied. "Cranston was taken aback for certain, but I am sure he comported himself gamely."

They continued talking. Gabrielle expounded on her favorites among the masculine virtues and Vivienne occasionally got a word in edgewise. The sandwiches were an unconditional success and Vivienne left Moses a five-dollar tip. After a couple of hours, Michael returned, floating on a cloud and smelling too clean. Vivienne strongly suggested that he smoke on the way home to cover the scent of the shower he had evidently taken.

Thursday had decided to make her own way home. She was invested in not being seen with either of the Blake twins in public for reasons Vivienne now understood. Michael had a car ready to take him and Gabrielle home. He escorted Vivienne to her own car, where the driver was engrossed enough in his book to startle when Michael opened the door.

And so Vivienne was off with Thursday's article promising some engrossing reading of its own.

Chapter 24:
A Nice, Polite Conversation

August 12th, 1921. Silkhaven.

Of all hotel employees, maids were the least loyal, not least because the work was so often seasonal. Silkhaven had an entire subclass of women who cleaned hotels only six months out of the year, during the four months of summer and two months of Christmas tourism. Eight such women were on an annual salary from the Walker Grand Hotel, passing along scuttlebutt from the competition.

Mrs. Irene Folger was currently employed at the Duke of Northumberland Hotel, affectionately known as the Old North Duke. From her intelligence, Cranston learned that Benjamin Syme along with twenty of his Atlantic Network goons were being put up there. Mr. Syme had a suite, 1103, which Mrs. Folger had cleaned twice. He also learned that Edward Blake was rumored to be looking into buying the place.

Cranston had learned to break into a hotel room in his teens. The first trick was to enter through the front door and go straight to the elevator. Elevators were good because you had to wait for them. It was perfectly natural for a guest to take those idle moments to enjoy the interior of the lobby. This let you familiarize yourself with the ground floor, which was useful when making your escape. If there was an alarm, someone going straight for the front door was suspicious. The smart burglar went to the restaurant and ordered lunch.

If you did not see the elevator as soon as you entered, turn right and keep walking until you found a place where a guest might stop—the bar, the restaurant, the restroom—and take a moment there to collect yourself. On this walk, you might spot the elevator. It was crucial not to deviate course. Sit down and have a drink or a leak, then go to the elevator. Always appear as though you had been there before.

Cranston and Odile entered the Old North Duke wearing the plainest clothes that the Red Widow could find in their sizes. Cranston couldn't remember the last time he had worn a suit that wasn't tailored. It was strange how loose it was, but it was not uncomfortable. Cranston had raided the lost-and-found at one of the docks the Walker Company owned and there found an assortment of long-abandoned luggage. The Stalker and Fortuna costumes were put in a suitcase which Cranston carried, while his sword cane and her cutlass were in the golf bag over his shoulder. Their pistols were in the daintier case that Odile carried.

They closed their umbrellas and Cranston led the way to the elevator and to find one already waiting. This was the trickiest part of the whole scheme. There were only two people likely to rumble you in a hotel: the floor manager and the elevator operator. The trick with elevator operators was to give them as little time to think about you as possible, which meant engaging them in small talk.

"11th floor, please." Cranston told the operator, a particularly dark negro. "Say, I didn't get your name before."

"It's John, sir."

"What do you know, that's my name, too." Cranston replied. If the operator's name had been Abimelech, he would have said the same thing. "Small world, isn't it?"

"Yes, sir."

Cranston grinned, despite the operator not looking at him. "Just a joke, that. So, John, how long have you worked here?"

"Fifteen years, sir."

"How do they treat you?"

"They treat me fine, sir."

"Good to hear. I wouldn't want an elevator operators' strike. Whatever would we do?" Cranston laughed at his own joke.

"There are stairs, sir."

"Of course, just another joke."

He eased the elevator to a halt. "11th floor, sir."

"Thank you," Cranston said and tipped the man a nickel. "Come along, dear." He exited the elevator, keeping his face turned away from the operator.

Bland conversation was less memorable than none at all. If they had been silent, the operator would have had time to reflect on how few people came up to the 11th floor and possibly see through the sham. Answering all of the usual questions once again tended to make someone's mind go blank.

The maid, Mrs. Folger, had shown Cranston her skeleton key for the rooms. It was a Holston, stamped with the company's mark. Cranston had one just like it in his old kit. As a youth, Cranston had loved parties. There were always lots of pretty girls, and the good parties were so busy that it was easy to disappear in one. They were also desperately boring for those new to society. While the adults discussed business, the younger attendees had very little to do, apart from dancing to old music and looking for secluded places to kiss. Learning to break into hotel rooms—which usually meant finding ways to acquire skeleton keys—had given Cranston an advantage in the latter department.

With the old skeleton key, he opened room 1103 as easily as if it were his own room. The Old North Duke was neither among the oldest nor newest hotels in the city. At around forty years old, it was in that awkward position of having no great stories attached to it and no freshness to make it an attraction. Syme's suite was nonetheless spacious, though its decor had not been redone since the turn of the century.

They entered first into a sitting room where winter clothes could be kept and a valet could attend to matters out of the gentleman's sight. One door from the sitting room led into an apparently unused servant's quarters, and the other into a combination dining room and parlor. They located the fire escape in case they needed it. Four more doors led out of the parlor: one to a well-appointed bathroom, a second to the dumbwaiter where the valet could pick up his gentleman's food, a third to the bedroom, and a fourth to a study.

Here, Syme had stacked several boxes of documents; more than they would be able to get through unless Syme was out until morning. Not knowing when he would return, they put on their costumes. Odile—Fortuna—had most of hers on under the white blouse and brown skirt she wore, while Cranston—Stalker—needed the room for a full change. Once dressed, he packed their street clothes into the suitcase. They put on their weapons and Fortuna began wiping the luggage of fingerprints.

While she did that, Stalker found a small pad of paper and wrote four things on it: 'vaccine', 'Edward Blake', 'Della Caine', and 'Neon

Jezebel'. He handed Fortuna the paper. "Look for these in that box." He pointed at one of the boxes of documents. He took up another and they began scanning through the things Syme had brought with him to help identify the Virago. When Cranston found something potentially important, he put it into a satchel they had put into the suitcase under their costumes.

Syme was thorough. The box contained records of various lawsuits and complaints filed against Saint Moon, perhaps looking for old enemies. Further in, Stalker found a folder of Edward Blake's public writings on eugenics, as well as responses that had been published in various newspapers.

Edward insisted that eugenics did not discriminate on the color of one's skin, that fit people could be found in every nation. 'The apparent concentration of fitness among whites,' read one passage that Syme had underlined, 'is due only to environmental conditions that promote the fit to accomplishment while the unfit languish.' The opposing views ran a gamut. Some of his detractors accused him of jingoism for his stance, while others argued that no, the negroes and Indians were by nature feeble-minded. One newspaper clipping had the headline: E. BLAKE WANTS TO SACRIFICE BABES AT THE ALTAR OF SCIENCE. Quickly scanning it, Stalker found it claimed that Edward proposed killing infants with deformities immediately after birth.

The second box he went through contained updated delivery schedules and routes, which Stalker put in the satchel. He was only halfway through this box when he heard voices. Stalker poked his head out into the parlor. Syme, along with at least one other man and a woman, were in the sitting room.

"You look more handsome." Stalker whispered to Fortuna. "I will distract."

She tossed him his mask and picked up her own, tying it over her eyes. Stalker did a quick check on his pistol, though he had no intention of shooting anyone, then picked up his sword cane, just in case Syme did decide to get violent.

He closed the study door silently, then found a chair facing the sitting room door. He positioned himself with his left hand holding his cane upright. It was near the liquor cabinet, and he was tempted to pour himself a glass, but his mask didn't have a mouth hole. So, he just sat in wait. Enough time passed for the waiting to get tedious, but the door did open.

"Good evening, Mr. Syme." Stalker said in his gruff, American accent.

"Who's that?" A woman asked, peering over Syme's shoulder. "It's a vigilante." She said soberly. Then, to someone Stalker couldn't see: "You have your papers?"

"I don't think he's here for you." Benjamin said in his deep and drawling Boston Brahmin accent before strolling into the room.

"Let me deal with this." Said another man, shouldering into the room. It was Governor Farrar. He scowled at Stalker without recognition. "Who are you? What committee are you with?"

"I am the Stalker." He replied, keeping his eyes on Syme. "Saint Lawrence VC."

"Never heard of you. And this is breaking and entering."

"I am conducting a registered investigation, but you know where to file a complaint."

"Alright," Benjamin said, dragging a chair into place so he could sit opposite Stalker. "What's your business?"

"I'm looking for a woman, and you are her last listed employer." Stalker said. "I have reason to believe that she is still in your employ."

Syme nodded. "This sounds like a private conversation."

"Your guests are excused," Stalker replied.

"Excused?" Farrar scoffed.

"It's fine, Harry," Syme said. "I've been expecting this. It's a little theatrical, but I can't say I'm surprised. See the ladies out, if you would."

Farrar bristled a little more, then waved a finger at Stalker. "You'll be punished for this."

Stalker only grunted in reply.

"Harry, please," Benjamin said. "Leave this to me. I wouldn't want policemen getting involved in something delicate if it can be avoided."

"Hmm...That's fair enough," Farrar gave Stalker one last disdainful look. "Come along, ladies." Farrar ushered the women out and shut the door behind him.

Benjamin Syme was in his late-50s, stocky, with narrow eyes and a handlebar mustache. He wore a four-button coat, wingtip collars, and a tie knot that could have used a woman or valet's attention. Still, he looked every bit the Brahmin save the cauliflower ear on his left, a slight rightward curve to his nose, and a wayward pinky that had once been broken and never set right.

It was hard to say if he was still a brawler and no telling how much of his bulk was muscle, but he had clearly seen more than his fair share of tussles.

"That's us alone, then. So, what's the name?" Benjamin asked when he heard the hallway door click.

"Della Caine," Stalker told him.

"Yeah, that's what I thought. It means you're the fellow my niece hired to protect her last year. I heard you were a Praetorian Guard. Very fancy. Not that it mattered in the end, but all's well that ends well, right?"

"Yeah," Stalker nodded. "Congratulations to your brother on his election. I heard it was a landslide."

Syme spread his hands in a shrug. "The Reverend Campbell was foolish, getting himself tied to a kidnapping just months before the vote, but there's no shame in benefiting from someone else's stupidity. Not in my book."

"Hell of a coincidence."

"That's life. You know, I never heard how it all happened. We didn't even know it *had* happened until it was already over."

"Why don't you ask your niece?"

"We aren't on speaking terms. She's got this mad idea that I was involved. That's women, though: always on you for something you had no hand in. One thing I did hear, though, is that Miss Caine got a bullet in the head and then tossed in the river. So maybe you should be inquiring about her whereabouts with Davy Jones."

"I saw her." Stalker said portentously. "After we'd cut our way through the kidnappers."

"I see." Syme grinned, but there was no surprise on his face. "Yes, she's harder to kill than that. Della is one of the most dangerous women I've ever known and I don't mind telling you, I like them dangerous. Wouldn't mind stepping out with one of your kind, rather than...uh..." He gestured at the shut door behind him. "Well, what I got."

"So where is she now?"

"Why do you care?"

"Because I saw her."

"She is a sight to behold. You want to strap her to a table? Cut her open?"

"No. Sincerely, I think she might be able to further research into a treatment for EDAD." Stalker said. Without vivisection." He added.

"Hmmm...you got honest eyes." Syme said in a non-committal tone. "You seen a lot of that ailment? 'Over there'?"

"More than enough."

"Mmm, yes, when I heard Rosamund got herself a pair of real soldiers guarding her, I expected better. Disappointing performance, letting her get taken. But that's par for the course with Praetorians, is it not? I have friends at the War Department. None of them were impressed by your performance, either."

"It wasn't us that made the promises." Stalker said, then kicked himself. He was letting Syme bait him. "So," he interjected before Syme could continue. "Where is Della Caine?"

"Sincerely," Syme said, leaning back in his chair. "I have no idea. The last time I talked to her, I told her to get on a boat and report to our London office. She never got on the boat, and no one in London has heard from her."

"I thought finding people is what you did."

"I also train my people in not getting found. Della knows how to stay out of sight. Where she is, what she's plotting; I don't know."

"You think she's plotting something."

"Oh yes, that's the kind of woman she is. After her accident, I offered her work behind closed doors, but she's gotta be out there, in the world, getting her hands dirty."

"In a secure hospital?"

Syme barked a quiet laugh. "You really don't know much, do you?"

"Enlighten me."

Syme shook his head. "I don't think I will. Then again, they say a Praetorian can get answers out of anybody. I heard stories from some Germans about it, that hypnosis thing you do. I wouldn't mind seeing it in action."

"The Voice is for the enemy," Stalker said, shifting a little into Cranston's accent.

"Yeah, I heard that, too."

"There isn't much you haven't heard."

"*Crazy Blues,*" Syme replied. "Now, you don't have much time here left. I don't know how long it's going to take Harry to tell my boys downstairs about you, but when he does, they'll come running. So, if you want to leave here with more than nothing," Syme leaned forward, elbows on knees; eyes alight with excitement. "You better show me how that voice of yours works."

It was more than his usual reticence that made Stalker hesitate. This wasn't the first time someone had asked him to use it on them, either, but those circumstances could not have been more different. What was Syme trying to get? Maybe it was something to talk about at a dinner party. Maybe he wanted to learn how to counter it. And maybe he thought he didn't need to, that he had a will too strong.

"Every day, they made us recite that," Stalker began. "The Voice is for the enemy." He was speaking in that tone one used at the beginning of a story. "There was a lot of distrust among the other units. They worried about how the brass might use us to order them over the top or keep them charging when the battle had already been lost." He took a deep breath and arranged the muscles in his neck as Syme's attention hung on his every word. "<u>Where is Della Caine?</u>" He asked in the Voice with its uncanny doubling effect.

Syme's eyes went glassy. "I don't know. I told her to go to London, but she didn't get on the boat and no one in London has heard from her." His voice was flat, like a student reading Plato aloud.

"When did you speak to her?"

"Last year, end of September."

That was after Cranston had watched her sail away. "<u>What was she doing in the hospital?</u>"

"It was for show, only on paper."

"What was she doing in 1919?"

"Looking for a cure."

"<u>Where?</u>" That was five questions. Stalker wanted to get at least to seven.

"Lots of places. She thought Nikola Tesla could help her."

"Did he?" Six.

"Not yet."

"Where would you look for her?" That was seven.

"Wherever Tesla is."

The hallway door opened.

One more for good measure. "You owe Rosamund the truth. She is a practical woman. She will understand."

"She's a daughter of the House of Whispers." Syme said.

Stalker was taken aback by that, but he didn't have time to ponder what it meant. He jumped to his feet and popped his cane under one arm. "Fortuna! Allons-y!"

That use of his true voice—albeit in an affected accent—broke the spell on Benjamin Syme, who keeled over and nearly fell from his chair, catching himself weakly with one hand on his knee. He dry heaved once. There was a loud knocking.

"Mr. Syme?" A voice bellowed. "Are you alright?"

Syme heaved again and groaned.

"Mr. Syme?" The voice called again, as Stalker watched the study door, wondering what was keeping Fortuna.

"Interesting," Syme muttered, recovering himself. "Thank you for indulging me." Then he shouted: "Allegro!"

Two doors opened at once: the study and the sitting room. A man in a brown suit threw the sitting room door open and took two steps in before drawing a pistol and training it on Stalker. A second man, in a grey suit, moved quickly past him on his right side, heading for either Stalker or Syme. Meanwhile, Fortuna came running out of the study with the satchel thrown over one shoulder and her cutlass raised. The man in grey caught sight of her, turned his head and, seeing the sword, changed his footing so that he could back quickly away. This sent him through the first man's line of fire.

The man in brown reflexively raised his gun just before seeing Fortuna himself. He wheeled to aim at her, but her sword was already coming down on his gun arm. Stalker surged forward, leaping onto the arm of Syme's chair and vaulting over the back of it. Fortuna's cutlass sliced into the man-in-brown's forearm and slid across the bone. He fired into the wall.

Stalker collided, knees first, into the man-in-grey's chest, knocking him to the floor as the goon was drawing his pistol. When the man-in-grey's back hit the floor, the shock sent his pistol spinning across the floor. Stalker somersaulted into a four-point stance, dropping his cane to the ground; the clatter hardly registering in the wake of the gunshot. He turned on one knee to face the henchman.

The man-in-brown grabbed his cut arm protectively and ran forward into the room, turning so that he could shoot at Fortuna from his protective posture. Fortuna made a long lunge at the man-in-brown and dodging it sent him backwards over Syme's chair. At the same time, the man-in-grey rolled towards Stalker, left hand outreached to grab him. Stalker took up his cane with his own left and jabbed it like a pool cue at the man in grey's face.

Fortuna, seeing the man-in-brown go over the chair, dove to the floor to use the chair as cover. The man-in-grey slapped the cane down, even as Stalker's hand tightened around its base and the vigilante's knuckles hit the floor smarting. The man-in-brown stood and fired again at nothing. Fortuna stabbed upwards at his gun hand. Using his left hand as a pivot, Stalker scrambled widdershins around the floor. The man-in-grey rolled himself onto his back. Stalker raised his right knee and brought it down on the man-in-grey's left thigh. He bellowed.

The man-in-brown screamed as the cutlass bit into his finger bones and he dropped his pistol. Stalker knelt on the man-in-grey's leg and raised his cane, grabbing it with both hands and driving it towards his man's face. Fortuna kicked the pistol in mid-air as the man-in-grey caught the pommel of the cane with both palms stacked and deflected it over his shoulder. The man-in-brown ran for the bedroom. Stalker tilted the cane down to bash the man-in-grey's face, but hit the floor instead. Fortuna let her man go and turned to Stalker, jumping to her feet. The man-in-grey heaved himself up and threw Stalker onto the floor.

Fortuna saw the second goon rise up and she extended her sword arm so that her cutlass' point was even with his face. Stalker slid and his head bumped into the man-in-brown's pistol and he saw Syme get to his feet. A meaty hand wrapped around Fortuna's arm.

"Koulye a, se yon batay reyèl!" Fortuna yelled and stomped on Syme's left foot before whipping her boot up to kick his right shin.

Syme grunted and started to buckle, but did not release her. The man-in-grey cast about for his gun. Stalker kicked up onto his feet while drawing the sword from his cane. Syme dropped to one knee, pulling Fortuna's arm down with him. The man-in-grey crouched to pick up his gun. Fortuna yanked her arm away from Syme's body, but against his fingers, not breaking his grip but unbalancing him. Stalker lunged at the man-in-grey's shoulder with his rapier, the cane low. Syme's other knee hit the floor and he clasped both hands to Fortuna's arm. The man-in-grey barely got his fingers on the gun before he was throwing up his right arm to block the stab. Fortuna kneed Syme in the chest, sending him toppling backwards. Stalker kept his rapier high and cut through the man-in-grey's sleeve with the cane, drawing a little blood. Still, those fingers closed on the gun.

Fortuna, free of Syme's grasp, swung her sword towards the man-in-grey. Stalker withdrew the cane and saw two more men running into the sitting room, guns drawn. The man-in-grey's pistol clanged as it hit the flat of the cutlass. Stalker ran forward, sheathing his sword, and kneed the man-in-grey in the face. Fortuna pulled her sword back as she saw the newcomers. The man-in-grey went down and Stalker landed behind him, rolling up to his feet as Fortuna did a backflip to land behind Syme's chair.

Stalker drew his pistol and fired at the open door to the sitting room. Fortuna bounded over Syme's prone body, heading for the fire escape. Syme grabbed her by the leg and she hit the floor shoulder first. Stalker vaulted and slid across the dining table, landing with both feet on the other side, gun trained on Syme.

"Crossing!" A man called from the sitting room.

Stalker fired at the floor near Syme's head. Benjamin recoiled, releasing Fortuna. A third man ran into the room and fired twice in Stalker's direction. Stalker ducked as Fortuna pushed up onto her side to sheath her cutlass. The third man took cover behind the liquor cabinet. Staying crouched, Stalker began walking back towards the fire escape while Fortuna crawled ahead of him.

"How many?" The fourth man called from the sitting room.

"Don't know." The third replied. "Too dark."

"Two." Syme replied as he hauled himself behind the chair Stalker had occupied.

"Lights?" The fourth man asked.

"By the door." Syme told him.

Fortuna pushed the window halfway open, letting in some of the rain that was drizzling away outside. Stalker fired at a spot he was sure was empty. He had six rounds left. Fortuna slid on her belly over the window ledge, then stood, back to the wall. The lights in the whole room came on, and the third man poked his head out, seeing nothing.

"Window," the third man yelled. "My twelve."

The fourth man broke cover, gun ready. Fortuna carefully opened the window further without exposing herself while Stalker hid behind the table.

"You okay, Mr. Syme?" The fourth man called from the foot of the dining table.

"Good enough," Syme replied.

"Here," the fourth man kicked the man-in-grey's pistol towards the boss.

There was another window to Fortuna's left. "Stalker," she whispered. "Ready." Her own guns drawn, she bent and fired four shots wildly through the left-hand window. Syme and his men took cover, and Stalker leaped out onto the fire escape.

"I save ou!" She shouted as they ran down the clanking stairs.

Chapter 25:
Escape the Old North Duke

Very few countries executed women, even for piracy. Any time the tide turned on a prize, it was extremely dangerous to help a comrade escape the men retaking their ship. Sometimes, it was worth it, as your own ship needed as many hands as possible; but that was why raiders had no essential tasks aboard. Those first men could be lost and the rest make a getaway.

The corsairs frequently traded prisoners for work. A handful of men get captured by Spain, the Caribbean negotiated their release in return for taking a Dutch ship. It didn't always work, but corsairs were trained to be model prisoners for this very reason; the women more so. If the crew was evacuating a ship that wasn't sinking, the women were the first to be left behind; especially if they were officers. Fortuna herself had been imprisoned three separate times.

That moment when Stalker had lifted Fortuna off the fortune teller's floor had felt, to her, the way land-women felt being showered by roses or having a song written for them. A man who would do that was a man you kept close and nothing kept a man close like proving you were willing to return the favor.

The fire escape was narrow as a gangway with landings, just wide enough to accommodate a body, circling around to the next flight of stairs. When they got to the first landing, Fortuna squinted up against the light rain to see a tight lattice of thin beams making up the landing. You couldn't shoot through that, not without a serious risk of ricochet.

That meant every level they put between themselves at the men in the hotel room, the safer they were.

On the third landing down, Stalker halted. Fortuna stopped and immediately heard the iron fire escape still ringing out under footfalls. Two men were coming up the fire escape to box them in. Fortuna looked over the side and caught a glimpse of something two landings beneath them. Stalker began trying to open the nearest window.

The poor land-man had his head on the ground. Everything was side to side with land-people. Sailors—especially those who cut their teeth on the old, three-masted ships—they thought up and down, as well. Fortuna listened for the men below as Stalker failed to open the window and began planning how to break the glass. She holstered her pistols and drew her knife, which she stuck in her teeth. With both hands gripping the outer railing, she listened.

There were footsteps above them, but very cautious and quiet. The ones below were in a hurry. The stairs rang differently than the landings. When she heard the first of them reach the landing directly below, Fortuna vaulted over the railing. She'd never done this without ropes, but the math was all the same. She twisted in mid air, reversing her grip on the railing so that she was falling straight down. Then, she let go for just a moment, the railing flew away and then she grabbed the supporting I-beam of the landing she had just left.

Feet swinging up, her fingers caught the support and shifted her trajectory, her gloves providing sufficient friction against the wet metal. Fortuna kicked a man in a black suit with both feet and he went over the inner railing, hit his head on the ascending stairs, then fell onto his partner coming up the descending stairs. The two men clattered and clanged down a few more steps and then were silent. Hot damn, she felt alive!

Stalker raced down a few steps and then leapt over the inner railing to land next to her.

"Allons-y!" She said, the long absent elation of victory coursing through her veins.

They both hopped the inner railing onto the stairs, then again to the lower landing, avoiding the unmoving bodies of the men that had tried to trap them. Then, they were running down towards the final landing and a ladder that their would-be trappers had already pulled to the ground.

When they got to the ground, Fortuna started for where she

remembered the car being.

"No," Stalker said, grabbing her wrist. "This way."

Running again, they were headed towards the rear of the hotel. Fortuna stayed a few steps behind Stalker, not knowing when he would stop. Part of her mind was expecting to hear gunfire behind them; the men from the hotel trying to snipe them, but they never came. Stalker led her out onto the opposing street. There were little shops and restaurants here, all darkened for the night. Without stopping, Stalker ran into the street just as a car rounded the corner and screeched to a halt in front of him. Instead of stopping, Stalker jumped and slid across the car's rain slick hood, then continued running for the opposite block.

With a whoop of thrilled delight, Fortuna followed suit, even as the driver shouted at them from behind the windshield. Running felt good, not as good as fighting more of those andouilles back there, but she would take it. So, it was somewhat disappointing to see Stalker opening a door. He was in an alley, using another one of his keys to open the back door to one of the shops. Red Widow had said he was from an important family, but did this man have keys to everything?

He waved her inside and she went, running right into total darkness and stopping as quickly as she could. Stalker followed, slamming the door behind him and throwing a bolt closed. A moment later, he turned a light on.

They were in a store room. The walls were covered in shelves and crates were piled around in a semblance of organization. It was not tidy, but it had the look of a place where a certain man could find anything quickly.

Kote nou ye? She thought. "What is here?" She said.

"The back room of a pharmacy." Stalker explained. "Le propriétaire est parti pour la nuit."

She understood 'pwopriyetè' and 'nwit'. It was sweet, him using French like she understood it better than English. To a point, she did. The main words were pretty similar to what they spoke back home, but all the little extra words that connected things were all different. English was the same story, though. On the sea, they used a form of English with none of the connecting words. You just had to look around at the situation and figure things out without the connectors.

(One day in the future, someone would teach her the words 'creole' and 'pidgin'.)

Looking around at her current situation, they were laying low until the storm passed. "More thieving us?" She said in her pidgin English.

"Not at all," Stalker said, pulling off his mask and becoming Cranston again. He tapped on a crate stamped with the words 'Walker Drug Stores'. "My name's on the sign."

"Ou place?"

He raised a flat hand and wiggled it. "Close enough." He replied.

"Now what?" She asked; a very common question from the English-speaking captains of boarded ships.

"Attendons." He said, then leaned against the wall.

Both of them were still catching their breaths. Odile took off her own mask and put the satchel on the floor. She still had some fight in her and she looked for signs of it in Cranston's face. When you get out of a fight, there's often a tiredness that sets into the face; but Cranston still had a hawkish awareness in his face, the look of a man who is ready for an attack to come. That was good enough for her.

Odile marched up to him. He straightened as he saw her coming and she grabbed him by the shirt and pulled him into a deep kiss. Her mouth was hungry, her body needed to be active, and he had refused to leave her behind. Cranston's arms wrapped around her, pulling her tight into him. It wasn't close enough.

She pushed her arms up and around his neck. They were nearly the same height, but she still pulled herself up off her feet, getting her legs around his waist and forcing him to turn his neck up to keep kissing her. Cranston responded by grasping her bottom with both hands. He spun her around and slammed her body against the wall. It knocked the wind out of her for a second. It felt like the fight she was spoiling for and she loved it.

Odile threw her head up to breath and Cranston took that as an invitation to start ravenously kissing the parts of her breasts that were exposed by her bodysuit. His mouth sucked on her and he raked his teeth across her skin. He was hungry, too; hungry for her body and she wanted to be hungered for. She wanted him pacing around that big house of his thinking about her body and feeling like he might go mad if he couldn't get his lusting hands on her.

Feeling that hunger as he licked and nibbled the insides of her breasts, Odile dug her fingers into his hair—which was strangely soft... like a puppy—and pushed his face even deeper into the cleft. She humped her cunt against his chest. She was sucking in hard breaths through clenched teeth and thinking she wanted him to suffocate in her flesh. What a lucky man to die that way! But she didn't want him dead, she just wanted him dying.

The weight of his body was pressing her against the unyielding wall and if he pressed a little harder, she would have trouble breathing. Odile let herself moan at that thought. The two them killing each other in a fit a carnal passion. Her hips were going like she was running and she crested what she thought of as the crystalizing wave.

This was how sex was for her. Once she was excited, she went into a frenzy and that frenzy brought her to a little orgasm. Not satisfactory, by any means, if anything it made her even more needy; but it had the effect of focusing her and she knew with crystal clarity how she wanted it. Usually, she wanted to be taken, hard and animalistic. But as her body tightened around Cranston and her throat growled, she knew it was the opposite this time.

Odile fell down the little wave, feeling she needed that second orgasm more than she needed air. "Down," she said, pushing Cranston back. He disengaged and set her down on wobbling legs. Then just stood there. "Down." She repeated.

"Ah," he said and laid himself on the floor.

She doffed her coat and reached between her legs to undo the buttons that closed the legs of her bodysuit. Odile had sewn the garment herself with ease of toilet use in mind. It had taken her a few tries to get the button placement right. Once unbuttoned, she pulled off her briefs and shimmied them down over her boots. With Cranston on the ground, Odile walked to his head and knelt down so that she was facing his feet.

The man knew what to do next. Cranston's lips began kissing deeply into Odile's bush until they laid her oyster bare and he attempted to suck the meat off the shell. Odile's hips were moving almost of their own accord in little circles across his face, but she wanted more. Even when he found the pearl, she wasn't satisfied.

Odile pulled the shoulders of her bodysuit down her arms. She grabbed Cranston's hands and brought them up to her breasts. He kept his grasp low, squeezing the undersides and obviously avoiding the nipples. Grabbing a nearby shelf, Odile steadied herself and continued to rub her cunt across his mouth, lips and tongue doing an admirable job of keeping up.

Oh and she was gushing now. She hadn't been this wet on dry land in over a year. With every exhale, she moaned, even yipped as

Cranston gently bit her throbbing labia. That second, larger wave was coming and her eyes locked on his cock, still wrapped in his trousers. That's where she wanted to crest, but not yet.

Cranston's fingers closed around her nipples then, sending a blue-white thrill through her. She went stiff for a moment, thrusting her breasts deeper into his hands. He squeezed them whole for a few seconds before grasping the hard points and pinching them tight.

"Wi!" She cried as her brain mistook the pain for pleasure. A fresh cascade erupted from her cunt. It felt like such a deluge that the man really might drown, but he continued consuming her nethers like a man dying of thirst.

His hands cupped her breasts and dug into the soft flesh. The touch itself was not the delight, but the neediness of it; the feeling of a lusting boy finally laying hands on a woman. The want was palpable and it tightened wonderfully in her stomach. Again, he pinched her nipples and she called out, pressing her juicy cunt into his face. She braced a hand on his arm, resting her weight on him, while keeping his hand where it was. He did not let go like before. His fingers kept squeezing her poor, pink nipples until they felt like they would burst.

That was it.

Odile threw Cranston's hands aside and flopped down onto his stomach. She unbutton his suspenders and opened his trousers as she listened to him gasp; whether it was more excitement or a need for air didn't matter, not to her. She just wanted that hard rod in the open air. Cranston lifted his hips so she could push his trousers and trunks down his thighs.

It was a good cock. Straight and thick, if not especially long. Odile pulled herself closer and wrapped her lips around it, tasting the half-dried sweat. The taste itself was awful, but it meant something grand. Her mind connected it with strength and vigor, the taste of a man that acted boldly, worthily. Pushing herself forward, she swallowed as much of it as she could and felt it pulse a little in her mouth. Men absolutely adored that move and she wanted him hard as a rock. A couple swallows like that and he was ready.

Odile crawled down his body and somewhat awkwardly turned herself around. He deserved to see this next part with how well he done so far. She rose up and held his cock up. Her long labia dangled down, practically dripping their juices, and she ran the head of his cock through the folds. Nothing felt better against that skin than hard cock.

Nothing. And she wanted it absolutely drenched.

With her hand soaked along with his rod, she nestled the head right at her opening, then dropped her whole body down on it. The cunny juice made it slide in like a spike being driven into her body. The girth made her feel like she was being split apart. Odile screamed at the ceiling and Cranston groaned beneath her. She just sat there for a moment, breathing fast and loud; the pain invigorating her like cold water. Her hands reached under his shirts and began rubbing his body as her own waited for the pain to dissipate. She wanted him to slap her, but she knew better than to say so their first go around.

Once the sharpness had dulled, Odile began slowly fucking herself on his cock. Gradually she picked up speed until she got to the fun part. Cranston's eyes were locked on her breasts as they quivered with each rise and fall. It entranced men, that view, and it brought a bewildered sort of lust to his eyes. Mouth gaping, eyes wide; oh, men were so beautiful when they were mesmerized.

Odile rode that cock and lust up to her second wave. She bent forward, steadying herself on his chest and choking out howls as the wave washed over her. It was like rings rippled out of her gut and ran along her body expanding with each surge until they threatened to break through her skin. Black spots appeared in her vision and her fingers tightened on Cranston's shirt. Her head fell against him as the orgasm pulsed through her body. She kept grinding her pelvis against him even as the waves grew weaker and weaker.

She could stop, now. That second orgasm was enough, as always, but—as always—she didn't want to. Besides, he hadn't had his yet and returning the favor was how you kept a man close. Once her strength was back, she took a firm grasp on his shirts and rolled him on top of her.

"Fuck," she told him. "Hard." Remembering things French captains often said to her, she growled: "Pute ta! Casse-moi!"

Cranston had that animal look in his eyes. He rose up, still inside her, and pulled his shirts off, then grabbed both of her legs and pressed them together against one of his shoulders, tightening her opening around his thick cock. Using her legs for leverage, he began drilling into her. Teeth bared and breath ragged, he pounded into her with speed and violence. It hurt and her mind went blank as the delicious pain overtook her.

A feeble series of whimpers escaped her as he fucked for all he was worth. She felt like she was melting into the sea as her third wave rose. Then, almost before she knew it, his movements became erratic and he stiffened. She felt the warm jet of him coming inside her and that launched her to the top of the wave. She cried out as she lost the ability to feel anything at all for a brief moment. Then, it crashed and she was scrambling away from him.

"Sispann! Sispann!" She said, pulling away. He let her go and she went limp on the floor, catching her breath. There was a terrible electricity dancing over her skin, like the numbness on your tongue from eating good, spicy food. She couldn't bear to be touched, then. It was incredible.

With every breath, the feeling dissipated until her muscles loosened and she began to feel a kind of spiritual cold. Odile reached out a hand. Cranston, still kneeling by her feet and catching his own breath, took her hand and shuffled over to her. His trousers were still around his calves. He eased himself down behind her and she wrapped his arms around her; needing now to feel as much of his touch as possible.

PART 6
The Victims

Chapter 26:
The Better Detective

August 12th, 1921. Silkhaven.

FIVE INFANTS POISONED
by Thursday Johnson

Eugene Reed. Doris Powell. Vera Miller. Donald White. Howard O'Malley.

These are the names on the latest graves in Notre-Dame-de-Mer cemetery. The oldest was twenty months of age. Few families have not been touched by the death of a newborn, either immediately or through a sister or cousin. Census records estimate that, before the war, approximately ten percent of infants never reached childhood.

These five, however, are extraordinary for the manner of their deaths. They were all treated by the same doctor, who has requested anonymity, and this doctor made note of each because of the unmistakable signs of poisoning witnessed in the babes: very dilated pupils, sanguine diarrhea, and swelling of the mouth and throat, which were the direct cause of death. Most alarmingly, these deaths spanned a mere two weeks, raising concerns of an encroaching epidemic.

Our anonymous doctor gathered all possible

information about the circumstances surrounding
these tragedies. The babes lived in two separate
tenement buildings within a few blocks of each
other. The mothers were all familiar with one
another and saw the pattern in the passing of
their little ones before the good doctor.

The tenements of that neighborhood are home
to dozens of children, from the most vulnerable
infants to heartier schoolchildren. Such signs
of poisoning have never before been witnessed,
according to other residents. One might also
expect such signs to appear, but weaker, in older
children, but no such signs were reported by
residents interviewed. This frustrated the first
theory put forward by our doctor: that some
dust or fungus was responsible. A fungus could
appear rapidly, particularly in the humid summer
weather, and affect many in a short time. However,
the catastrophic effects seen in the babes have
not appeared in others, and, under our doctor's
examination, the neighbor children are in perfect
health.

Our doctor now raised a new certainty: that
something unique to the circumstances of the
infants had led to their poisonings. With the
permissions of the mothers, an inventory of their
homes was taken, so that similarities might be
found. Neighbors also consented to have their
homes examined for information which our
doctor called a "control group".

In the field of medical research, it is known
that false associations might be found if one
merely examines the sick. Peculiarities of region
or profession may be mistaken for symptoms,
misleading doctors and delaying the discovery of
cures. Therefore, modern doctors making a study
employ a group of healthy people from the same
sort as their patients to reveal commonalities that
are unassociated with the malady at issue.

Once the inventories were completed, there were no items only found in the afflicted homes. Here, the investigation may have ceased, but our good doctor had another theory. It was thought possible that two foodstuffs, benign on their own, may become poisonous when mixed. Testing this theory, the inventories were re-examined. After an exhaustive comparison, a possible culprit was revealed.

The tragic homes alone had two certain products in their inventories: Yippity, a near-beer for women, and Saint Moon Milk Fortifier, a powder to be mixed with mother's milk to improve its nutritional properties.

Substances within mother's diet are transferred to baby's milk, hence the general warning against the consumption of alcohol during pregnancy. However, this near-beer contains less than one per cent alcohol, while maintaining the refreshment of its legally fraught counterpart. One can then imagine how a new mother might feel safe consuming it soon after, or even during, pregnancy.

It seems, however, that one of the ingredients of Yippity, when combined with Saint Moon Milk Fortifier, produces a toxin. Our doctor intends to investigate further, but the results of that study are still pending. It is the opinion of this writer that, until the study is released, mothers ought to refrain from drinking Yippity.

Further evidence of this theory is that both products have become available only in the last three months. Both products are made by the Saint Moon company, which has been importing its products to King Charles Island since spring in preparation for the opening of its own factory in Régence.

The two-story windows of the penthouse's living room were

mirrors. The city was asleep, and the light from inside turned those few lights still shining into mere dots that may have reflections.

Vivienne sat in one of the great sofas, staring down at the documents she had gotten at the Pink Lady's Slipper, spread out across the driftwood table which had been in her family as long as her family had been in Silkhaven. Thursday had included transcriptions of her interviews with the mothers, a signed testimonial by the doctor—one Marion Lambrie—and a set of Saint Moon delivery schedules annotated to demonstrate that Yippity was being sold almost exclusively in shops that also carried their milk fortifier.

There was also a copy of the Winter 1917 issue of the New York Eugenicist newsletter. It included an editorial written by Edward Blake, and Thursday had circled three passages. In one, he advocated for the "humanitarian quieting of the lives" of babies "at the earliest detection of deformity"; the second was a passage where he included "women of the night" among a list of persons "whose hopeless condition intolerably burdens the progress of the human race"; and lastly, this sentence: "It is therefore the duty of all men to act, as much as it is within their power, for the betterment of our race, even by methods that the present would rail against, knowing that the future will praise them for doing so."

Vivienne seethed. Nothing about Edward Blake's philosophy was new to her, not least the intensity of his adherence to it. The man took every opportunity to evangelize for his diabolical ideas. Ideas which he was carefully theoretical about at dinner parties. He was trying to win hearts and minds, not rally anyone to action. Rich men with horrifying theories were nothing shocking to Vivienne. Her father's peers had plenty of ideas about women that she had long ago learned to disregard only because they were nothing more than theory. Those men's own daughters rebelled against them, often with little to no recourse from their fathers: Lee Roosevelt, Elsie Whelen, Gertrude Whitney, and so on.

It was endearing, even, to hear 'Uncle' Theodore or 'Old' Cornelius complain about the state of the fairer sex, but only because the women knew full well that the men would do nothing about it. (Theodore had long been a supporter of women's suffrage to vote, though not to smoke.) Blake, it seemed, was a different animal. To think that those of good stock ought to marry and produce children with others of good stock was so common and ancient an idea that it did not warrant a name. But 'eugenics'—contriving a scheme to destroy the lineages of the "unfit", especially in such a way as it appeared accidental—was monstrous.

It was exactly what the Rose & Chain had feared Blake was up to. Until now, it had been only a suspicion. The reality was like cold water in her face.

Legs curled up on the couch, Vivienne contemplated opening a second bottle of wine and auditioned her own responses. She could confront Edward directly with fire and brimstone or she could more femininely discuss things with Mrs Blake, who could by no means be in support of this operation. Then again, she might go and burn the factory down herself. In reality, she would do nothing, of course, save to pass this intelligence to Cabot and let the society mete out its justice.

As hot as she burned, she had her responsibilities and there were plenty of other people whose responsibility this was. Vivienne did not confront partners about their business dealings. There were lesser account men and a battalion of lawyers to do that. You only got to meet with the CEO when you were playing nice; that was part of her mystique and mystique had been crucial to her success. If she went off and did something overt, it could rob her of everything she had earned for herself. Any embarrassment to the company and it would not take too long for the board to vote her and Cranston out and put cousin Martin in her chair.

Yes, she did need another bottle of wine.

That was when Cranston sauntered in. He was dressed like a stevedore, had a satchel over one shoulder, and carried himself so jauntily that she half expected him to burst into song.

"What are you doing still up?" He asked from the entry hall, pulling off a pair of workman's boots.

Vivienne snatched Thursday's article off the table and marched to him. "I am ordering up another bottle of Chateau Margaux. What can I get you?" He had that look on his face when he thought he was in trouble but could not imagine why. Men in general pulled that face so often that it deserved a name.

"Two fingers of the Four Roses, please." He said, minding his manners.

Vivienne stormed up to the small dining room, wrote her order on a card, and sent it down the dumbwaiter. She poured Cranston his drink. "Rocks?" She shouted down to the living room.

"No, thank you!" He called back up.

While she waited, Vivienne wondered how difficult it would be to hire some toughs to break into the Blake home, inflict grievous bodily harm on Edward, then abscond with all the cash in the house. The cash would surely be enough to cover the funeral expenses for those poor children, and, perhaps, death was too good for a eugenicist. Leaving Edward paralyzed or an idiot was far more poetic, was it not?

But that thought brought her to the mothers mentioned. In not one of Thursday's notes had she mentioned a father. No father had been interviewed or referenced, and now that she thought of it, Thursday had never used the word 'family' for them. 'Home', yes, but 'family' no. Nor had she mentioned any mothers by name, to say nothing of their addresses. That was when her mind dropped the second marked passage from Edward's editorial into place.

The women were sex workers. The fathers may be entirely unknown. The fathers may be men like Edward.

Naming the women could have direct consequences, and she assumed, that knowing their addresses would reveal to some what sort of women these were. No one mourned a prostitute, less so her children.

The bottle arrived. Vivienne uncorked it and poured herself a large glass, then padded back down to the living room where Cranston had, evidently, finished the article and was now reviewing the other documents.

"Where do the sex workers live?" Vivienne asked.

"Pardon?"

"Is there a neighborhood with a great many sex workers living in it?"

"A couple," he nodded. "Dockside is where most of the full-time entertainers live, which includes the dancers, the hostesses, and the guides."

"Guides?" Vivienne asked.

"Men come to Silkhaven on business or vacation and they hire a young woman to show them the sights. Legally, they aren't sex workers and...well, it's a complicated arrangement."

Vivienne considered this. "Do you remember Dorothy Plouffe?"

"She wasn't a professional." Cranston shook his head. "She just preferred men from out of town. Anyway, the more traditional prostitutes are in Bellevue, mostly. Even the girls at the St Amour Hotel are put up out there."

"The St Amour? Is it a brothel?"

"Not strictly, but the ladies in the restaurant and bar are all staff."

"How have I not heard this before?"

"It's something of a secret." Cranston shrugged. "Their clientele is overwhelmingly local and the gentry of Silkhaven aim to keep it that way. We wouldn't want the tourists putting us on a waiting list. Why do you ask?"

"These women," Vivienne indicated the article. "I think they are prostitutes."

Cranston scowled at the paper in thought. "That would explain why none of their addresses are given. Where did this come from?"

"The lady herself, Thursday Johnson."

"How did she get it to *you*?"

"Through the Blakes. I pretended to be Michael's date to a private dinner tonight. Thursday was there to spirit him away for a few hours while Gabrielle and I chatted. Before they left, she gave me that, saying I should know who I am doing business with."

"You saw Thursday Johnson with Gabrielle Blake?"

"Briefly, Thursday seemed eager to get Michael to herself. Not as eager as Michael, but that is men for you."

"What the hell happened there?"

"Thursday seduced Michael at the picnic, remember?"

"Yes, and then Mrs Blake sent some toughs to ransack Thursday's apartment as a warning to keep away from her son."

"Oh, yes, Gabrielle mentioned that. Apparently, it is de rigueur in China."

Cranston scowled. "Plausible...but how did Gabrielle get Thursday to go along with her charade? Is she in love with Michael?"

"Among her many possible motives, I believe Thursday saw the opportunity to give this to me."

"Well," he said, looking disappointed. "It seems Miss Johnson is the better detective." He set down the paper, picked up the satchel, and pulled several thick files from inside.

"What is that?"

"Information on Saint Moon gathered by Benjamin Syme." He explained. "I was going to comb through it for clues, but this"—he gestured at Thursday's documents—"is more than I could have hoped for."

"You look disappointed."

"It was not easy to get."

"Why are you not angry?" Vivienne felt her control start to slip.

He looked confused. "This is what we expected, isn't it? That is to say, I *am* angry. I thoroughly disapprove of Edward's conspiracy, here—it's evil incarnate—but I have suspected that for some time. Haven't you?"

"Only in abstraction. That it is real and in action...." She trailed off.

"Ah," he nodded. "In that regard, I am more sad than angry. We had hoped to stop his plan before it could do any damage. We have failed. But I take solace in knowing that it will be easy to foil."

"Poisoning breast milk," Vivienne uttered. "It is inhuman."

"Agreed. We'll take this to Cabot in the morning."

"Tomorrow is Saturday. Do you know where he goes on Saturdays?"

"No, but he'll be at mass on Sunday. From there, the society will decide our next steps."

"Damn the delay."

"I know how you feel."

Vivienne sighed. "I think I have also solved the other mystery, too."

"Which one?"

"The Virago." She pointed at the article. "Miss Johnson seems like a prime suspect."

"Yes," he said, looking deeply unconvinced. "Assuming it's all true."

"What do you mean?"

"As damning as all of this seems, it's easily forged. You only received these documents *after* Mrs Blake had Thursday's apartment ransacked. This doctor, Marion Lambrie, does she exist? Is that truly her signature? These children, are they in fact recent interments and did they die of poisoning? Pearl...Rebecca knew of our suspicions about Saint Moon and she is friends with Miss Johnson. She could have manufactured all of this on a borrowed typewriter this afternoon. Everything in this article must be confirmed before we can move forward."

"You think she made all this up as petty revenge?"

"She's a journalist. They have accused presidential candidates of crimes on this scale simply for belonging to the wrong party. And the things they say about Communists? The devil himself would be scandalized."

That thought was something of a blow. One that threatened to knock the anger out of Vivienne, which, she found, she did not like. She had spent so many hours now being angry about it that to stop being angry felt as if that time had been wasted, all for nought. If Thursday's story was not true, then Vivienne had been foolish and she was not ready to entertain that idea. (There was a comforting note, though, in knowing why she was thinking this way.)

"How did you get these files?" Vivienne indicated the ones from the satchel.

"Breaking and entering."

"Cranston," Vivienne started, but her thoughts collided and got clogged up on the way to her mouth.

"It's the Atlantic Network. They're like the Pinkertons but with fewer scruples, remember? Light burglary is merely playing by their rules."

"Do they have an office in Silkhaven?"

"No, Edward is putting the whole crew up in the Old North Duke, which, alarmingly, I'm told he is attempting to buy."

"He is what?" And the anger was back.

"According to one of the maids we employ there, the owner has been taking meetings with Edward all summer."

"And we are just now hearing about it?"

"Believe me, the first thing I did when I found out was order all of the maids on our payroll to be called in and made to report."

"That bastard!" She was imagining violence against Edward again.

"I'll talk to legal on Monday, ask if that violates our contract in any way. Once all this is resolved," he gestured at the stacks of papers on the driftwood table. "It may be relevant. But for now, we should get to bed." He threw back the last of his whiskey.

"Alright," she agreed.

They went upstairs together before departing for their own rooms. Cranston gave her a goodnight kiss on the cheek, which was not his custom. And it was the second kiss he had given her today. Suddenly, she was worried that he was dying. That concern piled onto her growing doubt in Thursday's article. The Rose & Chain would verify the information for themselves, but now Vivienne felt her own reputation was at risk. Except that was not it, she realized climbing into bed. Preserving her reputation only required her to express her own doubts about the article. If she equivocated, her reputation for shrewdness would remain intact.

It was the anger. She was not ready to let it go or even temper it. She wanted to be angry; either at Edward for killing children or at Thursday for lying about it. As she laid down and let the tide of wine carry her out to sleep, she admitted the selfishness of it to herself. Was her time really so valuable that she deserved justice for having it wasted?

Part of her believed it was. She had become precious about her time. In the office, naturally, she had to be, but it had bled over into her social life. And it was not that she had nurtured a belief that all people's time needed to be respected; it did not bother her in the slightest to keep others waiting. She considered it her prerogative as a woman.

But what value was her social time to anyone else? Mother had been a true socialite, not merely hosting parties and keeping up with the gossip, but using those things to further various causes. Vivienne had hosted nothing resembling a party since her parents' wake. Her social time was dedicated to shedding the slings and arrows of her professional time. Lying in the darkness with the clock approaching midnight, Vivienne wondered if her life beyond her office was a waste. She was childless, nearly friendless, and content—so she thought—with ambitions handed to her by others who made threats if she resisted.

What if that contentment was a lie and it was making her spiteful? She had been spiteful of Gabrielle for letting girlish wonder get the better of her manners. She had been spiteful of Oracle for being both clever and darling. Her nascent spite for Edward Blake or Thursday Johnson was more justified, but she had jumped to it so quickly without the charity of demanding proof of wrongdoing.

This was not how women were meant to think of each other and this was not how Christians were meant to think of anyone. She would have to take this to confession on Sunday, but she also wanted to make some kind of penitence immediately.

Vivienne decided she needed to verify Thursday's story herself. Her conscience needed to know who was lying to her and those anonymous mothers deserved names.

Chapter 27:
Ladies in the Morning

"Rebecca's not home yet." Said the old Mi'kmaq woman from her rocking chair, doing some native form of needlepoint. If she had a weapon, it was well concealed.

It was just after five in the morning and Vivienne stood in the doorway to 13 Rue de Roi with a bottle of wine in her hands and Thursday's article in her purse.

"Where is Mrs Cord?" Vivienne asked.

"Sleeping." The old Mi'kmaq woman said. "Where else?"

"And what is your name, ma'am?"

"I'm Mrs Christmas. You can wait here if you like." She patted a wooden bench on the other side of her chair. Her attention returned to her needlepoint, but she kept Vivienne in the corner of her eye.

Seeing no sensible alternative, Vivienne took the proffered seat and waited for Rebecca to come home; hopefully alone. This conversation would be complicated if she had an expectant man in tow. The price of the seat, it turned out, was a crafts lecture from Mrs Christmas.

What she was working on was "quillwork", a form of embroidery long practiced by the Mi'kmaq. The threaded needle was looped around a porcupine quill, which was prepared by soaking it in a bowl of water. The quill was bent time and again with new loops of thread binding each fold. Mrs Christmas had a variety of colored quills that she was using to make the design. With each new quill, Mrs Christmas had a length of antler that she used to flatten the needle and a small knife with which she trimmed the barbed ends.

So it was that Rebecca, arriving unaccompanied, found Vivienne watching over Mrs Christmas' shoulder.

"Vivienne!" Rebecca declared in exasperation. "It has barely been a day!"

"I know." Vivienne said and squeezed through the gap between the stairs and Mrs Christmas' knees. "Excuse me and thank you very much. It was a genuine pleasure." She told the old woman.

"You're welcome," the matron replied without looking up from her work.

"I brought a peace offering." Vivienne thrust the wine at Rebecca.

She took the bottle like it might crumble in her hands and frowned at the label. "1915? Where's this from?"

"Burgundy," Vivienne replied. "But I assure you, it is an excellent vintage, despite the war. They had something of a surplus and we bought more than usual, as a nod to the humanitarian side of the war effort. It has become one of my favorites."

"I'm not going to marry Cranston." Rebecca said firmly.

"I never asked you to."

"You're here to ask me for something," she held up the wine. "And it's big."

"Ah, yes, sort of." Vivienne said, understanding. "I do not think it will be too much effort for you, but after last time, I knew it would strain sociability."

"Out with it."

Vivienne took the folded article from her purse. "Do you know any women by the names Reed, Powell, Miller, White, or O'Malley that have recently lost children?"

Rebecca's face went pale. "Yeah, why?"

"I would like to make their acquaintance." She handed the article to Rebecca and took back the wine. "It seems my new business partner may be responsible for the passing of the children."

Rebecca's eyes shot up and blood rushed back to her face. "What?"

"As you can imagine," Vivienne forced herself to speak evenly. Seeing Rebecca's anger felt like a vindication of her own. "I cannot act on mere rumor. I need at least to know that the tragedy is real before I accuse anyone of causing it."

"Yeah," Rebecca said through her teeth. "Thursday," she added, to herself.

"How do you know Miss Johnson?"

"Her mother is Madame Juteau."

"The..." Vivienne caught herself. "The courtesan?"

Rebecca rolled her eyes. "The one and only. Reed, Powell, and Miller are her girls. They'll be at the Retreat. We can catch them before they go to bed."

"You mean they are still working?" Vivienne was aghast. That mothers of young children were working was startling enough, but that they would be working so soon after losing a child.

"As long as they've got bills to pay." She gave the article back. "Wait here, I'm going to change my dress and then we can go."

Rebecca hurried up the stairs.

Gabrielle had always risen with the sun, regardless of the season or continent. It was a quirk that her mother cheerfully complained about to her friends. All Gabrielle's life, she had heard her mother talk about how, as an infant, she had woken at the slightest trace of light coming through the window in that happy exasperation that parents do.

It was 6:30am and she had just sat down with one of the novels she had brought with her from Hong Kong. Thus far, English romance novels were, to a page, disappointments. The women were indelicate creatures, lacking the grace and manners that made one wish to see them happily enamored. Heroines pure of spirit could be found in books written by men, but they were always rank innocents. Their manners were the products of a sheltered existence, not a force of character. They seemed like they would turn into the heroines written by women, if only they would venture beyond the garden wall.

Chinese romances were vastly superior. Male and female, the characters were beset by exciting injuries of circumstance—not mere boredom—and, looking upon the unkind world, chose to be everything their situation was not. They were, in short, deserving of love.

Unfortunately, this morning, Gabrielle didn't get through one page before there was an insistent rapping at the door. She stood and fixed her housecoat and went to answer it. It was Benjamin Syme.

"Miss Blake," he said. "I'm sorry for the early hour, but I've got an urgent matter to talk about with your father."

"Good morning," she replied. "Do come in. I will fetch Father for you."

As he entered, the butler came hurrying out of the basement

where the staff were quartered.

"Good morning, Mr Syme." The butler said. "My apologies for..."

"It's alright, Jeeves." Mr Syme said. "In here?" He pointed at the sitting room door.

"Yes, sir." The butler said, moving to open the door for him.

"Miss Blake," Mr Syme said to her. "If you would."

"Yes, Mr Syme." She bowed and then scampered up the stairs.

After a few minutes, during which she pondered what 'Jeeves' might mean, her father was dressed and she accompanied him back down the stairs. Mother was not deigning to rise for Mr Syme, evidently.

"Benjamin," Edward Blake said going into the parlor. "What's happened?"

"There was a break-in." He glanced at Gabrielle. "Should we have some privacy?"

"It's alright, unless there was violence."

"Nothing to speak of."

"Go on, then. Actually," Edward turned to Gabrielle. "Darling, could you get us coffee?"

"Yes, Father." Gabrielle left for the kitchen, where the bleary-eyed cook was already percolating a kettle.

She dutifully prepared the tray with the sugar bowl and filled a small jug with the last of yesterday's milk from the ice box. As was proper, she sniffed the milk to make sure it was still potable. Gabrielle despised the scent of milk, no matter how fresh, but she could tell healthy sourness from unhealthy. Once the percolator was done, she poured the cups and returned to the sitting room with the tray.

"I can't be sure." Mr Syme was saying. "I only saw two, myself, but I suspect there were more."

"Thank you," Edward said to Gabrielle as she set the tray down. "But," returning his attention to Mr Syme. "Do you know what's missing?"

"Yes." Mr Syme gave Gabrielle an untrusting glance. "They took quite a few things related to the state of the business," she could see he was choosing his words. "Including all of the sales data."

"All of it?" Edward asked.

"Yes. Everything."

Edward sighed and pinched at his lip. "This is disappointing, Benjamin."

"I understand that."

"There must be an inquiry. Your conduct from here on will be subject to much scrutiny."

"I'm aware, Ed."

"Gabby," her father said. "Fetch me the phone, please."

She gave a little bow and then went to the nearby table where the big black phone rested. As yet, she hadn't had the opportunity to use it herself, but she was excited to. Not today, obviously. When the next opportunity presented itself, she intended to ask Vivienne to teach her how to use it. For reasons she couldn't quite identify, she felt that her father would not want to teach it to her.

Edward was a doting father when his attention was on his children. Naturally, his attention was on Michael more than her and he seemed to have real pride in her brother, just as he might a prized stallion. Her, more like a pet, a beloved puppy to fetch his slippers.

But that was alright. She had seen worse and wanted no more.

Gabrielle brought her father the phone, then stood back, ostensibly waiting to be dismissed, but hanging on every word and motion of his call. He connected in a few seconds to an operator—what an awful job that must be, the phone operator at dawn—and asked to be connected to a four-digit number in Chateau de Cygne, one of the city's more opulent districts.

There was a much longer wait, which the three of them passed in silence. Mr Syme kept looking at her like she was a spy. She considered giving him a look as if to say 'maybe I am', but decided rather to continue looking the perfect daughter; awake before the butler, ready before the cook, attending before the maid had made her first appearance.

If Mr Syme had suspicions about her, there was nothing he could do about them, but that was no reason to stoke them.

"Harry?" Edward half shouted into the phone. "Apologies for waking you. ... It is urgent. I just heard that some documents were stolen from Benjamin. ... Yes, vigilantes. ... Oh, you were? ... No, I didn't, hold on." Father turned to Mr Syme. "Did you get their names?"

"Stalker," Mr Syme said. "Just the one."

"Harry?" Father said into the phone. "One was called Stalker. ... You did? That's alright. We've known they were after us. Listen, Harry, we need to scrub everything from phase one of the vaccine experiment. ... Yes, the whole thing needs to go away. As quickly as possible. ... He knows, Harry. Let's deal with that later, shall we? ... Yeah, scrub it clean. Thanks, Harry. ... *Sto ónoma tis tétartis moíras.*"

With that, he hung up.

"Keep your boys searching." Edward told Benjamin. "But get a couple more to the warehouse. We are going to pull all of the Yippity from the shelves. We can do that without alarming anyone, what with America cracking down even more on alcohol. When the vigilantes get wind of it, they might come for the stores. What's important is diverting them from the plant."

"I'll be at the warehouse, myself." Mr Syme said.

"Harry said he was there. Why am I only hearing about this now?"

Mr Syme's face went red. "I thought it was about another matter. I've had agents working here in the past and apparently there are scores yet unsettled. It wasn't until we finished our inventory that I realized the vaccine project was wrapped up in it."

"Settle them fast."

"I will." Mr Syme said.

Edward stood. "Let's get to work." He turned to her. "Gabby, tell your mother that there has been a security matter and I need to be at the plant right away. I'm very sorry I won't be home for lunch. If I'm going to miss dinner, I will call."

"Yes, Father."

"That's a good girl." He beamed and patted her on the head.

Chapter 28:
The Ladies' Retreat

August 13th, 1921. Silkhaven.

The Ladies' Retreat was that rarest of tenement buildings: one with a yard. The space was large enough for another building and its grass grew in patches between dirt trails cut by hours and hours of children's feet until the ground was packed near into rock. The yard was fenced off and the fence extended a foot across the front of the building, so there was no doubt whose yard it was.

Vivienne's driver—another trainee—opened the door for her and Rebecca and then returned to his seat, where he had an apple and a story magazine waiting.

The Retreat, Rebecca had explained, was a private lodging for women who worked in one of Madame Juneau's establishments. It was free as long as they were working, but everyone had to chip in for the water and gas. It was a recent building, red brick; the sort that held heat well enough that the windows could be left open during the winter to discourage influenza.

Vivienne had worn one of her Sunday dresses today, hoping to project the sorority she would need to be trusted. Now that she was here, though, she felt simultaneously overdressed and like an ingenue. Rebecca's dress was much more practical, which felt like the natural order for such a residence, while Vivienne's had tiered skirts and an overabundance of sleeve.

They were stopped at the door by a woman in curlers and an unflattering nightgown. She was older, but her skin was well cared for.

Assuming she was a sex worker, Vivienne imagined she catered to men longing for a maternal embrace.

"Can I help you?" The woman asked Rebecca, casting only a queer look at Vivienne.

"There's a couple ladies we'd like to talk to." Rebecca said and pulled her sex worker's license out of her purse.

"And the turtledove?" The woman asked after giving Rebecca's license an approving look.

"She's a philanthropist."

The woman frowned. "Fancy word for 'tourist."

"I have heard a disturbing report about some of the ladies in this house." Vivienne asserted. "I am here to confirm before acting on it."

The woman shook her head. "There's not a drop of opium in the place and no one under sixteen here works. So, consider your fears allayed." She turned to Rebecca. "Why are you bringing us trouble?"

"I am concerned about Saint Moon." Vivienne added before Rebecca could speak. Seeing the woman straighten, she added: "Thursday Johnson told me I should come here to see what sort of company they are."

"And just what," the woman growled. "Are you going to do about it?"

Vivienne locked eyes with the woman. "Tie him up in litigation so pubic and costly that he'll make Tutankhamen look like Betty Blythe."

The woman scowled in confusion.

"She's gonna sue him 'til he's broke." Rebecca clarified.

"Oh, could've just said that." She looked unimpressed. "That's big talk."

"This is Vivienne Walker." Rebecca said.

"Like the ships?" The woman asked.

"That's her."

"Huh," the woman stepped back into the building, allowing Rebecca and Vivienne to enter. "Wait, here," she gestured into a parlor. "I'll see who I can find."

"Thanks," Rebecca said.

"Yes, thank you." Vivienne added.

The room had a variety of sofas, all in good repair. While none of them exactly matched, there was enough uniformity that it would look intentional if there were enough people to obscure the finer differences. They had a respectably large library, though most of the books were readers, including two complete sets of McGuffey's.

"What do you suppose they are in need of?" Vivienne said, glancing around at the tidy room.

"Stockings, probably." Rebecca answered. "Girls like us got about as much time for darning as you do. With winter coming up, I'm sure warm clothes for the children would be appreciated. Or one of those sacks of money robbers have in the pictures."

"Sacks of money?"

"You know, the ones with the big dollar sign on 'em."

"Do they have those?"

Rebecca laughed but stifled it as a woman entered the room. She was in a pale beige summer housecoat with a shock of blue thread on one cuff.

"I heard you were looking for me." This new woman said. Her voice wavered as she asked: "Is it about Vera? Oh," she exclaimed. "Rebecca?"

"Hi, Alice," Rebecca went to her and they took each other's hands. "How you holdin' up, doll?"

"I'm up." Alice sighed.

Alice Miller was a gaunt woman with all the usual signs of a diet that was spare on vegetables. While her face was well cared for, her neck wanted moisturizing and her hands were notably pinker than the rest of her skin. Now, Vivienne understood why Saint Moon had chosen a milk fortifier, rather than baby's formula. It was a foodstuff of the poor, the "unfit".

Of course, they would have been careful to avoid an attack on any family with the money to file a suit against them. The beer had been an obvious choice. Women of means were not known to drink such things. Whereas doctors often prescribed beer for those who could not reliably get clean water. While a city like Silkhaven could provide clean water for all through the municipal plumbing, buildings with cheap pipes and cheaper faucets could put back into the water what the city's processing had taken out. Beer, however, was sanitized by the brewing process and the pleasing flavor was only a bonus.

"Hello, ma'am," Vivienne stepped towards Alice. "My name is Vivienne Walker and I have recently learned of your loss. The story was so shocking that I hardly believed it. I came only to be certain of the horrible truth before I took action."

Alice nodded, attempting stoicism. "Is it going to be a class action? A...a fella I know, he told me about them."

Vivienne had not considered litigation, but now that this woman had said so, it would certainly be one of their steps. "If there are sufficient plaintiffs, yes. My company has been involved in Saint Moon's distribution." She was thinking aloud, now. "If we can prove that Saint Moon knew that combinations of its products were hazardous, that would have made us something like accomplices and opened us to lawsuits. We could sponsor your suit separately to provide evidence that Saint Moon's endangerment of our company is real. So, even if your case were dismissed, we would have grounds for complaint."

"I believe." She added. "My lawyers would need to assess the facts to be sure. So, I am here to gather those facts."

"Alright," Alice nodded. "Let's sit." She gestured at the nearest sofas. "I'll do my best."

They took opposing sofas with Rebecca joining Alice. Miss Miller had her eyes on the floor as she began.

"Vera was my first to make it through. I'm pretty careful about making customers use a mercury, but accidents happen and sometimes I get a bit drunk and reckless, just like anyone else. After my second miscarriage, I thought I just couldn't have kids and I thought maybe that was a mercy. But when Vera opened her eyes at me, I just..." She choked. Rebecca was there to rub her back.

Alice sucked in a breath to push the tears down. "I thought that I gotta do whatever I could for her." She paused for a few breaths. As she was fighting to keep herself together, a pair of women entered the room. They didn't say anything, only went to Alice and one held her hand while the other stroked her hair. She found her strength and her mouth became a tight scowl. "That's why I bought that milk fortifier. I always was a real skinny girl and never any good in school on account of being hungry so often. I thought that if I could get Vera good and plump, she'd...well, she'd be better off than me." She drew a long breath in through her nose. "I got the beer..." she sniffed. "Just to relax a little. I thought...I'd be a better mommy if...I was cheerful around her. You know...a little girl with a cheerful mommy, she's gotta grow up to be a cheerful woman herself, you know...and the world is just kinder to cheerful girls."

Alice broke then. The three other sex workers descended on her like cooing doves. But Alice wasn't done. She grunted and picked her head back up. A few thick breaths and she said voicelessly: "I lived... to see that girl smile." She was breathing loudly through her nose. "But damn my eyes, I saw it coming. She didn't like my milk the morning after I'd had one of those beers. She didn't like it. But I was just...too stupid to see..." Sobs racked Alice's body.

"That's enough, right?" Rebecca asked Vivienne.

There was a cold knot in Vivienne's throat. "Yes, thank you, Alice."

"I'll go next." One of the two new women said. "Go on." She told the others. Rebecca and the third prostitute helped Alice off the couch and out of the room. "Hello," she said to Vivienne.

"Hello, my name is Vivienne Walker." She extended a hand.

"Betty Reed." She was dark-haired and tan, more robust-looking than Alice. "I heard you were planning to bring Saint Moon low."

"That is the plan, now, yes."

"Good," Betty reached into the top of her nightgown and pulled out a trio of photos. She pulled one out and handed it to Vivienne. It was a baby, all round-faced and expressionless, wearing a white dress and propped among pillows. "That's my Eugene." Betty's voice was hard and flat. "I got two others. They live with my brother and I visit them every Sunday and Monday. Eugene was going to join them once he was weaned. I keep them here," she patted her left. "Next to my heart."

Vivienne handed back the photo.

"I'll keep Eugene, too." Her brow furrowed. "I'll be buried with this, so when I get to Heaven, I can prove I'm his mother." Her eyes were wet, but her voice was firm. "Folks think we ain't got hearts just because we don't want husbands. But I spent a day's pay on each of these and I send everything I can to my boys. Every Sunday, when I see them, I got candy for them or new socks or a comb; the things a mother buys her sons.

"A lady like you," she waved at Vivienne's relatively expensive dress. "Might wonder why I don't get myself a job as a secretary or the like and I'll tell you: I make more money spreading my legs for a couple hours than I could a whole day at a desk. I'm premium. I keep myself healthy and fed, and that lets me charge more. It gets me regulars. Maybe you don't see it, but I do right by my boys; as right as I can."

"I believe you." Vivienne said.

"Most girls don't think to get pictures of their little ones." Betty went on. "A lot of girls have nowhere else for them to go, but my brother understands. So, he raises them like family should and he tells everyone I'm a singer, which I am. He makes my boys as proud of me as I am of them. What I mean to say is don't listen to Alice about knowing. None of us knew. There were no signs until it was too late. The moment—the very moment—I thought something was wrong, I took Eugene to Dr Lambrie." She went still, dropping her eyes for the first time. "He was gone before we arrived. He was too gentle for this world." She raised her chin up, but the voice had drained from her words. "He was the quietest baby...anyone had ever seen. He was going to be kind, deep in his heart. Even when he was suckling, he was gentle." Her face drew itself into a hard neutrality. "This world doesn't deserve boys like him."

Vivienne waited a moment before asking: "And you are sure it was the Yippity?"

"Yes, ma'am. I had three bottles with the girls the night before. We were celebrating. In the morning, I mixed my milk with the fortifier and gave him a bottle. I didn't always. It was just that day I thought I should." She looked at the floor again. "Eugene never cried in the morning. At night, sure, but never in the morning. He opened his eyes and he saw the light coming through the window. He wondered at it. That boy had the soul of a poet. He was born that way. Now, I will not say that I am glad that he is gone, but I do take solace in knowing that he will never have that kindness or poetry trampled on."

Again, she raised her head, eyes staring sharp and bright at Vivienne. Her voice shook as she spoke: "I loved him and I gave him a perfect life. All he ever knew was love and wonder. If the Lord had wanted him to stay here, he would have healed my Eugene. But I believe that the Lord knew better and He wanted that pure, loving, poetic heart by His side before the world could grind him down. Some say I will go to Hell because of my profession, but the Bible says that a woman will be saved through childbearing. And I bore a child too wonderful for God to allow to stay on this Earth. When he calls me home, my Eugene will be there to greet me."

"I have no doubt." Vivienne said. "Thank you."

She stood, meaning to look for the third woman, but was distracted by the rumbling of a fleet of vehicles filling up the street outside. Vivienne and Betty both went to the window. A dozen police cars and wagons were pulling to a stop on the street outside.

The Retreat was being raided.

Chapter 29:
Skull Cracker

Vivienne had heard stories about raids. Newspapers painted them as wild, cowboy affairs with the police all but firing their guns in the air the moment they got in. Vivienne had seen a couple of raids—once at an upscale bar and one in the Walker Company offices—and they made those accounts laughable; it was the district attorney marching in at the head of an army of paralegals with some high-ranking police officer at his elbow.

The raid on the Ladies' Retreat renewed Vivienne's faith in the fourth estate.

The women of the tenement building were already in a fuss, seeing the vehicle pull up, so Vivienne could not say for sure if the officers announced themselves before they kicked in the door, but she did not hear them do so. After that, a dozen officers raced in, shouting at everyone they saw. Half of them, brandishing their nightsticks, went running up the stairs where the cries of children joined the commotion.

The officer who took the sitting room looked wildly between Vivienne and Betty. "Licenses!"

Betty had her hands up, Vivienne's found her hips. When neither moved, the officer shook his stick at them. "Licenses, now!"

"It's upstairs," Betty said. "In my room."

"Sit!" He told her. "Hands behind your head." Then he advanced on Vivienne. "Yours up in your room, too?"

"I am not a sex worker." Vivienne replied, trying to keep her voice plain lest she offend Betty.

"I got one!" The officer shouted. "You're coming with me."

"On what charge?" Vivienne demanded.

"No lip, now." He said, unhooking a pair of handcuffs from his belt; there were several.

"Officer, you may not arrest an individual without making them aware of the charges on which they are being arrested."

"Oh, look who 'knows their rights.'" He said mockingly. Then, he smacked her across the face with his nightstick. Vivienne reeled and fell onto a nearby sofa. "You're under arrest for resisting arrest. How's that sound?"

This was not the first time a man had struck her, but the blow made her feel as if she had been knocked into someone else's body. The room took on a strange cast, as if she was seeing it for the first time. Then, she tasted her own blood and she returned to herself.

"It sounds," she said, pushing herself up. "Like my lawyer is getting a new boat."

The officer grabbed her wrist and hauled her to her feet. In a move she did not fully understand, the officer twisted her arm so that her body was spun forty-five degrees with the arm now behind her. It was a deft move; she would give him that.

"I am terribly sorry," Vivienne went on as he fastened the cuff to one wrist. "But I did not get your name."

"Gonna file a complaint?" He said, yanking her other hand behind her back. "You can call me 'Cracker', Officer Skull Cracker."

"Is that a family name?" She asked as he thrust her towards the door.

"Don't move!" He told Betty. Then, out in the hall, he said in a more respectful tone: "There's one in there; says her license is in her room."

"Doesn't matter." Came the reply. "We found kids. We got everyone for conspiracy."

"Conspiracy!" 'Skull Cracker' whooped. "We're breaking up a whole illegal prostitution ring! We're getting medals, boys!"

As the officer pushed Vivienne out into the street, she saw that her driver was missing, but that the car was still there. Vivienne was taken to one of the wagons and handed off to another, politer officer; not through force of character, it seemed, but rather a dearth of passion. During the handover, Vivienne noted the number '37' on Skull

Cracker's badge.

This second officer was holding a large, burlap sack which he held open. "Personal effects?" He said sleepily.

Still handcuffed, Vivienne replied: "No, I left my purse inside. Would you be a dear and go get it for me?"

The sleepy officer stared at her confused. "No." Then, he grabbed her arm and helped her into the back of the wagon. There were two wooden benches running along the sides of the wagon's rear area. Vivienne did not know what the proper term was. She took a seat at the far end and waited. This was going to be delightful.

Father had prepared her for just such events. In a company as large as theirs, raids were inevitable. Perhaps an upper manager got into something dirty, perhaps a client, and perhaps a rival forged sufficient evidence to warrant an immediate seizure of documents. Whatever the cause, Father's instruction had been to follow all orders quickly and quietly. The less trouble you made, the less they could accuse you of. There was no need for her to raise her voice. That is what lawyers were for.

After a few minutes, more women were brought in, including Rebecca.

"Rebecca," Vivienne said, leaning in and speaking quietly. "Are you alright?"

"Yeah," she said forlornly. "They said they're charging me for unlicensed prostitution."

"You said this place was not a brothel."

"It isn't." Another woman said. "It's not a damn brothel!" She repeated louder to the officer outside, who did not seem to notice.

"What she said." Rebecca told Vivienne. "They knock you around?" Now, her voice sounded concerned. There must have been a bruise.

"A little, but that just means I shall be using that particular officer as a footstool, this Christmas."

"You're taking this awful calm. That is, you don't seem like the kind of dame that takes a beating lying down."

"Many years ago," Vivienne began, but was interrupted by the woman next to her suggesting that she and Rebecca trade seats. Once they were situated, she began again. "Many years ago, I was serving coffee at a meeting and the president of another company tripped me as a gag."

"You were serving coffee? I thought you were the president."

"This was when my father held that seat. Being tripped, I accidentally spilled coffee into the lap of the man who had tripped me. For this consequence of his own actions, he backhanded me. Now, I rather expected Father would challenge the man to a duel, but instead he only put himself bodily between me and the attacker and ordered them all to leave. Initially, I was hurt by my father's apparent inaction, but by the end of the year, we had sued that company into bankruptcy and even acquired the president's summer home. Father had the place torn down and sold the wood to a manufacturer of outhouses."

"Golly." Rebecca replied. "Think you can get me some of that kind of justice?"

"Darling, I have three criminal lawyers on the fifteenth floor of my building. You can take your pick."

"I suppose you need 'em."

"Why do you say that?"

"Every time I go out with you, I end up in the biggest trouble of my life."

"It is funny that you should say that: I was just thinking the same thing about you."

"Hell of a coincidence, these guys showing up just after we got here. Do you think they knew you were coming? What if you've got a rat problem?"

"Oh, I would not worry about that. If they had known *I* was here, this would have gone very differently."

Being under arrest, it turned out, was quite the process. Vivienne was made to stand in a line along one wall of a police station along with the other women from her wagon. Before them was a cramped office space with officers sitting at paper-laden desks. One by one, they were brought to a scale where their heights and weights were taken, then escorted to a desk and asked for further information.

"Name?" Officer #45 asked her.

"Vivienne Alexandra Lillie Walker," she answered truthfully.

The officer cocked an eyebrow at her. "Vivienne Walker?"

"Of the Silkhaven Walkers."

The officer sighed. "Address?" He said in a tone that suggested he thought this would be a lie as well.

"45 Rue de Cygne, Penthouse; Silkhaven, King Charles Island."

He nodded ruefully, but copied the information down. Next, he produced a sheet of paper with ten boxes along the middle and a pad of ink. To Vivienne's mounting horror, he made her soil each of her fingers and then leave an impression of them on the paper, first individually and then one hand at a time. When this was done, he handed her the filthiest handkerchief she had ever seen and proceeded to run the paper through a typewriter, copying her information onto it. He asked a few more questions as he went: her age, marital status, whether she was Jewish, etc.

Once that was done, he walked her to a back room that had a number of jail cells in it. In she went and there she waited. Vivienne was not sure how long she waited, only that fifteen other women were brought into the cells before a man in a very fine suit came marching in, scanning the detained women with nervous interest.

Vivienne smiled and stood up. "Governor Farrar!" She said. "It is so good of you to come and see me." She turned to the other women in her cell, voice dripping with sarcasm. "Is it not wonderful to see a friendly face in one's time of distress?" The others did not see the humor, but she intended to make it up to them in time.

"Get that door open immediately!" Farrar shouted at the officer with the keys. "Miss Walker," Farrar began before the door was open. "There has been a terrible mistake."

"Yes, I know. I was there for it."

"Of course, of course," he said, ushering her out of the cell.

He led her back into the big office and towards a row of doors with frosted windows. As she went, Vivienne caught sight of officer #37 and waved at him with her fingers. She watched as the blood drained from his face seeing her with the governor.

Harry opened a door to an office not his own and bid Vivienne take a seat. He then made himself relatively comfortable in the chair of whoever this room has been commandeered from.

"Again," he said. "I must apologize from the bottom of my heart for the misunderstanding. One of our fine, young officers saw your name and alerted the chief, who alerted me, and I came as quickly as I could."

"I am sure you did. I would like to phone my brother now, please."

"Of course, we'll get to that. However, for the sake of due diligence, I must give you a sort of...shall we call it...an exit interview. After all, there is now paperwork saying you were arrested. If I release you without a statement, it will look like cronyism."

"Well, I certainly would not want anyone calling you my crony."

"No, of course not, no." Harry took a deep breath. "What precisely were you doing at the Ladies' Retreat?" He said the name with a little too much familiarity.

"Philanthropic research." She said. "Did the police happen to pick up my handbag?"

"I wouldn't know." Harry replied, pulling out his pocket square and dabbing at his forehead. "What sort of philanthropic research was this?"

Vivienne considered. Her father would have told her to say nothing without her lawyer present, but she was suddenly very suspicious of the whole affair. Farrar had been at Edward Blake's home earlier and, now, on the morning after Cranston stole a bag full of documents about Saint Moon, the victims of Blake's scheme were having their home raided. Neither Blake nor the Atlantic Network had the pull to make that happen, which cast a very unbecoming light on Farrar. She wanted to see if he was part of it.

"I heard that there had been a number of infant deaths in the building." Vivienne told him, watching his face. "I thought I might be able to help to prevent future instances."

"Ah," he replied, his mouth turning in a way that made him look guilty as sin. "That's charitable. And did you...*learn* anything?"

"I learnt what a police baton feels like at speed." She turned her head so he could see where she had been struck.

"An unfortunate accident, I'm sure."

"Yes, I believe he was aiming for a passing baseball. Credit where it is due, that man might give Babe Ruth something to sweat about."

"Did you get the officer's name?"

"Skull Cracker," she replied innocently. "I think it is Polish."

"Now, Miss Walker..."

"You will give me access to a phone. Yes, thank you."

Harry's face hardened. "Listen to me. These are the lowest sort of women and I feel it is my civic duty to discourage you from further entanglements with them."

Vivienne saw him winding the rope around his own neck and decided that, now, she would be following her father's advice.

"They are where they are," Harry went on. "Because they are constitutionally incapable of living in civilized society. No amount of money can make them productive members of the community. They simply aren't the kind. *And* as it says in the Bible, they reproduce after their own kind. I admire the softness of your heart, Miss Walker, I do. I wish I could be afforded such a luxury in my position, but as tragic as the passing of a small child may seem, in these cases, it really is for the best. Whatever happened to those children was mercy incarnate."

Vivienne wanted to laugh. "Good luck fitting that on a re-election poster."

"It is a more popular notion than you realize. Popular enough that coming out against it could threaten your place in society. Larger companies than yours have been brought low by failing to see which way the wind is blowing."

"I employ ship captains to tell me that."

"Virtue, Miss Walker. Good, Christian virtue. That is the wind that is blowing and it will blow away the whores and the drunks and the kikes until this city is a safe place for the good Christians to live."

"Good Christian whites?"

"I resent..."

He was interrupted by the door being opened. Vivienne turned to see a cowed little policeman standing beside a portly, jowled, bulldog of a man in a grey suit and yarmulke.

"Miss Walker," the bulldog shouted through the door's glass. "Do not say one more word."

Vivienne grinned at the man—Obadiah Schwartz esq—and then back at Farrar. The governor waved his hand and the officer opened the door. Mr Schwartz entered and dropped his briefcase on the desk Farrar was occupying. He was followed by Cranston who opened his mouth, but was silenced by Mr Schwartz's hand.

"I speak for both of you." The lawyer said.

Vivienne silently turned her head so that Obadiah could see the bruise on her cheek.

"What is this?" The lawyer shouted at the governor.

"Miss Walker," Farrar replied in the voice of a master correcting a fumbling apprentice. "Was arrested on suspicion of unlicensed sex work and made certain gestures that the arresting officer considered threatening."

"Can you hear yourself?" Obadiah asked. "Which judge were you going to take that to? Please, tell me the name of the judge that was going to believe that Miss Vivienne Walker, the single richest woman in Silkhaven, was moonlighting as a prostitute."

"I know the charge is false. I was taking her statement before releasing her."

"You don't take statements. You're the governor. This whole thing reeks of corruption. My client will now leave."

Vivienne, taking her cue, stood and went to Cranston, who embraced her as if she were in some great distress.

"Miss Walker," Obadiah addressed her. "Do you have the name of the officer that assaulted you?"

"Badge number 37." She answered.

"Good enough," he heaved his briefcase off the desk. "I will meet you both in the car."

The lawyer nodded and Cranston escorted Vivienne out of the station.

"How did you know I was here?" Vivienne asked as soon as they were outside.

"Your driver," Cranston replied. "They questioned him but didn't put him under arrest. He called as soon as he was free."

They were greeted at the car by Williamson, who looked ready to storm the police station himself. That made three men steaming at the ears on her behalf and she was almost disappointed that they were not each getting an opportunity to raise Cain in there.

She and Cranston got in the car and Cranston insisted upon taking a closer look at her cheek. "We'll take you to a hospital," he said. "But I don't think it needs more than a cold compress."

When Obadiah came out to meet them, he said he would take care of matters and that they should go on to the hospital. Vivienne asked him to bring in the company lawyers to prepare a class-action suit and that one of them should be assigned to Rebecca's case specially. As they drove, Vivienne regaled both her brother and driver with the tale.

Before the hospital, she insisted on returning to the Ladies' Retreat. There, she had the honor of meeting Madame Juteau, come to check on this property of hers in its hour of need. Vivienne informed the famed courtesan that she already had several lawyers on the case and was prepared to bring in more come Monday.

Madame Juteau expressed her gratitude and also returned Vivienne's purse, left behind on one of the sitting room sofas. When Vivienne checked the contents, everything was there, save Thursday's article.

Chapter 30:
A Favor for Rebecca

Mass had been a to-do. Vivienne had made no effort to hide the fat, purple line across her cheek where the policeman had struck her. She had intended it to give her testimony a bit more weight with the elders, but it had sparked the well-meaning attention of every woman within a two-block radius. She had told the story so many times that, by the time they got to talk with the elders, it felt like a recital.

When they returned home, it was Cranston's turn to dote on her, which was sweet, but a little tiresome. Vivienne could not say what sort of bedside manner she preferred, but Cranston's military practicality was not it. No sooner was she out of her Sunday dress, but he was knocking on her bedroom door with a cold compress for her bruise.

She was still in her slip, so she invited him in. That she was in her underwear dissuaded him not at all. He just settled the cotton-wrapped ice against her cheek and then bound it in place—too tightly for her comfort—with a strip of cloth knotted below her chin like she had just had a cavity filled.

"How am I supposed to talk?" She asked through her teeth.

"I'll get you a pad of paper." He smiled.

Vivienne threw on a light housecoat and went down to the living room to read. It was a glorious day outside and the two-story windows let the light bathe the room, so it almost felt like she was outside, only without the pervasive noise of the city. She lingered at one window before deciding on what to read. Just two blocks to the west was the

North River and the broad expanse of Riverside Park. The river was only a few hundred meters across and, the weather being what it was, already filled with little sailing boats. On the far side was the Bellevue district, home to small-time fishermen and the majority of Silkhaven's negro community.

She wondered, cheek numb with cold, what the police were like over there. Quite a few would be negroes themselves, she imagined, but that guaranteed nothing. It was a fact of history that elevating a servant to the rank of master created the harshest slave-drivers. That is what had happened in Liberia—former slaves finding themselves suddenly a privileged upper class—and they had conquered half of West Africa.

With that thought, she turned away from the window. It was making her gloomy and she had no desire to be gloomy on a day as lovely as this. She went to the bookshelf nearest the stairs and found a PG Wodehouse book she had not gotten to yet. She took it to one of the sofas by the old driftwood table just as Cranston was coming down with drinks, including a straw for Vivienne.

He set the tray on the table where she could reach it as she reclined. After a brief glance at the book's cover, he went to the same bookshelf and took out another Wodehouse. It was strange having him there. Comforting in its way, but also distractingly unaccustomed. Book in hand, Cranston went to the record player and thumbed through their collection, yet put nothing on. Instead, he turned and regarded the room with dissatisfaction.

"What is it?" Vivienne asked without opening her jaw.

"How difficult would it be to hire a piano player?" He asked, eyes on Mother's old piano sitting unused—and probably out of tune—on the other side of the room.

"I am..." she stopped, realizing the sentence she was going to say was too long given her present handicap. "By dinnertime." She summed up.

"Hmm," Cranston replied. "They really should make records longer. It's not very relaxing having to turn the disc over every three minutes."

"Radio?" Vivienne suggested.

"I can't choose what's playing and whoever is choosing is liable to follow Schumann with Al Jolson."

"Or Liszt." Vivienne added.

"Precisely." Cranston said, then stood paralyzed by indecision.

Vivienne set her book down and went to the little cabinet beside the piano where they kept Mother's library of sheet music. She grabbed one at random and walked over to Cranston, thrusting it into his hands.

"Learn," she said, then returned to her sofa.

Cranston looked at the sheet music like he really might have a go at it—which would not help her read, but would entertain—then set the paper song on the table. He next picked up the record player and set it in the gap between sofas. It was too close to the fireplace, but in summer that was not a concern. Next, he brought the entire record collection to the table and set them in a few stacks.

"A compromise," he said before cranking the player and putting on 'There's a lot of Blue-Eyed Marys in Maryland'.

Vivienne started in on *Their Mutual Child*, only to find the main character—in the third paragraph of the first chapter—espousing eugenic ideas and could not go on. She returned that unpleasantness to the bookshelf and decided to reread *The Little Warrior*. After a page, Cranston put on 'I Might be your Once-in-a-While' and the elevator dinged. Vivienne swore internally.

"Miss Costa-Cortez to see you, sir and ma'am." Hornsby said from the receiving hall.

Vivienne set her book on the table and got to her feet, crossing to Rebecca as quickly as Cranston did. Rebecca was wearing a plain, tan dress; the sort where the skirt began well below her hips. She had a dark brown summer scarf knotted at her sternum and a sun hat in her hands.

"Pearl!" Cranston said, coming in to hug her.

Vivienne hung back, not being on such intimate terms with her, and saw the melancholy in her face.

"You are free." Vivienne said, trying to sound cheerful without moving her jaw.

"If I'd known you were getting out," Cranston told her, "I would have been there to pick you up."

"It's alright." Rebecca said, looking like she was screwing up her courage for something.

"What is wrong?" Vivienne asked. "Damnit!" She untied the cold compress and slowly stretched her jaw.

"Golly," Rebecca said. "That's a shiner and a half."

"I have had worse." Vivienne replied.

"You *have*?" Cranston exclaimed.

"Remember, I broke my arm that one time."

"Oh, yes, the matador."

"Rebecca, dear, do come in. Have a seat. Can I offer you..." she looked at the pitcher of drink she had not tried yet. "This?"

"It's orange juice and a little rum." Cranston added.

"Sure, why not?" Rebecca said and took the offered seat on the sofa Vivienne had occupied.

Cranston sat beside her, which put Vivienne on the opposite sofa. Cranston poured.

"I am so glad to see you are alright," Vivienne went on. "But you do not have the look of a woman making a social call." Gosh, but it felt good to speak in full sentences again.

"No," Rebecca sipped her drink. "I gotta call in that favor."

"By all means," Vivienne said.

"So, they let me go, obviously, but I'm still being charged with violating the terms of my license. Your Mr Schwartz says it'll be a real simple thing. We got a paper saying where I was arrested and another paper saying the Retreat ain't a brothel and that'll be that. The thing is, it's gotta be sorted out by a judge and the court date I got is in November. To make things worse, once the charges are cleared, I gotta reapply for my license and that's another month at least.

"All that to say, until January, I guess, I'm unemployed. Sure, I've got some money saved up, but it isn't going to get me through to January."

"I see." Vivienne said, unemployment being as alien to her as sex work. "I will have to think about what I can do."

Rebecca shrugged. "A girl's gotta eat."

"Of course," Cranston said, his brow knit in thought. "Can you type?"

"Not really. Besides, and no offense or nothing, but it might be a little strange for both of us, me working in your office. Look, it's hard enough, me asking for charity like this and being in your office, you know, I couldn't ever forget it."

"I can see that, though relationships like ours are not unheard of in the secretary pool."

"Sure, but those things develop the other way around." She tried to chuckle, but it did not come out right. "I don't really have skills for anything other than what I'm doin'. If I did, I wouldn't be here with my hat in my hands." She raised the literal hat.

"There are schools." Vivienne suggested.

"And I'd be happy to take the tuition off you, but my food and rent, too? That's too far. I mean, negotiating an allowance with you? I'd rather move back to New York. And, even as I say that, I know it sounds ungrateful. I'm sorry."

"Not at all."

"I'll take a boat ticket off you and call it square."

"Listen," Cranston said, looking uncharacteristically unsure of himself. "Being frank, you don't need a license to be a kept woman."

"Yeah..." she nodded. "But that ain't us, is it?"

He drew in a long breath. "No, it's not."

"Listen, I know I sound like a beggar tryin' to choose, but I'm thinkin' about the future. If I am gonna get my license back, I don't want nothin' changin' between us, you know? And if I'm not, I gotta find some kind of life for myself that I can really live. Stayin' so close to you," she reached out and squeezed Cranston's hand. "Things would change and I don't know if I can ever be a one-fella sorta girl."

"You like to listen." Vivienne blurted, recalling her very first conversation with Rebecca.

"What's that?" Rebecca asked.

"When we first met, you said you liked your work because you like to listen."

"Oh, sure, fellas unloading their problems...it's like I get to see the real man, you know?"

"Yes and I think I know someone who could use an apprentice with just such a proclivity."

"Who?" Cranston asked.

"Rosamund,"

"Of course!" Cranston turned to Rebecca. "And an apprenticeship is just the thing for you; learning a new skill while also earning your keep."

"I know what an apprentice is."

"Sorry,"

"It's okay." She smiled at him, then turned to Vivienne. "Who's Rosamund?"

Vivienne briefly explained the Syme Retreat and Rosamund's work there. "Shall I give her a ring?"

"Yeah, that'd be peachy."

An hour later, arrangements were being made. Rosamund wanted to interview Rebecca, naturally, but she seemed optimistic about the situation. With her Uncle Benjamin in town, though, she preferred to stay in Montague. So, Lucien would drive in the next morning and pick Rebecca up.

Nothing was guaranteed, but it was a start. Rebecca looked so relieved that Vivienne half expected her to cry.

"Golly..." Rebecca said when things were settled. "I had myself prepared to move back to New York. I don't know what to do with myself now."

"I have a couple of ideas." Cranston said.

Rebecca smiled and her mouth hung open like she was going to say something, but nothing came. The smile faded and still silence hung between them. That was answer enough for Cranston and Rebecca knew it, but she had to say something yet. "I'm not Pearl." She said finally. "I'm just Rebecca."

"Of course," Cranston replied. "I'm going to miss Pearl."

"Yeah, me too." She grabbed his hand. "It would feel like she wasn't comin' back." Her voice choked on the last word. Her mouth screwed up as she fought down the emotion. "Besides, it sounds like I gotta pack."

"Yes. Yes, you do."

Vivienne watched them just sit there, holding hands, as her mind scrambled for a reason to leave.

"How about," Cranston said. "I drive you home one l—...one more time?"

"Yeah," Rebecca nodded, eyes misty. "That'd be real nice."

Vivienne gave Rebecca a hug good-bye and walked them to the elevator, then was struck by that same sense of not knowing what to do with herself. Under normal circumstances, she would have simply gone out. The city was chock full of tea houses and such where a woman might pass the time. There would doubtless be other ladies of her set there, but that was the problem. She still had quite a large bruise on her cheek and she did not feel like explaining it to yet another gaggle of concerned women.

Still, the seclusion of the office proved insufficient. She picked up the phone on the desk and asked the operator to connect her with the Prosecution. It took a little more effort to get the right number, but she was eventually put through to the St Lawrence VC's phone. The Red Widow answered.

"I was wondering if Tiburon was in today." She said. "He is? Excellent. Would you keep him there for me? Thank you."

As Williamson drove her, it occurred to her that she might be imposing. Rebecca had been none too happy about her turning up at the Mermaid Club, after all. Then again, she was going to Tiburon's place of business, as it were, offering him sex. However inconvenient that may be, she could not imagine a man having any serious objections.

PART 7
The Virago

Chapter 31:
The Ghost Song

August 15th, 1921. Silkhaven.

The Dockside district extended from the east bank of the North River to Wright's Creek, the largest tributary to the East River. This whole stretch of land bristled with docks. The further east you went, the more modest the harbors became until you reached the marinas where Régence's landed gentlemen had their little, sporting sailboats.

Harbor 1, at the crux of the North and East Rivers, gazing out on the Northumberland Strait, belonged to the city and was largely used by the North American Combined Forces Navy. Despite its wealth, King Charles Island was too isolated to be of strategic importance. Any military assault on the island would have to pass through the Cabot Strait, between the American Navy on Cape Breton and the Canadian Navy in Newfoundland.

However, given the island's historical significance—most importantly, the Treaty of 1812 being signed in New Versailles—there were frequent visits by presidents and prime ministers. As such, a small military presence was needed on the island. The Combined Forces, which included Navy and Marines, were a sort of honor guard and were renowned for being the best-mannered military unit in North America. It was a place for the respected, but unambitious. Not a man among them lacked a medal on his uniform and the internal competition between Canadians and Americans kept everyone at maximum discipline.

The parades held in honor of either nation's head-of-state were a tourist attraction in their own right; the absolute height of martial performance in a civilian context.

Harbors 2-7 were owned by the Walker Corporation and they held leases on Harbors 8-10. Three of Harbor 6's docks had been designated for Saint Moon's exclusive use until the end of the year. It was here that the trucks had been arriving all day to unload every case of Yippity beer that the shops and bars still had to part with.

It had been a busy day for the dock's staff with all the unscheduled entries. The drivers had to produce manifests, which had to be verified, then the trucks were checked incoming and outgoing. They had had to call in two forklifts from Dock 2 to handle the logistical nightmare of rearranging a warehouse and, even then, the guys had clocked three hours of overtime. According to Mr Grafton, the dock-master, the only time it was this busy was early November when the produce exporters were clearing out their storehouses and the luxury goods importers were stocking up for Christmas.

All in all, it was a hell of a first day on the job. Oliver Little was apprenticing to the dock-master for the next three months to get familiar with the operation and would then be assigned to whatever specific job they needed more hands on. Mr Grafton said it was important for every man in the warehouse to understand what every other man was doing, thus all new apprentices starting in the dock-master's office. When everyone understood the big picture, they better knew what their responsibilities were and weren't, which helped with communication and camaraderie.

Oliver didn't feel like he knew a damn thing, just then, and wasn't feeling optimistic that he would ever learn. With the sun setting, he finally got a chance to rest in "the crow's nest", the third floor of a narrow tower of offices that gave the dock-master a great view of the dock and the bay beyond. He really hoped to get assigned to the radios up here. Sitting at the big window with one of those headsets on, telling the big ships where to go sounded keen.

What boy didn't want to get his hands on some state-of-the-art technology?

He was about to ask if he could finally go home—having put in a few hours of overtime himself—when he saw a light flashing on the radio console.

"What's that?" He asked.

"Security alarm," Mr Grafton said calmly.

The man operating that part of the machine cut in: "That's a warehouse alarm." The man said. "Something's disturbed a window."

"Alert the watch." Mr Grafton said.

"Is it a break-in?" Oliver asked.

"Nine times out of ten, it's a bird." Mr Grafton replied. "We get break-ins, but it's more likely that a crate was unbalanced and slid out of place. But it's probably a bird."

It wasn't a bird. The watch called in that the whole window had been cut free of the frame; definitely a break-in.

"Alright," Mr Grafton wearily commanded his staff. "Call the vigilance committee and inform the client."

"We're not calling the police?" Oliver asked.

"Nah, they'll just break stuff. It's why they're called bulls. The vigilantes will inform them, later."

Stalker pulled the Farman up to the warehouse gate where the watchmen opened the gate for him. He parked beside the watchmen's truck on the land end. The pier was a 600-foot structure extending out into the water with a warehouse on either side and a long row between them. On one side, the warehouses opened directly onto the water for ease of loading onto the ships.

There was a dock in front of and behind the warehouses, where crews could disembark, but it was 550 feet and two stories of warehouse between them. So, when Tiburon and the Sheik pulled up in their car, Stalker ordered them to drive down and stake out the window that had been the intruder's entry point, while he and Fortuna went in.

The dock-master had received a phone call from Vivienne Walker almost as soon as the vigilance committee had been called. On her order, all of Harbor 6 had been locked down and the incoming vigilantes were to be given full access to the buildings. So, when the Stalker asked the watchmen to open the warehouse office's door instead of the main door, they complied without scruple.

The warehouse office was a small room for filing paperwork that was separated from the rest of the warehouse by four thin walls, which would block the light from the street lamps outside and muffled the sound of the door opening. The door from the office into the warehouse didn't quite reach the ground and opened in near silence. This route ensured that no one inside the darkened warehouse would notice that someone else had entered behind them.

Fortuna had worn an eye patch on the ride over. When they

entered the dark warehouse, she flipped it up, that one eye at least prepared for the deep gloom. Stalker let her take the lead until his own eyes caught up. His partner also had a bandolier of loaded magazines for their pistols slung over one shoulder. She had insisted after the way their last mission had gone.

The interior of the warehouse was packed with towers of crates. Thick white lines were painted along the center of the warehouse, marking boundaries for the crates to ensure that the forklifts had room to move. A network of narrow catwalks was suspended at the second floor to allow inspectors to easily access those higher crates. Of course, there were no railings up there, as they would get in the way of the forklifts.

Stalker and Fortuna walked quietly down the center of the warehouse, looking for signs of the intruder. Whoever they were looking for would almost certainly need a flashlight to do whatever it was they were doing. About 200 feet down the row, they saw it on the upper story. The intruder was being careful, so it was only a narrow shaft of a crate that they saw, but it was a telltale all the same.

"You here." Stalker whispered as quietly as he could to Fortuna. "Me up."

She made a gesture of bringing the fingertips of both hands together to show she understood that they were doing a flanking maneuver. Stalker found the nearest set of stairs and crept slowly and softly up to the catwalk. He really hoped she was in a talking mood. He didn't relish the idea of yet another catwalk fight with the Virago, especially without railings.

Once on the catwalk, he gently touched his cane to the outer edge of the steel platform to keep it in mind. He moved slowly enough that the grating of metal on metal was barely a whisper. From up here, it was easier to see the intruder's flashlight. About three crates away from the light, he found a place where he could take cover. One stack of crates was significantly higher than its neighbor, which was a few inches below the level of the catwalk. He took the small step down, careful to make no noise and found the crate stable footing.

If the intruder stepped out onto the catwalk, they would not see him. From this position, he acted on a hunch: "Thursday?" He shouted in his gruff American accent. "I want to talk."

A moment passed. "I don't." She replied in that strange francophone accent. It was the Virago.

"I think we're on the same side."

"We aren't."

"You want to stop Saint Moon killing children, right? I do, too."

He heard her moving around, but not footsteps on metal.

"If you know what Saint Moon is doing, why are you here?" The Virago asked.

"I'm hoping to gather more evidence." He called back. "Bringing down a big company like that, it takes a lot of paperwork."

"If I had that kind of evidence, I would not be risking myself this way."

"But you've got some, right? I've got some, too. If we put it all together, maybe it'll be enough."

"Or maybe you are lying. How could you know what Saint Moon is doing unless you work for them?"

"I might ask you the same question."

"Well," she said, her feet making a soft ringing as they touched the catwalk. "I am rigging dynamite and you are not."

"I'm gathering evidence. You are destroying it."

"So, you gather your evidence. You take it to court. What happens when the judge agrees with him? Powerful men have powerful friends. By the time you understand how big this conspiracy is, it will already have done its work."

"If you already know..."

Stalker was cut off by the lights in the warehouse coming on.

"Your friends are here." She said and then she was running.

There was no time to investigate what she had done to the crates. If it was another bundle of dynamite, he didn't see a fuse. With no thought to stealth, he ran after her. In fact, he stomped a little to tell Fortuna where he was. No sense letting the Virago know he had backup. She was approaching an intersection and Stalker readied himself to leap between gangways if she did.

Her hand grabbed the support pole at the junction with her left and the Virago leapt and launched herself around at his feet first. Stalker leaned out of her arc and slapped the back of her legs with his cane. She let go of the pole and tried to land, but her legs buckled beneath her. She landed on her back. She rolled halfway around and she flung a black something at Stalker.

He ducked and felt the thing graze his hat. When he looked up, she was in a deep stance holding two weapons in reverse grips. They were black metal blades with fat bases and so angular they were almost pyramidal. Stalker held his cane just below the handle for better balance and eased into a fencer's stance.

"We don't have to..." he started, but she launched herself at him, daggers high.

She attacked with her right hand first. Stalker raised and tilted his sword hand. Her right wrist hit the cane and Stalker swung the cane back as she slashed with her left to hit her left forearm with the cane's pommel. He bent his wrist, jabbing the cane at her face. She raised her right to parry with the dagger.

As she did, she swung her left arm up, flicked her wrist and opened her fist. The dagger spun into a forward grip and she tried to stab him in the arm. Stalker retreated, bringing the cane with him. He jabbed again. The Virago turned to dodge and punched at him with a right cross.

Stalker grabbed her wrist with his left hand and twisted it back. He tilted his cane up to block her right hand. He had the wolf by the ears, though, so he pushed her away from him with his left.

They both retreated a few steps. Stalker switched the cane to his left and drew the sword. The goal was to disarm her. Meanwhile, she flipped her right dagger so that both were in the forward grip. Stalker advanced. He feinted a lunge. She took the bait and turned to let it pass her and try to get inside his guard, but this being a feint, he never fully extended. Instead, he turned the sword to slash her across the stomach, forcing her into defense.

The Virago parried with her left dagger, which left a moment's pause before she could stab with her right. In that moment, Stalker swung the cane and hit her in the neck. When she slashed at him with her right, he pulled back the sword for another jab. She abandoned her attack to deflect the sword, then lunged, crossing her left hand over her right to stab.

Stalker deflected that attack with the cane. The Virago followed the direction of the cane's swipe and spun. Keeping her right dagger on his sword, she reversed her left dagger again and widened her stance so she could stab him in the leg. Stalker saw it and pushed forward, pressing her right dagger aside as he went past her.

The Virago continued her spin until she was facing him and immediately went on the attack. This time, the left dagger came high, aiming for his neck. Now, she was inside his guard, too close to stab. Stalker parried her left dagger with the cane. He lowered his sword and tipped it up, knowing the right dagger was coming. When she adjusted her weight to stab for his chest, he smacked her wrist with the flat of the blade.

From here, he tried to beat her in the chest with the pommel, but she retreated. He chased her with a lunge, but she got both daggers under his sword and pushed it above her head, then stepped in again to kick him. Stalker smacked her in the shin with his cane. Her foot stomped onto the catwalk and she wrapped her right arm around his left, trapping the cane in her arm pit. Still locking his sword with her left dagger, she kicked again, hitting him in the thigh.

Stalker felt his leg go numb and it began to buckle. He slid his sword down across her dagger and turned his wrist to smash the pommel into her stomach. The Virago released his left arm and staggered back. Stalker was kneeling on the catwalk, pins and needles aching in his left leg. It still wasn't ready to have weight on it.

The Virago recovered herself and moved in on him again. Both daggers reversed, she slashed at his weapons, trying to open his guard. Stalker threw himself onto his back, pulled his left knee to his chest, and then kicked. His boot connected with her hip bone and it threw her off balance. She stabbed as she went down, but her back slammed into some crates and she lost focus.

Stalker kicked up onto his feet, back throbbing. He was expecting her to stab at his feet. Instead, she tried to trip him with both feet. Stalker jumped her legs and landed unsteadily. He took a few steps to right himself and turned. The Virago was halfway onto her feet already. She was breathing heavily. They both were.

The Virago ran at him again. Now, she kicked when she was at the edge of his guard. He tried parrying with the cane again, but the force of her blow sent it wide as she screamed. He barely kept his grip on the cane. Stalker retreated until he got his rapier between them. "Stop!" He shouted in the Voice, though he hadn't properly prepared his throat, so it faltered a bit. Nonetheless, the Virago hesitated. It was long enough that he could set the muscles of his throat. "Don't fight me." He said, but as soon as the first was out, the Virago shouted back:

"床前明月光!"

It was the Voice. That was one of the techniques they had learned in the academy; speaking the Voice to counter the Voice. If another Praetorian was giving orders, you hummed in the Voice to not be swayed by it. Shouting some gibberish worked just as well. How had a journalist learned it? How had a woman learned it? There were no women in the Praetorian Guard.

"You sing the ghost song?" The Virago said. She was walking backwards with the pyramidal daggers in icepick grips. Stalker held his cane across his guard with the sword resting on top of it; ready to strike and parry.

"We just call it the Voice." He replied.

The Virago darted back, then she did a no-hand cartwheel off the side of the catwalk. Stalker followed her with his eyes as she landed on a wide stack of crates, then leapt again to the floor. He sheathed his sword and jumped over the side after her, landing not nearly as gracefully as she had, but leapt again to land on the warehouse floor.

Pain shot through his shins and he needed a moment to steady himself before running after her, but he hadn't lost sight of her yet.

Chapter 32:
Pinstripes and Colt 1911s

Stalker limped a few steps and then found his gait as he chased the Virago. He saw her disappear behind some crates and locked his eyes on them, ready to be ambushed there. Unfortunately, he was ambushed much earlier. A man in a pinstriped suit suddenly stepped into his path. The shock of it made Stalker skid, falter, and drop onto his back.

The man had a gun drawn and was raising it. Instinctually, Stalker threw his cane at the man. He flinched and blocked the cane with his free hand, but it delayed him long enough for Stalker to plant his boot into the man's groin. The man doubled over and Stalker launched himself up, getting inside the man's reach before he could fire. He grabbed the pinstripe suit by the shoulders and pulled the man deeper into his bend. Stalker rolled backward, kicking the man in the stomach, but leaving his foot in place to propel the man over him.

They both landed on their backs and Stalker heard the gun clatter on the ground. He rolled over and scrambled on top of the man who was trying to sit up. Stalker got his arms under the man's armpits and then put him in a Nelson hold. Pinstripes kicked against the floor, trying to push Stalker onto his back. Stalker threw his own weight to the left, spinning them both to the side.

They fell with Stalker riding the man's back down. Pinstripe's forehead hit the concrete floor with an almighty crack and he went limp. Stalker retrieved his cane and popped it under his arm, then found pinstripe's gun. It was a Colt 1911, the same as the one Stalker had strapped to his leg. They'd made enough of these during the war to arm every adult man in North America.

He released the clip and stuffed it in his pocket, then pulled back the slide and ejected the last round. He snapped the slide back in place and popped the recoil spring before pushing the slide back to where he could remove the slide stop, which plinked down on the concrete floor. He pulled the slide off the frame and set both on the ground. It was a sequence he accomplished in five seconds.

Standing up, a distant voice shouted: "Stalker!" It was Benjamin Syme. He was a hundred or so feet away and dressed in what looked like a hunting suit. Still, Stalker could make out the gesture he made towards pinstripes on the ground. "He dead?"

"No!" Stalker replied. A braining like that could kill you, but not yet. Four more men in suits, pistols drawn, were coming up behind the boss. "Evacuate!" Stalker waved at the catwalks. "Dynamite!"

"And you with no detonator!"

He had a point and Stalker hadn't seen any fuses. It almost made sense, too. The Virago may have planned to set all the dynamite, then run a single fuse from the last back to the first. Stalker didn't actually know enough about dynamite to be sure if that would work or not.

"Your conspirators have abandoned you!"

"No conspiracy!" Stalker said. If he didn't draw his gun, they would take him peacefully. If he kept Syme talking, the others could chase the Virago. "I'm trying to catch her, too!"

"Not important!" Syme drew his own pistol.

Being taken peacefully, it seemed, was not on the table. Still, Stalker raised his hands, but he tightened his legs, which had the effect of making it look like he was about to kneel. Suddenly, the ground felt softer and Cranston could smell the lingering particles of freshly dug trench hanging in the air. There was a bitter taste in his mouth, like a Forced March tablet dissolving. His sidearm was slung too low, out of uniform, but there was no time to adjust it. Jerry was right in front of him.

Sound was not your friend in no man's land. It traveled slower than bullets and obscured itself in echoes. Muzzle flash was another story. One bright spot appeared in front of Syme and Stalker hurled himself behind a stack of crates.

He rolled to the ground and sat, back to the wood, as a burst of fire came from Syme and his men. If he was hit, his body didn't think it was worth noticing. Stalker got to his feet and fired two shots blindly around the side of the crate—six left—then immediately started climbing the boxes. There was a plateau and he crossed to where another stack jutted out. He fired once in the air—five left—letting the echo obscure his movements, and jumped down to the floor.

When the roar died, he heard Syme's men moving forward. Stalker dashed out into the row and fired three times—two left—and was greeted by a half dozen shots in return. As Syme's men kept shooting, Stalker scrambled up a stairway of crates that let him up onto the catwalk. The Atlantic Network goons were running after him now. He jumped up onto the catwalk, fired twice down at them, expending his clip, and then jumped back down behind the crates.

During the return fire, he dropped the empty magazine and fished the other out of his pocket. He ran across the crates, now heading towards the main entrance. They heard him and followed. Suddenly, the crates became even and his cover was gone. Four shots rang out and someone shouted: "Reloading!"

The catwalk was a foot above Cranston's head. It would be too slow to climb it, but he needed to get to cover. So, he holstered his gun, turned towards the aisle, and jumped, grabbing the railing with his free hand, then swinging himself forward. He felt a bullet hit his leg as he swung out, but then he was falling below the hail of gunshots.

"Reloading!" Two more called and Stalker hit the ground in a crouch that made the bullet wound burn like hell, then somersaulted behind crates.

Above him, there was a clinking of chains and a grinding of metal wheels as Fortuna—coat flapping behind her—threw herself off the catwalk holding the chain of a loading device that ran on a track across the warehouse. One hand wrapped in the chain, her other unloaded a pistol magazine on Syme and his men as she flew like an angel of death across the warehouse.

Stalker drew and ran out after her. He saw one goon take a bullet in the neck. Syme was firing up at her. Stalker fired three times at Syme, catching him somewhere on his right side. Then, he aimed at one of the reloading goons with three more. A third goon was retraining his gun from Fortuna to Stalker when he took two to the chest. He stood there frozen with his hands held out in shock as Stalker decided to conserve his last three and took cover. His last view of the enemy was the fourth goon grabbing Syme and pulling him to cover as the third, stunned goon dropped his gun and grabbed his chest.

"Formation!" Someone bellowed in the relative quiet. "Formation!"

Stalker looked up to see Fortuna jumping down the crates. She landed within arm's reach of him, grabbed him, and kissed him harder than he remembered being kissed in a long time. She let him go and growled, smiling. She moved to the edge of their cover.

"¡Listo!" Fortuna shouted, then pulled a clip from her bandolier and handed it to Stalker.

"¡Ve!" Came the reply, presumably from El Tiburón.

Someone came running towards them on the catwalk, firing judiciously as he went. Then, another runner echoed along the far catwalk, firing more aggressively. Fortuna was reloading. Stalker looked up as the feet approached to see the Sheik dropping to cover above them and reloading. Across the way, Tiburón was firing with two pistols and clicked both empty, before getting to cover. In the brief glimpse Stalker got, he saw that Tiburón was using extended magazines. Still, he didn't like Tiburón being all by himself over there.

"¡Vienen más!" Tiburón shouted.

"¡Baja! ¡La puerta!" Fortuna called back. She turned to Stalker. "Nou tire." She gestured between the two of them, then pointed up at Tiburon and the Sheik. "Yo desann. One, two, three." Then she spun around and stepped out into the row.

Stalker scrambled after her. Fortuna crossed the row in a scissor step, firing with every footfall. Stalker stayed behind cover and fired his three at anything that looked like fabric. He assumed they were just trying to keep the goons back. Meanwhile, Tiburon and the Sheik were climbing down from the catwalks.

Stalker hid to reload and the Sheik tapped him on the shoulder. "Nice to see you." He said, getting a thumbs up in reply. Across the row, Fortuna was reloading as well.

"Team 2!" came a voice from further down the warehouse.

"Team 1!" came a reply.

"How bad?"

"Pretty bad, Boston."

"We're two men down, Philly."

"Four shooters, Boston."

"We're covering the bottleneck, Boston."

That was clearly a code, but Stalker couldn't begin to guess what it meant. Fortuna hazarded a look down the row, then pulled back. She held up four fingers. From down the row came shouts of "crossing left" and "crossing right". Evidently, Syme had a second team covering the rear of the warehouse and that team was now moving in after hearing the firefight.

But then...where had pinstripes come from? A group this organized wouldn't send one man into the middle by himself. 'Philly' was a lie. They weren't two men down, they were one man down: pinstripes. If Fortuna had only seen four in the row, there was another team with three that was either hanging back or they were on the catwalks.

"Crossing left! Crossing right!" They continued shouting, possibly masking the sound of men walking along the catwalks.

Stalker pointed an angry finger up at the catwalks, then started walking backwards. It kept him out of sight of the row, but let him get a wider view of the catwalks. He saw two more approaching Fortuna's position. It was a terrible day to be right.

Fortuna was watching him and he held up two fingers. She seemed oddly happy about that news. He supposed that was corsairs for you. As quietly as he could, Stalker climbed back up the crates, his leg burning with every exertion. Staying behind one stack, he peered around, keeping his eye just at the bottom of the catwalk and really regretting that he had red lines stitched onto his mask. There was only one up here.

Stalker ducked down and crossed around to the far side of the catwalk. There, he got up onto the top of a high stack, putting him in deep shadow three feet above the goon's head and giving him a startling look at the enemy as a whole. There were two lying in the row, with Syme and two others behind cover as not four, but six more goons approached in a leapfrog fashion. He double-checked that there was only this one on this catwalk. But it was just the two of them.

Fortuna was watching him and he aimed, hoping she would take the silent signal. Stalker fired once at the goon on the catwalk, hitting him in the head. He teetered and fell down the crates as Stalker fired three more times at the goons on the far catwalk. Below, Fortuna and the Sheik stepped into the row and fired on the leapfrogs, while Tiburon ran closer to the door.

Stalker jumped down onto the catwalk and fired twice more at his opposites, hitting one in the leg, who had to abandon the fight briefly to keep himself from falling. Sheik and Fortuna returned to cover as Tiburon unloaded on the row, giving them the cover to run to his position. Stalker made for the stairs, which would provide more protection than anything else in the building. Tiburon spent his rounds and then dashed to cover with the Sheik stepping back into the row to continue firing.

The main door to the warehouse was open, but it was also in a direct line with the row. As Stalker reached the floor, he called for the Sheik and directed Fortuna and El Tiburon towards the office.

"Guns down!" Boomed a voice from the warehouse door. "Guns down!"

The Sheik got out of the row and ran to join the others.

"Stand ready!" Was the order from the Atlantic Network. Three of the goons crossed into the open, guns out and down, but stopped as they watched six more people enter the warehouse.

The newcomers all wore purple uniforms with white eagles stitched into the fabric: Silkhaven's Finest. At the head was a man wearing a pair of motorcycle goggles from which hung a triangle of purple fabric like a modern-day highwayman. This was the official leader of the vigilance committee: Paragon. He was holding a large revolver in one hand. Behind him was Strong John Blonde with a Thompson and Cheetah with a pistol in a policeman's grip. Oracle ran in and dropped to one knee beside Paragon, holding a scoped Springfield bolt-action. A fifth member, wearing a white, bauta mask and a long purple coat over black clothes, entered and trained a shotgun on the St Lawrence vigilantes. The sixth had two pistols drawn and was turned away from the rest, watching their backs.

"Guns down!" Paragon bellowed again, eyes on the Atlantic Network goons.

Stalker led the St Lawrence vigilantes by raising his hands and crouching—leg wound screaming—to set his pistol on the ground. The others followed and the Venetian ushered them closer to the door, behind Strong John Blonde.

"Last warning!" Paragon told the Atlantic Network goons.

"Presto!" One of the goons shouted.

Three shots rang out and the goons yelped as their guns spun out of their hands. Smoke rose from Paragon's pistol. Three shots, all to the weapons, before one of them could get a shot off. Stalker made a note to never get in a firefight with that man.

Syme's goons didn't get a chance to surrender, though, because that was when the first dynamite package exploded. The sound hit

Stalker in adrenaline-slowed waves, like an artillery salvo. The battle-trained part of his mind counted the explosions as his body reached out for his nearest compatriots and pulled them back, trying vainly to get some distance. You needed to count the shells per second, like the time between lightning and thunder, to know just how much trouble you were in.

That cold, calm part of his survival brain realized why he hadn't seen a fuse. The Virago had put her sticks of dynamite close enough together that one detonation set off another in a chain. It was clever, he thought as the concussive force lifted him off his feet and threw him back onto the dock, knocking him unconscious.

Chapter 33:
SS Thomas Canty

August 15th, 1921. Silkhaven.

As soon as the shooting started, the Virago kicked out a window and ran for the rear of the warehouse unmolested. There, her fuse hung from an upper window. She struck a match, set the string burning, and then dove off the pier into the water.

She didn't understand the fight going on inside the warehouse. Her initial assumption that the vigilantes were working with the Atlantic Network was clearly wrong, but that didn't change the fact that both seemed to be trying to stop her. It was just as the wise man had once said: "the enemy of my enemy is my decoy."

As the warehouse went up in a rapid chain of explosions, culminating in the ignition of the bag of dynamite she had abandoned to fight the vigilantes, the Virago swam beneath the water's surface and cursed the fact she was wearing leather. It was extremely practical for crawling through broken windows and quite the opposite for a long swim.

She made for the nearest boat that was actually at sea. It was a small sailboat drifting along at half sail. Night sailing was quite popular in the summer. There was no better way to take in the lights of the city and very few of the large ships were active. The city was a magnificent sight. There was an incredible glow in the air above the dark lines of the harbor buildings. It made you realize you really were living in an age of progress, a new world was being born; a world that had no place for men like Edward Blake.

The Virago approached the little boat quietly, staying below the water's surface as much as her lungs would allow. There were two figures on the deck, but their eyes were fixed on the burning warehouse. Climbing up onto the deck, she saw the words 'SS Thomas Canty' painted on the side, which she thought was an odd name for a boat. Employing every bit of stealth she could, the Virago stole into the lower deck of the boat.

In the little galley, there was a bench seat behind a folding table. As was so often the case, the seats could be lifted up and the space beneath used for storage. On this ship, that compartment was almost completely empty. She climbed in and replaced the seats above her, then just lay back and waited. She focused on keeping her breathing quiet.

In what felt like a short time later, the Virago heard a motorboat approaching. That would be Harbor Patrol, the main reason she was in this little compartment.

A man's voice shouted something, but the Virago couldn't make out the words.

"Just sailing, sir!" A man replied from the deck. "Is that a problem?"

The Harbor Patrolman's words were lost again.

"It's just me and my sister."

Several minutes passed as the motorboat came closer and then the grumble of its engine was cut. "I have to come aboard." The patrolman said.

"Of course," said the Canty's sailor. "Do you know what happened?"

"I'm sure it'll be in the papers tomorrow. Stay here, I need to check below deck. Make sure you didn't accidentally pick up a stowaway."

"Yes, sir."

The Virago heard a single pair of feet come down into the galley. He checked the other two rooms down here and then left.

"It's all clear." He announced once he was back on deck. "Can I get your names?"

"My name is Michael Blake." Said the other voice. "This is my sister, Gabrielle."

"Blake?" The patrolman said. "You don't look like 'Blakes'."

"Our father is American. White American."

"Uh huh," the patrolman sounded unconvinced. "This your boat?"

"No, sir, we rented it."

"I'll need to see the registration."

"Of course,"

Now, two pairs of feet came down into the galley. There was the sound of a drawer opening and a minute later, the patrolman said: "Alright, just procedure, you know."

"I understand."

The drawer was closed and they went back on deck.

A few more words were traded and then the patrol boat's motor kicked back on. The Virago listened as it sped away, quieter and quieter by degrees. When the motor's sound had disappeared into the regular noises of the night, including the sharp sounds of the burning warehouse, another pair of feet came down into the galley.

"Gabby?" A woman's voice called. "경찰은 갔어."

The Virago pushed the seats away and sat up. Bo Myeong stood there in a casual evening dress with broad square collars, as were traditional for boating.

"예 아래에 있어!" Bo Myeong shouted up to the deck.

"그래, 그럼 배를 다시 움직여 보겠네." Michael called back down.

She came over and helped the Virago out, then led her to the cabin. Together, they peeled the wet leather off and Bo Myeong produced a towel. It wasn't enough to fully dry herself.

"누가 물어보면 그래 넌 물에 빠진 거다." Bo Myeong said, handing Gabrielle a much humbler dress.

Gabrielle looked at the cheap dress. "이제 난 내가 아닌건가?"

Bo Myeong reached out with a finger and poked her neck. It ached to high heaven. "멍 들었잖아."

"당연하지, 나 떨어졌지 않았나?" Gabrielle replied, taking the cheap dress.

It was fine, though. Being the seamstress just meant she had to sleep at the dress shop for a few nights. Showing up at the house with a bruise would raise questions and the less lying they had to do, the better. In the short time they had been in Silkhaven, Father had never shown the smallest sign that he noticed when she and Bo Myeong traded places. If Gabrielle came home with a bruise on her neck, Father might really start looking closely and then the jig would be up.

Spending a few days at the dress shop was marvelous, really. Having all that space to herself was a revelation. There were no rules! None at all. Tonight, she decided, she was going to walk around naked. She would eat dinner and have tea and read a book completely nude. She'd never done that before. It hadn't really crossed her mind before, but now that it was an option, it felt like her heart's dearest desire.

When they came out of the cabin, Michael was in the galley getting a drink of water. His eyes lit up when he saw her.

"欢迎！好的！" He said, stepping past Bo Myeong to give her a hug. "我很伤心."

"一定就是那样." Gabrielle said, giving him a kiss on the cheek to signal the end of the hug.

"瘀伤也很棒！" He said, inspecting her neck.

"나아질 때까지는 우리 가게에 있어야 해." Bo Myeong said.

Michael looked crestfallen, but didn't argue. He had never quite warmed to Bo Myeong. They did their best to pretend, but it was never up to Mother's standards. The High Master in Hong Kong had suggested Michael and Bo Myeong sleep together to improve their relations, but Mother had been adamantly opposed. Instead, she took to softly chiding Gabrielle for being too affectionate when they were in public or around Father. It made Bo Myeong's coolness look like obedience and no one really questioned it when Oriental family members were a little cold towards one another.

"我必须回到甲板上." Gabrielle told her brother.

"是的." He sighed, gave her another quick hug, and then went back up the stairs.

"차를 준비해 줄게." Bo Myeong said.

Gabrielle returned to the bench and flopped down on it, letting the mission melt off of her. It was a slow process, but the tea would help.

Vivienne had been standing at the window since the phone call had come in. Hornsby was standing by to fetch whatever refreshment she might need through her vigil. She knew exactly where Cranston was headed. The vigilance committee had phoned to tell him about the security alarm and she had put in a call to the dock master to make sure the vigilantes were well received. Then, she had called Silkhaven's Finest. If they wanted to stop a war, this was their opportunity.

Then she waited.

She could not have said what she thought she would see. The warehouse was ten blocks away and even with her bird's-eye view, she could barely make it out past the many buildings between and the peripheral glow of the city. The explosion, however, was difficult to miss.

For a moment, she saw the graves of her parents lying open before her. Mother had wanted the whole family buried near a tree, that way the ravages of time upon the dead would serve to reunite them in the years that would follow. Vivienne placed a hand on the glass, half expecting to feel the fire's warmth on it.

"Ma'am?" Hornsby asked.

"The warehouse exploded." Vivienne said in a choked whisper.

"Ma'am!" He rushed to her side. His hands hovered at her back and elbow, not touching her but still sensible.

Vivienne's eyes remained on the distant fire and she braced herself against the glass. The portion of the dock she could see, furthest from shore, glowed brighter and brighter as the fire spread from the warehouse to the pier itself. Fireboats swarmed, casting what looked like tiny threads of water onto the blaze. Not that it mattered, in the end. Before the flames were out, the entire dock collapsed into the water.

Burning detritus floated out into the river, bobbing along before their flames were extinguished. Minute by minute, the dock returned to darkness with only the fireboat lamps remaining like stars in a black sky. Vivienne vomited.

The heaving doubled her over and brought her to her knees. Hornsby was ready and eased her down. He drew her hair away from her mouth in preparation for a second bout, but it never came. Her hand never left the glass.

"I will clean this." Hornsby said when he felt confident she would not be sick again.

Vivienne just stared down into the small, grayish pool on the floor in front of her knees. It was bumpy with the nuts she had been eating to fend off the effects of the wine. It felt strange, in that moment, to look at something that had come out of her. There was a part of her mind trying to protect her from the horrid emotions clamoring to reach the fore of her thoughts; that defensive part wondered if there was a metaphor to be found in the vomit, but even part of her mind was itself too scattered and desperate to find an answer.

Then, Hornsby was cleaning it up, starting at her knees and wiping away to prevent it from soiling her trousers. It left Vivienne staring at a fuzzy reflection of her own face and she decided that was undesirable. She slumped to one side. Hornsby reached out for her arm and eased her landing a little. Vivienne was sitting with her back to one of the legs of Mother's piano, tasting the vomit.

Hornsby hastily finished cleaning and carried away the cloth. He returned a moment later with a glass of soda water. That washed the taste out.

"Oracle was right." Vivienne said, quietly.

"Ma'am?"

"That is a war out there." She gestured limply at the window.

"Mr Walker survived a much larger war." The butler primly eased himself down to sit beside her. "Has Mr Walker told you much of his time in France?"

"No," Vivienne said voicelessly.

"I had the pleasure of being regaled by Mr Gabriel some months ago. According to him, Mr Walker charged German machine gun batteries with, and I quote, 'nothing but a pump-action shotgun, a cavalry saber, and a rakish grin'. Then he came home. It seems to me such a man is unlikely to meet his end facing one masked woman, no matter how much dynamite she is carrying."

Vivienne turned to look at Hornsby. His face was alight with pride. Hornsby had been employed by their family since Cranston was in short pants, but it only now occurred to her that he might have something akin to paternal feelings for them. He was not much older than Vivienne, perhaps ten years, so maybe it was more fraternal, but it was familial pride nonetheless.

Vivienne wrapped her arms around one of Hornsby's and cuddled into his well-pressed sleeve. He placed a gloved hand on her arm and gently patted it. If her mind had not been in a whirl, she might have fallen asleep.

Despite Hornsby's reassurance, Vivienne found herself shuddering at the realization that there was now, indeed, a war on. That explosion had not touched Edward Blake. It must prove a setback to his plan, but anyone who would stoop to infanticide was too committed to be stopped by something so remote. It was not as if one of *his* children had been in that inferno.

Edward would try again and the Rose & Chain would try to thwart him again. They had known the Virago was a dynamiter and they had sent Cranston to face her anyway. If he survived this, there was no reason to think they would not ask him to do it again. Indeed, he may not need to be asked. Surviving that blast might fill him with a desire for revenge.

Nor was it only Edward. Governor Farrar was involved. How many others were part of this conspiracy? How much of this city was bent on destroying the 'unfit'? How big was the army that the Rose & Chain meant to take on? Her mind conjured an image of the whole city in flames as masked men and police officers clashed in the streets; a civil war raging through the city. Her city.

That was what she had told Oracle: la ville, c'est moi.

That protective part of her psyche reasserted itself. It reminded her that, throughout history, the personification, the spirit of great civilizations had always been a woman: Athena, Marianne, Columbia, Britannia, Mother Russia. She felt them gather, a cloud of witnesses, to urge her to action. If there was to be a war, here, the city deserved to have a say in it. *Vox urbis.*

It was a thought that should have stiffened her back, brought her to her feet, but Vivienne could not move. Instead, she clung to her butler's arm and, she now realized, cried. Distantly, she heard the phone ringing.

"Shall I?" Hornsby asked.

"No," Vivienne said, discovering fresh strength in that little bell. Hornsby helped as she rushed to her feet and crossed to the phone in three long strides. "Hello?"

"Miss Walker?" A woman said. "It's Red Widow."

"What news?" She breathlessly demanded.

"Cranston's being taken to Holy Vigil Hospital. Tiburon talked to him and said he was in as good a shape as you could expect."

A sob burst out of Vivienne, a long moan of feeling escaping her like water bursting through a dam. She steadied herself on the phone's little table. Hornsby was at her side still, close enough that he had likely heard the news already.

"He's okay." Vivienne sputtered.

"Yes, Miss." Red Widow replied patiently.

"If I may," Hornsby said, touching the phone receiver.

Vivienne released it and Hornsby spoke into the horn: "One moment, please." Then, he helped Vivienne to a chair where she could spend her tears. Hornsby finished the conversation with Red Widow, then went upstairs. When he returned, he was carrying one of Vivienne's kimonos. "Mr Walker is at Holy Vigil Hospital. I thought you would not want to wait to dress."

"No," Vivienne said, sniffing to compose herself. "Of course... thank you." She rose and took the kimono, pulling it on over her silk shirt and trousers. Given the lateness of the hour, it was acceptable evening apparel.

Williamson had the car ready by the time Vivienne and Hornsby arrived in the lobby.

Holy Vigil was a hospital that catered to the vigilance committees as well as the police. The doctors were discreet and there was an unspoken truce at play between those factions which so often clashed. Vivienne insisted Hornsby join her. At the hospital, Williamson presented his long-expired vigilante credentials and got the trio as far as a waiting room.

It was nearly midnight when a nurse came to tell them 'the Stalker' had been informed that his sister was here and had requested that she be allowed to see him. To her shock, Vivienne was required to wear a blindfold for the journey to Cranston's room, lest she discover the identities of any other vigilantes. Williamson assured her this was praxis.

Once blindfolded, the nurse guided Vivienne to an elevator and up two floors. When they stopped, Vivienne called out for Cranston before the nurse could take off the blindfold.

"Ma'am," the nurse said. "Noms de guerre only, please."

Cranston, unmasked, was sat in a bed curtained off from the rest of the room. He had a few bandages on, but looked whole. Vivienne threw herself on him and he winced, but did not push her away. It was strange for her, but it was what she wanted to do.

Once the storm of emotion had passed, she found a chair and sat beside him, holding his hand, as he recounted the evening's events. It was, she suspected, a watered-down version of the truth. There was a bulge on his leg where it had been bandaged and he never mentioned how it had been injured. Vivienne had nothing to say in return, only that she was glad to see him with only cuts and bruises.

Eventually, he began to drift off to sleep. Vivienne wished him goodnight and put the blindfold back on before finding her way to the hall where a nurse took her arm and guided her back to the waiting room.

"Hornsby," she said once they were back in the car. "As soon as we get back, please contact Saint Moon. They should be informed of tonight's events. I would like a meeting with Edward Blake first thing in the morning."

"Of course, ma'am."

Vox urbis vocata.

Chapter 34:
Breakfast Cocktails

August 16th, 1921. Silkhaven.

The executive dining room of the Walker Grand Hotel had once been the gateway to the family penthouse. Lolita Walker had used it to host luncheons with charities, a few bridal showers, and sundry meetings deserving better than a restaurant. Likewise, James Walker had invited new business partners and the like here if he wanted the meeting to have a defined end time. It was a known thing that a meal in that room was an audition. Getting invited to the executive dining room was considered requisite to getting invited to the grander soirees held upstairs.

In recent years, though, it had seen little use. Vivienne rarely used it because there were so often good reasons not to. Hosting a new client required a retinue; at minimum, a lawyer and whichever account man had made first contact with said client. Such retinues made her the only woman in the room and the casual nature of this room tended to fling men into their usual habit of ignoring the women in the room. Vivienne, though, was not in the habit of being ignored.

She could host clients individually, but private meals with men, even on the second floor of the hotel, would send tongues wagging. Today, that was not a concern. The warehouse fire was a better story than Edward Blake having an affair.

Vivienne had called in a charcuterie board and a wheeled bar with a specially curated selection of ingredients. When the floor manager brought Edward to the dining room, she was standing at the bar stirring a pitcher of opaque liquid so purple it was almost black.

"Edward!" She called across the table which seated twelve. "Come in and have a seat."

"Vivienne," Edward sounded a little out of breath. "I don't even know where to begin."

"Begin by sitting and catching your breath, old sport." She smiled.

"You are calmer than I expected." He approached the head of the table and took the first guest's chair.

"The time for urgency has passed." She gave the pitcher a final, unnecessary stir. "My people have already been in touch with the papers with an initial statement. I sent a man to liaise with the police last night." She brought the pitcher and a pair of Collins glasses to the table.

Edward was still standing. She moved to the opposite side, instead of sitting at the head of the table.

"I said 'sit.'" She added lightly.

"Thank you," Edward looked rattled, more so than she had thought he would be.

She set the glasses down and began to pour the purple fluid. It had the consistency of a milkshake. "A breakfast cocktail," she handed him one of the glasses. "The secretaries in my office swear by these. Wine and vitamins along with some malt powder. In a pinch, it serves as a full breakfast."

He eyed the opaque drink uncertainly. Vivienne took her seat, careful not to disturb the containers she had placed on the floor, obscured from casual view. "I am told there was a break-in," she said. "And a vigilance committee responded." She sipped her cocktail.

"Yes," he followed suit and paused for a moment to give a surprised, yet approving look at his glass. "I had a couple of private security men there and they informed me."

"You and I need to discuss the Atlantic Network." She said and watched as his face shifted. When she said no more, he knew then this was not going to be a companionable meeting. This was his opportunity to appease. To show her some appreciation and buy himself some time, he took a long pull off his cocktail. Vivienne sipped hers.

"Yes," Edward said, chasing the cocktail with a deep breath. "I spoke with Benjamin Syme on the phone this morning. My lawyers are on their way to deal with the police now."

"He is in jail?"

"No, a hospital, but under police watch. The vigilantes have apparently been cleared, but the police are keeping Syme and his men under arrest. We filed all of the relevant paperwork, but that intelligence has not reached the police yet."

"And Syme's men attacked a vigilance committee. That is one step down from attacking actual police officers."

"They *fought* with a vigilance committee." Edward corrected her. "The matter of who struck first remains to be settled."

"Quite," Vivienne took a ladylike sip of her drink. It was actually very nice. Edward mirrored her, though with a more masculine gulp. "What do you know," she loaded a slice of bread with meat and cheese. "About the fire?" She took a bite of the little, open-faced sandwich to cue him to speak.

"According to Mr Syme," Edward began slowly assembling his own comestible. "The Masked Virago placed a number of explosives in the warehouse. None of his surviving men engaged her directly and he believes the vigilance committee was protecting her."

"Surviving men?"

"Yes," he stifled a burp. "I believe he said five were killed in the explosion."

"How terrible. And the vigilantes were working with the Virago?"

Edward gave a few final chews, then swallowed his sample of the charcuterie. "That was Benjamin's impression, yes."

"Edward," Vivienne said, spying a gleam of sweat appearing on his forehead. "You look a mess. Here, the cocktail will settle your nerves." She raised her glass and he touched his to hers. She took a bigger drink than before to encourage him. She was down about a fifth of hers and, when he set down the glass, it was two-thirds empty.

"I'm sorry, Miss Walker." Edward said, taking up the jam spoon and another slice of bread. "Nothing like this has *ever* happened to me before. The contents of that warehouse represent nearly fifty percent of Saint Moon's stock in Silkhaven. Our entire supply of...um... Mother's Tomatoes, Yippity beer, Canned Mixed Greens, and...um... Bean Bonanza were destroyed. Mother's Tomatoes is our best-selling product in Silkhaven, so far."

"Did you know that the dock sank? It will be at least a month before it can be rebuilt. We will have to halt any further imports for a while. I will do my best to find room for your goods, but it is a tall order."

Edward nodded vigorously, then appeared to regret it. Green was seeping into his face. "Yes, we still have the second warehouse and the supply at the factory. We can bring some goods there directly from the ships." His breaths were heavy, like the room had suddenly become stuffy. "Once we have settled those logistics, the tomatoes will take a month to replenish, and even then."

"No need to panic over profits. The insurance will certainly cover the damages."

"Mostly, yes," He reached for his cocktail and took another drink. "But the lack of products will damage our customer base. New products on the market are exciting, draw people in, but if they disappear, the customers we won over will return to their old favorites, and there's no telling if we can get them back."

"That is a concern." Vivienne said, feeling her own stomach start to turn. "This is unrelated, but since I have you here, I had a disturbing conversation with Governor Farrar. Are you aware that your Yippity beer has been connected to a string of infant deaths?"

Edward sputtered. It did not help that he was visibly becoming sick. "It's not a drink for children." He managed.

"No, but some new mothers drink it. There is a theory going around that the Yippity gets into the mother's milk and then mixes with certain ingredients in your milk fortifier to become toxic."

He shook his head and drank. "That's poppycock."

"Well, I discussed it with Governor Farrar." She took a drink. "I thought it deserved more investigation and I know the two of you have become friends. What disturbed me was that he did not seem to think further investigation was warranted. Indeed, he seemed to think the deaths of these children were to society's benefit; their mothers being prostitutes. Most concerning was that he used several eugenicist expressions in his little speech. Are you worried he has gotten the wrong impression from your evangelism?"

"Um..." Edward looked like he was about to vomit.

"Never mind, I already know the answer. By the way, you did not lose your entire supply of Yippity."

Edward said nothing, only gave her a distracted look of inquiry before wiping the sweat off his brow.

Vivienne reached down to the containers by her feet. "You gave me a case, remember?" She placed two empty bottles on the table. Edward's eyes flicked between the bottles and his drink. "I apologize for lying about the wine, but I did not want you to feel emasculated by drinking a beer for women." She lost her train of thought for a moment, feeling the sweats break out on her face as well. "I thought, since I was hosting you, it would be a nice touch if I served some of your products."

Again, she reached down. This time she lifted a can up to the table: Saint Moon Milk Fortifier.

"'Chock full of vitamins'," she read off the can. "Quite the wholesome combination."

Edward suddenly tried to leap up from the table, but he wheeled unbalanced and slammed into the wall behind him, then tripped over his upturned chair and landed in a heap on the floor.

"Edward?" Vivienne called calmly. "Are you alright?" She stood slowly, steadying herself on the table. Even so, her head spun when she rose. "This is strong stuff, Edward." She came around to him. "Can you imagine..." black spots appeared in her vision. "Can you imagine if children drank it?"

He was jerking on the floor, eyes bugging and face drained of blood. His body was trying to vomit—a thin stream of putrid liquid was leaking from his lips—but his throat was closing up and trapping the ejection.

Vivienne stumbled around the table and dropped to her knees beside him, trying to slow her descent by grabbing the drink cart. "Children, Edward, even the *fittest* children...I do not think they could handle it."

His lips were turning blue as he futilely gasped for air. Vivienne did not blame him. Her hands and feet had gone numb and she could feel her throat tightening. "And you drank so much more than they did." Something changed in his eyes. Her mind was too clouded to register exactly what it was, but it set off an alarm in a deep, instinctive part of her mind. "Edward?" She asked innocently. "Can you hear me?"

There was no reaction; only the small, abrupt tightening of muscles all over his body. She detected the smell of feces and noted a dark stain appearing in his trousers.

"That is most..." Vivienne nearly swooned. "...ungentlemanly of you...Edward." She grabbed the bell on the drinks cart and rang it as vigorously as she could manage. It was the only sound, the last sensation to reach her brain as the black closed in around her. She did not even feel herself collapse on top of him.

EDWARD BLAKE DEAD

Poisoning has been ruled the cause of death for Mr Edward Blake, President of the Saint Moon food corporation. Mr Blake's body was found in the Walker Grand Hotel yesterday morning and an ambulance immediately called. He was taken to Silkhaven Central Hospital where he was pronounced dead.

Mr Blake, 47 years old, newly of 68 Rue d'Acer, was a native of New York City recently moved to Silkhaven to oversee the expansion of his company into King Charles Island. He is survived by his wife, Martha Blake, 46 years old, and twin children, Michael and Gabrielle Blake, 22 years old.

Vivienne Walker also poisoned

Attendants found the unconscious body of Vivienne Walker of 45 Rue de Cygne alongside Mr Blake. Hospital officials say Miss Walker, 35 years old, is in stable condition and expected to recover. Furthermore, they say she is the victim of a lower dosage of the same poison.

The two victims were found in a private dining room of the hotel. The hotel manager said the two were having a breakfast meeting to discuss the harbor fire of 15 August. The harbor was owned by the Walker Corporation of which Miss Walker is Acting President and the warehouse which caught fire contained goods belonging to Saint Moon.

Poisoning Linked to Masked Virago

Since 5 August, Saint Moon has been harried by a vigilante dubbed the Masked Virago. The Virago is accused of attacking multiple delivery trucks belonging to the company and for setting the explosives which destroyed the Walker Corporation's dock. Police believe this same figure is responsible for the poisoning. The identity of the Virago remains unknown.

An emergency meeting at the Saint Moon headquarters in New York has been called and Michael Blake has been named the new President of the company pending unspecified conditions.

Chapter 35:
Horse Head Cane

August 18th, 1921. Silkhaven.

The first clear memory Vivienne had was of Gabrielle. The girl was sitting beside her, reading something with a young man waxing poetical about socialism. That could have been anything, these days. Vivienne looked around; the movement did not seem to alert Gabrielle to her. She was lying in a hospital bed and light was coming through thin blinds suggesting morning or late afternoon.

Vivienne was immensely calm. It was the calmest she had felt in as long as she could remember. Later, she would learn she had been sleeping for two days and that went quite a ways towards explaining things. It had not been a solid two days. She had had moments of apparent wakefulness accompanied by coherent, yet disjointed speech. So, when she said: "Gabrielle?" The girl only replied: "Yes, still me."

"Where am I?"

"Still at Silkhaven General Hospital. And, yes, you would rather be at St Joseph's, but they lack facilities for poisoning."

"Oh," Vivienne replied. She had not been thinking that, but it now occurred to her as something she would think. "Not to be rude, but what are you doing here?"

"Reading." Gabrielle said, holding up the book and turning to look at Vivienne for the first time. "Oh...are you really awake?"

"I am not counting out the possibility of this being a dream," Vivienne said. "But I believe I am, yes."

"Wait, please." Gabrielle got out of her chair and ran out of the room.

She returned with a doctor in tow and there was quite a bit of fuss. Vivienne only half paid attention to the doctor. She wanted to know what had happened to Edward and what sort of trouble she would be in. As her mind played through the possibilities, she decided it was acceptable if he had survived. The plot had been exposed. Of course, Saint Moon would deny and deny, but the crucial parts of the truth would be out.

The doctor proclaimed Vivienne ready to leave and went on his way. Alone again, Gabrielle brought a dress box over to the bed.

"They already called Cranston." She said and Vivienne saw her cut off one of her monologues before she got going. "Listen, you already made your confession—a few times actually—so I'll just skip ahead and tell you it was all an accident. I understand why you feel guilty, but you needn't; not on my account, anyway. So, that's that, alright?"

"Yes, alright," Vivienne replied.

"Here," Gabrielle opened the dress box and revealed the Chinese dress Bo Myeong had made. "There is a gaggle of reporters outside. I thought you should have something nice to wear. Come along, I'll help you dress."

Vivienne did not speak during the process, only followed Gabrielle's instructions. It was not a complicated garment, essentially a robe that buttoned up one side and fit a lot more snugly. They ran into some trouble when Vivienne tried to stand and found her right leg was not entirely in working order. A nurse was fetched and she said it was nerve damage, according to the doctor, and she should try to walk on it at least one hour a day, but not more than three, until the nerves had healed.

All of this, the nurse said in the tone of a woman who has said this a dozen times before, but understands why she must do so again. Then, she brought in a wheelchair for Vivienne to use before disappearing again. At St Joseph's, she would have had a dedicated nurse.

Not long after, Cranston arrived. He presented Vivienne with a cane. It was some pale wood with a silver handle shaped like a horse's head.

"I was of two minds." Cranston said, taking over the wheelchair from Gabrielle. "I wanted something that would invoke a speedy recovery. My first thought was some animal known for its speed and my second thought was something so hideous you would will yourself mended just to escape it. In the end, I decided you were too likely to walk without the ugly cane and injure yourself further."

"I see." Vivienne replied, inspecting the cane. She did not own a horse, but perhaps she should.

"It was between the horse and a rabbit and...well, you're not a prey animal, are you?"

Vivienne reached back to touch his hand.

There was indeed a gaggle of reporters outside the hospital. Each of them seemed to already have a story written about what happened and merely needed Vivienne to confirm it. They asked leading questions and she gave them simple, honest answers. It helped that none of their apparent versions of the meeting were at all correct.

It didn't take long for one of them to let slip that Edward was dead. Vivienne took the opportunity to play up her shock—she truly hadn't known—and that was enough to get them free. Cranston pushed her through the crowd, berating the reporters for upsetting her. An upset woman could hardly be expected to give an interview.

As they drove home, she managed to bring herself to tears. This was mostly for Gabrielle's sake, but it proved additionally useful when they got home to find a detective waiting. Instead of grilling her, he walked her through that fateful morning's events. He asked a few questions, which Vivienne answered quickly, then confirmed the version of the story he had written. He got a few things wrong, but nothing which could be proven wrong, so Vivienne never corrected him.

She never corrected anyone.

Epilogue:
Red Silk

Mr Sen Hongfei was an up-and-coming dye merchant taking a long walk from the Central piers to one of the great houses at the foot of Victoria Peak. He was barefoot and naked under a long, red, silk robe. On the back of the robe was a camel stitched in gold thread. As he walked, more than a few dubious characters looked him over and then gave him a wide berth.

Hongfei had come to Hong Kong five years ago to get into the dye-selling business. His father owned an indigo farm in Yunping on the mainland and the local farmers always complained about the dye merchants exploiting them. This was how things were now: those who produced were paid the least and those who did nothing but sell kept the most. There were some people back home who believed they could lead a revolution against the new government and establish a system where no one was richer than anyone else; but Hongfei was no dreamer. In his mind, if this was how the world was, the best thing to do was become one of the sellers.

At first, Hongfei had struggled the same as any newcomer would, but he had built up a few clients and then convinced his father and his father's friends to sell exclusively to him. That had made all the difference. By 1919, he felt he was well on his way to becoming a major player in the dye business. However, Yunping had been hit with a famine last year.

It seemed that every day, hundreds were dying in the province.

Desperate to spare his family, Hongfei had attempted to burn down one of his competitors' factories. He thought he could drive those customers to his own business, double his income, and send the money back home.

Through this misadventure, Hongfei was inducted into a mystery that had sat beneath the surface of China's high society for two thousand years. Long, long ago, the silk producers of China, Joseon, and Japan had banded together to protect their products from the vicissitudes of governments. They fixed prices, protected routes, and shared news of untrustworthy buyers. It grew into a secret power, behind thrones and pirates, capable of waging wars.

The factory Hongfei had attempted to burn down belonged to one of their members. He was indebted now, not only to his competitor, but to the entire Red Silk Society. Tonight, walking like a beggar in an expensive robe, he was paying off a little of his debt.

When he reached the assigned house, he was shown to the servants' entrance and, from there, to a basement room. The room was like nothing he had ever seen. A large, round area was surrounded by bookshelves packed with books, scrolls, and porcelain objects. Above these bookshelves, there was a gallery; three rows of big, wicker chairs. Two people awaited Hongfei: a young Chinese man in a European-style suit and a Eurasian woman of about thirty in scholar's robes.

The Chinese man told him to go to the center of the room where a fat pillow lay on the floor. Hongfei stood in front of the pillow, afraid to kneel before he was bade to. So positioned, the man told him to wait and he did. For a long time, the three of them stood in silence until a door behind the gallery opened and people began wandering in and sitting.

There were no lights among the seats, so Hongfei had only rough impressions of the people, but he could tell some were women. At least one was wearing a cheongsam. In the dim light, he could see the distinct shape of white shirts under suits and ties; perhaps Europeans, perhaps Chinese who spent a lot of time with Europeans. The quiet in which this all played out gave Hongfei the impression that these were highly educated people; privileged, elite.

The Chinese man told Hongfei to lower his eyes, then muttered something about the poor manners of rural mainlanders.

Hongfei knew what had to come next. Only one thing made sense to come next, but he had had no idea what circumstances it would happen under; all these people, some of them women. He was not prepared. At the same time, he did all this in exchange for keeping his business running. He got to continue making money and sending what he could back to his family and maybe deliver them from starvation. His family lived because he did this.

The Eurasian woman came to his side and began addressing the audience. It was a formal address, a greeting; well practiced and probably traditional because Hongfei didn't recognize some of the words. He did have some education and he could read and write enough to run a business. The fact that he didn't recognize some words made him think again of how educated the audience must be and, by extension, how powerful.

When the address was finished, the Eurasian woman stepped in front of Hongfei. She was a head taller than he was. Some of that would be her European heritage, but it spoke more to her childhood diet and the family wealth that went with it. Mixed children were usually the offspring of whores and lived off the same sorry diet as the rest of the mean class. They did not grow taller than a landlord's son. If she was the daughter of a prostitute, her father must have been a very kind and generous man. It never even crossed his mind that her mother might be European; such a coupling could not exist in his mind.

Without speaking to him, the Eurasian woman reached out and untied his robe, as Hongfei knew she would. He wanted to weep as she gingerly pulled the robe off of him, exposing him completely to the audience. Of course, it was not his body they cared about; it was the message written on him. For an hour, Hongfei had knelt in a quiet room onboard one of the ships as someone copied a missive onto his skin. The brush had tickled as it painted character after character onto him.

It was a smuggler's trick. Any mail coming into Hong Kong was liable to be inspected by the British. People coming and going from the ships were rarely strip-searched.

His head hung low, Hongfei could see the lines of characters running down his chest all the way to his ankles. He recognized less than half of them. He was not a person now; he was a book because books cannot read themselves.

The Eurasian woman inspected him and found the beginning of the message. She read the words audibly, but quietly, pausing often. It was the Chinese man, standing close, who communicated to the audience. Every time the woman paused, the man spoke; but he spoke more and stranger sentences than the woman had. This much, Hongfei understood. China had always been a nation of nations and, it seemed, the audience originated from all the disparate parts of the country. The man was relaying the message in Yue, Guanhua, Ngu Ngei, even Xiang.

It was only now Hongfei understood what the message was. The audience was some sort of organization which had agents working in secret in America. A man they called 'The Black King' was dead. This result had not been part of whatever plan the organization had, but was seen as a good thing, though they would have preferred it to happen later. Now, a Black Prince had taken his place. This was part of the plan, but again premature.

The agents of the organization insisted that they had not killed the Black King, but rather he had been poisoned by one of his business partners. The event, they claimed, had been outside of their control. Now, they asked for guidance.

With the message concluded, the woman addressed the audience to conclude the meeting. The people got up from their seats and filed out of the room. Hongfei was taken to a washroom where two servants bathed him in a stinging liquid and scrubbed his skin until it was red. It felt like they were trying to abrade him down to the bone, but he understood they wanted no sign of the message to remain, which suited Hongfei.

The clothes he had worn to the ship were waiting for him, evidently delivered by someone else. As he dressed, the Chinese man in the European suit returned to him. He reminded Hongfei that his debt was not yet settled and that he was not to breathe a word of what had happened to anyone, ever; then sent him away.

Hongfei didn't need to be told to keep this secret. If his family was not starving—was not relying on him to send them money for food—he would have killed himself. As it was, their lives mattered more than his dignity. Walking home, he resolved himself to bear this humiliation, knowing it would keep his nephews alive; but he swore he would never have children of his own.

THE END